The Killing of Butterfly Joe

RHIDIAN BROOK is an award-winning writer of fiction. His first novel, *The Testimony of Taliesin Jones*, won several prizes including the Somerset Maugham Award. His third, *The Aftermath*, was an international bestseller and has been translated into twenty-five languages; it has also been made into a major motion picture. He has written for television and the screen and is a regular contributor to BBC Radio 4's 'Thought for the Day'. He once had a job selling butterflies in glass cases.

'Part travelogue, part ... is a bold ... the biggest joy of the part fantasy, *The Killing of Butterfly* ... the biggest joy of the novel is in the brilliantly teased out sense of dread that starts the moment you pick up the book and read the title ... a beautiful story, and beautifully told too.'

Culture Fly

'A compelling, unusual, character-rich novel; a great pleasure to read.'

Gerard Woodward, Man Booker Prize
shortlisted author of *I'll Go to Bed at Noon*

Times (South Africa)

... r of *Arrested* ... *den Girls*)

'An ent ... ques are a good wa ... ng number of adults) want to go to Hogwarts. Everyone who has read Donna

'A mixture of thriller and ...
style. Like having all th...
my thoughts into o...

...enthra...
mo...t while r...
nove...th humour,...
highl...ough'

'A fast-p...d, neo-gothic thrille...
Scott Fit...rald. Brook unpacks ...
dream in a...w and refreshing way.'

'F******* hilarious.'

Sunday ...

Jim Valley (Writ...
Development and Gol...

'A true original. Impossible to put down. One of the most orig...
al books you'll read this year.'
Western Mail

'Beautiful, ingenious and rather sinister. A skilfully plotted tale
about butterflies, a deeply dysfunctional family; and a maverick
salesman'
Notreallyworking

'This rollicking, entertaining road novel is as much about
make-believe and truth, loyalty and friendships as about the
agonies of cold calling . . . The prose is a marathon of brilliantly
sustained folksiness and linguistic invention, a riot of erudition,
both faux and real. A triumph.'
Richard Hopton, *Country and Town House*

You have to get the new book by Rhidian Brook. It's bold, brilliant & beautiful. Highly recommended.'
Omid Djalili

RHIDIAN BROOK

The Killing of Butterfly Joe

PICADOR

First published 2018 by Picador

First published in paperback 2018 by Picador

This paperback edition first published 2019 by Picador
an imprint of Pan Macmillan
20 New Wharf Road, London N1 9RR
Associated companies throughout the world
www.panmacmillan.com

ISBN 978-1-5098-1616-3

A CIP catalogue record for this book is available from the British Library.

Typeset by Palimpsest Book Production Limited, Falkirk, Stirlingshire
Printed and bound by CPI Group (UK) Ltd, Croydon, CRO 4YY

Visit **www.picador.com** to read more about all our books
and to buy them. You will also find features, author interviews and
news of any author events, and you can sign up for e-newsletters
so that you're always first to hear about our new releases.

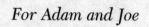

For Adam and Joe

Well…
There we were.
We were working like that
And then who should come up
But the CAT IN THE HAT!

Dr. Seuss

I.

I tell this tale of Butterfly Joe
The adventure, wonder, trouble, woe;
But how to let unfold and flow
To save my butt as well as soul?
I'd hail a Muse (but they've kept shtum
E'er since Cupid swapped bow for gun)
Leaving the Music of their name
And ten thousand spent writers seeking fame
And glory and lead in pencils,
An orally delivered, full-blown story.
No. I'm not waiting for them.
I'll just get on with it
Open with the opening:
A first encounter with my hero
And his selkie-sister, naked
In the cool waters of
The Kaaterskill Falls
Not far from where
Rip Van Winkle took
His twenty-year snooze.
This is where the adventure starts
And this is how my story goes . . .

CHAPTER ONE

In which I meet Joe Bosco and his sister Mary-Anne
at the Kaaterskill Falls.

I met him a butterfly-life ago. That's six months if you're an exceptionally strong, large, lucky butterfly. It was the beginning of May. I was lying by the side of a river in the Catskill Mountains, reading and smoking, when I fell asleep and into a dream. It was one of those lovely in-and-out dreams that come with shallow sleep. I'd been reading about Rip Van Winkle, the man who took a nap outdoors and woke twenty years later to a world that had moved on without him, and he was in my dream. There was a butterfly – yellow, white and black. And I was at my father's funeral. Scattering his ashes. I knew I was dreaming and I was enjoying the illogical bleeding of disparate things into one another. But someone was trying to get into my dream. I could hear a voice coming from outside it, pulling me rudely from my semi-sleep. I even remember thinking – in my dream – 'Don't wake up, don't wake up!' But the intruding voice was as insistent and enthusiastic as a toddler's. The voice of someone who enjoyed interrupting and who paid no heed to what people thought of them.

It's a monster. A total monster!

It was an American voice. But of course: I was in America.

I opened my eyes and there he was, eclipsing the sun. He was naked from the waist up, shoeless, holding a butterfly net in one hand, grinning down at me. The lenses of his glasses magnified his eyes to bushbaby saucers. His hair was short on top and long at the back which made him look less intelligent than he turned out to be. I guessed him to be in his twenties, a little older than me perhaps. A boy in a superman's body.

'Don't move, sir,' he said. He made this snorted chortling

3

noise and curled up his nose in concentration. 'You should see this, Mary. It's a giant!'

He was addressing someone in the water. I sat up and saw a young woman, maybe seventeen or eighteen years old, swimming in the pool beneath the main cascade of the falls. She was completely naked, her skin ivory-green, her long hair snaking across her back. I wondered if some spirit of those witchy-woods had put a spell on me and that I had, like Rip, woken up to a world that had moved on without me.

'It's a *Papilio glaucus*!' he said to the girl.

'Not so special as all that,' she shouted back.

What were they? Naturist entomologists? Prelapsarian hippies? (The Woodstocks were not that far away.) Or maybe, this being the top end of the Appalachia, they were a couple of feral in-breds.

'Don't move, sir. If you just could stay . . . very . . . still.'

He brought the net down over the huge yellow, black and white butterfly that was sunning itself on the rock next to me. He reached in to the net and pinched the butterfly dead, pressing its thorax with his thumb and forefinger (if I couldn't actually hear the crunch I imagined it). He then held the butterfly in the palm of his hand and stretched out his arm towards me.

'*Papilio glaucus*. Eastern tiger swallowtail to you. Ain't she super-beautiful?'

What with its wings folded over its back and it being dead it was hard to agree.

'Aww. Don't look that way. She'll give people more joy dead than alive. You'll see.'

He slipped the specimen into a glassine paper triangle that he produced from a Tupperware box.

' "A thing of beauty is a joy for ever",' I said.

He gave a 'hmmm' of assent, although I'm not sure he'd caught the sarcasm. He looked at me, curious now. Maybe he was sizing me up before netting, stunning and pinning me? He thrust out his hand.

4

'Joe Bosco, *"Alexandrae boscensis"*.'

'Llewellyn Jones.'

'Llewhat?'

'Lew is easier.'

'OK. Lew. That's my sister Mary-Anne. *"Paradoxa boscensis"*. I apologize for her in advance.'

I was unsure where to look: the colossus on the rock or the naiad in the water. Joe was vast: six foot five with absolutely no fat on an athletic frame; he had perfect proportion, built like a statue of a Greek discus-thrower. His stunning physical presence made his voice all the more incongruous. It was whiny and childish and so unlikely I thought it might be a disguise, a voice to lure you into an underestimation.

'What you reading there?'

'Just a book of stories,' I said.

I showed him the cover of my book – *Classic American Stories*. It depicted a painting of the Headless Horseman of Sleepy Hollow.

He squinted at the cover and looked unimpressed. He swept his hand towards the waterfall and woods behind. 'The real story's here, my friend. Here, over there, and beyond that.' He opened his arms and turned a 360 to take in the waterfall, the hemlock trees, the cornucopia of life within. 'Don't you just wanna dive in?'

'I'm working up to it,' I said.

I tried not to look at the figure in the water but I could 'feel' her there even without looking, her nakedness more threatening than any predator.

'Don't mind her,' he said. 'My sister hates men.'

'I what?' she snapped back, clearly listening, her disinterest a pose.

'I said you hate men!'

'Ain't met one yet!'

She was now swimming on her back, her breasts breaking the surface of the water.

'So . . . where you from, Lew? I'm hearing England. You from England?'

I nodded, not bothering to explain that I was Welsh and the differences therein.

'You travelling? Working? What's happening here? What's the plan?'

What's happening here? My plan was vague: see America; have a good time.

'I don't know yet. I'm just living in the moment.'

'You ain't depressed or nothing?'

'Depressed? No.' I laughed but it was such a pathetic laugh I despised myself for it. 'Why?'

'You seem kinda blue.'

'Really?'

'Well. You're right by a cool river on a hot day lying next to the most beautiful natural wonder and you're reading a book.'

I shrugged.

'Well am I right or am I right?'

I was a bit down but I wasn't going to tell a complete stranger about the recent death of my father or my tendency to get high when I was low.

'I'm fine.'

'Ha! I don't believe you. But I like that voice. Hey, Mary, you should come up here and listen to this. This is how to talk right!'

From the start I think Joe heard something in my voice he could use. I have a good speaking voice: clear, neutral-accented, with just enough Welshness to give it a good timbre. I realize a British accent has a disproportionately mesmerizing effect on the natives here, but to Joe's ear my voice was a door-opening, deal-closing voice.

He laid down his net. 'You coming in or what?'

'Maybe.'

He placed his specs on his net and stepped onto the rocky overhang that served as a diving board. He lifted his arms into a vee and stood there as if about to conduct the foliage; he milked the moment of delay then dove with great theatre and surprisingly poor coordination. He re-emerged and let out a tumultuous *whoop!*

'You don't know what you're missing here!'

I knew exactly what I was missing: what I was missing was the un-self-consciousness required to just strip down and dive in whilst his sister was still in that pool, her nakedness now more tantalizing for being obscured by the eddying waters directly beneath the falls.

'Mary! Don't embarrass the man. Put some clothes on!' He turned to me with a shrug. 'It's her protest. She thinks it's her right to swim naked, as Eve would have swum before the fall. 'Cos she ain't done nothing wrong. She has Bad Theology, see. Mary, come on!'

She trod water. I couldn't read the look she gave me; but it wasn't completely hostile. She slowly swam back to the bank and stepped out – one step, two step – whipping her head to catch her hair in a bunch and squeeze out the water, all this while leaning over, ignoring me but checking to see if I was looking, which I was, like a mesmerized frog before a hypnotist snake. Out of the water, her skin was milky pale and she had a boyish skinniness. She picked up her towel and mercifully wrapped it around her midriff. There was something un-American about this show of immodesty. She could have been French.

'All yours, mister,' she said. Unlike her brother's, her voice was smoky and deep.

I wanted to show them (her mainly) that I had more than just an inner life. I stood and stripped down to my boxers, turning away from the pool, conscious of some arousal. I took off my watch – an heirloom from my late father – and laid it carefully on top of my shorts. I walked to the ledge feeling, with the gaze of that girl on me, like I was walking a plank to shark-ridden waters. I stood there for a while looking down into the pool, calculating its depth. I thought for a moment about the tricksy refraction of the light, my fear making the distance to the pool greater and the pool itself shallower. Joe coaxed me from the bank. 'Go on! Dive in!'

I dove, my whole being focused on keeping my legs together and arms dart-straight, determined to make a good impression on the girl. The bottom of the pool came to meet me quicker than I expected, my hands touched and dispersed gravel, making little clouds. The sun carved chutes of light around me. I stayed under for a few beats, to prove I had puff to spare, enjoying the new cool world. When I resurfaced I cried out, as much to catch my breath as praise existence. It was May and the water was still ice-fresh. I was expecting applause or acclaim of some kind but I was greeted only by the sound of water falling on water. I looked up to the pedestal rock but there was no sign of Joe or his sister. I thought little of it and swam breast-stroke across the pool, stopping in a silky warm patch in the sun to float on my back. A bird of prey flew across the waterfall spray. (I know now that it was a bald eagle.) Then I heard a shout from the creek, a man's voice, followed by a crack of wood and a cackle of girl's laughter, then another shout from the man. Dopily I wondered if more people were coming to spoil the idyll, and then it hit me: this whole thing – the butterfly netting, the engagement in conversation, the encouragement to dive, the naked girl – had been a sting. And I had been stung. I swam to the bank, pulled myself from the pool and ran up to the perch where I'd left my watch with my clothes. The watch was still there lying on my shirt, glinting gold in the sun, but the wood fairies had stolen my book. I looked down the creek and thought about giving chase but they were too far gone and, anyway, it was just a book, a book I could replace without my aunt ever knowing.

The blue tints of the uplands were turning purple as I tramped back to my aunt's house. The robbery was a mild violation but it left me feeling unsettled and foolish. I like to think I'm a good judge of people but I hadn't seen that coming. Yes, the girl had been aggressive and sullen but the guy had seemed sincere in his friendliness. They probably scammed day-trippers like this all the time. I felt I'd been robbed of my discernment as much as my book and, as I descended the creek, was sure the trees and the rushing waters were laughing at me. I know this is just a projection of my feelings but from the day I arrived in the Catskills I felt that the landscape had a spooky intelligence, as if it knew things about me, things about my past, things about my future, things I didn't even know about myself. And if I'd been better at reading the signs I might have seen a warning.

CHAPTER TWO

In which Joe brings me an offering and makes me an offer.

That night, the sleep that embraced me so sweetly during the day played hard to get. My encounter with the butterfly people had stirred up an over-stimulating cocktail of obvious desires, exciting possibilities and abstract anxieties. Who were they? Where were they from? Why had they taken the book and not the clearly more valuable 1950s Omega Seamaster wristwatch? Had I really met them? The ghost of the gone-book at my bed-side table confirmed that I had but the dreamy overlapping of the day's events and an evening spliff fuzzed my sense of what was what. As I lay in bed I noticed – for the first time since I'd been at my aunt's – the animal sounds of the forest. Trying to identify them, I ran through a hierarchy of American predators from cicada to bear via frog, snake, owl, lynx, coyote and cougar with the butterfly guy's selkie-sister at the top of the tree. She was still out there, naked in the cool pool beneath the falls, horn-ier than a frog, more cunning than a snake, more powerful than a bear, making siren sounds to lure me.

But if I could dispel her image with corny fantasy and a few flicks of the wrist, I couldn't get the butterfly guy from my head. His presence had been burned on my retina in that first sun-eclipsing glimpse, and his observations about me – so pre-sumptuous, so judgemental, so true! – repeated on a loop in my mind like an annoyingly catchy pop song.

'You ain't depressed or nothing?' 'You seem kinda blue.' 'The real story's out there.'

It was as if he'd read my mail (as they say here). I'd come to see America, but since I'd arrived two weeks before things hadn't quite gone to plan. I'd got myself fired from my first bar job for oversleeping. My aunt, feeling sorry for me, offered me work painting her barn but, being impractical, I found this work hard and slow. I also got distracted by and lost in her vast collection of American literature. The barn contained ten thousand books and she'd asked me to catalogue and alphabetize them, a job that I was only too happy to do but that saw me retreat to the fictional terrain of American literature instead of getting out and exploring the actual land in which many of the stories were set. I told myself, 'Why leave the beautifully turned world described in books for the messy, contingent reality that required sweat and blood and money to see when it was all here and available to me?' Truth is, the reading encouraged my introspection. And I was smoking too much.

I woke the next morning – oversleeping the alarm by two hours – to the long-noted, American-style telephone ring (these differences were still novel enough to surprise me then). I felt heavy-limbed and hungover. My right arm was dead. Pins and needles spread up from my right calf. When I set my feet on the floor my spine felt dislocated, as though I had wrestled all night with a strongman and lost. I vowed that I'd never smoke dope again.

'Did I wake you, honey?'

I covered the mouthpiece and cleared sleepy phlegm from my throat to make my aunt think I'd been up for a while.

'Not at all, Aunt Julia.'

'You're not getting lonely and bored up there, Lew?'

'No. I have good company. I'm working my way through the library.'

'Pa had some weird things in that barn.'

I decided not to mention the stolen book or the butterfly people. I didn't want my aunt to think I was losing my mind as well as her possessions.

'How about the car? You get it started?'

'I took it up to Hunter. It drives fine.'

This was also a lie. In the two weeks I'd been at my aunt's I had not taken the car out once. The reading and the mild agoraphobia that excessive smoking of weed tended to bring on had limited my excursions to the waterfall and the general store.

'Listen, I won't be coming up this weekend, Lew. But if you want a break you're welcome to come to the city for a few days. We have room.'

'I'm fine. Thank you. I've found a good rhythm here.'

'So how is the barn coming on?'

'I'm a bit slow. But I'm enjoying it. It's very therapeutic.'

This was not a lie. The manual labour was helpfully thought-neutral, goal-achievable and outdoors. I had settled on a routine of painting nine to twelve, stopping for lunch, walking to the falls, reading, cataloguing in the afternoons, leaving evenings for more reading, smoking and, supposedly, writing; but the painting was the best part.

'And the book? You getting some writing done?'

'It's really flowing. Like the Kaaterskill Falls, Aunt Julia.' I winced at this embellishment.

'Lew, that's wonderful.'

My third lie in as many minutes. It was interesting how easy I found it to deliver these lies. I consider myself to be an honest person but over the years I had learned to tell lies largely to avoid disappointing people, seeing it as both a sort of kindness as well as a self-protection. In the year since I'd left university I had started telling people that I was a writer. This was a lie that grew in the soil of my failure to get a decent job and a need to differentiate myself from my professionally successful siblings and friends who were thrusting ahead of me in the world, and a way of placating my father who had despaired at my failure to find a real profession. It was also an enigmatic and purposeful (as well as handily hard-to-verify) answer to the question: 'So what are you doing these days, Lew?' When I first tried the line on a girl at a party she had been so taken with it I decided that I would use it for as long as I could get away with it. It seemed to work a kind of magic on people, granting me favours and, at the very least, unwarranted admiration from strangers and even friends. Only my father dissented; laughing in my face when I told him of my plan to write a book, a travelogue written in verse and set in America. (My Americodyssey). My aunt, however, loved the idea of me – someone, anyone – writing a book almost more than I did and she indulged me by setting up a desk and typewriter in the barn and politely asking after my progress whenever she called, which was every other day. I went along with the pretence, discussing the things I had not-written as though they existed on the page. Sometimes I liked the sound of what I was not-writing so much I wondered why I wasn't actually writing it. In truth, I had written something the night before but it wasn't 'The Book' I'd set out to write. It was a poem inspired by my strange day at the waterfall; but I didn't want to tell my aunt about this lest it led me to telling her about the stolen book and the butterfly people or, worse, her asking me to read the poem to her. It was somehow easier telling her about a book I was not-writing than the poems I was.

'I'm pleased things are working out, Lew. You're OK with everything now?'

'I think so. I'm getting there.'

By 'everything now' my aunt meant the death of my father, still four weeks fresh at that point. I had not disabused her of a belief that I had taken his death badly. My 'loss' gave me leverage, permitting me to request things that might otherwise seem cheeky; things such as asking if I could stay longer in her house than the original two weeks she'd offered.

'Grief does strange things,' she said. 'I know I felt weird when my Pa died. I couldn't face people for months. I think you're doing great, Lew.'

When I got to work on the barn that morning I found myself picking up the argument with the butterfly guy – really an argument with myself that I'd had the night before. It was about 'reading' versus 'experiencing' and I was winning this argument handsomely when a car pulled up the drive, country music blaring. It was a sedan of unidentifiable make or model; its bonnet was metallic blush-red, the rest of the car was cobalt-blue. A man in a baggy yellow cotton jacket, lilac shirt, green shorts, white socks and trainers stepped from the car and it took me a few moments to realize that it was Joe Bosco. Joe's jacket was too small for him and his shorts were a two-tone moss–lime green. Despite the appalling, ill-fitting, uncoordinated get-up, his sheer animation and wonderful physique made it all work.

'Hey there, Lew!'

It is a measure of my neediness for contact that someone speaking my name came as a pleasant surprise, even when that person was someone I regarded, at that point, as a thieving hick. But I was immediately glad to see him. He was carrying a book and a glass box and came up the path looking all around, assessing the premises as if measuring it out for his own purposes.

'Oh my!' he said. 'Would you look at this.'

My aunt's house was pretty enough but hardly exceptional. It was a standard white clapboard 'New Englander'; it had a veranda with wicker chairs and roses growing on the timbers, a white picket fence and an average-sized barn for those parts. It could have been transposed to any Midwestern town without causing comment or offence.

'Here.' He held out the book to me. It was my stolen *Classic American Stories*. 'My goddamn little sister. She ran off with it. I only caught up to her at the bottom of the creek. She does these things. She's a klepto.' The book's spine was broken but its return was so unexpected I didn't complain. 'This is for you, too.'

He handed me a 6" by 4" glass box with five clear sides and blacked-out base. It contained the swallowtail he'd caught and killed in front of me the day before. The butterfly had been mounted upon a piece of smooth, pale-grey driftwood and its wings were fully expanded. I could clearly see their intricate venation, like the lead lines holding in pieces of stained glass. It's easy to overlook that kind of detail in the blur of brilliance that

14

is a butterfly flying by, but caught and displayed in a box you noticed things. It was just as he'd said to me the day before: '*She'll give people more joy dead than alive. You'll see.*'

'This is a fine barn you're working on here.'

He left me holding the butterfly and the book and marched up towards the ladder. He grabbed the rails and shook them to test the steadiness. He looked at the tin of paint and sniffed it. 'You need a hand here.' It wasn't a question and he wasn't asking permission. I'm not sure Joe ever asked permission.

'What about your clothes?' I offered, lamely, not wanting him to mess up my system, such as it was. (If there was a system, Joe would mess it up.)

He took off his jacket and threw it on the grass, rolled up his shirt sleeves, picked up the brush and dipped it in the tin and started to layer on the paint thick and fast, with great splashy strokes, singing to himself as he did: 'Dee dee dee. Dee dee dee.' He had such a superabundance of energy and it could not be contained.

'You've done this before, then.'

'I've been varnishing barns since I was eating Gerber. You gotta get it on quick. One time, when we lived in Michigan, I was painting the barn just hours before we had a tornado. When the tornado came our two dogs would not come inside the shelter. We were yelling at them but they just wanted to bark at that twister. So the twister comes and it picks them up and slams them against the side of the barn and leaves two doggie-shaped imprints there on the un-dried paint.'

He painted manically, for about ten minutes, covering twice what I would have done in the time, and as he painted, he asked me questions as though I were the visitor and he the host. How had he done that? How dare this guy barge in to my nice, ordered life and turn everything upside down, with his theologies and entomologies and mangled etymologies!

'I'm curious. What brings you here, Lew? You didn't come all this way just to paint a barn.'

I set the case with the swallowtail on the garden table and explained my family connection, how my mother's sister had married an American and moved here when she was just twenty. How I had always wanted to see America. I spoke euphemistically about my travel plans. My intention to work here and there. For good measure, I told him I was writing a book. I gave him a fair bit of myself and as I talked it became clear that my need to talk was greater than I cared to admit. The information poured out of me with a candidness almost inappropriate outside of a counselling couch or lover's bed.

Joe didn't appear to be listening. He nodded away but – like an actor in a badly dubbed foreign film – the timing of his nods and his cod-meaningful expressions didn't quite synch with what I was telling him. Then, as abruptly as he'd begun painting, he stopped, descended the ladder, tossing the brush to the ground, spattering the green grass blue.

'Gotta see inside this barn.'

He climbed the side steps to the open door in two bounds. He was always moving, like the Cat In The Hat, setting a plate spinning and then moving on to the next plate, then the next. He never heard the crashing behind him because he'd already moved on.

'You must be kidding me!'

When I caught up to him, Joe was running his hand along a bookshelf, shaking his head.

'How many books are here?'

'Ten thousand. Exactly ten thousand, apparently.'

'It would take you twenty years to read them all.'

Joe stopped and pulled a book from a shelf. He started to read from it haltingly, in a robotic, flat monotone giving the prose no chance of success whatsoever: ' "At the clubhouse the next morning, the unshaven Knights were . . . lumbering and red-eyed. They moved around list . . . listlessly and cursed each step." ' He stopped reading and tossed the book aside whilst reaching for another. He read from the next in the same manner,

16

managing to make a different author sound like the last. ' "Cheese it, the cops," whispered Bettina. "Why, Blake," she said loudly, "you . . . angel ape . . . angel ape . . . of a stud, who do you think I'm talking to?" Eeuuu, that sucks.' He threw the book to the floor, its pages flapping as it landed spatchcocked, a broken bird. He grabbed another: ' "Some months after, dragged to the gibbet at the tail of a mule, the black met his voiceless . . . his voiceless end." ' He paused, deigning to look at the cover. I reached out this time and took the book – *Billy Budd and Other Stories* – from his hand before he threw it across the room.

'Please be careful. They don't belong to me. Besides. It's hardly fair, is it? Reading random extracts like that. To make some kind of point.'

'The point is this, Lew: there's a time for reading stories, and there's a time for making them. You read too much about other people's lives, you forget to live your own.'

He moved on, measuring the floor with his metre-length strides. When he reached the end he saw something in the corner. 'What have we got here?' He was inspecting a spider's web in which there was a single butterfly wing. He extracted the wing from the web taking care not to break the threads. Joe could be tremendously gentle when he wanted to be and, despite the violence of things to come, I believed then and still believe now that he wouldn't hurt a fly (unless severely provoked) or a butterfly (unless he could sell it). He studied the brown and – to my eyes – featureless wing the way a person might read a text. He was at his most calm and contented when 'lepping'. As I watched him studying the insect I studied him and noticed discolouring on his wrists and forearms, scarring that looked like skin-grafts.

'*Papilio ulysses* here? Can't be,' he said. 'Met a bad end.'

A butterfly named after my hero? I took that as a sign.

The cat then put back his hat and resumed to turning things upside down. The typewriter was next in his sights and he was on it before I realized it still had my previous night's effort sitting on the platen.

'This your book?' My heart flopped then spluttered.

'No . . .'

He bent over and twisted the platen knob to release the sheet. Then, to my horror, he started to read the poem out loud, in the same sense-crushing way he'd read from the random books.

'"At Kaaterskill Falls
  I met a man
  Who killed a butterfly
  With bare hands;
  Then saw a girl,
  In the brook
  Who killed me, too
  With one bare look."'

'Please. It's not really for . . .'

'This is great. I'm in a poem! This is me and Mary, right?'

'It could be. It's just . . . thoughts.'

'Well. I like these thoughts . . .

'"They stole my stories
  Then my pride
  The book no longer
  At my . . ."'

I had to physically retrieve the sheet to stop him. I put out my hand. 'It's really not meant for others to read.'

'Aw . . . don't be so sensitive. This is funny.'

'Well it's not actually meant to be.'

He handed me the poem back. He seemed genuinely tickled by my efforts but I'd rather have swum naked in front of him than have him read on.

'I tell you, we could use a wordy guy. I'm looking for one right now.'

He started rubbing his hands together and then he struck the pose of someone about to make an offer: hands out palms up, the purpose-driven smile.

'Look. Llewellyn, Lew . . . whatever, – and we have to do something about the name – I'll be straight with you. When I first saw you I thought, "Who is this pale, puny, good-for-nothing European guy lying by the river, smoking weed and reading a book?" I saw you from the top of the falls before we got to the pool and I thought you looked dissatisfied, like some philosopher, the way you were lying on your side with one leg up. I mean it was hot as heck and yet there you were, nose down inside this book, reading it as if it contained an answer to life's mysteries. I was sure that it contained no such thing and that even if it did you weren't going to put it to it any use. When we talked I kinda liked you, and some of what you said about beauty and such, though I knew you were looking down your nose at us, like you thought we were a couple of redneck retards. You didn't disguise that too well.'

'I wasn't thinking that.'

'It's OK. I'm used to it. But I was impressed you made the dive. I didn't think you would do that. That showed me you had some life – some daring – in you. But then Mary-Anne steals the book! I chase after her. We get back home and later I am lying in bed feeling bad about this, and I'm half thinking about the day and some of the things you said, and the way you said them, and it comes to me that maybe you could be the answer to my prayers. At the precise moment when my business is growing and I am in need of intelligent, articulative people, I meet you. You could be the right man at the right time! With that voice and your way with words and your understated manner. So I came here not only to return your book but to make you a proposal: to offer you a job working for us. I'll put you in charge of marketing. You will be paid well. You'll have a car. And, as a bonus, you will get to see this great country of ours. Although its greatness doesn't necessarily lie in what Americans say or think is great about it. But I do promise you this: if you come and work for me, I will show you America.'

Joe was raising a severe challenge to my continued days of hermitry. When he was selling hard, when he wanted something, words and thoughts poured out of him like an Ontario over a Niagara. He worked up a flow and rode the froth and foam.

'I did some telesales once. But I'm not sure I'd make much of a salesman.'

'That'll be your secret weapon. Modesty. Understatement. This country's overrun with guys full of their own gas and there's no trick of the trade the public hasn't seen or heard. But you'll bring something new. With your cynicalistic European ways and your way with quotes. I can see you are an educated man. A refined person. You are not easily impressed. These are things we need. Qualities I need.'

'What would I have to sell? I don't even know what you do. What your business is.'

'Come and see.'

He led me back to his car. Despite my above-average knowledge of American makes and models, I really couldn't identify this vehicle. Its front grille didn't look like it belonged to the rest of the car and was tilted down on one side. The radiator chrome had a Buick emblem but the side signs said it was a Chevrolet. A bumper sticker read *What the hell, it runs*.

'What make of car is this?'

'It's my Chuick. Maybe the only Chuick in the world. Rarer than a five-winged morpho. I hit a deer in Pennsylvania and had to rebuild the front. It used to be a Chevrolet Caprice Classic but after the accident I had to fix it up with a Buick Delta 88 grille and the front fender. I came pretty close to meeting my Maker that day. The car flipped a full one-eighty and drove into a spruce. I got cut up pretty bad.'

'Is that how you got . . . those?'

He scratched his forearms and paused for a moment (Joe's state of perpetual motion made any pause seem like a meditation). Then he laughed. 'Nah. I got these when I was a kid.'

He leant in the driver's side to pop the trunk then went to

the back and lifted the lid, inviting me to look in. Was he about to show me something awful: a body perhaps, guns, or some illicit contraband? No. It was a trunk full of butterflies. Butterflies in glass cases. Small, medium and large cases with one, two or three butterflies per case, all mounted on driftwood, some decorated with dried flowers. The colours and patterns flew out in a dazzle of visual information, black blotches, blue crenels, cinnabar eyespots, neon blues, parakeet greens (phrases I would come to learn and use later).

'You sell these?'

'We sure do.'

'Who to?'

'To gift shops. Flower shops. A few department stores. And pretty soon to America's Number One retail chain. J. C. Penney. We sell in eleven states so far. But we're about to go national. And that's where you come in. I'm gonna need extra hands on the wheel. Extra heads in the room.'

'Is it . . . I mean, is it OK to sell them?'

'Sure.'

'Do you catch them yourself?'

'You're kidding me!' He picked up a case containing an extravagantly marked little lime green and black beauty. 'This one's from Australia. That one's from Alaska. And then . . .' He reached in and held up a case containing a single, large, neon-blue giant. 'These blue morphos are from a farm in Costa Rica. Our Number One Seller. Although we're trying to rear our own.'

The stunning specimen was as big as a man's hand. 'It looks rare.'

'Nah! These bugs are as common as ants. We offer seventy-two different species in total. All legally sourced and CITES approved. I'll explain that later. Look at it.'

He put the beauty in my hands and started to sell it to me, adopting a slight Southern drawl.

'Sir. For fifteen bucks you get something that reminds you that there is beauty in this world and that creation is calling out to us and saying, "Look! How amazing!" I mean: look at this! This creature before you started life as an ovum and then grew through the fixed order of insect metamorphoses – larva, pupa, imago – having come out of one male adult and one female adult, in a primordial act of creation, and then reproduced their own kind through time – and is now here, captured in this setting for your pleasure, for as long as you are alive to see it. It's more than just a piece of scientific data, it's a message from the Lord himself – a message that says, "Look how much I love you and see what I can do!" For fifteen bucks that's not bad. What do you say?'

This was pure Joe: a mangled three-way tug between the salesman, the scientist and the saint. I laughed. 'You almost make me want to buy it.'

'That's my Bible Belt pitch. For atheists (and I'm guessing that's you) I have a different spiel. If I'm in Virginia or Georgia, I pile on the creation stuff. If I'm selling on the east coast, we go for nature and environmental matters. In the Midwest they like some combination of guns, God and America is Great. If I'm in California, I talk about spirituality and a person's "inner butterfly". But the pitch that works for everyone is the story of how we came to sell butterflies. That works most places, with adjustment for prejudice. You have to use all your powers of observation and sympathy to try and understand what the potential purchaser thinks and wants. Like the butterfly itself, you have to adapt to the environment to survive. I think you'll be a natural, Lew. Help me spread the word. What do you say?'

'It's an interesting offer.'

'Interesting! It's a lifetime's opportunity! You can stay here reading books about people who don't even exist, written by people who are dead, and try to write about things you ain't experienced. Or you can get out there and live! You can't serve what you ain't cooking. You only wrote that poem because of me. Follow me and I'll give you a whole book to write.'

Joe had the knack (handy in the salesman) of making you feel your life could be so much more interesting if you dropped everything and followed him; he took delight in making your existing plans and alternative prospects seem bleak whilst identifying your deeper desires and suggesting he could meet them. His methods weren't subtle, he always ran the risk of insulting or crushing you whilst flattering and bigging you up; but he had my number before I had his. He'd diagnosed my malaise and his medicine sounded sweet.

'Here.'

He reached inside his suit jacket pocket and produced a little box of business cards. The box was still sealed but had a sample card taped to the outside. He pulled the sample card off and gave it to me.

Joseph Bosco

President

Butterfly World.

'Lovingly hand-crafted gift items'

Cellphone 201 345711

There was no address.

'Where are you based?'

He nodded towards the mountains. 'Over the hills, not far away. We operate from home. It's a family business: "Lovingly hand-crafted gift items".'

I ran a thumb over the script to see if it was embossed, but it was smooth.

'Think about it. Just don't take twenty years getting back to me, like the guy in that story!'

'You do read then.'

'Sure I do. And if that story had a message for you I'd say it was: "Wake up, Rip! Before the best years of your life pass you by." Hey. Maybe that's what I should call you. Rip.'

He threw his suit jacket on the back seat of the Chuick, a seat still covered in the detritus of recent journeys. He got in and started up the car. The raspberry purr-growl of its V8 was a sound full of prospect and road-yearning, pulling me with it.

He drove off at speed and honked his horn. I stood there and watched him until the car vanished up round and into the side of the hemlock hills. I felt the sadness of the person left behind, the envy of the person not going anywhere. As I walked back to the barn, I almost shuddered at the thought of carrying on the way I had been and not ever getting out on The Road.

I picked up the case with the yellow swallowtail. The base of the case had the little gold sticker with its Latin name – *Papilio glaucus* – but beneath this there was a hand-scratched message:

'A *thing of beauty is a joy forever.*'

Joe Bosco. How I underestimated you. I thought you weren't listening but you'd heard everything, seen everything, clocked everything. You had given the impression you were an impatient, boorish fool, and then you went and showed a delicacy and a thoughtfulness that won me back.

I can't overestimate how easy it was to underestimate him. You think you have him pinned down, identified, named and categorized, then he changed colour, or sprouted a fifth wing, or turned out to have different underside markings to the ones he really should have. It would have been easy to write him off, with his grating voice, his dime-store blagging, hyperbolic hawking, his invasion of personal space, his anti-intellectualism, his spiritual certainties, his exploitation of nature for commercial gain, his assumptions and presumptions. Most people I know would have had nothing to do with this guy and given how things have turned out, maybe I shouldn't have either. I should have thrown his cheap, un-embossed business card in the bin, stuck to my routine, finished the barn, read some more books, smoked my weed and set out to see America on my own and in the usual way. But it was too late: The Cat had set me spinning in his Kingdom of Spinning Plates.

CHAPTER THREE

In which I am re-baptized and re-located.

I was re-named Rip Van Jones in a panoramic lay-by overlooking the Hudson River plateau upon which great American families – the Roosevelts, the Vanderbilts and Van Cortlands – had built their prodigious homes. The ceremony was conducted by Joe and witnessed by Elijah, a sixteen-year-old black kid Joe had found trying to steal his car in Albany and who now worked as a butterfly-case maker for 'Butterfly World'. As Joe finger-splashed me with Coca-Cola he delivered his own mashed-up baptismal rites: 'In the name of the Road that leads to sales and glory, I baptize you Rip Van Jones, butterfly salesman. We here gathered commit to pray for your soul for as long as it needs prayerfulness and see to it that you deliver as much product to the people of this great nation – although let's never forget that its greatness doesn't necessarily lie in what the American people think makes it great – and that you do this work to the best of your ability under His Grace. Can I get a witness?' Joe looked around. Elijah was eating a bag of Lay's potato chips and staring at his feet. 'Can I get a witness?' Elijah mumbled a 'yay' and Joe brought proceedings to a close with a souped-up preacher's 'A-men!' He then produced a little box of business cards and handed them to me.

'I got these made up in Lexington, on the way to Mississippi.' Again, the sample card was taped to the outside of the box.

Rip Van Jones
Head of Sales & Marketing
Butterfly World.
Cell no 214 3213421
'A thing of beauty is a joy forever'

The script was embossed. As I ran my finger over it Joe giggled with pleasure. 'I saw you turning up your nose up at my card. So I got these and some new ones for myself. You see, Rip! These are the kind of improvements your sophisticated ways are going to bring to us. See I changed the motto.'

'You got them made before I said yes?'

'Oh, I knew you'd say yes.'

When it comes to making important decisions, my grandfather said you should sleep on it, and then sleep on sleeping on it. Just to be sure-sure. Before calling Joe to accept his offer I gave it the overnight-overnight test, to allow time for a change of heart or fate to intervene; but I knew what my decision would be. I knew it when he'd driven off, leaving me with a chasmic feeling of missed opportunity; I knew it when I saw the Keats quoted back at me so unexpectedly from the base of the butterfly case. And I felt it in my animal desire to see his book-stealing sister again. In the two days before I made the call, I did what I sometimes do when anxiously wanting confirmation of a decision already made: I looked for omens in everyday phenomena. I said: 'If the numbers of his phone add up to a significant number I will do it; and, lo and behold, they added up to twenty-three, my age at that point. I said: 'If I see something very unusual, something I do not expect to see, I will accept'; and, would you believe it, at breakfast the next morning a black bear walked across the lawn right before my eyes (in the twenty years since she'd had the house my aunt had never seen a bear in the Catskills let alone her garden). I even granted fate a last-minute intervention. As I dialled Joe's cellphone number, I told myself that if his phone rang three times before he answered it was meant to be. He answered on the fourth ring:

'Butterfly World. This is Joe Bosco!'

A country and western ballad was playing loudly on the car radio: 'gonna make my man see, gonna take him home, see'.

'Joe? It's Llew Jones.'

'Rip! It's you! So – you decided to come work for me!'

'I think so.'

'You think so? Or you know so?'

The music remained at yell-forcing volume. 'I'd love to work for you! If you still want me!'

'Of course we want you! Hey, Mary, turn it down will ya? This is great! This is great! You are not going to regret this decision, Rip. We will take this country by storm. States will fall. Right now I'm in the Magnolia State. Know which one that is?'

'No.'

'Mississippi! We're heading north to the Volunteer State. Then it's the Bluegrass State. Then we drive through Almost Heaven State up to the Keystone State and back to the Empire State! I'll come by and pick you up in a couple of days.' In a few state-swallowing sentences, Joe shrank the nation to Sunday-afternoon-drive size.

'You got a suit?'

'I have a smart shirt and a jacket.'

'That's OK but we gotta get you a suit. Get you in front of some honchos. I been using your "thing of beauty" line on people all week. Like today, when I was selling, I said it to the store owner and she went all quiet. I thought, hell I've blown it. Then she just said: "Mr Bosco, that is the most beautiful thing I have ever heard." She took a box of twelve mixed cases right there! You see, Rip! Your words are doing business for me already.'

'I'm glad. Although they're not my words.'

'Take the credit here! No one's gonna know! Oh. Mary says hullo by the way. And she says sorry for stealing the book. Right, Mary?'

I could hear Mary saying no such thing. But I could picture her: denim dungarees, bare feet up on the dashboard, painting her toenails black, and I confess the prospect of seeing her again was a draw more powerful than America itself.

'So. I'll be there to pick you up late Friday afternoon. Take you to meet the family. They'll all be lovin' on you! I'll show you the ropes. We'll stock up and be out on the road before you can say Kalamazoo. Ever seen the great monarch migration?'

'No.'

'You'll see it. One of the greatest wonders in nature.'

'I just have to tell my aunt what I'm doing. But that should be fine.'

'Tell her you'll be working for one of this nation's most entre-preneurialistic persons and helping to bring joy and beauty into people's lives.'

'What about my things? Do I bring everything?'

'This is a family business, Rip, and you're going to be part of the family. Bring it all.'

'But you . . . have room?'

This made him really laugh. 'Aww! He's asking if we have room, Mary. You hear that? Tell him. Tell him how many rooms we got.'

'Tell him yourself.'

'There are many rooms in my mansion, Rip. You'll see.'

He broke into song, the way he did when he was excited, mimicking the tune still playing on the radio and adapting the lyrics to the moment: 'I'm gonna make my man, see; I'm gonna take him home, see; see the folks he's gonna see, how many rooms he will see! Rip is gonna work for me! Dee dee dee dee dee, dee; dee dee dee dee dee, dee!'

I still had Joe pinned for poor-white-trash-done-good at this point. I had pictured him living in a tumbledown shack with jalopies on concrete blocks in the yard, wire-mesh fencing running the perimeter, and siblings sleeping three to a bed. I had not and could not imagine him living in a mansion. Butterfly salesmen didn't live in mansions.

My aunt seemed genuinely pleased when I told her about the job. I admit I made it sound more kosher, more formal, than it was, partly because I didn't want her to think I was getting involved in something weird, or working for a cowboy outfit; but also because I didn't want to disappoint her or seem ungrateful in any way. She had been kind to me. I said I'd met the CEO of a national company that specialized in making 'a range of gift items' and that they were looking for someone to help them take their business 'to a new level'. I seasoned the whole dish with phrases like 'sales and marketing', 'promotional literature', and threw in the likely J. C. Penney deal for good measure. I summarized it all as being, at the very least, a way of seeing America and getting paid for it. I didn't describe Joe or mention butterflies, but nothing I told her was untrue.

And so, five days later I sat on the veranda waiting for Joe, packed and ready to go. The sky was overcast and I could feel the electricity of a gathering storm. Clouds were forming, bulging full of threat. I realize that I might be seeing everything through omen-tinted spectacles now, but these clouds were shaping up to be just like clouds you'd want to convey a message that change was coming. Change, and maybe trouble. *Cumulo portentous*. The first drops started to hit the road and that lovely smell of rain on hot tarmac filled the air. The downpour was torrential but quick, unlike the rain where I come from which is timid and persistent; this rain passed so fast that by the time Joe arrived the sun was out and the road shining from the storm's aftermath. He turned up in a brand-new midnight-blue Cadillac Seville with Elijah sitting in the passenger seat. Joe beamed proudly as he came up to the veranda to greet me. The mullet was gone. As were his terrible clothes. His hair had been cut conventionally and gelled back and he was wearing a new dark suit, a white cotton shirt, sober, silk polka-dot tie and black Oxford shoes. He looked like a Mormon coming to convert me: a comparison he would utterly reject on the grounds that he believed Mormonism was based on a bogus revelation and was as perfect an example of Bad Theology as one could find in this world. He opened the flap of his suit jacket to show me the lining.

'What do you think?'

'Very smart.'

'The President of Butterfly World needs to look the part. You like the tie? It's the same colour as a malachite. You like the Caddy?'

'Yes. You . . . just bought it?'

'No! It's a rental. When you pull into the lot of a bank you got to look like an executive with national ambitions. We get the big deal done we'll buy our own Caddies. Think of it as an incentive.'

It looked a little stubby for a Cadillac and lacked the trailer-trash-charm of the Chuick, but it was new and expensive and suggested success, which was the point. I could feel questions forming in my mind but in the whoosh of those first days obvious questions rarely got from my head to my tongue because there was always a fresh distraction to delight in, some new surprise to absorb.

Like the fact that a young black kid was sitting in Joe's car.

Joe waved at the kid, who was listening to a Walkman, moving his head to another beat. 'Hey! Elijah! Elijah! Come say hi!' Elijah pulled off his headset and got out of the car. As he loped towards me, he scratched his hands and avoided eye contact.

'Say hi then!' Joe said to him, with sudden exasperation.

'Hi.'

I said 'hi' back and shook Elijah's hand, which was dry and calloused and covered in little prickly rashes.

'Say something then!' Joe coaxed the kid.

'Do you have cars in England?' Elijah asked.

'Yes. We do.'

'Do you have Cadillacs?'

'Well. There might be some but we don't make them.'

'Do you have Fords?'

'Yes. We have Fords. Smaller than yours. Everything is smaller than yours.'

'Oh.'

This seemed to satisfy him.

'Elijah used to be called Leroy, which is no help in this country, and in Albany a sure-fire passport to the state pen. I gave him a name to make folks sit up and give him some respect. Now he's Production Manager for Butterfly World and is the fastest case-maker we ever had. He makes them quicker than my sister Isabelle. Isn't that so, Eli?'

Elijah gave a modest nod.

'Rip here is going to be bringing you in so many orders you won't be able to keep up.'

Joe's philanthropy was admirable but I was a little irritated to hear this. It undermined my newfound sense of self-importance, as well as my hope that Butterfly World was a company going places. If a gauche teenage kid could be a Production Manager for Joe's company then my speedy rise to Head of Sales and Marketing was not such an achievement. Joe's hyperbole notwithstanding, I wanted to believe his rhetoric about me being 'the right man at the right time'; I wanted to be chosen on merit not randomly rescued.

These cusp-of-journey fears were soon forgotten in the pure thrill of setting off in a car named after a French explorer and an Andalusian city, with a man built like a Titan and a boy named after a prophet who was carried off to heaven in a golden chariot. I looked back at my aunt's house and the freshly painted barn for the last time. I was saying farewell to introspection, sedentary contemplation and going nowhere; hello to sensual experience, the great outdoors and the pull of The Road. I was saying goodbye to Llewellyn Jones too, for within the hour I would have a new name, a name charged with American myth, and I was full of hope for things I could not see.

As we ascended Hunter Mountain, Joe jabbered away. I think he was even more excited than I was. He drove like an

31

actor in an old movie, where they deliver their lines whilst barely glancing at the road and a fake background is projected onto the back window.

'The whole family are curious to meet you, Rip. I told them you are a charming, cultured fellow of fine tastes and opinions, so you mustn't let me down on that.'

'I'll do my best.'

'I told them to call you Rip. No offence, but that old name of yours just isn't serviceable. You can't have a name people can't say right. It's death to sales. So we're going to conduct a little ceremony up here, at the Hudson Panorama. Elijah, hand me that Coke.'

So Joe re-named and re-baptized me with the sweet liquid of his land. I actually liked the no-nonsense brevity and associations of my new name. It was good to be free of my phlegmy L's. And when we were done, he put an arm round my shoulder and showed me the vista as though he owned everything in it and was about to offer it all to me. 'There she is: America. When we moved here I brought Ma to this spot and told her the names of the great families who lived down there on the Hudson and I made her a promise that the Boscos would do for butterflies what Carnegie did for steel, the Vanderbilts for railroads and the Rockefellers for oil. We are about to take it to the next level. And you are going to help us get there, Rip. You've been sent for a time such as this.'

Joe was a person who found books in brooks, sermons in stones and the good in everything. I didn't believe any of this for a second, and I am not sure Joe did either, but I went along with the theatre of it because there was foolish pleasure to be had in such wild fancy and sometimes wild fancy brings about impossible things. I had a feeling that people must have at the beginning of all great voyages, a root feeling, a radical stripping-back to the absolute of journeying, where you feel like you are starting afresh, without the hindrance of history. It's ridiculous, but from the moment Joe gave me my new name I really did feel like a new person.

❋   ❋   ❋

Joe was vague about where he lived and the time it might take to get there. It was simply 'over the hills, not far away'. It is only thirty miles from the east of the Catskills to the west as the bald eagle flies, but it seemed to take hours to get there; I can recall my feelings that day more clearly than the route to his house. I remember the summer-stalled ski-lifts of the Hunter resort, the hippy paraphernalia of the other Woodstock. And I can picture passing through forests of black Norway spruce and by white churches with slim steeples and narrow peristyles; but my mind was on what was round the corner. Mention of Joe's mother had got my thoughts driving on ahead to his family and their 'mansion with many rooms'.

'You have a big family, then?'

'Let's see. There's me. Ma. My sisters: Mary-Anne, you met. And Isabelle. She is the serious one. Then we have Little Celeste who we adopted. Old Clay who we found in a garbage truck. And Elijah here. And now we got you. That makes eight. If you count the dogs, Nancy and Ronnie, that makes ten.'

'What about your father?'

Joe went quiet for a few seconds – an era of silence in his case – and then he made a groaning hum like a dying animal. I immediately regretted asking the question.

'Sorry.'

Joe looked like he was weighing what to tell and what not to tell. He checked the rear-view mirror. 'Elijah?' The boy didn't stir but Joe repeated his name louder just to be sure. Then he turned to me.

'One thing I have to tell you now, Rip. We don't talk about my father. He is The Unmentionable One. He's the cancer

33

you've just been diagnosed with. The haemorrhoids you got. The elephant in the china shop.'

'Bull. You mean bull in a china shop. Or elephant in the room.'

'You see, Rip. It's this kind of refininering I need. Out there, you'll be the polisher of my rough edges. What I'm saying is, don't raise that question around the house. Especially around Ma. Never around Ma.'

Was this permission to 'go there' with him? It was the sort of prohibition you immediately wanted to break. 'Sorry. I didn't mean to be nosy.'

'It's OK. I just don't want you asking Ma the wrong thing and getting on the wrong stick!'

'I'll keep . . . mum.'

'But you should know how we got to where we got. That's important. You need to know the story. In case you have to use it yourself. It's part of the sales pitch.'

And that was when Joe told me his version of the Bosco family history, a history that (I would learn) would mutate in the telling and vary with the teller:

Joe (twenty-five) was the eldest of three children: Isabelle (twenty) and Mary-Anne (nineteen). Joe's father was a leading entomologist and lecturer in zoology. Joe's mother, Edith, was from a poor Southern family but savvy enough to teach herself bookkeeping and earn extra money as an eye model. He described her as pedigree hillbilly turned middle class. They were a reasonably prosperous couple living in Palos Verdes, a suburb near Long Beach, California. Joe's father spent most of the year away on expeditions to South America, in search of rare and new species of butterfly. His long trips away were a source of tension between Joe's parents. Sometimes he'd disappear for months into the jungles of Yucatán, or the rainforests of Colombia, in pursuit of his obsession, sending packages of incredibly rare specimens in glassine envelopes back in parcels which Edith kept in a naphthalene-laden trunk. The long absences already put a great strain on the marriage. One day Joe's father called, from Bogotá, to say it was over. He was leaving. Not coming back. That same night a fire destroyed the home and nearly killed Edith, who was eight months pregnant. The fire was caused when his preserving chemicals ignited. That was the 'straw that flipped the camel on its back'. Joe's mother filed for divorce. The father didn't contest it. Edith moved the family to Tucson and then to Michigan where she got a job as PA to a university administrator. It was in Michigan that Joe became a keen bug collector and butterfly chaser. One day, when Joe's mother was sick and in bed, he set his prize *Colias eurydice* on a piece of wood inside a 4" by 6" glass box, made it look pretty with some dried flowers and gave it to her as a get-well present. Joe's mother took one look at it and said, 'We should make these and sell them.' Joe knew where to source the butterflies in sufficient bulk; they just needed some glass, some silicone and bits of wood on which to mount them. The local flower store took an order of two dozen cases and sold them all in no time. Encouraged, Joe and his mother started to sell on the road, going farther afield, down to Ann Arbor, up to Saginaw and west to Kalamazoo, loading up the trunk of the Caprice Classic and driving until it was empty. It was unsolicited cold-selling and not everyone took the product, but once a store took an order repeat business usually followed. Before long the order-sizes increased and they began to venture across state lines into Wisconsin, Indiana, Ohio, Illinois and Pennsylvania, selling butterflies from the trunk and taking sample boxes to get pre-orders. The family business was soon taking in regular orders from gift and flower shops in six states. Then, about a year ago, the Boscos decided to move further east, 'in search of new opportunities'. They found a house in the Catskills with enough space to create a factory to meet the increased orders that were coming in. They started to employ people to help and Joe started making plans to pitch the products to the big chain stores and get the 'national order' they were looking for.

That was around about the time he met me.

If someone you don't know well tells you their family history, particularly a history with trauma at its centre, what can you do but accept it at face value? I had no reason to disbelieve this account at the time and nor did I; I believed he was telling me the truth, even the truth about the untruths.

'Thanks for telling me that.'

'I mix it up sometimes, Rip. When I need to tug the heartstrings during a sale that's flagging I can call on that history to win a few extra orders. Maybe get into the detail of how I saved my ma from the fire. Sometimes I might tell them my father went missing in the jungle. How I was the main "bread and butterfly winner" from the age of around ten. Folks love that rising from the ashes stuff. And they love how I saved Ma from the fire. And everyone loves a story where someone gets killed. That really greases the skids. It's a straight road to sympathy. Every time.'

I couldn't tell if he was being serious or not until he giggled. 'I'm just kidding.'

'About your Ma nearly dying in the fire?'

'Nooo!' he squealed. 'I wouldn't make something like that up! That would be twisted!'

'Of course not. I'm sorry.'

'But if it's your story, you can do what you like with it. They usually ask me how I got these anyway.'

He lifted a hand from the wheel and held out the scarred wrist that I'd noticed in the barn. He then started to hum some as yet un-composed tune, signalling an end to this line of talk. The fire at the heart of this history had supplied quick kindling for my speculations, but I decided not to ask any more about it for now.

We were at the western end of the Catskills and climbing again, along a road that narrowed until it became track. A hood of vapours had collected around a peak and with the sun going down there was a glow to the sky that my new namesake would almost certainly have described as sanguine (a word that seems better applied to sunsets than people). For the first time in days I desired a spliff.

'There are a few other things you should know about my mother,' Joe said. 'She swings from calm to crazy like that.' He flicked his fingers. 'One minute she is as sweet as maple syrup. Take you in as her own son. The next she'll curse you to hell. And when she curses she does it like she's paid by the word. It's hard to take at first but you'll get used to it. It pretty much started the day after the fire. She's still angry with God, the world and the Unmentionable One. When we get there she might act as though she has no idea you are coming even though I told her a hundred times. I'll need to go and explain things again. She might swear like crazy at me, she will say all kinds of stuff but she won't really mean any of it. She'll blow herself out like a twister in April. At her centre there's this calm part, the generous, kind part of her. Remember to hold on to that in the middle of the storm.'

'But she does know I'm coming to work for you?'

'Sure! But she forgets stuff. And she gets mad at me for bringing people back to the house. Ain't that right, Eli?'

Elijah was now awake, face pressed against the windowpane, looking out sadly at the passing trees. 'I guess.'

'When I brought Clay home that was something. She always taught us to practise charity. I found Clay literally in the back of the truck where they throw the garbage. I thought I'd bring him back home. When I turned up I thought she'd kill him. I had to hide the gun. She keeps a gun in her bed, under her pillow, for effect. She likes to get it out and shoot the chandelier some days but it's nothing to worry about. Now she loves Old Man Clay like he's her own. It'll be the same with you. There might be a little test for you when you meet her but you'll be good.'

'A little test? What kind of test?'

'If I told you what the test was it wouldn't be a test. Just don't speak too much. It'll make her think you're conceited. And don't speak too little. It'll make her think you're timid and if

37

there is a thing my mother will crush, it is timidinicity. She hates weakness and she hates pride. It's a tightrope you gotta learn to walk. And tell the truth. If she looks you in the eyes and asks you a question, tell the truth! She'll know when it's not. If there is nothin' she hates more in this world it's a liar.'

The sun was almost down when we came to the entrance gates of the house. The pillars were the height of a man and had balls on the pediments. The wrought-iron gates themselves were drawn back and one was off its hinges. The drive curved away out of sight, bisecting a wood and unkempt lawns. The uncut grass in the middle of the drive brushed the undercarriage of the car and Joe drove slowly, to draw things out for my benefit. He kept looking at me, giving me his 'I bet you weren't expecting this' grin.

Two dogs – an Alsatian and a Dobermann – bounded up to the car, barking and snapping at the wheels. I remember thinking these were either the dogs of a rich man with something to protect or the dogs of criminals with something to fear.

'Here's Nancy and Ronnie!' Joe yelled. 'Don't get out until they are chained. They don't know you, they'll rip your throat out.'

The dogs gave us a barking escort up the long, long drive, Joe taunting them with little dummy swerves, accelerations and decelerations. 'Come on, crazy dogs! Come on, crazy dogs!'

We continued for maybe a mile through thick forest, on a slight camber, and then the track straightened and a house came into view. I was still, even at this late stage, expecting a shack, or perhaps a lodge or a cabin in the grounds of a rich man's estate. When Joe had used the word 'mansion' to describe his home I had assumed euphemism, or more Joe-oversell. But the house was a huge neo-Gothic stately pile, and with the sinking sun making a silhouette of its gables, turrets and folly attics, it was a splendid sight, a house worthy of any of those Captains of Industry who had made their homes over the hills not far away, and

Joe was drinking in my surprise, slowing the car to eke out every drop of it.

'It used to belong to a gun-manufacturer. It's the house that homicide built!' He laughed at this joke, a joke that seemed well rehearsed. 'It was sitting empty for thirty years. No one would touch it because there was some stupid superstition about all the crimes that paid for it. But the real crime was that a place like this was empty for so long. So we moved in and fixed it up. Made a few improvements. Mended the pipes, sanded the floors. We got a priest to anoint the doors with oil. Its reputation has been well and truly exorcised.'

'So . . . is it yours now?'

'Like everything in life, Rip: it's just on loan.'

As Joe swung the Caddy around in front of the house, the sun no longer flattened everything out and I saw its true condition. Hardly any of the windows on the ground floor had glass or frames and large parts of the roof did not have tiles. One whole section of the outside wall was exposed to the elements, with a rough tarpaulin draped over it. There must have been power because there were lights on in the upstairs rooms, and signs of life within, but it was, essentially, a ruin.

'Welcome to my mansion, Rip.'

— Is he dead?

— I can't say.

— You can't say, or you don't know?

— Like I said, I can't say.

— I didn't do it. I know how it looks but I didn't do it. I know you have to ask me a lot of questions but I need to say that now. Before my memory and the pressure of remembering confounds things. Plus, my head hurts.

— I understand, sir. And it's your right to say what you believe to be true. We're going to go through everything. Believe me. We have time. But, first things first. Why don't you start by telling me your name?

— Llewellyn Jones.

— Can you spell that for me, Mr Jones?

— L.L.E.W.E.L.L.Y.N.

— Your business card here says 'Rip Van Jones'?

— That was my working name. Joe said I needed a snappier name for selling.

— You mean Mr Joseph Bosco?

— Yes.

— And how old are you?

— Twenty-four. Last week.

— From England, right?

— Wales. But yes, I'm British. Is he OK – is Joe OK?

— We can't tell you that right now.

— He's alive, though? You can at least tell me that?

— I'm sorry. Can you tell me what you were doing in the United States? Was it business or pleasure?

— *Pleasure. I intended to do a bit of manual work, bar work here and there, to pay my way. But I came to see America.*

— *Seems you done that. Thirty-two states. In six months. That's some going. So how did you meet Mr Bosco?*

— *Do you have a cigarette, Sheriff?*

— *Sure.*

— *I was staying at my Aunt Julia's. Near Hunter. I was doing odd jobs for her but I intended to get out and see the country. Maybe write about it. And then I met Joe – at the Kaaterskill Falls. I told him I wanted to see America; he offered to show it to me. I needed money; he offered me a job. He was very persuasive. He could sell you . . . anything. And I liked him. I thought he was unusual. But good-unusual. I think most people in my shoes would have taken the job.*

— *Selling butterflies?*

— *It was a good business.*

— *You didn't see anything that made you think you should steer well clear of this guy?*

— *Well, yes, plenty. He was annoying and constantly attracting trouble. Winding people up. He really didn't care what anyone thought of him. He was afraid of no one. Except for one person perhaps. He'd do all kinds of things – not exactly breaking the law – but trouble-making. You might say these were warning signs, but nothing that prepared me for what came.*

— *What kind of signs?*

— *Well. He would get into arguments. He talked about having Good Theology and Bad Theology. He had a particular beef with religious authority. Well, any authority, really – especially male authority. He'd go into churches and sit at the back and wait for the sermon and then he'd start asking them questions. 'What are you doing for the poor?' 'How much do you get paid, Reverend?' 'Do you really need that Mercedes?' That kind of thing.*

— *He was an atheist?*

— *No. He just had a thing about religion. And what it did to people and what America has done with it. He wanted to help*

41

the poor and would give money away, willy-nilly. Including money that was needed for other things. Like bills. It was a chaotic kindness.

— Sounds like he was always headed for trouble.

— You say 'was' like he is no longer with us.

— This his car?

— Yes.

— It ain't a model I recognize.

— It's a Chuick. He gave it to me when I made my first big sale.

— Not exactly screaming success at ya.

— Maybe not. But it was reliable. And trustworthy. It got the job done.

— We found this in the glove box. This belong to you?

— Yes.

— You do a lot of cannabis?

— I smoke to escape, or when I'm stressed. It helps me not think.

— And were you smoking a lot when you met Mr Bosco?

— What are you suggesting?

— Would you say your judgement was impaired, at the time you met Bosco? That you weren't thinking straight?

— Possibly. I'd got into my head too much. I was sleeping a lot. Twelve hours some nights. And I had recently lost my father.

— I'm sorry about that.

— Don't be. He was not a pleasant man.

— You want to take care saying things like that. 'Honour thy mother and father so that you might live long in the land.'

— Tell that to Joe. I'm not sure how you honour parents like his.

— All the same, losing a parent is a big deal. Maybe it affected your judgement.

— About what?

— About Joseph Bosco. I mean, I'm finding it hard to understand how you got involved with a guy like that. A man arrested

42

for disturbing the peace in seven states. A man wanted by a government agency. Driving a car like that claiming to be pulling big deals here and there. Seems like a regular huckster. What were you thinking?

— *I already told you. I was looking to see America and I was offered a chance to do that. And I liked him. Infuriating though he was – is. I felt . . . somehow bigger in his company, that life was more interesting. He was a force of nature. And it wasn't just him either. The whole family was – extraordinary. I got . . . involved. You could say lust had something to do with it. At the beginning. Lust and trying to prove something. And just being caught up in . . . an adventure.*

— *Lust for who?*

— *His sister.*

— *Is that . . . Miss Isabelle Bosco?*

— *That was . . . no. I meant his younger sister. Mary-Anne.*

— *At what point did you realize what was really going on?*

— *With what?*

— *With the bugs.*

— *Too late, I suppose. Although I don't know if I ever really knew what was going on. I thought I was ahead of things. But I wasn't. I think a part of me is still hoping I'll wake up and discover it was . . . you know.*

— *A dream?*

— *Not real.*

— *Well. It's real, Mr Jones. As real as you and me sitting here in this cell. And we're gonna need you to remember as much as you can. Get your statement clear. Get your story straight. You owe your future to it. I see you made a start.*

— *Yes. Although I'm maybe giving too much detail. I don't know.*

— *If it's relevant to the case, write it down. Some say the Devil's in the detail but I'm inclined to think it's the Lord who has a preference for exactitude in the small things. In the end it's the details that will save you, Mr Jones.*

II.

So Butterfly Joe said:
'Drink up your tea
Leave your book
And follow me.
The story's out there
You oughta know
The time is now
And we gotta go.'
So I dried my quill
Broke off my labours
Hit The Road
And took its favours.
Freshly named and re-baptized
I drove to a mansion
'Neath burning skies.
I faced a test
(Which I survived)
I looked a monster
In the eye.
Then given the choice
'Tween woman and girl
I took the oats
And saved the pearl.

CHAPTER FOUR

In which I meet Joe's family and face 'a test'.

Joe's home was more than a mansion.

'Wow.'

He was giggling at my response. 'Isn't it great?'

'It's . . . extraordinary.'

'Not what you expected, huh?'

It wasn't what I expected. It was probably the first (it wouldn't be the last) instance of reality matching Joe's hyperbole. The house was a Frankenstein of inspirations – Scottish hunting lodges, Victorian English museums, French châteaux, Welsh castles. There were jalopies lined up against a tumbling orchard wall. I could see Chuick parked up next to what must have been the rest of the Buick that had supplied its front; there was a flatbed Ford pick-up and a Chevy Camaro Z28 on blocks. The whole premises combined a faded Gothic grandeur with the whiff of hick, neither quite winning.

The dogs, meanwhile, were jumping up on my side of the car and Joe wasn't exactly encouraging them to calm down. 'Hey dogs, say hello to Rip! They won't bite ya! Once they know you're family.'

The dogs didn't look or sound convinced and neither was I.

'Are you sure?'

'They'll be licking your face tomorrow. Eli, why don't you tie them up.'

I waited while Eli led the mutts towards some outbuildings and then I followed Joe towards the house where an elegant young woman and an impish black girl appeared on the veranda. The little girl hop-scotched down the stone steps, leaping into Joe's arms and hugging him with fierce affection.

'Hey, Ceelee. Say hi to Rip.'

'Hi, Rip.'

'Rip, this is Celeste. She's a little cuddle monster.' Celeste was like a fairy-elf: white frock, grown-out Afro, bare feet. When Joe set her down she started touching my shirt, poking me to see if I was real, pulling at my hands, then hugging me as though she'd known me a lifetime. The young woman was less enthusiastic with her welcome. She put out a hand to call the little limpet off: 'Ceelee, leave the man be. I'm sorry. She hugs anything that moves!'

'I don't mind,' I said, but the limpet obeyed the instruction and let go before running off.

'Rip, this is Isabelle. Izzy, meet the new Head of Sales and Marketing.'

Joe had described Isabelle as the serious-minded one in the family and I gave her my most serious-minded look. We made little head-bows of hello to each other.

'Rip's here to help bring beauty and joy to the world.'

'That's a fine ambition,' she said.

'I'm not sure it's my ambition.' I didn't want her thinking I was easily led, or incapable of independent thought.

'What is your ambition?' she asked. It seemed a little early in the day for such a question but I felt the need to justify myself and impress her.

'Rip's going to be a writer,' Joe bawled. 'He's gonna write a book about his adventures with me!'

Whenever Joe told people of my ambition to be a writer, I felt the push and pull of opposing emotions: I wish you wouldn't say that but I'm glad you did!

'Joe's usually able to make everyone else's ambitions serve his own,' Isabelle said in a calm, un-judgemental way that sounded perfectly true.

'Aw, that's not fair!' Joe protested, feeling no offence whatsoever. He was looking at something in the house, upstairs. 'Is the volcano ready to spew?'

A figure stood at the window looking out, watching us.

'She's been simmering all week. You'll have a hard time talking her down today.'

'You show Rip around. I'll go deal with her. What's for dinner?'

'Clay's doing moose burgers with corn bread.'

'Moose! You ever had moose, Rip? It's something. Like the tenderest beef. We need to put some muscle on you. Get you combat-ready.'

I wanted to follow him, just to see what it was he had to do to talk his mother down.

'Do you have any luggage?'

'It's in the trunk.'

'I'll have Clay bring it to your room. Shall we go in?'

Elegant-gangly, olive-skinned Isabelle was more obviously Joe's sister than Mary-Anne. Like him, her face was not pleasing in particulars but there was beauty in overall effect. In personality, however, she was still waters to his mad rapids. She had a gentle disposition and was languid of movement and speech; qualities the noisy people around her served to amplify. Even so, as she began her tour, I was wondering where the wild sister was.

We entered the house through the door-less doorway to what was once the main hall. Broken fittings and fixtures lay all around, a grounded chandelier, a rack of wooden skis, the head of a stag. The house had history but the customizations of its current inhabitants gave it a futuristic, post-apocalyptic feel. It was like entering the headquarters of some survivalist remnant set on re-making the world. A carpenter's workbench had been set up near the gaping windows and a window frame was waiting to be set.

'Joe wants to restore it all. He's hoping we will be able to buy this place one day. For now we live upstairs.'

'Joe said you were "borrowing" the house?'

'Yes. He did a deal with a collector. He sold a set of rarities from our collection.'

'Wow. They're that valuable?'

Isabelle nodded, but made it clear that she did not want to discuss this further by ushering me onward towards the staircase. The stairs were bare wood but became carpeted at the turn to the first floor. The burgundy and gold pile faded to brown and yellows and was patterned with what I assumed to be a family crest – pistols and doves.

'The bedrooms are on the next floor. We'll probably put you in Ceelee's room – in the attic. I need to tidy it for you. Let me show you the factory.'

I followed her along the landing and entered a vast room through double doors. I was hit by a smell of dried flowers and naphthalene that made me sniff and blow.

'This is where we make the cases. You get used to the smell.'

The wood-panelled room had a full-length snooker table with retractable light box over the baize. The table itself had been converted to 'factory floor'; it was laid with all that was required to make a butterfly case: butterflies, glass, silicon tubes, dried flowers and driftwood.

'We stopped production for a while because we ran out of driftwood but we just had a fresh delivery. Clay collected this from the Finger Lakes.' Driftwood had been dumped in a pyre-sized pyramid in the alcove where there were two large baskets either side of the pile. Isabelle went over and picked a piece from the pile. 'We separate the rough from the smooth.' She felt the piece to gauge the rub then handed it to me.

'Smooth?'

'That's actually a "rough".' She pointed to the appropriate basket and I tossed it in.

'Is this what you all do, full time?'

'We all contribute. Joe does the selling. Ma used to sell too but she mainly does the bookkeeping and the running of the business now. Mary sells too and she likes to drive. You met Mary already, right?'

'I . . . saw her. Briefly.'

'I'm sure she made an impression.'

'Well, she was naked. I tried not to look'

'If there's something Mary cannot abide it is not being looked at.' Isabelle blushed at her bad-mouthing of Mary; she then muttered something as though inwardly castigating herself for it.

'What about you? Don't you sell?'

'I am a terrible sales person.' Her voice had a tiny vibration, and the smallest tremor was perceivable in her hand. 'I help with the production of the cases and the administration but I mainly look after the Collection.'

'I hope you'll show me.'

She nodded, withholding full endorsement.

'Do you have other ambitions – beyond butterflies?'

'I am hoping to go to university. A bit late, but I had to delay things. 'Cos of Ma and . . . well, financially.'

'What are you going to study?'

'I'd like to do European Literature. Majoring in the Russians. What about you? Joe told me you graduated already.'

'I did Classical Studies. Fat lot of use it's been so far. My father was right about that.'

'All that thinking. Some of it must have rubbed off.'

'Maybe.'

'Joe described you as Britain's greatest salesman.'

'Of course!' I said and we both laughed, finding common ground in our understanding of Joe.

'He also said you were someone looking for meaning.'

I was amazed Joe had thought this let alone described me in such a way. 'I'm not sure there is any to be found in this life.'

'Maybe that's why he said it.'

She led me to an adjacent room, an antechamber where men must have once smoked cigars whilst plotting new ways to exploit the masses.

'We call this the Operations Room.'

A huge map of the United States was laid out on a table. It was the kind of map a five-star general might pore over whilst plotting a great campaign. Different-coloured pins – the pins

51

used to pierce the thoraxes of butterflies – pierced towns, cities and states. A cluster of pins along the eastern seaboard and Great Lakes area gave the impression of a beachhead established. There were also random, single pins in some of the big cities elsewhere – San Francisco, Dallas, Denver, Santa Fe, Phoenix, Seattle (there was even a pin in Anchorage, Alaska).

'The black pins mark places where we have sold butterflies. The red pins indicate repeat orders. Those are important.' The south and east were well pinned but the west was largely butterfly-free. 'Joe's ambition is to have a pin in every state and a butterfly case in every home by the end of the century.'

'Thirteen years. Do you think that's possible?'

'My brother gets these giant ideas. Sometimes you have to tie him down, like Gulliver. He's not a bad person but his eagerness can create casualties. He needs people around him to keep him grounded.'

Isabelle looked at me carefully, as if to make sure I'd understood this. Yes, I was here to help sell butterflies but my real job was hammering Lilliputian guy-ropes into the earth to keep the giant from hurting himself and crushing others.

'How do you do that?'

'We all try. In our different ways. Ma shouts at him – as you'll hear. Any second now, I guarantee. I try to catch him when he's still. Which is not easy these days as he's always on the move. Mary just laughs at him.'

'What's in there?' I asked, pointing to the door at the other end of the 'office'.

'That's the library. It's where we keep the Collection.'

Yelled expletives from above cut across our dialogue and saved my blushes. It sounded as if Joe's mother was giving him both barrels of her sawn-off swear-gun.

'Why do you go and do that? Fucking ape! I already got bills enough.'

Isabelle looked at me with concern. 'Joe did tell you about Ma, yes?'

'He said she has a temper. But that she can also be sweet.'

She nodded. 'Did he tell you anything else?'

'He told me the family history. About – the fire and the divorce.'

Isabelle still seemed to want to verify something but the exchange between Joe and his mother became even more audible. And it was now clear they were talking about me.

'He's here to help us, Ma. Super-smart and literary. Great salesman. Wait till you hear his voice.'

'I'm not paying him a cent. We got an army to feed here. I'm here all day while you gallivant.'

'I'm not gallivanting! I'm working hard. Goddamn it! Who do you think is bringing in the money here?'

'Don't you swear at me, you goddamned sonofabitch!'

'Well I am that!'

'You cock-sucking bastard!'

'Well you know I'm not that!'

'You may as well be. For all I care. You may as well be. Asshole!'

'Count to sixty, Ma. Come on. I want you to come downstairs. Come and meet Rip.'

'I saw him already. He looks lame.'

'Come on. He's gonna help us. He speaks nice. He's got charm and will help get me in front of some people. And he writes nice.'

'He looks like a punk. A useless punk.'

Being conventional in dress and moderate in attitude, I liked the sound of being a punk, even a useless one, but Isabelle was embarrassed for me and waved off the description. 'Take no notice.'

'Sixty, Ma, come on. That's it . . . there . . . that's it.'

It went quiet then.

'When she's bad, Joe's the only one who can get through to her and help her get back to herself. It's OK. The swearing is a kind of tic. When you see her she'll be a different person. She'll be like the First Lady meeting the King of England.'

As it was, Edith Bosco's etiquette was not the most challenging thing I had to face. Why hadn't Joe told me what so obviously should have been mentioned? Was it that, after nearly twenty years, he'd grown oblivious to it and was unable to see what would strike anyone else were they meeting her for the first time? She entered the room with one hand crooked through Joe's arm and her other using a cane for support; such a picture of maternal and filial respect that it was hard to believe they'd been at each other's throats just minutes before. Joe didn't even give me a helpful 'yes I know this must be quite a shock for you' look. He simply said: 'Rip. This is Ma. Ma, this is Rip.'

Edith Bosco's face was disfigured, the scar tissue and skin grafts forming ridges on one side of her face, one of her eyes a dead black glass, one half of her nose rebuilt. I could see straightaway that even this must have been a miracle of reconstruction and that time had allowed some settling and natural regeneration, but not even two decades of plastic surgery and natural healing could disguise the grotesque.

This must be the little test, I thought. Don't look away. Don't stare too much. Look her in the eye. Look her in the good eye. An eye she used to model.

'Hello, Mrs Bosco.' I put out my hand but she waved it away.

I fixed my gaze on her good eye, which was, if you could somehow isolate it, a quite lovely eye, full of green and yellow flecks. From this eye you could almost reconstruct what might have been.

'It's good to meet you. Thanks for letting me stay.'

'Not my idea. Shit-for-brains here tells me you are some hotshot salesman with a top-dollar education and that you're going civilize him and us and teach us how to transform his bullshit into gold.'

I couldn't stop myself laughing.

'The fuck you laughing at?' Her voice was so smooth-sounding it seemed ventriloquized.

'Sorry. That's . . . a . . . it was a funny metaphor.'

'Metaphor? I'm being damn serious. You work for us you gotta bring something in. You do want to come work for us?'

'Yes. I . . . well . . .'

'Hesitation? I hate hesitation. We can't have a hesitator. Joe?'

I stood up straighter, trying to compensate for a perceived lack of backbone. 'I really do want to work for you.'

'Why?'

Remember: not too timid. Not too cocky. 'Well. I have always wanted to see America and . . .'

'We're not a goddamn travel company!'

'And, I think you have a product that can bring a little joy and beauty into people's lives and I'd like to be a part of . . .'

'Sentimental bull-crap!'

I looked for help, but Joe was revelling in my discomfort, smiling like a fool, while Isabelle was behind me, out of sight.

'Tell me. Rip! Do you think I am an attractive woman?' She leant forward on the cane, studying my reactions.

So *this* was the little test. Whatever you do: speak the truth. I tried to look her in the good eye, and I could see past the scars to what she might have been. Her mouth was pretty. There was a good underlying structure to the face. Her pre-fire eyes must have once entrapped someone into falling in love with her. Come on. She's waiting. You have to say something.

'Notwithstanding your scars, yes.'

I thought this was a good answer and, feeling emboldened, I stood up even straighter and held her gaze.

'Scars?'

'Yes. You've been . . . Joe told me. About the fire.'

There was a silence. Was she so deluded as to think I might not notice? Had I failed the little test already?

'Damn right, I got scars. What of it? Answer the question.'

I took the dive.

'I can see that you were – you have – a natural beauty. The scars make this harder to appreciate but they are not represent-ative of who you are.'

She continued to look at me and I stared into her good eye trying with all my will not to look at its dead, black counterpart.

'Flatterer.' She looked to Joe. 'I hope he's going to do better than the last guy you brought here.' She pointed her cane towards the window. 'We buried him somewhere in the woods. Over there somewhere. English? Irish? Bolivian? I can't remember. Another lamo, anyhow.'

Joe was sniggering.

Then she came towards me, taking my hands, feeling them and flipping them over, like a slave-owner.

'Soft and pudgy. I have no use for soft and pudgy. And you been painting your nails?' There were flecks of barn paint on the nails of my right hand.

'I was painting my aunt's barn.'

'Stick out your tongue. Tongue!'

I looked at Joe. Is this really necessary? He nodded: you better do what she's asking. So I stuck my tongue out and kept it there for a couple of seconds, or until I noticed Joe really laughing, unable to contain himself any more. Edith let go of my hands. She was laughing too! And then she said: 'If you can make me sound like Miss America then maybe you got a future selling. But I'm going to give you a tip, Rip! A dishonest pitch is way easier to deliver than an honest one. Honesty pays, but dishonesty pays better!'

It seemed I had passed the 'Little Test'.

As Edith and Joe walked on through to the dining room Isabelle drew alongside me. 'I don't like it when Ma does that but she does it to everyone, so don't feel too bad. No one gets to work for us unless they are prepared to say what is so.'

Later, we – that is, Edith, Joe, Isabelle, Celeste, Elijah and I – sat around a piece of plywood mounted on boxes in an assortment of chairs that put us all at different heights to each other. Isabelle brought in the moose burgers cooked by the still unseen Old Man Clay, who seemed to have many roles: servant, cook, valet, porter, wood-collector. Joe was halfway through a rambling and profane grace when Mary-Anne entered, all the lovelier for being clothed. He improvised a sign off: '. . . and we also thank you for Mary, who is slowly learning the ways of the humans after years in the forest. Amen.'

'Amen.'

'Fuck you, Joe.'

'Language, Mary?' Isabelle said, attempting to keep order. Everyone in the family was a fluent cusser, except for Isabelle who never gave up trying to keep a lid on it all, mainly for the benefit of Elijah and Celeste.

'It's English ain't it?' Mary said, picking up her burger and perching on the arm of my armchair, working hard on her non-chalance whilst knowing she had become the lightning rod in the room. She bit into her burger and began to make speaking and eating at the same time look alluring.

'You working for us now?'

'Yes.'

'Rip passed the test!' Joe confirmed. 'Better than anyone, so far. Wouldn't you say, Ma?'

'He did OK, for a Limey.'

Joe's termagant mother was now – if not quite the First Lady entertaining the King of England – friendly. She concentrated on eating her food and let the next generation have their say.

Mary was keen to mark her territory. 'How did it go with the bank?'

'They're all fools,' Joe said. 'We don't need no bank. I been working on getting us the super-deal of the century. Plus we got Rip here to help out. As soon as he's learned the ropes, we'll get him selling on the road. They are gonna be lovin' on him. We'll be heading into the Midwest. You are gonna be our secret weapon, Rip.'

'I get to drive, right?' Mary said.

'It's Izzy's turn to make a trip. And you just been with me to Mississippi.'

'But she don't drive.'

'It's fine if you go, Mary,' Isabelle said. 'I have plenty of work to do. Books to read.'

'Our Izzy's going to Yale,' Edith said, with pride.

'We gotta sell a lotta bugs so Izzy can learn about all those depressed Europeans,' Joe said.

'I appreciate it,' Isabelle said, flushing.

'You had your chance, Joe,' Edith cut in.

'I know. I ain't complaining. I'm learning every day.'

'Reading ain't working though is it, Iz?' Most of Mary's remarks were aimed at puncturing Joe's fancy or undermining Isabelle. She really had it in for her sister and I sensed early she was upping things because of me.

'You OK with that, Iz?' Joe asked.

'I'm OK.'

I looked from Isabelle to Mary-Anne and then to Joe. I was not unhappy about this configuration. Mary-Anne seemed happy with it, too. 'You don't want to be with my brother on your own for that long,' she said. 'All those words tumbling out of him and most of them meaning nothing. You need somebody to interpret that bullshit.'

Joe laughed, these sisterly slights sliding off his back. But Isabelle seemed agitated by her younger sister's brazenness and she started pouring water to channel it.

'Have you been to Europe?' I asked Isabelle.

'Not yet. I would like to go. Joe thinks I'd find it too decadent and the people too cynical.'

'It's older so it's got more to be cynical about,' I said.

'Maybe America just needs more time to get cynical,' Isabelle said. 'To experience the decline first.'

'I don't see America in decline,' I said. 'Even if it does decline it always bounces back.'

'Oh, you'll see the decline,' Isabelle said.

'But you'll see the wonder, too,' Joe said. 'Such wonders that you'll blub like a babe.'

'I can't wait.'

The end of the meal was signalled by Edith pushing her plate away. 'I'm turning in. Where you putting our guest here?'

'We've put him in Ceelee's room,' Isabelle said. 'Ceelee can share my bed.'

'OK. You better show him where it is.'

'Maybe Ceelee can show him,' Mary said. 'Izzy's got to study. Ain't that right, Izzy?'

'Sure. I don't mind.'

If Isabelle cared about being ousted as my chaperone she didn't show it, but from day one my presence was stirring trouble between the sisters.

Then Edith stood and fixed me with a look. 'Well, it's nice to have you here, Rip; but remember. If you fuck up, I'll kill you.'

CHAPTER FIVE

In which I get high with Mary and she tells me things.

Celeste showed me to my quarters and the fearless little thing took my hand and pulled me along, firing question after question at me like the Elephant's Child.

'I am adopted. You know what that is?'

'Yes.'

'Mama Edith chose me out of a hunnerd chillen. She says she picked me 'cos I looked smart. You think I look smart?'

'You do. You are.'

'I know the names of a hunnerd butterflies. My favourite is an Alexander birdwing 'cos it's green and big and rare. Joe says when I get to eighteen he will give me one and if I sell it I will be able to buy my own house with it. We got five which is more than the museum in Washington.'

Celeste's bedroom was in the eaves at the very top of the house and reached via a bare wooden staircase. The walls of her room were covered with her own drawings.

'I did all these. Do you like to draw?'

'I can't draw to save my life.'

She laughed at this. 'That's funny.'

The pictures were portraits with detailed outsized heads and generalized stick bodies. 'Can you guess who they are?'

I paused to identify each of them, calling out the names:

'Let's see.' (Male. Filling the whole page. Huge glasses and smile. A butterfly sitting on his head and another in an out-stretched hand.) 'I recognize this one. This is Joe.'

'Yeah.'

'And this . . .' (Female. Hair up in a bun. Big eyes and long lashes. Book pressed to chest with one hand. Other arm out like Julie Andrews.) 'Isabelle?'

'Uh-huh.'

'OK. And this is . . .' (Female. Exaggerated bosom. Barbie waist. Large nose. Cigarette. Cowboy hat.) 'Mary-Anne?'

'I got her face wrong. Who do you think is the prettiest?' Celeste asked me. 'Mary or Izzy?'

I starred at the two sisters for a bit and eventually placed a finger on Mary.

'Izzy says it's better to be prettier on the inside. Man looks on the outside, but God looks on the heart. Do you know that song? We sing it in Sunday school.' Celeste started to sing the song and perform accompanying hand signals: 'Man looks on the outside, God looks on the heart' (hand pointing outward; hand on breast, repeat).

It was a noble sentiment – one I should have heeded – but 'inside-prettiness' could wait.

'And who is this?' (Female. Warm smile, bright eyes and big yellow-gold hair. Friendly. Pizza box. Gun.).

'That's Mama Edith, silly!' By process of elimination I assumed it was Edith but there was no indication of her deformity; either Celeste was being kind or she just didn't see it. Or, she saw 'on the inside'.

'Why does she have a gun?'

'For the Boogie Man.'

Celeste moved on to the next. 'Guess who?'

I identified Elijah easily enough from his baseball cap and coloured-in brown face. And I correctly assumed the portrait of a black man with silver hair to be Old Man Clay. There was a joint portrait of the dogs, Nancy and Ronnie, looking as loveable as puppies. Celeste's self-portrait was a little girl in her trademark dress, standing on a mountain-top with a sky holding sun, moon and stars simultaneously.

'This must be you.'

'Uh-huh.'

'Ceelee – you let our guest alone now! It's bedtime.' It was Isabelle calling from the bottom of the staircase.

'I think Isabelle wants you, Ceelee.'

'How long you staying? Will you stay for ever?'

'Well. That's a long time.'

'Ceelee?'

'I'm coming!'

'Thanks for letting me have your room.'

Isabelle poked her head round the door. 'Ceelee? Let our guest alone now.' Isabelle turned to me. 'I brought you a towel. There's a restroom at the bottom of the stairs. Don't mind the colour of the water. It's just the rust.'

'Thank you.'

I looked at Isabelle's eyes. The lashes were indeed thick and dark around small almonds. Small eyes are always prettier in my view.

'Anyway. If you get too hot there's a fan in the wardrobe there. Come on, Ceelee. Say good night to Mr Jones.'

Ceelee gave me a hug goodnight and I half hoped Isabelle would do the same. Instead, she made a little bow and left, closing the door carefully behind her.

Alone in my room I had that feeling – a feeling that I kept having in those first weeks with the Boscos – of wondering if I had actually met these people, or whether their eccentricities and grotesqueries were proof that I was still in an elaborate dream that had begun back at Kaaterskill Falls. To counter this, I thought I'd write something down, share something of what was happening with someone else out there, before it evaporated or I woke up! I dug out the airmail letter pad that my mother had given to me. 'You will write to me, Lew?' 'Yes, Mum. Of course.' But, other than a phone call upon my arrival in New York, I had not communicated with anyone back at home. I sat there, stuck at 'Dear Mum' for several minutes, long enough for my hot hand to stain the paper and force me to start again with a clean sheet. I couldn't decide what address to put – Aunt Julia's or Joe Bosco's – and instead settled for the compromise of 'The Catskill Mountains'. As for the date, well, I literally did not know what day it was, let alone the date, so I wrote 'evening' which seemed enigmatic and writerly to me. But when I started the letter I felt like a man writing with his mouth; I was unable to be precise about what I had actually been doing. I tore up another page and started for a third time and ended up writing one of those letters I despise, the kind my sister Fran writes: competent, full of information but saying nothing of true feeling and offering no original insight. I dutifully and mechanically worked through the things my mother would want to know: how I was, how her sister was, sights I had seen. But the thing that I really wanted to explain – the phenomenon that was Butterfly Joe and his exotic family – just would not be explained. I kept the letter to a single page with the promise of a longer one to come, creating the not entirely misleading sensation of being on the hoof. My mother would have been pleased enough with it, not having heard from me in weeks, but she would remain ignorant of what was really going on. When I got to the end I shocked myself by signing off as Rip rather than Lew, bracketing it with the explanation: 'my new nickname'. I folded the letter and sealed it in an airmail envelope, writing my mother's name without my father's for the first time in my life. As I wrote my home address – a simple act I found strangely difficult, as though I was worried I might be transported back there just by writing down the names – Mary-Anne entered without knocking.

'Hey.'

'Hey.'

'You got weed?'

'Yes. Of course. It's OK? I mean, will your mother mind?'

'She smokes it herself sometimes. For the pain.'

I rummaged through the jumble for my doobie-tin and my Kents. I then set the tin on the toy box and set about rolling.

'Does Joe smoke?'

'Joe hates me smoking. He's pure like that.'

'What about Isabelle?'

'You kidding?'

Mary lay on my bed and saw my notebook on the bedside table next to the letter pad.

'Joe says you wrote a poem about me.'

'Well. I mentioned you, yes.'

'Maybe you could write another about me. I can just lie here and when you're done you can read it to me.'

I lit the joint and took a long, deep toke before passing it to her. I went through the motions of the idea, picking up my notebook and pen and sitting in a chair opposite her as though I was sketching her which, in a way, I was: trying to catch her likeness. Mary was darker skinned than her siblings, there was something Native American about her. It was hard to believe she was Isabelle's sister. They weren't just different in appearance, manners, taste and deportment; they seemed to be from different eras.

'You did OK with Ma. Some people can't be in the same room with her. Joe tell you how Ma got those scars?'

'In the fire, yes.'

'I weren't born when it happened. I was inside her. They said I was a miracle baby. Sometimes I get close to a flame I scream. If I get hot, I have to get into water. That's why I go to the lake here. To put the fire out. Like the lake of fire in the Bible. I don't believe in all that baloney. Hell. The Rapture. You know about the Rapture? That's when the good people get taken up to heaven. And the bad get left behind. I wish Jesus would hurry up and take them religious folks away and leave me in peace to get on with my life.'

'What do you want to do, with your life?'

'I got plans. I like to drive. NASCAR. I like to go fast. Like Shawna. Shawna Robinson. She's going to be the first woman to win the touring series. I wanted to be a dancer when I was younger. You wanna see me dance?' She got up and did perfect pirouettes around the room, spliff between lips.

'You're good.' This wasn't flattery.

'When I was little I wanted to be a ballerina and when I did lessons the teacher said I was a natural. But we were always moving, and lessons was expensive. I think in a past life I was a queen,' she said, chewing her hair. 'Like a 'Gyptian. Or something. One of those tribes from the olden times. You ever feel you don't belong where you are? Like maybe your family ain't your family?'

'Sometimes I wished they weren't.'

'Are you done with your poem yet?'

'I have a verse. But it . . . let me keep going here.'

'You have a girl in England?'

'Not any more.'

'You been with many girls?'

I'd 'been' with two. 'Five.'

She turned on her side and reached out to pull an imaginary piece of stray cotton from my shirt.

'You prefer Isabelle to me?'

'I hardly know either of you.'

'You don't have to know someone to know if they're the person you wanna be with. The knowing comes later, don't it?'

I was enjoying this moment, listening to her girly, stoner platitudes and watching her perform (to my eye) flawless arabesques and pirouettes; I didn't want to think about Isabelle. Isabelle appealed to what my mother would call my 'higher nature' and acted as a cold shower on my intentions.

'I saw the way you talked. But she won't let you in. She is saving herself. And unless you believe that Jesus Christ is Lord you can't have her. So I guess that leaves me.'

Mary was wearing shorts and a T-shirt that exposed her everted navel. The downy hairs of her belly were standing up, the breeze goose-bumping her skin that was as flat as a dining-room table. How I wanted to eat off that table. She had one leg up, like a sail, one leg straight, tilted out, and her legs were touchingly unshaven. I could smell skunk smoke, shampoo and naphthalene. And her. She passed the joint to me. I made another long, last-requester's draw.

65

'She don't believe in sex before marriage. But I say sex is for when you want it.'

'I agree.'

'Would you like to fuck me?'

'Yes.' (I couldn't think of another answer quick enough.)

'I'll let you fuck me on one condition.'

It felt low asking, but I had to know. 'What's that?'

'You don't try to go with Isabelle. Not ever.'

Sometimes it takes a prohibition to alert us to what we really want. I wanted Mary-Anne with all my body, but even then to retain a little bit of my soul for Isabelle.

'Vow it.'

'Vow it?'

'Vow you won't try and sleep with her.'

'I . . . this is silly.'

'Vow it!'

'OK. I vow.'

'You vow what? Say it!'

'I won't try and sleep with Isabelle.'

'On your life.'

'On my life!'

With the terms and conditions of our future union secured for now, we finished the spliff in silence.

'We can't do it under my mother's roof. We'll get our chance on the road.'

What an offer, what a promise. Come, Road, sex me here! We'd drive through the land like some sexed-up Bonnie and Clyde, making sales and love.

'So how many boys have you been with?'

'That ain't for a lady to say.'

'Really? Why not? I told you how many girls I've been with.'

'That's different.'

'Why different?'

''Cos.'

'Come on. One? Three? Ten!'

'I'm no hussy!'

'None then?'

'Fuck you,' she lashed out, with her bare foot. The way she reacted you'd thing being a virgin was worse than being a hussy.

'OK. It's not a judgement. Either way. It doesn't matter.'

But it mattered to Mary. More than I then understood. She shifted her weight and sat up, her hair hanging down evenly each side of her face, a lovely curtain leaving half eyes, nose and lips visible.

'You ever had a naphth-hi?' she asked. 'You mix mothballs with varnish and tobacco you can get a really good high and it gives you crazy dreams. Naphthalene dreams are the best. You ain't lived until you had a naphth-hi. When I'm high on naphth I can tell you things . . . about the future. About your future.'

The concoction sounded awful but I didn't want to displease her in any way or look feeble. She told me to keep going with my poem and left to fetch the necessaries. I sat there with my undiminished erection, painful against my thigh. I got up and tried to walk it off. Visions of me and Mary in some motel sating our desire didn't help, so I thought of Isabelle sitting in her bed reading some Russian novel perched at the side of her single, spinsterly metal cot. After five minutes Mary returned with the equipment. She had a glass bulb jar for a bong, some mothballs in a cellophane bag and nail varnish. She knelt on the floor and set to constructing her materials with the dexterity of a pro. She coated each ball in varnish and dropped them into the jar. She lit them with a piece of paper and started cooking up the vapours. The fumes came off pinky-yellow, the bubble-gum smell of the varnish veiling the repellent naphthalene odour. She then pulled her hair back with one hand and leant over, holding the jar with the other, guiding the funnel to her mouth, which covered the lip. She then passed the bong to me and I inhaled the vapours. It was like breathing in the essence of old wardrobes and my grandmother's dressing table. At first there was no discernible hit.

'You don't mind my belly button?'

'It's cute. You don't see many outties.'

'I hate it.' She fingered her protruding navel, circling it with her index finger then pressing it in and holding it there. 'I used to press it in with my finger and hold it in to make it stay. Ma says it's 'cos I was born in an unnatural hurry and they didn't cut it right. They were more concerned with her, what with her burns.' She lifted her finger away and the button pinged back all erect again. It looked like a colourless nipple and I wanted to suck it. 'Most people have innies. I bet you got an innie.'

She stretched out her foot and lifted my shirt with her toes to reveal the hairs orbiting my own inverted belly button. She then dropped her foot down and almost-caressed the fly of my jeans. I wanted to ask her more questions about the fire, and about her father, but I was unable to hold any intention for more than the moment of thinking it.

'I like that I can change your body without even touching. Like I did at the falls. When you went to make that dive.'

I needed to gain some control.

'Why did you take my book that day?'

She flicked her hair and looked annoyed. 'I didn't take your book.'

'Joe said you took it.'

'Is that what he told you?'

'Yes.'

She tissed, but her indignation was convincing enough. 'That fucker. He took your book, not me.'

'But . . . he doesn't like books.'

'Joe? He's read more books that anyone I know. Even Isabelle. I'm going to get him for that. He really tell you that?'

'It doesn't matter. He brought the book back. It's just odd he blamed it on you. Why wouldn't he just say he took it – I wouldn't have minded.'

'Don't be a dumb-ass. It's obvious why.'

'Why?'

'Why? Because my brother is a lying sonofabitch, that's why.'

I didn't have Joe down for a liar; a bullshitter, an exaggerator, a spinner, a huckster – but not a liar. The disconcerting thought that I had got Joe all wrong coincided with my first hit from the bong. My breathing became noticeable to me and I thought I could see my pulse – on my wrist. Mary took on that shamanic, earthy quality she'd had when I'd first seen her at the falls.

'I feel a bit weird,' I said.

'You look weird.'

'No, you look weird.'

'No, you look weird.'

Something was happening to Mary. The narcotic showed me something I was unable to see in my sober state. It was as though I could see beyond her outward allure right into 'the heart of her'; there I saw a heart of fire, consumed by passions and rejections and envy and crass manipulations.

'I can see your future,' she said.

'I don't want to know it,' I said.

'I can see your future,' she repeated, not hearing me for some reason. 'You know what I see?' The smoke came out of her mouth and her words seemed made of smoke. The smoke mingled with the words like magical punctuation. She was talking to me in smoke signals, she had gone back to some root ancestral skill. 'You are going to go far. But there will be trouble. I see smoke. And fire.'

'Don't tell me that,' I said. 'I have a right not to be told.'

She frightened me. Her voice was slowing, like a voice on a 45rpm record clicked to 33, and her smoky soprano was getting deeper and deeper. 'Don't speak like that,' I said. 'Speak normally.' She smiled at me and chewed on her hair that was falling over her mouth. 'Don't eat yourself,' I said. 'What's wrong with your face?'

She stood up then I went to talk to a man on the other side of the room.

'Who are you?' she asked him.

The man was my father. He told her to have nothing to do with me. That I was a waster. A freeloader. A disappointment.

'It's not true,' I said.

'It's not true,' Mary agreed. 'Rip is going to go far.'

'That's not his real name,' my father said.

'I can feel I'm changing,' she said. 'Can you feel it yet? Are you changing?'

'No. I like you the way you are.'

She turned away from me and slowly lifted off her top. Her back was nut-brown and flawless, but where her shoulder blades were there were wings. Not feathered, but gossamered butterfly wings. And then she turned round and revealed the rest of her metamorphoses: her nose a proboscis, her mouth a labial pulp, her ears antennae. She stared at me with her two great compound eyes and asked: 'Ever fuck a butterfly?'

CHAPTER SIX

In which I wake to an empty house and a nasty surprise.

Blue paper butterflies were turning in the heat. I could smell mothballs and wood smoke. I was hellish thirsty. My tongue was furry and fat, my mouth dry and the taste in my craw was vile. I felt the dislocation of waking in a strange new bed. Then, with a hazy dawning, I remembered: I was sleeping in the bedroom of an adopted girl called Celeste, who was part of a family that included two sisters, one of whom I admired the other whom I desired. The one I desired had come to my room in the evening and we'd got high; she'd told me she could tell the future and that I was heading for trouble. Then she'd . . . turned into a butterfly!

I sat up, slapped my face and shook my jowls. The cause of my muddle (and Mary's metamorphosis) lay on the floor, its sides stained with the vapours we'd inhaled. Burned, varnished mothballs sat in its base like the evil eggs of some mythical creature. I went and took a shower to wash off the coagulations of the night. The water came out brown just as Isabelle warned me it would. After my shower, I stood in front of the mirror, cleaning my teeth, making the pose I make when thinking myself handsome: a slight tilt of everything – head, mouth, eyebrows – and my mouth pouted askance. I remembered my new name and I practised saying it, like an actor doing exercises before taking the stage. 'Hello. My name is Rip Van Jones. Rip. Van. Jones. Van Jones. Ripvanjones. I have something that I think you will like.' I felt good about the new, improved iteration of myself looking back from the steamed-up mirror. Llew had always had a credibility gap between his ambitions and his ability to realize them; he had always been afflicted by idle indecision and procrastination. Rip had the appearance of someone who was not only going places but going to arrive. Having established who I was, I got dressed and went in search of souls and sustenance.

On the landing I paused outside a bedroom strewn with girl's clothes. A duvet had been scrunched into a ball at one end of the bed. A poster with swirl paisley print saying *If it feels good do it* was stuck on the wall above the bed-head. There was a chest of drawers with the top two drawers out and tilting, the clothes over-spilling; a dressing table draped in jewellery and tat; and a wall festooned with idols cut out of magazines. It had to be Mary's room. The next bedroom was organized and had little adornment. There was a chaste and made single bed, a bureau with books and a shelf full of copies of the *Entomologist's Review* and *Butterfly Monthly*; two Tolstoys and a Dostoevsky on the bedside table. In the corner of the room there were collecting boxes, killing jars and nets, including what looked like an antique net, a strip of muslin held between two poles. Isabelle's room? The room at the end of the landing had a mattress on the floor, no bed. Not even a pillow. The only furniture was a chair draped with a blue and white striped cheesecloth jacket. A large open suitcase full of clothes jumbled pell-mell lay in the corner of the room. By the side of the mattress there was a well-thumbed little red Gideon's Bible, like the ones you find in the drawers of motels. Indeed, the room looked like it was being used by someone who never stayed in one place for long and had left in a hurry. Joe.

In the kitchen I found the remains of a breakfast eaten a few hours before: an unfinished bowl of Golden Grahams, the milk honey-yellow and grainy; a pot of coffee and a half-eaten waffle drenched in maple syrup. I ate the waffle feeling as guilty as Goldilocks, poured myself a mug of cold coffee and set off to continue looking for the bears.

The factory was empty, the production line paused with a row of topless glass cases waiting for their butterflies to be mounted and lids to be sealed. There was no one in the Operations Room either although the map of America – the America that Joe wanted to conquer and that I wanted to see – had an unfinished mug of coffee sitting on Massachusetts and loose pins lying on their sides as though someone had been plotting a route west. The door to the library that housed the collection was open. Instead of finding books and bookcases I found myself in a canyon of seven-foot-tall, twenty-drawer mahogany chests. I opened one of the drawers and it slid out smoothly and silently on felt lining. It contained a case of spotted green butterflies, with creamy forewings and spiralling red hindwings. The introduction of such colour into the dark space was a pleasant shock, like finding a drawer full of jewellery (indeed, I would soon discover that some of these specimens were as valuable as gemstones). I left the drawer open and opened another. A card – written in spidery cursive – indicated the name of the species. Blue-yellow *Nessaea batesii*. There was a system here that was at odds with the rest of the family's chaotic poetry. A more ordered hand and mind than Joe's was behind this. I opened another drawer containing *Asterope* sapphire. Another. Much larger and more dazzling, primal butterflies with huge yellow abdomens, green and blue wings. As the brilliant ghosts of dead butterflies lit up the room, their colours pushing against the glass, I had this feeling they wanted someone – me! – to set them free! Then the drawers began to creak. It was such a creepy phenomenon and the timing so uncanny (Isabelle would explain the cause later as heat expanding the wood) that I closed the drawers and backed out of the room, talking to myself out loud, splitting myself in two for company:

'Maybe everyone's outside.'

'Why don't you have a look then?'

'Yes. Good idea. I'll go and have a look.'

'Yes. Do that.'

The interior of the house was so dark it was a shock to discover that outside it was a fine day. Joe's Cadillac was gone, as was the flat-bed Ford that had been parked by the outhouses next to the Chuick. I decided to walk up the track to see if the family were at the lake that Mary had mentioned, but when it came into view I saw that its waters were as flat as a mirror, teak-dark and naiad-free. I thought about calling out 'Is anyone there?' but fear at having nothing but my own voice echo back prevented me. It's a risky thing asking an empty landscape if anyone is there.

I started to walk back to the house when I saw the dogs – Nancy and Ronnie – sniffing around, unchained! I kept walking, praying they would not see me; but dogs always see you when you don't want them to. In the same second I broke into a sprint I caught the black blur of the chasing dogs in the corner of my eye. I wasn't going to make it to the house before they got to me so I swerved towards the Chuick and reached it with Nancy (the Dobermann) just a few bounds behind. The door was locked and as I tugged the handle, she launched herself at my leg. I lashed out with my other leg and caught her hard in the eye. Seconds later Ronnie (the Rottweiler) arrived and sank his teeth into my buttock. I did a peculiar squat thrust, holding the door handle and lifting both feet off the ground, and then double-kicked my feet into Ronnie's haunches, forcing him back. I rolled forward onto the boot and scrambled to the roof. Nancy (the smarter of the two) ran around to the front of the car and took a running leap onto it. She managed to get all four paws onto the bonnet but couldn't grip it properly and went scrabbling off the side, whining in frustration. I stood up on the car's buckling roof. Those hounds were relentless! They must have tried thirty, forty times, their claws making an awful mess of the car's paintwork. But they couldn't get to me and once I realized this I started taunting them: 'Come on! Crazy dogs! Ha! Ha! Ha! You can't get me! Ha! Ha! Rar! Raaaar! Raaaaaaaar! I'm the King of the Castle! You're the dirty rascals!' Ronnie stood on his hind-quarters, his front paws on the side window, his peeled-back fangs inches from my feet, mouth snapping, drool spattering. I remember thinking how embarrassing this would have looked had any of the Boscos seen me! Then, without apparent reason, the dogs stopped, turned and slunk off towards the outhouses. I was so relieved and deranged by adrenalin I taunted them. 'Awww. Come on . . . doggies! You scared of me now?' But they continued to trot towards the outhouses where I could see a man, speaking calmly but firmly to them, pointing them towards a metal spike and a chain to which he then tied them. Once he had secured the dogs the man came towards me – the loon on the roof – with a look of amused puzzlement.

'I think you can come down from there now, sir.'

He was dressed in dark-blue dungarees, a check shirt and a trilby that sat tilted back on grey hair, tight and white against his black skin. His eyes had teabag folds of world-weariness beneath them and his voice was mellow and lifelorn. Despite his reassurance, I didn't want to move. I could see the dogs up on their feet, straining at their bonds, still having doggy fantasies about ripping my throat out.

'Joe said they'd be chained up.'

'They're all chained up now.'

I stepped down, my heart hammering, my legs shaking, and when I slid off the bonnet I felt the bite and yelped.

'You got bit?'

'Yeh.'

'We better take a look at that. Lord, they messed up the car pretty bad.' He ran a wetted finger over the scratches and rubbed them. 'Good job they took the fancy new one. I'm Clay by the way. You must be Mr Rip, right?'

'Yes.' How quickly my new name was becoming my name.

'Does it hurt?'

'It does now I think about it.' My buttock was burning; my legs were visibly shaking.

'That's the 'drenalin. You were like a crazy man up there.'

The knowledge that he'd seen and heard my rooftop ravings was as painful as the throbbing in my arse. I followed him past the outhouses to a detached wooden shack that was next to a long greenhouse thick with plants and opaque with sweated panes. I caught a flying flash of electric blue. Then another.

'Are those butterflies?'

'Uh-huh. That's the blue morpho farm. We had a good crop this year. Near on a thousand. Miss Edith ain't sure it's worth the sweat. Joe says it makes more profit than raising cattle. I'm in the middle. Jury is still out.'

Outside the front door of Clay's shack there was a mat saying 'home sweet home'. Inside there was a Zed-bed, a storm light, a fridge, a camping gas cooker and a wardrobe. The only other adornments were a Harold Robbins paperback and a signed picture of an American football player.

'I know we just met, but you're gonna have to drop those pants and let me see your butt.'

The pain was over-ruling my self-consciousness now and I undid my belt and buttons and let my jeans slip over my boxers to my ankles, wincing as the material snagged my bite. I then lifted my boxers over my cheek to let Clay look.

'It ain't pierced. But we need to get this cleaned just in case. Hold on.' He went to get something from the wardrobe.

'Let me see . . . When everything comes to an end I got all I need in here . . .'

Clay's wardrobe was part larder, part medicine cabinet, part war chest; a storehouse built for the End Times. He rummaged around and found a bottle of purple liquid and some gauze. He soaked the gauze with the liquid then made me stand up straight. 'Gonna hurt some.' I anticipated the sting of the astringent by taking a deep breath. The pain was delayed for a few seconds but when it came I groaned. It was as if he'd applied a burn to a burn. I had to lean forward and use the table for support.

'OK. Hold that there. I'll get you some Tylenol.'

He went back to the war chest. Found some painkillers. He ran a tap and filled a glass with brown water and handed it to me, with the pills. 'Those dogs won't forget your face in a hurry. Or your butt.'

I swallowed down the pills thinking that what I really wanted was something for the embarrassment. He went to a fridge and found an iced tea which, under normal circumstances, I disliked. But I swigged it back and let the vileness of it distract me from the pain.

'Where is everyone?'

'Church.'

Of course: it was Sunday. Since being picked up by Joe I'd really lost any sense of what day it was, what date it was, or even what era I was living in.

'Did they all go?'

'Miss Edith insists on that.'

'Mary too?'

'It's a house rule. 'Cept for me.' Clay chuckled. 'Miss Edith took me to her church one time and I stuck out like a snake in a chicken coop. Music so gloomy it would make you want to take your own life. Lord forgive me for saying so. I like my worship upbeat. Assemblies of God. I explained to her my way of thinking and in time she unnerstood. I go to my own meetings too, at the AA in Hancock. I ain't touched a drop of liquor for ten years.'

'How long have you known the family?'

'Ten years, near enough. Miss Edith took me in on July 5th 1977. I started getting my independence back the day after Independence Day. Not a day gone where I don't thank the Lord for her. I don't care what people think. Or say. She's some woman. What that fire done to her would finish most people. She raised a family single-handed. She started a business. I can't say a bad word about Miss Edith after what she done for me.'

This praise seemed too quickly offered to me. There was a 'but' hovering in the silence after it, a silence I let sit for a bit.

'Joe said how he . . . found you.'

'Oh, I got Joe to thank, too. That boy saved my life.' Clay pushed his mouth sideways into a pout and whistled slowly, a note up and a note down. 'I was so drunk back then that I booked myself into the Plaza. Turned out to be the back of a

77

garbage truck. Joe hauled me out and took me home. That boy was stronger than a man even then. Miss Edith agreed to take me in on condition I gave up the liquor and helped with the butterfly business. That was when they were living in Michigan. I been working for them ever since. They got some faults, like us all. But they showed kindness to me and kindness is the only currency that counts in this life. Anyways. What's he brought you here for? Joe don't normally take on people with credentials. Educated types, I mean. Most people who land here are in trouble of one kind or other. Needy and desperate. You needy and desperate, Mr Rip?'

'No. I don't think so. He offered me a job. Wants me to help build the business. Take it to the next level.'

'That sounds like Joe. Everything taken to the next level. Ain't no mountain high enough. He promise you the earth?'

'He said he'd show me America.'

'Well, that's a start. As long as you dilute everything he says with a gallon of salt water you'll be right. But I guess you probably know that already.'

'Am I making a mistake? Working for him? Should I be worried?'

Clay looked at me and thought for a few seconds; caught between loyalty to family and courtesy to a stranger.

'You just gotta know what you're in for. Joe is a human hurricane with a heart of gold. He is strong, and he has energy – dear Lord such energy as will not be contained; if you find a way to harness that then you could power a city. Natural law can't contain him, and the laws of man, well, they are like bars of a prison cell. He will never be told what to do. Or where to go. Or let you know where he's going! I mean, do you know where he is now?'

'I thought you said he was in church, with the others?'

'Lord no. He's banned from Miss Edith's church. He left last night going somewhere.'

'Last night? Do you know where?'

Clay laughed.

'He done say. He never done say. Always got some deal going on. He could be meeting the King of Siam. He could be having lunch with a hobo. He could have gone lepping. Even when he does have a destination he finds another along the way.'

'He didn't mention going anywhere to me. He might have said. What with this being my first day.'

'Don't take it personal. Mr Joe can't be in a place for more than a day before going crazy. One time he set off to get some parts for the car or something. In Albany. Next we heard was he was in the Blue Mountains of Jamaica, looking for strange fruit to make jellies out of. He will mention everything but the thing needs mentioning. And never the same answer to anyone. He might tell me he is going to Washington. He tells Miss Edith he is taking the car back. He prolly tells his sisters he was getting some groceries. And he prolly tells the Lord he is going to find some lost soul. Wherever he is it won't be where he said. He will ramble unaccountable to his dying day.'

This was not reassuring. Joe's spontaneous 'I am answerable to no one' approach to life was a singular and beautiful thing; until you were the one he wasn't being answerable to. But at least Clay was describing a Joe I recognized. It was the same mountain albeit from a slightly different angle.

'Why was Joe banned from church?'

'He got into an argument with the preacher. In the middle of the sermon. Does it all the time. Someday they'll lynch him for it.'

'I thought Joe had faith?'

'Oh yes. Not a journey made without some waif or stray rescued from somewhere. Or him giving away his every last dollar. Without faith he would be a danger to himself and everyone else. But he has his own notions about what is true and what in't. About what's man's and what's God's. He's a one-man denomination. Without a father around to tell him otherwise he learned to have his own 'pinions young. He's allergic to any male 'thority, see. He won't be told. He don't respect men much. Which is no surprise gi'n the example he been set by men. But I guess you know all about that already.'

I guess you know all about that already. Clay kept repeating this phrase and then making a quizzical look at me as if to see what I did and didn't know, to see how far into the confidence of the family I had travelled. For all his 'faithful and loyal servant' shtick Clay struck me as having a capacity to spill the beans.

I gave Clay my most ingenuous look. 'He told me something about his father leaving when he was young. But that they don't talk about him. That's he's called the Unmentionable One.'

'Uh huh.' Clay looked at me and narrowed his eyes.

The plate was tilting, the beans moving to the edge. I continued to tilt it. 'He said he was an entomologist. That he was always away. Left this incredible collection of rare butterflies. Said he loved bugs more than people.'

I was sure Clay was burning to tell me what he knew. Our knowledge of those close to us is often the only power we have over them, our only collateral in this life. And Clay was weighing up whether to spend it.

'Did you ever meet him?'

'No. He was a big deal in the bug world. But he had a—' Clay broke off, deciding to stop it there.

'He had a what?'

Clay shook his head and castigated himself. 'That's enough, Clay Cornelius Beauregard, that's enough!'

Clay moved away from me, tidying up my bottle of iced tea and rearranging his wardrobe. He continued to reprimand himself. Further disclosure was prevented by the sound of a car and those damn dogs barking.

'That'll be them back from church. All washed clean for another week. We'd better go.'

'Will you go first, make sure the dogs stay chained?'

'I'm on to it now.'

'Don't tell them about, you know . . . what you saw. The way I reacted, I mean.'

'That crazy banshee jig?' He laughed. 'Don't worry. Everybody's secret's safe with Clay.'

I let him go ahead, giving him enough time to make sure no one loosed the dogs. I watched him through the little window of the hut as he greeted the family, opening the passenger door for Edith like a chauffeur, holding an arm for her to steady herself on. Was there more than deference in the way he greeted her? He wasn't quite staff; he wasn't quite family. He seemed friendly enough, though the way he'd suddenly stopped talking about Joe's father was odd. This ban around any sort of talk about him was taken seriously and perhaps I should have respected it. But as everyone knows, the more you enforce a prohibition, the greater the temptation to break it.

CHAPTER SEVEN

In which I lose an argument and gratification is delayed.

'You kick my dogs? Hey. Lamo. You fuckin' kick my dogs?'

I'd just sat down on the rubber ring that Clay had given me to ease the sting of the dog-bite. I'd made an entrance, partly to win sympathy, but also to deflect any concern about the damage caused to the Chuick by the dogs' claws. Isabelle and Clay were serving the lunch. Edith was sat at the head of the table fixing me with her one-eyed gaze. She was wearing a pirate's patch over her dead eye, had her hands out, palms up, and mouth open feigning stunned offence (a mouth not in the least bit washed clean by the Lord). Mary, Elijah and Celeste were staring at me, waiting for my response. Only Isabelle continued dishing out the food, resolutely not looking at me, or her mother.

'Clay said you kicked them and cussed them. Called them all kinds of names. And Clay don't lie.'

I understand that loyalty to the house supersedes all others, but this little betrayal was disappointing. Clearly Clay was not the safe deposit for confidences he'd made himself out to be. And I couldn't shake the feeling that he'd let those dogs loose in the first place.

'I . . . I'm not sure, Mrs Bosco. It was all so quick,' I said. 'I was just trying to defend myself.'

'Those dogs wouldn't hurt a fly. You must have provoked them some. You been here barely a day and you're abusing my animals? Wrecking my property. That car is going to need a new coat of paint.'

Then Celeste contorted her face into a snarl, made claws of her fingers and started mimicking my rooftop rant with an excruciating accuracy. 'Rar Rar Rar! Crazy dogs, crazy dogs, rar,

rar, rar!' Clay really had given them quite a vivid account of my performance.

'They attacked me, Mrs Bosco. I'm sorry about the car, but I had nowhere else to go.'

The room fell silent. Perhaps challenging Edith was a new, revolutionary idea.

Edith wiped her mouth with a napkin and fixed me with her sparkling one eye.

'What I really would like to know is this. Was that dog's bite worse than its bark?' There was another long pause. Then she snorted, the way Joe did when childishly amused; and then Mary and Elijah were laughing too, all laughing at my expense. Oh what mirth I was providing! I raised my hands in defeat and joined in. A willingness to take the abuse without buckling was the price to pay for being accepted into the bosom of this family. No doubt, future generations of Boscos would one day recount *The Tale of Rip's Butt*.

'Seriously. How is your butt, Rip?' Edith asked, softening.

I shimmied into the rubber ring. 'It's . . . fine, thank you.' And then, for good measure, I added: 'Would you like to see it?'

This won the day.

Elijah sprayed his mouthful of food over his plate and clapped his hands in disbelief. Mary, who liked to think she had a monopoly on sass, looked genuinely impressed at the gall of it. There was a second's pause from Edith and then she pointed her finger at me, stabbing the air with it, her living eye sparkling. 'Son. Of. A. Bitch. You'll go far, Rip. You'll go far.'

What an endorsement. (The second such endorsement in less than twenty-four hours.)

Only Isabelle remained beyond my winning powers of self-deprecation. She'd been quiet since getting back from church and shown no sympathy towards me for the dog attack. She was still in her Sunday best and, whilst a lack of concern for fashion is commendable, she really wasn't making the best of herself. With her blouse pressing her breasts flatter and her hair in a little-too-tight bun she seemed wilfully dowdy. It was as if she was trying to be the very opposite of her sister. How had Edith spawned such different creatures? They were fire and water.

'Ain't you hot in those clothes?' Mary asked.

'At least I'm wearing clothes.'

I'd not known Isabelle more than a day but this seemed uncharacteristically sharp.

Mary wore her sister's criticism like a mantle of victory, sucking up her disapproval with a satisfied smile.

'You can dress like some governess from way back when if you like – but it's 1987, not 1887. In case you hadn't noticed.'

'It's just inappropriate, Mary.'

'You mean slutty?'

'I didn't say that.'

'Jesus loved sluts. The preacher said so today. Weren't you payin' attention? Maybe our guest should be the judge of what's OK?'

Mary was wearing a tie-dye vest without a bra and her full breasts easily filled the material and spilled out the sides; she also had on the shortest cut-off jeans it was possible to wear. It looked appropriate to me. Good enough for Jesus; good enough for me. But, people-pleaser that I am, I didn't want to get caught in this fight, so I pulled a diplomatic 'each to his own' shrug and made conciliatory gestures to both sisters.

'Whatever feels comfortable, I suppose. "If it feels good do it."'

Mary flashed me a look. *Coward.* She was in a merciless mood.

'This is the bod I got from God. I am fearfully and wonderfully made.'

All the Boscos could quote scripture when they needed to; even the ones who didn't believe a word of it.

'You shouldn't mock,' Isabelle said.

Mary mocked on. 'It's true. My body is a temple.' She straightened her nave and pushed out her transepts to prove it.

'Then why abuse it by smoking?'

'I don't hardly smoke. Not cigarettes anyways.' Mary gave me another look.

'You know what I'm saying. If you have to smoke don't do it in Ceelee's room.'

Isabelle flushed burgundy as she said this for it was a reprimand that extended to me. I finally twigged. How dull-witted I was being; how slow to pick up on what was going on! Isabelle wasn't really upset about Mary smoking in Celeste's room (Mary smoked all the time); she was upset about Mary smoking with me, in my room. She didn't care about Mary's scanty clothes (Mary wore nothing less than scanty most days); she cared about the effect that scantiness was having on me. She obviously knew about Mary's visit to my room and did not approve of our nocturnal pow-wow; she was just too polite or embarrassed to say so directly. Or perhaps too proud to let on that she might be jealous of my attentions towards her sister. Yes! That's it, I thought. Isabelle is in a cranky mood because she likes me and is disappointed I've already fallen for her more flagrant sister. Feeling sorry for her, I tried to help her into the conversation.

'How was church?'

She continued looking down at her plate, cutting the meat into minute morsels and taking an inordinate time to chew them so as not to have to speak. Naturally polite, it took Isabelle a lot of effort not to answer me. An over-confident Mary leapt in to the silence.

'That preacher is such a jerk. He so likes the sound of his own voice. Joe's right: why do we go to church and have to listen to one man talk for so long?'

'I like Pastor Jennings,' Edith said, showing an interest. 'Better than Rat-face. Remember how long he went on? He'd talk for an hour, making his three points beginning with the same

85

letter over and over like we were children. At least Jennings keeps it under half an hour.'

'Do you have church in England?' Elijah asked. Elijah's idea of England as being a primitive country lacking in all but the very rudiments of existence was profound.

'Of course they have church in England, Eli,' Edith said. 'England is a Christian country, right?'

'Not any more,' I said. 'Not many people I know believe in God.'

'But you believe in God, don't you, Rip?' Celeste asked, worried.

'I don't know.' It felt like the most honest thing I had said in days.

'That's stupid,' Celeste said.

'Where I come from people think you're stupid if you *do* believe in God.'

'Well that's stupid, too.'

I looked at Isabelle, willing her to get involved. I could guess her thoughts: *'I'll not throw my pearls to you, you pig. You think you are interesting, have intelligence and depth, but you are a shallow chancer, and the fact you've fallen for my sister's Venus fly-trap act proves it. And now you're talking garbage about something you don't know or care about.'*

'Your folks not bring you up in the fear of the Lord?' Edith asked me.

'They weren't church-goers. My mother would say she was a spiritual person. My father didn't believe. Until his dying day. He even asked that there be no religion at his funeral. He didn't want God to have the last word.'

'Good for him,' Mary said, more to provoke than out of conviction.

'Mary-Anne thinks she's an atheist,' Edith said, as if it was a craze Mary would get over.

'I know what I think,' Mary said.

Mary's atheism seemed more like emotional rebellion than

intellectual rejection to me but what surprised me was that Edith didn't seem to mind. Despite the mandatory church-attendance she was laissez-faire with what her children believed. She herself had grown up Catholic (Joe on Catholics: 'man, those people make a meal out of a simple instruction') and although her own faith was 'hanging by a very thin thread' (her own description) she wanted her children to have the ammuni-tion they needed to keep arguing about it either way. As a result the family were religiously literate and, I would discover, just as comfortable discussing the ontological as the entomological.

'So what was the sermon about?' I asked. Again, I looked at Isabelle, determined to hook her into the conversation before the meal was done.

Again, Mary intercepted. 'It was about Adam and Eve and who was to blame,' she said.

'Who do you think was to blame, Rip?' Edith asked.

I hadn't really thought this issue through but I knew enough, and if my expensive education had taught me anything it was how to stretch a little knowledge into sounding like a great deal; what people call bullshit.

'I've always felt slightly sorry for Adam and Eve,' I said, as if I'd carried this burden of sadness for our deepest ancestors all my life.

Isabelle took a deep breath. She half looked up, her eyes widened. She was nibbling my line.

'Oh?' Edith said. 'I always thought if the schmucks had just listened to the Lord we wouldn't be in this mess.'

'Well that seems a bit harsh,' I said, finding my argument. 'God told them not to do something but when someone tells you not to do something you're sort of inviting them to do it, really.'

Edith chewed on this thought and looked only semi-impressed. 'Hmmmmm. So. Are you saying God tempted them?'

'Well. Yes. In a way.'

Isabelle made a sigh – the kind of sigh a long-suffering

teacher might give out when all other ways of trying to help a stupid pupil grasp a simple maxim have failed.

'But they were free to choose,' she said. She was involved now!

I hit right back. 'But if God knew they would make the wrong decision he should never have let them.'

'If we're not free to make the wrong decision it isn't freedom.'

Her voice cracked a little with the saying of this and her pallor, which still hadn't recovered from the fracas with Mary, now included blotches on her neck around her frilly collar. She was not made for confrontation, or smart-arsery. She was a serious person with no glibness in her who argued only when it really mattered to her. And this mattered to her.

'You're saying desire is a bad thing?'

'No. It's what you desire that counts.'

I felt something hot rubbing up against my calf. It was Mary's foot saying, 'You're mine, remember what you desire, and remember your vow.'

Isabelle finally looked at me and for a brief moment I felt transparent. She had me but intellectual pride is first cousin to smart-arsery and I couldn't leave it there.

'I think they were curious. Testing the boundaries. Wanting knowledge. Like children. And then they were punished for their curiosity.'

'They weren't punished for being curious,' Isabelle countered, still that nervy quaver in her voice, but with a steely determination to hold to her orthodoxy. 'They put their faith in the wrong thing.'

This seemed reasonable, possibly true. Stuck for an answer I threw her the best that my education could offer.

'Ultimately, you can't trust in something you can't see or prove.'

This statement went unanswered for a few seconds and a

smirk from Mary suggested she thought I'd struck her sister a fatal blow.

'But that is precisely what faith is,' Isabelle said. 'Trusting in something you can't see and don't fully understand. Most people believe in things they don't understand – or can't see.'

'Such as?'

Isabelle looked at me, genuinely surprised I had to ask. 'Love?'

She let the theological fuck-you hang for a few seconds, to see if I had anything to say. Seeing that I didn't she stood and started to stack the plates. When she'd left the room Edith looked at Mary.

'What's got into her?'

'She's uptight,' Mary said.

'Why were you being mean to her?'

'I weren't. Maybe she don't like being challenged like that. She thinks she's so smart. You told her, Rip. You put her in her place real good.'

Mary winked at me as though we had won a victory, but it was Isabelle who'd had the last word. And it had been a good word. While Mary footsied my calf and I winked back at her, my thoughts followed her smarter sister from the room. I'll win you over yet, I told myself. But, for now, I was prepared to buy the lie that the serpent supposedly introduced to the world: that dark is interesting and light is bland and that to know everything is freedom. Joe was right in this regard: Bad Theology can take you down the wrong road.

* * *

Joe had said nothing to anyone about where he might be going and, apart from me, no one seemed to care. The general message was that Joe's whimsical flits were part of who he was and I should get used to it; for the sake of my sanity it was best not to fix Joe to a time frame or a particular place; Isabelle said he'd call soon enough. The phone was the umbilical cord by which he was still joined to his mother. As it was, he called three days later. We were all working in the factory putting together an order of fifty cases for a florist in Bangor, Maine. Edith took the call on her portable phone, seated on her 'throne' at the head of the factory table, and it was instantly clear who was at the other end of the line.

'Where the hell are you?'

Edith pressed a button on the phone so we could all hear Joe's answer. Not that she needed to. Joe always yelled when on the phone, as though having to shout above the noise of a crowd at a wild party. 'Ma! Can you hear me?'

'Yah: too loud; too clear!'

'Guess where I'm calling from!'

'I wouldn't care if you were calling from the Great Wall of China. You should be here. Working not gallivanting.'

'Dollywood! It's a total piece of serenicity, Ma. I was filling up with gas in New Jersey and I met a guy who sets up theme parks. He did Dollywood and when he saw my cases he told me I should get down there first thing.'

'Down where?'

'Hold on. Just turning here.'

'Down where?'

'The Volunteer State.'

'Remind me.'

'Tennessee! He said Dolly loves butterflies. She did that song. "Love is like a butterfly, soft as gentle, and that's no lie, da de da." She's thinking of setting up a butterfly house in the park. He told me to check it out. Then I got me thinking we should do a theme park and call it Butterfly World! It'll be like a cross between Disneyworld and the Smithsonian, all wrapped in an "entertainmentful experience".'

'You must think I'm no smarter than a shithouse mouse. No one wants a theme park for butterflies. You're up to something.'

'Ma, if they have made a theme park for a country singer they can make one for butterflies. Dolly will be lovin' on the idea.'

'And how are you going to pay for this cockamamie idea? Right now I got bills for these phone calls you keep making. And we got cases to make and sell. I need you back here focusing on reality.'

'Pretty soon Ma you won't have to worry about any of that. I'm working on a deal so big you'll be able to watch TV all day.'

'Enough of this.'

'So how's Rip doing? He learning the ropes?'

'He's been pontificatin' about things he don't know about. And he got himself bit by the dogs.'

'No! Ha! Really? Let me speak to him. He got bit?'

'King Crapola wants to speak to you. Don't let him off the hook. I'm not nearly finished with that ape.'

I went and took the receiver, standing next to Edith.

'Hi, Joe.'

'You got bit! Was it Ronnie? Or Nancy? I bet it was Ronnie.'

'It was.'

'Oh man. He's a one. How's it going there? Everyone lovin' on you?'

'Uh . . . sure. Apart from the dogs.'

'Ha! You met Clay yet?'

'I did. He saved me from certain death.'

'Clay's got a way. He showed you the morpho farm?'

'I saw them through the glass. But not properly.'

'Has Isabelle shown you the collection?'

'Not yet.'

'You need to see it! You need to know all about it. And tell Ma we need a hundred cases for our trip west. And tell Clay we need some travel packs. When I get back I want you to be ready to hit the road, Rip. We got some selling to do.'

'When will that be?

'Any day now. I'll call you. Learn the names of all the butter-flies we sell. There are twenty-six core species you need to know.

I want us to be super-prepared. I need you learning those names. Learn them good. You should prepare for this pitch like a NASA astronaut making a trip to Mars, Rip.'

'OK,' I said, not sure that NASA actually sent astronauts to Mars.

'I gotta go.'

'Your mum wants . . .'

I handed the phone back to Edith but Joe was gone.

Although I was frustrated at Joe's desertion of me, the days he was away gave me time to insinuate myself into the family's affections and learn the ropes – which, I later realized, was all part of Joe's chaotic plan. In the mornings I got involved in the construction of the cases. Working the production line made me feel a part of things and brought everyone together around a unifying purpose: Elijah sealing the case with the silicon gun, Celeste arranging the flowers, Isabelle mounting the butterflies and Edith adding the Latin stickers to the bases, me packing the cases in cardboard boxes and Mary and Clay sealing the filled boxes and taking them to the storehouse. It was truly a family production and if these gift items were not always 'lovingly hand-crafted', they were, as Edith liked to say,

'Made in America by American hands;

not by machines in foreign lands.'

My job was to pack the cases in boxes padded with ripped-up pages of *National Enquirer* magazines, and as I did this I occasionally paused to read a headline in my best received pronunciation – 'Ryan O'Neal's son: my father's a monster.' 'How To Be Richer A Year From Now: 42 Easy Tips to Put $$ Thousands In Your Pocket—' a little act that seemed to go down well with everyone. I also started to learn the names – English and Latin – of the butterflies that I would be selling. While we were constructing the cases Elijah or Celeste would hold out a butterfly to test me. I memorized the prices – retail and wholesale – of the five different sizes of case and the variations according to state: in some parts of New England you add 25%, in some parts of the South you knock off 25%. I was taught the difference between how to pitch to florists versus how to sell to gift shops (florists were friendlier – they had the happiest work of any retailer – and better if you needed quick cash, but they generally bought fewer cases than gift shops); and there was the golden rule: 'never pitch to a Muppet' (someone who didn't have the authority to buy). Or as Edith put it:

'Save your breath for the one who signs the cheque.'

After a few days I knew all the names of the butterflies and the catchphrases that would help me sell them on the road and felt ready to get out there. My desire to get going wasn't just about wanting to sell or to see America. Close physical proximity with Mary was an exquisite torture that the promise of satisfaction on the road did little to cool and she did little to ease. All that week the heat picked up; it was that oozy, itchy Appalachian heat that makes you yearn for cold showers, mountain rivers and outdoor rutting. It was opiate and aphrodisiac, slowing everything down and swelling everything up. The factory was airless and the odours of dried flowers, glue and chemicals and all that pent-up passion would leave me with a throbbing headache. I tried to break her resistance down; I'd tell her what I wanted to do with her fearfully and wonderfully made temple. I'd whisper crass sweet nothings: 'I want you.' 'I've never met anyone like you.' 'You are so beautiful.' The borrowed phrases of pulpy romance come easily when you're in an unsated delirium of desire. One afternoon, I asked her to show me where we were going on the map in the Operations Room so we could be alone. We were leaning over the map of the USA, me one end, her at the other. I started to drive my finger from east to west, towards the hot states, towards her. Mary was leaning over the map from the Canadian side, her breasts cascading over the 49th Parallel into Montana, her elbows planted in Alberta and Manitoba, her lovely smooth brown arms running down the Rockies and the

Badlands. She was looking at me running my finger from the Catskills along a rough route to the West, calling out the names. She reached over and started driving her own finger across from California, along Interstate 80, and our digits met somewhere in Nebraska where I drove my finger up onto the bridge of her hand and along her arm and up to her shoulder and then to her lips. She opened her mouth just a little and I pushed the digit in. She clamped my hand and lightly bit into my already clamped finger. My heart was hammering like the heart of a trapped bird.

'Can't we find somewhere to do it in this big old ruin?' I asked.

'Like I said. Not under Ma's roof. She would kill me. And then she would kill you. You'll be pushing your pin into me soon enough.'

'But where?' I asked, picking up a pin and holding it over the map. 'Here?' I put the pinhead somewhere over Pennsylvania. 'Or here.' I moved it West to Iowa.

'Depends.'

'On what?'

'How many butterflies you sell. You gotta sell two hunnerd and fiddy cases first.'

'You've changed the terms of our agreement.'

'I get to.'

'How so?'

'Supplier sets the price.'

'I thought it was demand that set the price.'

'You think you're the only one that wants a piece of me?'

'You have a boyfriend?'

'Two-fiddy cases.'

Never did a salesman have a better incentive to hit his targets.

CHAPTER EIGHT

*In which Isabelle shows me the collection and
Edith sets me straight.*

Since our theological clash I had not seen much of Isabelle. She tended to get to the factory before I was up, do her bit, then go to the library to continue working on the collection. I was sure that I had upset her and, despite Mary's warning, I was determined to win back her approval partly to sate my need to be liked, but also because she had got the better of me and I would not rest until I had given a surer account of myself. I used the excuse of needing to see the collection as a reason to seek her out and I was sly enough to wait for Mary to be out of the house (taking her Z28 to the race circuit in Watkins Glen) before asking Isabelle to show it to me. She was in her room, at a desk set in the alcove. Sunbeams lit up the square where she sat. She looked quite in her element and when you see people in their element, being what they should be, they are usually at their most attractive and Isabelle was, in that moment, an absolute picture. Her hair was up but long black strands hung down, against a pale, thin kissable neck. Such was her focus that she wasn't even aware that I was standing in the doorway. I knocked gently on the door so as not to startle her.

'Sorry to interrupt.'

She looked up at me and then quickly back at what she was doing. Was she still pissed off or just preoccupied? I couldn't quite tell.

'I was wondering if this might be a good moment to see the collection.'

'Oh . . .'

'Or we could do it another time.'

'I just need to finish setting these two. It'll take a few minutes.'

She had a setting board on her desk and was taping the wings of a butterfly with strips of paper. There was a little groove in the board to lay the body of the butterfly in so that it wouldn't be crushed and to allow the wings to spread naturally. Isabelle's jaw was slack with the concentrating, her tongue darting at her top lip, her eyes widened and narrowed at the tiny movements required to set the butterfly without damaging it.

'Where did you learn how to do that?'

'*Directions for Making a Collection* by Benjamin Wilkes. Would you pass me that magnifying glass?'

I handed her the magnifier and she examined her handiwork.

'How long does each one take?'

'If I get it right, then maybe five minutes to pin and tape it. Then a few days for it to set.'

'Looks fiddly.'

'I'm doing it the old way, pinning the forewings sloping backwards in the natural manner. Present day collectors set the dorsum – the trailing edge – at right angles to the body to expose more of the pattern of the hindwings. But I prefer this method. It's more natural. It's actually the old British method. The one . . . my father favoured.'

There was the tiniest hesitation before mentioning her father, but she mentioned him. The F-word.

The two butterflies she was setting were small but brilliant, with stripes and spots of turquoise on black velvet wings.

'What are they?'

'Blue glassy tigers. Male and female.'

'How can you tell which is which?'

'In this case the male is the slightly prettier one. In the wild they're easier to distinguish as the males usually patrol a fixed boundary while the females go where they please.'

'Unlike this household?'

She smiled at my dig at Joe.

'My father specialized in the Neotropical region. The most colourful and spectacular species. As well as some of the rarest.'

'So those were caught twenty years ago?'

'Yes.'

'They look as good as new.'

'These little envelopes are miracles of practicality,' she said. 'They used to just press butterflies in books, like flowers. But the specimens never lasted. A specimen can last indefinitely in these. So long as you keep the pests away. That's the big challenge for most lepidopterists.'

'You don't get bored?'

'I do my best thinking when I'm setting.'

'Thought any good thoughts today?' I asked this without agenda but she blushed again.

'Oh . . . Many things. And nothing. I'm . . . no. I am trying for a scholarship to Yale. And I have to write a five-thousand-word essay.'

'On?'

'You won't want to know.'

'Try me.'

'It's . . . Well. More theology, I'm afraid. I'm comparing and contrasting the different expressions of faith in the novels of Tolstoy and Dostoevsky.'

'As you do.' (I had seen *The Brothers Karamazov* and *Anna Karenina* on her bedside table. Looking at those books had made me momentarily envious of the inner life she was enjoying and that I, not so long ago, had exchanged for the experiential pleasures promised by Joe.)

'I've not done the Big Russians yet. Tolstoy or Dostoevsky?'

'Oh. I couldn't choose between them. I admire them both so much.'

How facile she made me feel. She wanted to get inside the heads of great Russian novelists, I wanted to get inside her sister's knickers.

'So what are the differences? In a sentence. Save me reading those big doorsteps.'

'Well. You *should* read them. If you care about literature and have aspirations to write. It's hard to say in a sentence. Tolstoy does the panoramic so well and the prose seems to come easy and elegantly. Dostoevsky's thoughts pour out with less polish but more passion. And he gets a little deeper into the troubled side of his characters. They are both men of faith but I think their responses to the claims of Christianity are very different. Which is what I'm proposing in my essay.'

'Go on.'

'Well. . . . Do you really want to know?'

'Yes.' How the angel of my better nature stirred in her company!

'OK. Well. It's my opinion that Tolstoy's faith was more theoretical, deist and actually unorthodox, whereas Dostoevsky's faith was more intimate, Christ-centred and orthodox.'

'Tolstoy Bad Theology, Dostoevsky Good?'

'Ha! Joe might put it that way. It's hard to know for sure what people really believe. Even those who are capable of expressing themselves better than others. What people write or even say isn't always exact testimony. Nearly done here.'

I was happy to wait, standing there watching her carefully tape the wings of butterflies whilst talking about God and great writers or the third instar of papilios. Mary was right: Isabelle was out of step, not just with her generation but with these times, which are brash and boastful and preoccupied with the need for instant gratification ('if it feels good do it'). But how original that made her. And it was certainly easier to appreciate Isabelle's quieter qualities when she was not sat next to her noisier sister.

'I actually wanted to say sorry if I offended you in some way the other day,' I said. 'When we were talking about beliefs. I was being glib.'

'I'm sorry if I was a bit strident.'

'I was brought up to have an opinion on everything – including things I don't know about. I didn't mean to upset you.'

'Thank you for saying so. My head was elsewhere.'

'In Russia?'

'In Russia. But in other places, too.'

I quite liked the idea of being in those other places with her – wherever they were.

'I thought Mary was being mean to you and I didn't want you thinking I agreed with her.'

'Mary likes to disagree with people. It's her way of working things out. She was probably trying to impress you. I think she's taken a shine to you. And you seem to have taken a shine to her.'

Isabelle said this without any trace of the envy I thought she might be feeling – or that Mary had hinted at. I laughed a phony, pathetic laugh. 'Really?' My fake surprise brought the most sudden and profound change of colour to Isabelle's face: a mortified purple.

'I'm sorry. That's presumptuous of me.'

'No. She's . . . attractive. Feisty. She has a strong personality. But I don't have feelings for her – in that way. I'm flattered though.'

Was that relief in her eyes? Let it be so!

'Mary can give the impression she's a confident, free-thinking young woman but really she's an insecure girl. More vulnerable than you might think.'

I felt transparent again, my intentions exposed. It sounded like a gentle warning. Was she protecting her sister or me? Or herself?

'I don't have designs on her if that's what you mean. She's not my type.'

I am slightly ashamed of my cold, chameleon opportunism. How quick I was to lie in order to keep the field open. I was prepared to demean both sisters in order to play them off against each other: when I was with Isabelle, Mary was a needy nymphet; when I was with Mary, Isabelle was a pious prude.

'Can a person really be a type?' she said. 'In novels, perhaps. We name types of things but every living creature is essentially unique.'

I had, once again, been put in my shallow puddle. With Isabelle there was a test (I was always failing): the challenge of the unobtainable. I really needed to up my game in her company.

'I . . . suppose we create types for convenience. Because life is too short to really find out who someone is.'

She seemed to like this.

'Yes. All categorization is shorthand. I think it's why I chose arts over science. Taxonomy is as much about our need to order things as understand them. If not more. You probably think I'm a type, too. I can see that you do. It's all right. I confess to doing the same with you.'

'And what type am I?' I asked her.

'Oh.'

'That bad?'

'You are . . . a charmer. Clever. Maybe a pleasure-seeker.'

'Thank you.'

'I think you want to be all things to all people.'

'A people-pleaser?'

'Is that rude?'

'No. It's true enough,' I said.

I'm not sure I liked the type she'd defined. Charm is a dubious quality to have. It implies a certain attractiveness and emotional intelligence, but requires guile and guile is demonic angelic. Clever is great at school and dinner parties but it suggests a lack of depth and was not the intellectual endorsement I was hoping for. As for pleasure-seeker. Well I couldn't really argue: I was a hedonist. Pleasure was my true goal, and pleasure at the expense of others a necessary part of that philosophy.

On the way to the library I decided to act as if I was seeing the room and its treasures for the first time in order to let her have the pleasure of showing it to me. (People-pleaser that I am.)

'These chests are incredible. Were they here when you came?'

'Joe found a cabinet-making specialist in a place called Hancock, a Shaker community. We sold some rarities to pay for them. But it was worth it.'

Isabelle opened a drawer.

'I presume there's a system?' I asked. (What taxonomist could resist answering such a question?)

'Yes. My father used a specially devised standardized system to record locality, frequency, early stages and collection serial numbers of every insect he captured. Every little envelope he'd send back carried the information. And he made a note of every single specimen he caught in his notebooks. He had a thing for aberrations. We have some species here that are not even in the Smithsonian.'

The collection – 'one of the most extraordinary on earth', I would later learn – was wasted on me. To my uneducated eye, the butterflies were wonderful but no lovelier, no more brilliant, than the butterflies we would soon be selling to gift stores and florists out on the road; but in the company of this Keeper I was happy to be educated. Isabelle was sensitive enough just to show me the highlights, including the wonderful and slightly frightening Queen Alexandra birdwings that made up – along with the Hesperon, Homerus and Chika –the Big Four rarest, most valuable butterflies in the world.

'We have all nineteen of the Appendix I butterflies. That is butterflies that it is a criminal offence to trade. Back then it wasn't an issue. But mankind is voracious. Species are dying out.'

'So how come your father didn't set them himself?'

'He never had the time. He was working in far-flung places and specialized in very large specimens. He would send the rarities back until he had time to mount and set and frame them. Ma would put them in his "collection chest".'

'The trunk she pulled from the flames?'

Isabelle nodded.

'She paid a heavy price for saving them.'

'She knew they were valuable. It's only in the last few years that we realized just how valuable.'

Isabelle walked to the far end of the room and pulled out two drawers.

'If there is ever a fire again – these are the bugs to grab.'

To my eye they looked like the blue morphos that were being raised on the farm and that were the business's most popular seller.

'Blue morphos?'

'Almost. But with something extra.'

I looked and couldn't see anything, spectacularly different other than a little appendage between the wings.'

'They're five-winged blue morphos. A new species. As far as we know, they are the only examples in the world. For a long time, it was considered to be a myth, a phantasm, like a Moby Dick of the skies. Rumours of its existence fluttered between the halls and drawers of the great museums and around the conventions of the great collectors. But no one had one or had seen one. Then my father found these. Twenty-four of them.'

The name card said 'Morpho wolffii.'

'Morpho wolffii?'

'Wolff is my father's surname. Ma reverted to her maiden name after they divorced. And we did the same.'

'You don't seem to mind talking about him. I thought there was a prohibition.'

She didn't answer.

'You don't remember him I suppose.'

'I have a vague memory of a man with a beard and long hair in shorts and sandals. I remember the trunk. It was like a treasure chest. When you opened it you were bedazzled by all the colours. Even in their envelopes. They were nearly all jungle butterflies so the colours were powerful and vivid. If you squinted you could imagine that trunk was full of sapphires and rubies, diamonds and emeralds.'

'Do you . . . regret not knowing him?'

'What's done is done. I sometimes think I am connecting with him in some way, when I'm setting, but I'm not sure what they tell me about him, other than the fact he was obsessed with them, that he travelled a great deal, that he was meticulous. I can admire that part of him. It will be sad to see it go.'

'Go?'

'Joe thinks he's found a buyer for the whole collection. Mind you he's said that before. He's been trying to net the big deal – the deal that changes everything – for years. But he seems certain this time.'

'Do you mind? After all the work you've done putting it together?'

'It would be good for us to not have to chase after money all the time. To escape the hand to mouth. Joe carries a heavy burden but he doesn't always show it. And there's no point in having these things in drawers, unseen.'

'How much would it be worth?'

'I don't know. Joe thinks it's a lot. But it's hard to know if the numbers he's quoting are Joe numbers or real; they seem a little too much to me.'

'What sort of numbers?'

'I don't even know.'

'Go on.'

'A year ago he sold a set of the Big Four for fifty thousand dollars to a Japanese collector.'

'Jesus. So . . . the whole collection . . .'

'It could be a lot.'

'But you don't seem that keen.'

'If it was up to me I would give them to the Smithsonian.'

'That's noble of you.'

'Yeah. But as Ma would say, "Nobility don't pay the fuckin' bills."'

Isabelle's impersonation of her mother's husky twang and expletive was surprisingly accurate and reassuring: her loyalty wasn't blind and her sense of humour wasn't dead. And when Isabelle swore it was rarer and just as beautiful as an Alexandra birdwing!

'What about Mary?'

'I don't think she really cares. She's never shown any interest in butterflies.'

Isabelle started to move along the canyon of mahogany, closing those lovely silent sliding drawers.

'Have you ever wanted to see your father? In all this time?'

She didn't answer yes or no but I took it as a yes. 'I wrote my father a few years ago. When I was sixteen. I don't know what I was trying to do. I posted it care of Princeton. It was silly. I shared blithe and bland facts about my life.'

'Why is that silly? Seems perfectly natural to me.'

'My problem was how to be honest about what I was doing around Ma who, as you know, would not countenance any mention of my father let alone correspondence with him. 'I still respected her position. And Joe's too. But Joe had some memory of our father. I did not. I was curious to know something. I still felt unfaithful writing those letters. And asking Clay to post them for me.'

'Did he ever reply?'

Isabelle hesitated.

'Isabelle?'

'Ma found out in the end.'

'How?'

'Clay told her. In his hierarchy of loyalty Ma is first. Ma said I couldn't have anything to do with him as long as I was under her roof, or until I was twenty-one.'

'And when are you twenty-one?

'In the fall.'

Just then Mary appeared without warning. I'm sure she'd been eavesdropping. 'Izzy been showing you her true loves?'

Mary was wearing just a T-shirt and knickers, her hair tied to one side. She directed the barbed words at her sister but the looks were for me. Isabelle closed the drawers and left the room, unwilling to fuel this fire.

'Ma wants to see you.'

'What about?'

'She didn't say.'

'How's her mood?'

Mary shrugged. 'Hard to say. She might shoot you, she might hug you. Take her an iced tea. That'll keep her sweet.'

Mary was stood in the doorway. She lifted her brown leg across it, barring my exit.

'Remember what you vowed.'

'I do.'

＊　＊　＊

I set off to see Edith without trepidation. She had become a little sweeter towards me over the last few days; my combination of self-ridicule and directness played well with her. I was confident in my ability to charm people of different temperaments, even the tightly strung ones. She must have heard the creak of the floorboards for she said 'come in' before my knuckles even rapped the door. Because of her troublesome legs, she spent most mornings in her vast bed with four carved posts, which she used as a desk, spreading invoices, orders and bills around her. She was sat propped up with several pillows and looked the queen of her realm. The room's original fittings and fixtures were intact. The only anomaly was a big television propped on a chest at the end of her bed. She was half-watching a romantic soap while doing the admin. I set the iced tea on the bedside table and stood, unsure of my next move. She continued to look from paperwork to television.

'Mrs Bosco?'

'No one calls me that except AT&T and I ain't friends with

them. Making money outta people just talking. Call me Edith or nothing.'

'I brought you an iced tea.'

'Sit.'

There were no chairs in the room, other than the cushioned bench in the bay window. There was a single cot bed the other side of Edith's. Later, Isabelle would explain that she would sleep in it on the nights her mother had the fire-fears, reading her to sleep with psalms or *National Enquirer* articles.

'I won't molest you or nothing.' I perched on the end of the bed, inches from her outstretched legs. She was wearing a silk dressing gown over a blouse. Her legs were out straight but covered by a counterpane. Her caliper was propped against the bottom of the bedside table that was stacked with *National Enquirers*. In her lap was a pile of just opened correspondence. She held up a letter, her nails immaculate purple almonds, and read:

'"Dear Mrs Bosco, Re: your application for a loan dated" blah, "we regret to say that your application has been declined . . ." Blah!" She screwed up the letter into a ball and threw it at the basketball hoop fixed at the end of the four-poster. 'Chase Motherfucking Manhattan! These people shit money but not one of them will help us. Cocksucking motherfuckers.'

I like a good cuss as much as the next person but Edith's use of the word motherfucker brought me up short every time she said it. She used it the way some people say damn and her off-spring – and I include the never-swearing Isabelle in this – hardly ever seemed shocked by it.

'I'd like to say that we don't need these people. But we do. Unless we get a loan we can't meet the orders we get. Constantly behind. We are close to sinking here. We got too many pigs for this tit. I mean, look at these bills.' Edith picked out the itemized phone bill and held it as though it was a live rat. 'This car phone is just another example. Three hundred dollars' worth of calls to

Wyoming? Who the fuck is in Wyoming? I think maybe Joe's started a family or something.'

She leant over for her iced tea. When she sipped it she had to rest the lip of the cup against her lip and tilt her head to stop it dripping. She set the iced tea back down and sniffed, her reconstructed nostril whistling strangely. She stared at me and I braced myself for another 'test'.

'Still gawping? It takes about a week to get used to me. After that you got no excuse.'

I sniffed my laugh. 'Sorry.'

Edith took another slug of her tea. 'Let's get one thing straight. I don't for a second believe you care about this business or want to be a butterfly salesman. Let's not pretend here. For you this is all an experience. It doesn't matter to you if it works or not. You can have your fun and go home. But it matters to me. And it matters to this family. This is our livelihood.'

'It's in my interest that you do well, Edith. What's good for you is . . .'

'Save it for the road. I'm already working with one champion bullshitter. I don't need another. I know when someone's paying you it ain't easy to speak your mind but I'm paying you to speak your mind.'

Being in the chrysalis of my butterflying career, it seemed churlish to point out that I had not yet been paid, or even discussed the matter of my remuneration. The terms of my 'package', as laid down by Joe that first day, were to be 'well paid', have 'a car' and see 'this great country', none of which had been delivered yet. But I'd not brought the subject up. The family had welcomed me into their home and adventures lay ahead. I was being fed, I had a roof over my head and I was having an experience. I certainly liked the idea of being paid to speak my mind. So far, it had been the best policy with Edith and the method most likely to promote me in her eyes.

'Before my legs got bad I drove probably more than twenty times around the earth selling. I built this business from nothing into what it is now and I don't want nobody – especially not Joe and his cockamamie ideas – screwing it up. Your job is to it to keep him on the right road.'

She grabbed an invoice from a different pile and held it up, pinched between thumb and index. 'You see this?' It was headed paper with the name Bangor Floral. 'This is a repeat order from a flower chain in Maine. They have faithfully re-ordered every quarter for ten years. Fifty cases. We got a hunnerd of these and we're doing OK. These kinds of people are the bread and butter. Now if we get A and P or J. C. Penney's they will want exclusive rights and we will have to stop selling to all these good folks. Trade in all that goodwill and loyalty for a big faceless corporation that doesn't give a single shit about us and who will screw every living cent from us. It's a big risk. And even if we get an order we might not be able to deliver it. We are a one-product company, like Coke. And you don't fuck with the recipe. Joe of course wants to fuck with the recipe. To "diversicate" or whatever the word he uses is. But he hasn't thought it through. He never does the math. He's too busy tossing dollars around like confetti. And coming up with crazy ideas. We have a good thing going here. This business has kept us all in houses and food and it's going to put Isabelle through college. It could have put Joe through college too if he'd wanted it. But he had other ideas. And lately, he's been getting notions too big for his boots. He thinks he can sell the collection for big money and it's given him this idea that he can act like he's already sold it. Buying fancy suits. Hiring Cadillacs. When he gets cash in his hands he spends it. Or he gives it away to some tramp thinking he's a great philanthropist. He has these notions about doing right by people and God but they are not compatible with running a successful business. I need someone to keep an eye on him. I only got one!'

Edith saw pretty well with her one eye. Up, down, forward – and backwards! She could tell the shape of someone trustworthy and the shape of a faker from twenty paces. I think she trusted me for now; but in the long run she trusted no one, which, although a cynical way to live, means you are proven right more often than not.

'You are here because I told Joe to go and hire someone who was sensible. Someone who had an education. Someone with intelligence but who weren't too original or liable to go and start their own business. Someone who would do as they were told and respect the law. Someone not like Joe in other words. You are meant to be that guy. So when you go selling, keep him on the highway, keep him away from trouble, and distraction; churches and preachers especially. And keep an eye on the money. Will you do that?'

I nodded. Although being told I'd been hired for my common sense and unoriginality was a blow to my ego and sense of mystery. It wasn't for my charm, my voice, or even my intelligence that I was being hired; or because of the serendipitous timing of the gods; it was to steer Joe a sensible course, and report back on his 'up-to-somethingness'.

'What if he sells the collection?'

'I wish he *would* sell those little fuckers. I have no affection for them. But Joe's been saying he's got a buyer for that god-damned collection for years and I don't see anyone smoking no cigar. 'The problem with Joe is he's got a streak of his father in him. I see too much of him in Joe these days. I see him in Isabelle, too. You can't deny that. Her brain. Her need for order. That comes from him. But lately I seen some of those same traits in Joe that I don't like.'

Edith looked at me, making sure I got the point.

'What traits are those?' I asked, trying to sound indifferent, lest I scare the moment away.

'An inclination to disappear when you need him. My kids saw more of the Palos Verdes blue than they did their father. That's an extinct butterfly, by the way. So I'm making a joke there. You know where he was when Joe was born? In a rainforest in

Venezuela. You know where he was when Isabelle was born? At a bug convention. When Mary was born he was gone.'

She paused, breathed, and exhaled the memory.

'I get the impression – from Isabelle – that he was an obsessive man.'

'Obsessive don't even cover it. What else she say?'

'Not much. She . . . seemed uncomfortable talking about it.'

She was looking at me now; her lovely green eye more exacting than a lie detector. Maybe this was the real reason for summoning me. It wasn't to discuss the business, or Joe's gallivanting; it was to check on what had been said about her ex-husband by her children to me. Like a paranoid dictator, Edith needed to control the story.

'We're not talking about a normal person, here. I used to joke that he loved bugs more than people – but it turned out to be no joke. He was as single-minded as an ant. I'm pregnant and he leaves me with two kids to go to South America because he says he's on the verge of a major scientific breakthrough. After months of nothing he calls from South America to tell me he's had a revelation. I'm thinking, "Maybe he's had the breakthrough!" But no. He says he's leaving. That he is not cut out to be a husband or a father and that the work demands his everything. So he leaves. He only communicates one more time. About a month after the fire. I was still confined to a bed. Mary on a ventilator. He calls me. From Bogotá. I can just about breathe. You know the first thing he asks me?'

I nod her on.

'"Are they safe?" And I think he means the children. And I say, "Yes, they're safe." And he says, "All of them?" And I say, "Yes, all of them." Still thinking he means the kids. And then he says, "The ones in the trunk, too? The freaks?" And then I realize: he isn't asking about the kids. And there's this long silence. I think I've lost the connection. And then there's this faint "Oh my God." And I swear he's weeping. Not from relief that his wife and kids are still alive. But because his life's work has nearly gone up in flames. And in that moment I know it's over. I can't let my kids be around that. No scientific breakthrough justifies that kind of behaviour. Not even the discovery of a goddamn talking butterfly justifies that.'

Edith stopped, opened her mouth and took a gulp of air, the memory of being in that fire and on that respirator triggering a bodily response. She mumbled a few more reassurances to herself as though still needing to justify the action she'd taken half a lifetime ago. Who could blame her for wanting her children to have nothing to do with such a man? A man who valued insects over his own kind?

'He's never tried to get in touch? See his children?'

'Why would he? He never wanted to when he was around. When he said he was leaving I told him he'd never see his kids while I was their mother. He accepted it. Not because he felt guilt or respect – but because he didn't care.'

'And you've not seen him since?'

Edith leant over to her bedside table and produced a pistol. It was a small 'woman's pistol', the kind a femme fatale might slip in her handbag before a dinner.

'I bought this for self-protection. After he left. But the truth is I would use it now if I saw him. Without hesitation.'

'What if . . . he'd changed? Expressed remorse?'

'Remorse needs a human heart. And he ain't got one of those 'cos he ain't human.'

It was flattering to have Edith share these painful memories. I was vain enough to think it was because of something intrinsically sensitive and trustworthy in me. But I could see that she was making sure I got the story straight lest I get it crooked from someone else. All the years Edith had controlled the story, its truth augmented by the telling and re-telling and by going un-challenged. The absolute guilt of the accused was testified to by her scars, which were a daily prosecution. But for all that I still felt those scars didn't tell the whole story. Just the parts she wanted the world to see. I believed Edith's straight talk on most matters – butterflies, business, religion – but on the subject of her ex-husband I couldn't help feeling the lady doth protest too much.

CHAPTER NINE

In which Joe returns with a new recruit and news of a life-changing deal.

Joe returned just as the storm broke, dispersing the electric tensions in the house and bringing with him 'the fresh breeze of 'optitude', the Western promise of vast horizons and news of a life-changing deal. We were all in the factory when we heard the scrunching of tyres in the drive and the blaring of country and western filling the air. It had been a week since he had set off without telling anyone where he was going, and two days later than he'd said he'd be when he'd called claiming to have had 'a heckish high-level meeting'. I was beginning to see that there was a relationship between the level of the fanfare and distraction Joe created upon returning and the amount of making up needed for whatever upset he'd caused by his sudden, unexplained absences. His entrance that day had a lot of Ta Da! And since my 'briefing' from Edith I was more alert to Joe's tricks. Even as the car door slammed I told myself I would not be distracted by whatever white rabbit he was going to pull from his hat, tales of life-changing deals, or odes to the glories of America's natural wonders he was about to deliver. I intended to get some straight answers about where he'd been and what he'd been up to.

If Joe's absences made the heart grow sceptical, when present he had this ability to obliterate any doubts you had about him by the sheer force of his Joe-ness. He looked effortlessly magnificent as he entered the kitchen, his shirt soaked from the storm rain, sticking to his skin, his shoulder muscles and pectorals stretching to bursting, his steamed glasses pushed up above his forehead. All the accumulated irritations evaporated. He was carrying an aerated cardboard box used for transporting pets, which he held in his spread palm above the shoulder, just out of reach of Celeste, who was jumping up to look into the box and asking, 'What is it? Let me see!' Joe beamed with the confidence that no matter how many grievances we had, the thing in the box would be enough to make us forgive and forget. He was like an adventurer who, despite being gone five times longer than he'd said he would, and having committed all manner of heinous crimes in the adventuring, had found the diamond that justified it all. Damn you, Joe Bosco, I thought. I don't care what the something you've been up to is. I've missed you!

'Good day, leppars!'

'Show me, show me, Joe.' Celeste stood on a chair to get a look inside the box.

Joe giggled with the vicarious excitement of us discovering what he knew he had for us.

'What happened to your face?' Mary asked.

In all the razzmatazz I'd failed to notice the cut over his eyebrow sealed with a butterfly strip and a faint bruising on the cheekbone.

'Skunk. Broke so hard I hit my head on the mirror.'

Mary's expression said 'skunk, my ass' but we were all too mesmerized by the box now to pursue it.

'OK. You need to be quiet.' He set the box on the table. 'Don't crowd round.' He pulled of the lid and stepped back.

'Ladies and gentlemen, I present to you . . . Jimmy Carter.'

It was a bird. Large as a crow but featherless and baby in every way except for the beak – which was hooked and formidable. The bird lifted its head and opened that beak anticipating food. Joe grabbed a piece of pizza that Elijah had left in the box and dropped it into the bird's maw.

'Know what it is?'

'It's a baby turkey,' Celeste said.

'No!'

I had no idea. It was ugly as a dodo and helpless as a lamb, except it ate like something born to devour. Its beak was monstrous.

'Is it a . . . crow?'

'Nope.'

'A buzzard,' Clay said.

'Close.'

'It's the goddamn national bird.' Edith was sticking Latin names stickers to the bases of the butterfly cases and buying none of it.

'Yay, Ma! Come on down! You've won a car! It's a little orphan bald eagle. Ain't he cute? I found him at Batavia Kill. Just sitting in the road.'

'We got enough lame birds around here already.' Edith said.

Celeste tossed the bird another slice of pizza. When it ate you saw more clearly the bird it was going to become.

'He's a hungry son of a gun. Needs constant feeding. I reckon he's grown about a pound a day. Clay, you think you can fix Jimmy Carter a coop? Needs to be dark but have a feeding hatch.'

'We can try.'

'I'm not feeding that little fucker a single scrap,' Edith said.

'You don't have to. He'll be coming with us, out on the road. We're going to set him free in the Grand Tetons.'

'You just get back from one bit of gallivanting and you're already bragging about the next?'

'Fear not for I bring tidings of great optitude.' Joe was beaming now, and the beaming looked sincere. 'We got a buyer for the Collection.'

'Oh here we go.'

'No. This time you gotta believe me. I met this guy. He buys for a private collector who lives in Wyoming. He says his patron is one of the richest men in America. He is building a museum called "The Museum of Extinction", which is full of species that are no longer found on the planet, from the brontosaurus to the Palos Verdes blues. I showed him the photographs of the

115

Collection. He said that he ain't, in all his days, seen bugs like it. When I mentioned the freaks he didn't believe me.'

'Makes two of us.'

'This is serious, Ma. This time. It's real. I showed him the sample.' (Joe carried this freak on him at all times, as a sort of emergency insurance/credit/calling card.) 'This guy was so super-impressed he called his client. I asked who this client was and he wouldn't say. Super-secretive. He just called him the Wizard. 'Cos no one gets to see him. He wouldn't even tell me his name. Just that he's like a super-private reclusive type who happens to have the largest private collection of butterflies in the world. Like Rothschild, Riley, Bretherton, Margaret Fontaine all rolled into one, Iz. He is "The John Paul Getty of Butterfly Collecting". He invited me to his house in Wyoming!'

I watched Isabelle during this announcement. Her mixed feelings were all there to see in her lowered eyes and little nods: resignation mixed in with gratitude, a necessary scepticism towards Joe but a desire to be pleased for him.

'You talk money with this Wizard?' Edith asked.

'Trillionaires don't talk about money, Ma.'

'So why don't he come and see the collection for hisself?' Mary asked, voicing what I was thinking.

'He's a kind of hermit. Apparently he never goes out. Lives in an oxygen tent. Never flies. Frightened of getting a disease.'

'So how come he's willing to meet you?'

'Ha! 'Cos I got what he ain't!'

'What about the Smithsonian, Joe?' Isabelle asked.

'I tried them. I took photographs and a couple of speci-mens. Met the Keeper of Entomology. This is a guy who's seen more bugs than most people on the planet. You know what he said? "Mr Bosco. This is a quite astonishing collection. Have you thought about bequeathing it to the nation?" "Bequeath",' I thought. "That sounds like a fancy word for getting for free." I said we had to get something for such valuables. He said they had a ceiling. Which is a fancy way of saying they're cheap. And that the ceiling was ten thousand. So I said that ceiling wasn't high enough. That I could get ten thousand for just one butterfly if I made a couple of phone calls. The Keeper got all frosty with me. He said, "Money can't buy you everything, Mr Bosco!" So I said no, but it can buy you a set of Queen Alexandra birdwing when you want one! He got mad at me after that.'

'How did this collector in Wyoming make his money?' Isabelle asked.

'Right. I said I don't want to be selling the collection to some oppressor of the poor, or no arms dealer or oilman. This guy said his client inherited his money from his grandfather who was an oilman. But his client, he reassured me, is a Philanthropist with a capital P. He supports all kinds of environmental causes, saving whales, Siberian tigers, rainforests. He said he was a man who wanted to save the planet from the abuses of mankind. What his father destroyed he wanted to put right. He's building his museum away from cities and the sea. In case something happens to the world. Like a nuclear war. Or a second flood. I held off telling him that this was Bad Theology as God made a promise he'd never flood the whole earth again. He sounds like one of those people who feels guilty about how much they have accumulated and wants to make up for all the stomping and accumulating they done.'

I could see Edith already placing Joe's story in the library of bullshit with all the other bigged-up biographies of Joe's composing. Being around a serial exaggerator for long periods of time inclines you to stop listening. Joe was the boy who cried, 'Wolves! Goddamn thousands of them!' I had subconsciously started doing what Clay had advised me to do: dividing everything Joe said by ten and then cutting that in half again. I was sure that this Wizard – like his famous namesake – was going to be all smoke, all bark; a silly little man pulling levers to trigger the machinery of special effects needed to make him seem more than he was. It sounded fantastic, even by Joe's standards.

'When this guy can turn your bullshit into gold, then I'll

117

celebrate. But for now I got a goddamn business to run here. And a letter from a bailiff.'

'Ma, while you worry about some florists in Bangor buying three fritillaries from us I'm trying to set us up a real deal, here.'

And then the two of them slipped seamlessly into bickering. Edith reminded Joe (maybe for the thousandth time) that she had started this business when he was in diapers and managed well enough without hiring Cadillacs with car phones or Limeys to help the business (I was still at this point, if not the enemy, part of the problem, an extension of and cheerleader to Joe's gallivanting ways) or arranging meetings with Wizards in Dollywood. Joe said he wasn't in diapers, he was eleven, and that without his making her that case that time they would never have started the business. He defended employing me saying I had already helped with the business. My educated ways were making a difference. Edith countered with my educated ways would count for dick at the coal face. Joe said that soon they'd no longer have to work at the coal face. She came back with the fact they were behind on the rent and that the banks were turning them down. But despite all the yelling, Edith needed the medicine of a good rant. She needed him to do annoying things so that she could rant some more. And Joe needed her to be angry with him to affirm his maverick unaccountability. It was like letting blood, with Joe her apothecary supplying the leeches. She and Joe were more like a bickering married couple than mother and son. One by one the rest of us drifted from the room leaving them to their necessary and eternal squabble.

Later, when we were packing for the trip west, I decided to confront Joe about the Wizard, Jimmy Carter, and the cut above his eye.

'Was that really a skunk, Joe?'

'Sure.'

Joe was actually a terrible liar. When he was lying it was so obvious it was as though he wanted you to know he was lying. You only had to call out the first lie and he'd fess up.

'OK. It was Baptists.'

'Baptists?'

'I got beat up by Baptists. In Virginia. They didn't like me questioning the preacher. This one preacher was preaching a gospel of prosperity in this life and justifying it with scripture from here and there – which even the Devil can do. And his congregation – who all looked pretty well turned out in their suits – were nodding and Amen-ing his every fart. The preacher said he had a Mercedes and that it was God's provision and reward and he wasn't ashamed to say it. He said a worker deserved his wages. And his congregation who looked like they all had good wages agreed. He said he was doing important work, more important than any CEO, and that he should get paid in a commensurating manner. So I put up my hand and asked if he could clarify for me, how much he was being paid as pastor of this church? And that's when they took exception and threw me out. These four guys took me to the parking lot. Escorted me to my car. They wanted me to fight them back. So I offered my cheek. And this one guy took it! They put me in jail for a night.'

'They put you in jail for preacher-baiting and that's why you been so long?'

'Rip, I have been setting up this deal. Believe me. And that was just for one night. But it was worth it. Just to see the look on those Baptists' faces when I interrupted the preacher in full flow. Talking about who was in and who was out. And being a real Christian. And how he was going to heaven! I had to! I had to interrupt that. Because that right there is the theology that's killing this country.'

'Why do you even bother going to church, Joe?'

'It's food, Rip. And like any restaurant, if the food's bad you send it back. Preachers are waiters dispensing heavenly chow – or at least they ought to be. They serve you something indigestible, or so rich and rarefied that it makes you want to puke, you send it

119

back. But they should not be charging for that food because it was already given to them by someone else. They charge good money too, some of them. That's why it should be asked.'

I suddenly realized that Joe and I were alone. It was so rare being on your own with Joe; there was always someone – a chaperone, a companion, waif, a sister, a stray – in tow. I was sure he always had a foil so he could avoid the questions that might come. I made the most of the opportunity.

'Your mother told me about your father. About what happened.'

'She did?'

'Yes.'

'Well, that's a sign she trusts you.'

'Her version was slightly different to yours. I didn't realize your dad was that . . . bad.'

'She's dramatic! People always give different versions of a story. You should know that. A writer. Look at the Gospels. Don't mean it ain't true.'

'Your mother has told me to keep an eye on you, Joe. Thinks you're up to something. You must be straight with me.'

He scratched his hands. The hands that he'd told me had dragged his mother from the fire.

'You think the Wizard really wants the freaks?'

'I do, Rip. In the world of lepping, it's the misfits that make it big. But let's talk about this when we're out on the road. We'll have plenty of time to share biographies. Straighten the twist and turns to your likeability.' He then whispered. 'When we're a thousand miles from Ma, I'll tell you everything you need to know. I promise. Come on. Let me show you where we are going.'

Joe led me through to the Operations Room. When we got to the map of America he spread out his arms, hands palm up, like a preacher revving up for a sermon.

'The world is divided into two kinds of people, Rip. People with butterfly cases and people without. You, my friend, are to be the bringer of good news, a fisher of men and women, a bringer of people into the kingdom of butterflies. Every town that has a church, a McDonald's, a gas station and a school will have a store selling butterflies. We are going to spread the good news of *Papilios* across this land. We will make it into a nation of lepidopterists. We will establish our empire of winged beauties, our cornucopia of colour. We will not stop until the Kingdom of Butterflies has been established here on this earth.'

One reason I think Joe was drawn to preachers was because he recognized kindred spirits. He was an evangelist, doggedly, even cheerfully enduring the boorish ignorance of the unsaved as he proclaimed his entomological gospel. And as preposterous as these words were, Joe made me believe again.

'You ready to sell, Rip?'

'I think so.

'Are you ready to sell, Rip?' Joe yelled it the way a sergeant major yells at a platoon and expects a shouted response.

'Yessir!'

'I said: are you really ready to sell?'

'Yes, sir! I am ready, sir.'

'Oh . . . I can feel it. We are going to take this land. You are going to rip it up, Rip. We are going to sell like crazy. And you are going to conquer. With charm and stories and salesmanship. Selling is stories and stories is selling. To sell something you gotta be a storyteller. Conjuring up pictures for people. Giving them hope. And if you want to understand this land, Rip, you have to sell. When you sell you will understand it. Selling is the language of this nation. And you are going to learn to speak it fluently. Having something people want, or need, or something they didn't know they needed yet: this is the beauty of it. And when you have a product that actually has real value and meaning, truth and beauty (you said it!) there's nothing better. And while we do this you will experience such glories, and see such wonders that you'll think yourself crazy for ever contemplating saying no to my invitation. But it ain't all a plain sail. We are like fishermen. Putting out to sea in our metal boat, hoping to net some sales, in various ports, crossing a land so huge you will think you are in an ocean. There will be storms. There will be sharks. Pirates even. But if we cast our nets we will catch them, Rip! There's plenty fish in this sea. Dee, dee, dee. Fish for you and fish for me.'

It would be easy to think Joe some kind of cheerleader for the American Dream. But I think he just took the tropes of the Dream and mashed them into a pumped-up pep talk to gee himself up. The can-do positivity was the language he needed to speak in order to survive and make it. It took me a while to see through all the bluster that 'making it' (financially, commercially) was not the goal for him, and that the only bit of the Dream he cared about (if indeed it is even what the Dream is about) was the freedom it might buy him, the opportunity to keep moving, to 'ramble unaccountable'.

I looked down at the map of America. It was a land big enough for Joe. A land big enough to accommodate all our delusions. A Quixote could make a go of it here, travel unhindered across the plains for a long distance before meeting a single self-doubt or being called crazy. I wanted to embrace her and I felt sure she wanted to embrace me. I was willing to be credulous, believe anything she told me, her impossible possibilities and crass creeds. I looked at all those lovely states with names so resonant and full of some elemental meaning and memories of things I had only dreamed but not yet experienced – and they called out to me: 'Come to me, Rip,' said Colorado. 'I have mountains higher than anything you've seen.' 'No. It's me you want,' said Wyoming. 'My mountains are prettier, my grasslands greener, my parks more spectacular.' 'Up here!' Montana said. 'Where the skies are bigger and the rivers cleaner.' 'It's my rolling plains you wanna roll over,' said South Dakota. 'Down here, boy,' whispered a smoky Tennessee.

I'm coming, America. I'm coming!

— Do I get coffee?

— This ain't room service.

— Where's Larson?

— Larson?

— My guard.

— Not my concern. I'm Deputy White. The Sheriff's asked me to pick this up. I read your statement to date. Or should I say 'book'? You sure got a frilly way of expressing yourself. And boy, do you go on.

— The Sheriff told me to be exact.

— Just writing it down in all this detail don't make me believe you any more than were it a few words. So why don't you put down that pen and just tell me why you did it and we can just save ourselves a few rainforests.

— I told you: I didn't do it. But I assumed just writing 'I didn't do it' wouldn't cut it.

— Well someone did it, Mr Jones.

— Did you actually read my statement?

— I have and you ain't being as honest as you think. Just because you're writing it down like this. You already shown yourself to be a top-dollar liar when you want to get your way. Using the death of people still living to get your way. A man can deliver a bare-faced lie like that he can lie about anything. What's to say anything you say is true?

— I'm being honest about the lying. Are you telling me you've never lied?

— Sure but some of these lies had scale.

— I've admitted to them.

— Look. I'm a 'this happened then that happened' kind of

123

guy. I don't want your opinions on America or what you were doing with your dick; although the way you bounced those sisters was impressive. You certainly played them for kicks.

— It wasn't that simple.

— Oh I think it was. You wanted the full buffet there. All you can eat. I don't blame you for that. Young man sowing his wild oats. But sowing wild oats means using the bad seed. And it seems you did that.

— What's your point?

— My point is, Mr Jones, I don't think all these words are going to justify you. Or are even helping people understand your case. I'm not buying it.

— There's no buying – or selling – here. I want to give a true account.

— Well, I ain't sure I trust you, Mr Jones. Or this tomb you're writing.

— Tome.

— Whatever. You're damning yourself with this statement.

— Why?

— I made a note of how many times you said you felt like killing someone, so far. Six times. Five different people, too.

— It's a figure of speech.

— Did you kill him?

— Joe? No!

— Did you ever want to kill Joseph Bosco?

— Come on.

— Answer the question, Mr Jones.

— Of course I did! Who wouldn't? But the wanting and doing aren't the same. You know that.

— Did you ever threaten to kill him – to his face or in front of anyone?

— I killed Joe once, in a manner of speaking. But not twice. Not in the way you mean. Everyone in that family was usually threatening to kill someone.

— Everyone in that family?

124

— Edith. Joe. Mary. Edith mainly, and practically every day.

— What about Mrs Bosco? Seems you and she had a grudge going on.

— I . . . we had a clash. But I never threatened her in that way. I might have thought it.

— Why don't you tell me about this?

— Mary borrowed it. For the journey west. Her mother said 'every woman should have a gun'.

— It had your prints on.

— That's because I held it.

— Mr Jones. I think I know why you did it. You didn't get what you wanted and you made sure they wasn't going to get what they wanted.

— That's absurd. This is really ridiculous.

— You seem angry.

— Of course I'm angry. I'm being held here under false charges.

— Because you were the only person found at the scene of the crime. Someone who had reasonable motive to do what they did. And who even admits to thinking about doing it. Don't seem so ridiculous.

— You're twisting my words. Or misunderstanding them.

— How do you think this is going to end, Mr Jones? You just think you can write the end you want?

— I'll write what happened.

— Well, the way I'm reading it, this isn't going to end well for you.

III.

O my America!
The dreams were sweet, at first.
The dreams you dream
When wide awake imagining
An idyll to fly to, a fleece to find.
I sprouted wings and crossed your land
Half blue morpho; half boy-man.
Took the road inevitable
Destiny manifestly get-able,
The signs were good
(The ones I saw
Other portents I ignored).
You lay before me
Open-armed and legged
On your back, flat
Canyons, valleys, eventual sea,
A country to finger, feel and bed.
I did all three.

CHAPTER TEN

In which Joe, Mary, Jimmy Carter and me head west.

We set out first thing – Joe, Mary and me – with the Chuick loaded up with 'two and a half thousand miles' worth' of butter-flies and a bald eagle called Jimmy Carter. Joe woke me at seven o'clock with a reveille: 'Rise and shine. This glorious world is yours and mine!' He said we needed to get a head start on the rest of America; that all over the eastern seaboard people with things to sell were waking up and we had to beat them to the opening of the stores' doors.

'The early bird gets the waffles, Rip!'

We ate a vast breakfast of bacon, eggs – and waffles – as though it would be our last meal for some time. Holding up the packet of Hungry Jack, Joe delivered a pitch on the simple beauty of making one thing well. 'You see this, Rip? These Hungry Jack guys were like us once, before they became a household name. They had a product that was home-made and they sold it in their local communities. They did nice business because everyone who tried it loved it. They could have carried on that way and done just fine. But one day a buyer for a national retailer tried it and now they sell in every grocery store in the land.'

'Difference is people want waffles,' Mary said, puncturing Joe's ballooning fancy like a good sister should.

'People shall not live by waffles alone,' Joe said, the syrup anointing his T-shirt.

We had loaded Chuick with as many butterfly cases as it could hold (about a hundred and twenty mixed in the trunk and another two dozen on one half of the back seat). Mary complained that we weren't taking the Cadillac but Edith had won the argument about taking it back. Joe said that we'd all be driving Cadillacs soon enough. As far as I was concerned Chuick was a more fitting vessel for our adventuring: faithful, trusted and true. Chuick was a rare instance of something that was claimed to be unique actually being unique. As we walked to the car, Celeste was pleading with Joe to let her come, attaching herself to his leg, making him walk like a giant with a limp.

'Let me come, Joe. Let me come!'

Joe was carrying three butterfly nets with folding sticks and his ridiculous, faux crocodile skin attaché case with the combination locks, which contained a 'travel' set of five-winged blue morphos for the Wizard.

'I'll take you next year, Ceelee. I promise. We'll do Disneyland this winter.'

'You promised that last time. Mr Rip, tell him to let me come.'

'It's not up to me, Ceelee. But it'll be a lot of driving. You'd get bored. Plus, we only have room for three people with all the butterfly cases and Jimmy Carter.'

'Dang! It's not fair.'

'You got school, Ceelee,' Joe said, setting down the case and lifting her up. 'I need you to be smarter than everyone else. For when you are the first black female President of America.'

Mary had already called shotgun on the back seat and was lost in the music of her Walkman. Jimmy Carter was next to her in the box Clay had made for him. It was wooden-slatted and had a slide top and a litter of ripped-up *National Enquirer*s which, Joe pointed out, meant the national bird could poop all over the nation's celebrities. I had the smaller of my two travel bags with a couple of changes of clothes. Joe was wearing everything he was bringing: canvas pants, collarless dress shirt and black moccasins. His only luggage was the attaché case.

'What about a change of clothes, Joe?'

'I'll buy some when I need them.'

Isabelle appeared, her hair down, dressed more loosely than usual. How typical that she should be looking her loveliest just as I was leaving. 'Ma wants you, Joe.'

'Someday she'll just let me leave.' Joe put the three butterfly nets on the back shelf and strode off.

What now? Would there be some last-minute thwarting? My desire to get out there, see the country and start my adventure on the road was so powerful now. I was a pulled-back arrow in a bow, ready to be fired out across the Mississippi and beyond.

Clay appeared carrying a big Tupperware container. 'This is if you need to make some cases in a hurry. If you sell out quicker than you thought, or you break some. You got the materials to make up fifty cases if you need to.' The box contained a tube of silicon, cut 6 by 4 pieces of glass, a hundred mixed specimens, stickers, driftwood. 'You can keep this. If you get bit again.' He handed me the haemorrhoid ring.

'Thanks, Clay.' I shook his hand.

'Be safe out there.'

We could hear Edith and Joe yelling at each other. I looked at Isabelle.

'She never lets him go without a fight. She's determined to keep all her chicks chicks. He's still her Li'l Joe.'

I put out my hand which she took and shook. Her hand was cold and small and white but her grip was firm. I decided last minute to give her a kiss on the cheek. She did that thing shy people do, bowing their heads when about to be kissed, and I ended up kissing her forehead which had the effect of making the kiss more meaningful than I had intended or she wanted.

I wished Isabelle good luck with the writing. She wished me well with the selling.

'I hope the collector turns out to be . . . true,' she said. 'And travelling mercies.'

Joe bounded down the steps. 'OK. Saddle up!'

'Everything all right?'

'Yeah! Everything's great. She gave me the usual send-off: "Go screw yourself. I hope you die. Don't expect me to be here when you're back. Why are you making this trip? It's a waste of time. You're worse than your father." She doesn't like me leaving, is all.'

When I got in the car Mary gave me a dagger look.

'"Good luck with the writing",' Mary sneered, mimicking my farewell to Isabelle.

Jimmy Carter was agitated, squawking and scratching in his box, sensing change. Joe fired up the Chuick and the V8 gurgle of the engine was a sound full of promise; a noise that said, 'We're going places.'

'See you when we see you,' Joe said, leaning across me to speak to Isabelle through my open window. As we pulled away Celeste ran alongside the car, her skinny gazelle legs springing and her feet hardly seeming to touch the ground. Isabelle waved and I waved back through the open window feeling a connection. And then I saw, standing like a sentinel in her bedroom window, Edith. She watched us all the way round the bend until we were out of sight.

The Road! I was following in the tyre-tracks of a thousand men and women – salesmen, desperadoes, preachers, lawmen, poets; the greedy, the sad, the optimistic, the crazed. The Road was no longer the borrowed road of other people's telling, it was my own, and it promised a sort of salvation, it was my Asphalt Messiah. The Road was infinite possibility. The routes we might take, the people we'd meet, the timing of all this and the contingency of the subtlest variations that lead to entirely different outcomes makes it so intense and so mysterious.

I was a participant in the quintessential American drama: the road that takes you from rags to riches via pitches. All over this land, hundreds and thousands of entrepreneurs were flitting to the headquarters of some giant corporation, or a store in a strip mall, their life's work in a briefcase, praying that their voice wouldn't crack, that their numbers added up, and that the cut of their cloth was right. Even though the statistics told us that only one of the twenty-five products being pitched cold that day would be successful, we had no doubt our flightless cargo would be the chosen one. Of all the dreamer moths being drawn to the burning lights of the American Dream, we would be the ones that flew right through the flames un-singed. Or something like that.

I felt elation in being a young, healthy man in the greatest country of the free world, in the company of interesting, unusual people, with the imminent prospect of sexual fulfilment and a means of making money that would keep us forever propelled on adventures. My thoughts raced on to the America I was about to see, the sales and love I was going to make (I was fifty cases from that ecstasy). I could see Mary in the wing mirror, her brown pins across the bench seat, painting her toenails with great concentration, trying to anticipate the bumps and turns in the road (is there anything as mysterious or appealing as a woman doing her make-up whilst on the move? No there isn't); she was humming along to a tune on her Walkman, her head-phones making an Alice-band in her lank hair that fell over her features in a perfect random symmetry.

If, for the first few miles, we were each alone with our thoughts, as soon as we left the perimeter of the Catskill Park something lifted. (That place really did have some kind of spell that broke the moment you left its range.) As we joined the highway, Joe snapped out of himself and yelled, 'The Road! The Road! The Road.' Up ahead there was a metal box-girder bridge and as we came to it he slowed. 'Listen to this,' he said. As soon as the car was on the bridge the tyres started to sing a distinct note, which Joe changed by accelerating and decelerating. He played the bridge with the car as if it were a giant tuning fork. As soon as we passed beyond the bridge the tune stopped, or rather, it reverted to a tune that had been playing all along but you didn't always notice until it stopped. He put out a finger and pointed to his ear. 'Now hear that?' It was like the noise of radio static or a rushing stream. 'The road makes sounds. And different roads make different sounds. And the weather changes the

tune. Heat makes the tyres scream. The rain makes it shush –
what a sound that is! The sound of a car driving in rain, Rip. That
is the most beautiful sound in the world. I wish it was raining
now so that you could hear it. Sometimes you have to be careful
though. It lulls you. Makes you sleepy. And I have fallen asleep
at the wheel twice in my time – once in Kansas and then in
Nebraska. But this hum is like a bass line. You hear that?' I listened to the sound and there it was, the rushing stream, just
behind the chug of Chuick's V8.

'I hear it.'

'The music of the road.'

He started to drum on the steering wheel, grip and flex it,
and then he started to sing one of his songs. When he was at the
wheel Joe sang songs – an appalling bastardization of popular
tunes and half-caught lyrics mashed up with his own words.
There was one he sang, to the tune of 'Yankie Doodle', that he
said was his hymn to selling; it was his theme tune. The words
to the first verse went:

'Will you buy my butterflies
From all around the world?
I pinned them here for you to see
How much do you think they're worth?'

And the chorus went:

'Five for fifty dollars,
Ten for seventy-five.
Buy some with the flowers,
To help us stay alive!'

We sang the song all the way to Ithaca.

Odysseus was born in Ithaca and I took it as a good omen that my
first attempt at selling would begin in a place named after such an
esteemed traveller. A cynic might laugh at the idea but I have no
difficulty in seeing a Homeric equivalence in my own voyage and
the business of selling. The cold-calling and hard selling, the

humiliation and rejection, the daily questioning of integrity and taste, the combination of confidence and humility required by the salesperson would have tested the wily Odysseus as severely as any siren, Cyclops or harpy. Joe said (and I would back him) that travelling salesfolk were the true heroes of this age, setting out in all weathers, covering great distances, risking body and soul, facing humiliation, rejection, destitution every day, away from their loved ones; facing more temptations, demons and beasts and beatings than your average hero – all to make ends meet. This Ithaca (population 30,000) was an elegant and civilized college town built around the southernmost tip of one of the Finger Lakes, populated (according to Joe) by educated, left-leaning people who were open to nature and a more poetic view of the world. By Joe's reckoning this was the ideal demographic for a rookie butterfly salesman needing to flex his wings.

'They'll be lapping you up,' Joe said.

'You gonna try him selling here?' Mary seemed surprised at the choice of town.

'Sure, why not?'

'You ain't even cracked it yet.'

'None of us have. Rip's gonna be our secret weapon.'

'Who is best at selling in the family?' I asked.

'Ma,' Mary said, as though it were indisputable.

'Nooowah!' Joe protested.

'Come on, Joe. She always outsold you.'

'What about her . . . ?' I drew a circle in the air in front of my face.

'People either feel sorry for her or are too scared to turn her away,' Mary said. 'She don't sell too much these days. But she always pitched it straight, no frills. Unlike Joe. Joe claims to be the best but he talks too much.'

'I bring in the deals, Mary. You know it.'

'You use ten words when one will do. And not all those words are words people know.'

'I got my method. Everyone got their own method.'

135

'Right. Joe makes up all kinds of shit to get the sale. You'd think us the most tragic family in all America the way he talks sometimes.'

'Don't listen to her super-negative talk, Rip,' Joe protested although I'm not sure he really cared about his reputation as a salesman.

'What about Clay?'

'Clay's good but being black ain't helpful – especially in this part of the world. Elijah's too shy.'

'Isabelle?'

'Isabelle!' Mary sneered. 'She couldn't sell if her life depended on it.'

I actually thought it was admirable – not to be able to sell – but I didn't say this to Mary.

'And what about you?'

'I can do it if I have to. Ma thinks women sell better than men because men are full of shit and never really say what's true about a thing. Ma wants me to sell more but I don't like it. I feel like I'm selling myself. I like the driving. I drive good.'

'You do.'

As Joe parked up, Jimmy Carter started squawking and scratching in his box on the back seat.

'I think he needs more food already,' Mary said. 'You got dough, Joe?'

Mary pulled her headphones down around her leg and was leaning forward into the space between the front seats. Joe handed Mary ten dollars from a roll he kept in his sock. 'See if you can get Jimmy Carter some fish. Fish is his natural diet.'

'I need some for hair dye.'

'Hair dye?'

'I'm thinking of going blue.'

'Make it blue morpho blue! Good branding.'

Joe gave her another ten dollars. Mary wished me luck. 'Two-fiddy cases,' she said, before winking and setting off to look for raw fish and blue hair dye.

The florist was in the centre of the city, in the car-free zone (a thing Joe decried as elitist arrogance and a restraint on trade as it meant having to park up and walk a few blocks). I was suddenly overcome with nerves. What if I wasn't any good at this? I had sold, cold, on the telephone and proven a success; but that was a faceless experience; rejection was disembodied and impersonal.

'Aren't you going to show me how to do it first?'

'The only way to see if you can ride the horse, Rip, is to ride the horse. I'll be right behind you. I'll stay quiet. I'll pretend you're the boss. I'm just carrying for ya. I will not say a word. Tell them I got a problem with my speech if you need to. Tell them I'm dumb.'

He continued to prep and gee me up as we walked. 'You have to read the signs real quick, Rip. Is this person happy or sad? Do they like their job or not? Republican or Democrat? Atheist or Believer? Or neither. Do I get heavy on the science? Or the business side? Or will they prefer the against-all-the-odds version? Should I lead with the blue morpho or start with the malachite? You'll get a feel real quick for these things. You'll soon learn when to goose the accelerator and when to ease off. Remember to smile. You got one of these faces that looks kind of grumpy when it's in neutral. Try and look a little more – you know – upbeat. In this world, a fake smile is better than an honest frown.'

I tried a smile.

'How about some teeth? We need to see your teeth.'

'They're a little yellow.'

'It don't matter. You can't smile without teeth. And you can't sell without a smile.'

I opened my mouth and flashed a toothy grin.

'Jeeze.' Joe grimaced. 'Don't you ever floss? You need to floss, Rip. OK. Keep the mouth closed mainly. Except when you're talking. We need to get those fixed. Maybe a writer can get away with bad teeth, but a salesman gotta have great dentures. It's kind of a given. And if you can you make the smile a little less . . . you know . . . smile from the inside if you can. From the inside . . . a sincere smile.'

'The smiling doesn't come naturally to me. I can't fake it.'

'OK. But you got to learn how, Rip. You gotta sacrifice your pride in the name of selling. You gotta be ready to be a fool for your fortune. Fake it to make it. And remember, every pitch a poem. Or a story. Bring the butterflies to life with your pitching. Make them fly. And make sure you admire their wares before you sell yours. And don't forget to compliment the way they look. Not just the women. Men, too – "Sir, I like that shirt. I been thinking about growing a goatee myself. Does it take much upkeep? You work out a lot? You must be bench-pressing two hundred pounds" – that kinda thing. And get them to talk about their product. Look interested. Let them show you their enthusiasm for what they do. Oh, and if you can get a name, or see their name on a name-tag, use it. I tell you. People love to hear their name spoken by a stranger. It has a magical power. Don't be afraid to make little variations in the story. You gotta serve fresh bread. And finally, whatever you do, never . . .'

'Pitch a Muppet.'

'Right! They taught you well.'

Kris's Flower Shop was sandwiched between a bookshop and a vegetarian restaurant. It was hardly a castle or an impregnable fortress but when we entered that store I felt like I was going into battle. I had more butterflies in my stomach than in the box Joe was carrying. I'll say it again and again: all over the world there are people in the front line, going over the top, once more unto the breach-ing, all in the name of making a living. And I salute them all because every sale you attempt contains the possibility of failure, rejection and a kind of death.

'You think I look professional enough?'

'I'd buy a crippled horse from you.'

I straightened myself out, tucking a lose flap of shirt into my jeans and brushing back my hair. I did a mouth stretch, pictured myself as a clever, charming winner, and stepped into the store.

I was hit by the smell that would become familiar to me in the days and miles ahead. The aggregated smell of flowers in a flower store is a sweet, bottomy stink, an odour so powerful and primal and sexy, at first. There appeared to be no one in the store. It was just after nine o'clock and we were almost certainly the first there that day. Classical music came from somewhere in the foliage. I stifled a sneeze.

'Can I help you?'

A disembodied, female voice came from behind the counter. A woman stood up from behind it, her face flush with bending down. She had a handful of ribbons that she started to tie into bows. She talked without looking up at me but seemed to know already that I was not a customer. I gave her my best smile and put on my best English accent, trying to sound somewhere between a newsreader and Shakespearian actor – sonorous, bassy and florid. It seemed appropriate to be florid in a florists.

'This is lovely. A . . . veritable floral cathedral.' (I never use the word veritable – as it's clearly pretentious – but I was nervous.) Out it came, at the head of a veritable tide of unctuous effluence. 'I've not seen such a dazzling array. You have a wonderful store. Perfectly wonderful. Really. The finest I've seen. Ever. You should be proud.'

'I just work here.'

'Well. You work in a lovely store.'

'Well, it's no picnic, I can assure you. You selling life assurance or what?' She nodded to my sample briefcase and shot Joe a suspicious look. She looked at me as though I was going to rob her and Joe as if he constituted some kind of criminal threat. This was going to be tough. Her accent and her attitude was pure New York City.

'No, no. Not at all. I uh . . . my name is . . . Mr Jones, this is my assistant, Mr Bosco. We work for Butterfly World, a company specializing in selling gift items to florists.'

Her name-tag said Anthony.

'Anthony. That's a pretty name.'

'It's Anth, "th".'

'Ah. Where I come from that's a . . .'

'Guy's name, I know. My father wanted a boy. I was a constant disappointment to him. So. What you trying to sell?'

'Well, Anthony. If I could show you, I have some samples here.' I lifted the sample case onto the counter.

'Don't put it there.'

'Sorry.'

'Put it there if you have to.' She pointed to a chair. 'This better not be life assurance.'

'No. Something far more life affirming.' Joe smiled at this line. So far, he was being very restrained.

'So what is it then? I got things to be getting on with.'

'It'll be easier if I just show you.'

I set the case down and opened it. The sample case was hollowed out to fit three 6 by 4s with one each of our most popular butterflies (fritillary, swallowtail and blue morpho) and some sample sheets showing the different sizes and a 'leave behind' brochure with more examples.

'Basically, we have . . . well . . . you can see . . . they speak for themselves. I think you'll agree.'

'Is it dead?'

'That's a *Morpho peleides* – more commonly known as the blue morpho.'

'It's real?'

'All our butterflies are real, madam.'

'You catch it yourself?'

'Well. That one is from Brazil . . .'

'You kill them?'

'No. No. Of course not. We just . . . They are all stunned. Put to sleep. In the most humane way.'

'Humane? How's that?'

'We use . . . It's a type of . . . It's painless.'

'Really? To be put to sleep and never wake up. Jesus. That's sinister. What are you – some kind of mass-murderer?'

Joe cleared his throat as though about to come and rescue my crashing pitch. It was going as badly as it possibly could. I was unable to relax, to be myself. I was letting her determine the direction of the pitch, and I was focusing on the product's least appealing but unavoidable aspect. I was sounding patronizing, even to myself. Patronizing and a bit weird. More crucially I was pitching a Muppet. I should have asked there and then to see the owner but instead I dug myself a deeper grave.

'We like to think we are extending the life of the average butterfly. Giving them a life beyond their first life, so to speak.'

'You ever ask a butterfly how it felt about that?'

'Butterflies have a short life span. Some live only a few weeks. So in a way we are giving them . . .'

'All the more reason not to murder them for financial gain. Jesus. I don't need this.'

'Ma'am.' I switched into auto pitch panic, drumming up the by-rote facts I'd learned the weeks before. 'There is no cruelty involved in the killing . . . capturing . . . of the butterflies. All the butterflies we sell are approved for sale. They are all sourced from reputable suppliers . . .'

'So someone else kills them?'

I looked at Joe. He was making a monumental effort not to laugh.

This woman was playing me, deliberately trying to humiliate me. She was immune to the charms of my accent or the charms of my charm. Maybe it was a kind of revenge for doing her shitty job, for working for someone else. She would not let me get one sentence ahead of her.

'Anthony, is the owner of the store available?'

'He's in Barbuda.'

'Barbuda?'

'On vacation.'

The bell dinged. Anthony looked past me and as she did a

141

radiant, as yet unsighted, smile burst forth across her face. A man entered carrying a plant he had selected from an outside trolley; he set it on the previously forbidden counter without objection from Anthony. Her transformation was profound and alarming. Now she was charm itself. She'd found a smile from somewhere and it was a stunning smile. (Maybe all Americans have a little box of smiles they carry around and stick on, like fake moustaches, when they need them.) Even her accent became homier. It was something to behold and she really went to town on being nice to him, in a shameless and shameful act designed to show me up.

'Acanthus. Is this for Maria?'

'Yah. It's our anniversary.'

'Well don't you think you should throw in some flowers? We got a special on today.'

'She loves irises.'

'We have the purple and the yellow. One bunch or two?'

'I'll take one of each.'

I wanted to kill her, for her shameless apartheid and her total condescension. While she wrapped the flowers, the man glanced at me and then at Joe. Finally, his gaze rested on the blue morpho on top of the sample case.

'Woah,' he said. 'That's not real, is it?'

'Yes,' I said. 'It's a blue morpho.'

'That colour. It don't look real though.'

In a way the deeply irritating man, who I wanted to kick, was right: with its metallic, shimmering shades of blue and green and the interference effects of its reflective scales (I learned this from Isabelle), the blue morpho doesn't look real. But I didn't say this to him. He didn't deserve to know. He left the store to a virtual ticker-tape parade of 'see-you-soons' and 'say hi-to-so-and-sos', as though this were the friendliest flower store in the whole of America. Once out the door that woman's smile fell off her face, just like a fake moustache, where it lay on the floor next

142

to my dead pitch. She made a told-you-so squish face and put her hands out towards the blue morpho.

'Mister. Take it from me. No one here wants a dead butterfly sitting in their living room. They should be flying free, not locked up in that glass tomb. Their life's short enough, ain't it?'

The awful thing is, I sort of agreed with her.

Joe's self-imposed silence finally came to an end. As he started to repack the case he set her straight on a couple of things.

'Ma'am. I can see you don't appreciate our wares. But let's be clear: these flowers you sell are dying a slow death. You have cut their lives short in the name of putting a little beauteousness in people's lives. And if you think a butterfly is living the life of Riley, flying free, flitting from flower to flower, let me tell you. It's a horrible existence: you got predators left and right, you got birds chasing you, people chasing you. You got cars squishing you in their grilles. You know how many eggs laid by females ever make it to adulthood? Two per cent. You may look at this bug and think, "How cute. What a wonderful life!" But butterfly society is brutal, just brutal. It's cannibalistic, incestuous, the young butterflies get molested, you got your little caterpillars eating their brothers and sisters trying to become pupae, or they get hijacked by the ichneumon wasp which lays its eggs inside the caterpillar, and then if you're a female you get to be cradle-raped by horny males desperate for females before you've even opened your wings. I mean really and truly some butterflies are better off dead.'

CHAPTER ELEVEN

In which Joe shows me how to sell and Mary
thinks we're being followed.

The humiliation and failure of my rookie pitch made me want to curl up and die. To have something to sell, and for that something to be a not unlovely thing, and for your success in selling that thing to correlate with your continued ability to have the experience that you crave, and for someone to dismiss that thing (and you) so comprehensively, well that is a crushing experience.

'Maybe I'm not cut out for this, Joe.'

'Aww, come on Rip! Don't be disheartened. You're sounding like the old Llew Jones there. I coulda jumped in but that was a good lesson. I knew that store would be a waste of breath before we even entered. I didn't want to tell you but I never sold a single case in Ithaca. I just wanted to see if you could do it. And to start with a failure. That way you know what you gotta do. Don't feel bad. She was not for changing. These stone-hearted liberals who think they've found salvation in yoga and granola, I swear they are more stuck in their ways than the rednecks. Had Abe Lincoln himself walked into that store she would have turned him away.'

'OK, but you do the next one. I need to see how you do it.'

'I'll do a couple for ya but don't take heed of my method. You gotta find your own style, Rip. You'll only find it by doing it.'

We kicked up the dust on Ithaca and moved on.

Mary started to tease me for my rookie failure, and her teasing was more about the postponing of our union than my commercial shortcomings. For the next few miles we danced a tango innuendo around her oblivious brother.

'How many cases you sell there, Rip?'

'Zero.'

'Two-fiddy cases seems a long way away.'

'I reckon we'll do it before Ohio,' I said.

Mary smiled and checked the mirror to see if Joe was picking up on this. He was feeding Jimmy Carter and seemed unaware of the subtext. (This guilelessness in Joe was something I admired. I found it reassuring. It was one of the main reasons I trusted him, even.) Mary ribbed on. Testing it.

'Can you wait that long, Rip?'

'Oh I can wait. Better to do it well than do it too quickly.'

'Not doing it at all, that's worse.'

'That would be a crying shame. But I'll do it.'

'I'm beginning to doubt you got what it takes.'

'Hey, come on, Mary. It was Rip's first go and I doubt even Ma could have swung that woman. Rip will come good.'

'I hope so.'

'He better.'

Joe showed me how to do it at a florist outside a small town near the Finger Lakes. After a flattering preamble (transparently false to my eyes and ears) about the beauty of the store to a reluctant looking Ken ('Ken, this is really the nicest flower store I've seen in upstate New York, maybe in the whole Atlantic seaboard') and a granted request to show Ken something that might 'enhanciate' that beauty (if that were possible!), Joe set the sample case on the counter and started to make the pyramid stack that formed the prop, stage and backdrop to his storytelling. His scars looked conspicuous as he laid out the cases and I waited for 'How I Saved Ma From The Fire'. Joe paused for dramatic effect, and to let Ken admire the tower of flying colour before him, then he picked out the orange swallowtail that he'd placed at the point of the pyramid.

'Before my father was killed by a jaguar in the jungles of South America,' he began, 'he taught me the names of all the butterflies. And this was the first one. The orange swallowtail. *Papilio thoas*. Isn't she pretty?'

The death of Joe's father and the manner of it was a shock

(and, frankly, news to me) but it had the immediate effect of creating the respectful pause into which Joe poured his story. Ken held the sample in his own hand, unsure how to react: caught between 'Yes, it most certainly is a pretty thing' and 'I'm sorry about your father but please tell me about the jaguar.'

'My last memory of him was him holding an orange swallowtail, just like that one there, and saying, "If people took the time to look at butterflies, the world would be a better place."'

Joe paused again, letting the pertinent fact sink in. He later told me he called this 'testing the levels of compassion'.

'I think your father was right about that, sir. I'm sorry to hear he . . . did he . . . what happened there . . .'

'Well. It was a long time ago. But he at least died doing what he loved. In the habitat of his favourite creature. He was certainly a remarkable man. By all accounts. I only have a few treasured memories.'

Another pause.

The storekeeper was now both respectful and not un-curious, the perfect state for a buyer to be in.

'He was an eminent entomologist, see. A professor. He was always away in a jungle somewhere searching for a new species. His particular obsession was the group of butterflies known as Morphidae, a Neotropical family comprising spectacularly colourful butterflies. He wrote books about them. My ma used to joke that he loved bugs more than people. Ha! She weren't far wrong about that! Anyway. One day, when I was five, he was in Colombia searching for the five-winged blue morpho.' (Joe pointed to the standard blue morpho case in the pyramid.) 'It was a super-rare aberration of this butterfly here. *Morpho peleides*. That's the blue morpho to you, sir. He'd been away for months. One day, we got a call from the US consulate in Bogotá telling us about his death. That was twenty years ago now.'

Out of respect for the dead, the man picked the case up carefully, aware that he was one remove from a great rarity as well as a touching tragedy.

'But he left a legacy,' Joe continued. 'A pure love of bugs. For which I thank him, daily. He took me to see the great monarch migration. I grew up surrounded by butterflies – green bird-wings from Australia. Malachites from South America, Indian moon moths; small blue Grecians from Venezuela, and that one, the blue morpho – our number-one seller. A cousin of that five-winged aberration my father literally lost his life looking for.'

'It's a very attractive colour. It almost seems . . .'

'Unreal! I know. That's what everyone says. But that blue is the morpho's great trick. It's a trick of light. It's a play of light, like the sky itself. It ain't really blue. My pa would bring home rare specimens. Valuable specimens. But this one – although quite common – was my favourite. And I remember when he gave me one – in a little frame – I had that strange feeling that I think every butterfly lover has of wanting to keep it and let it go all at once. And I also had this powerful feeling of wanting to share it with other people. For people to see how beautiful it is. It's why we started this business. That desire gave birth to a dream, a dream of putting a butterfly in every home in this land. It's in the pursuit of that dream that I stand before you today.' Joe held the blue morpho up to the light. 'You could say we're keeping the memory of my father alive.'

Joe was actually crying! All teared up.

'He taught me that butterflies transcedate politics. And bor-derlines. I mean when a monarch flies to Mexico does it care that it has crossed into another country? He taught me that.'

I can't say for certain if it was the man's attraction for the product or his sympathy for Joe's story that sealed it; but the pitch that had begun with little chance ended with twenty cases bought for cash.

As we walked back to the car $150 richer, I had to ask.

'Jesus, Joe. You took some liberties there.'

'Come on, Rip. It's called poetic licensing. You should know that! He could be dead. I don't know. I mean, he might as well be. We ain't ever heard from him. I have told and retold this story so many times I actually can't remember what the real version is. I don't know that it rightly matters as long as the deal gets done.'

'Don't you feel . . . bad? Saying that? Isn't it . . . dishonouring the dead or something? Your memories.'

'I can do what I like with the memories of my father 'cos I got hardly none. It's my history, Rip. I'll do with it as I please.'

'Were you faking those tears? You got me going, too.'

'Sometimes when I get to pitching I'm so in it I can't tell. It's like I'm there. Look, Rip, if you start telling someone about someone they never met, telling them what a great person they are, listing their achievements, then they are only going to be so interested. Tell them that person died, and died in a heroic or tragic way, then they really get to sit up. A death really greases the skids in a story. Try it.'

All families tell myths about themselves. My own family myth is that my parents were a faithful, happily married couple, and our family a close, brilliant, sociable unit, but at least we kept it to a single, consistent narrative. With Joe the myths were legion. When it came to pitching, that lacuna in his past was filled with whatever dramas he pleased. And because he delivered fact and fiction with equal conviction, melding them seamlessly in such a torrent of words and energy, it was sometimes hard discerning the truth of the tale. I don't think Joe was mendacious because once he got going he got so into it he believed it. The tears were not crocodile; the emotions were felt. But he was an absolute anarchist with his past. In one pitch he might start by talking about the day he saw his first butterfly (he was five, he was ten, it was an orange swallowtail, it was a blue morpho). He might have several brothers and sisters; he was an only, lonely bug-obsessed boy; sometimes they lived in Michigan, other times (if it fitted) they lived in California. He liked to open with the line, 'The first butterfly I ever saw was a dead one. And it changed my life.' Sometimes he'd stretch out his hands so the shopkeeper could see the scars and they'd ask and he'd tell them (faux-reluctant) how he saved his Ma from the flames. Other times he'd tell them about the day they heard his father disappeared or died (in Colombia, in Borneo, even in the Congo once!); he might have been seven at the time, he might have been twelve. His father was often the hero of this entomological tale. The Great American Lepidopterist who disappeared in the jungles of South America, and who never returned, and in whose memory the butterfly business was started. If it was Joe's way of dealing with the father who'd left him, I can't fault him for it.

Afterwards Joe started looking for someone to give his God Money to. Mary was driving but watching Joe as he counted out the money from the day's haul.

'How much?'

'Four hundred dollars.' Joe took $40 and then he started looking around.

'What you looking for, Joe?'

'Someone to give alms to.'

'Don't give no alms, Joe. We might need all that dough.'

'You know that's stinking thinking right there, Mary. We always give alms.'

As we passed a row of street stores, Joe called out, 'There. The old lady.'

An old woman with a mop was wiping the floors of the canteen. Mary pulled over. Joe jumped out and went and gave the lady the forty bucks. The woman looked bemused but after a little coaxing she took the money.

'Joe, is that wise?' I asked. 'Giving away money we need?'

'Of course it's wise,' he said. 'That money ain't ours. First fruits, Rip. You gotta give your first fruits. The Lord will make it up to us. You'll see. Now we can go eat.'

At first I saw Joe's random philanthropy as another form of distraction, another foil laid to enable him to keep distance; but it was sincere. Edith was right: Joe was too recklessly generous and economically profligate to make a successful businessman.

Mary pulled up at a drive-thru Taco Bell. 'I love Taco Hell,' Joe said, before scrambling his voice at the intercom to try and get an extra burrito at the pick-up counter. Having succeeded in confusing the girl at the intercom we picked up our food and drove on. Before we dispensed the food, Joe said one of his graces. He talked to his God with a familiarity and irreverence that was shocking, even to someone who thought it all nonsense. I had been brought up to be embarrassed by expressions of faith and usually I was, but with Joe I never felt that. His wild, comic God sounded inclusive and accessible.

'Lord, crush our enemies especially that bitch back in Granolaville (just kidding). Seriously. Thank you for this fake Mexican food. May it be a blessing to our bodies. Keep us from haemorrhoids.' He chewed a mouthful before continuing, riffing theological for a bit – (for my benefit, I think). 'Thank you that you are with us now, by your spirit, rather than just having died and not risen or been anything more than a good man with some nice ideas, but in fact God himself come to earth! I mean if you're not God then let's just quit pretending. And thank you for the fact there is nothing we can do to earn salvation. You have done it for us. No hoops to jump through. There's no standing up, no sitting down, no talking funny, no men in dresses, or bead-rubbing, no payments or do-goodery that will get us there – because you've done it! Oh boy. Forgive us for taking the poetic liberties with the stories and the quotes. And thank you for my new friend who has come to work for us, even though he doesn't for one second believe in you and finds this prayer embarrassing. Help him sell at the next store we find, Lord. Let him relax and let him fly. And I pray that before our journey's end you will have changed his atheistic ways by maybe blinding him temporarily so that he might see – just a few days, long enough to really make him think! A. Men.'

'A. Men.'

Mary gave Jimmy Carter some tacos. The national bird had been supine all day.

'I'm worried about him, Joe. He ain't right.'

'He's a major predator. He needs calories.'

Jimmy Carter came alive at the whiff of food, demanding his next pound of flesh. When he was eating you knew what he was: one of the world's great predators and symbol of its most powerful country. His mighty, full-grown beak open in a constant demand of 'feed me feed me feed me'.

The national bird chomped crackers, chips, bread and even apple cores. 'Look at him. He's growing so fast. I swear he's grown since we he last saw him an hour ago. He's a true patriot,' Joe said. 'He'll eat anything.'

Somewhere on the southern shore of Lake Ontario, Mary said she thought we were being followed. Joe had asked me if I could name the great lakes. I named three of them. He gave me the acrostic to remember all five by: 'Homes': Huron. Ontario. Michigan. Erie. Superior.

'Don't all look at once,' Mary said. 'This Grand Fury's tailing us.'

Joe put his great arm across the back of Mary's seat to look, trying to be surreptitious.

'I love those Plymouths,' he said. 'And that is a nice colour. The colour of a mimosa moth.'

'I'm serious, Joe. He's been behind us since Syracuse.'

'He could be going to where we're going.'

I turned sideways to look. The green Plymouth was being driven by a man wearing sunglasses who drove with that neutral frown that drivers drive with when they're concentrating. It was hard to tell if he was tailing us but the trouble is once you think a car is tailing you it's tailing you. I felt a faint alarm at the time, but it was like hearing a fire bell in a disused factory at the other end of town that everyone ignores and that after a time you think isn't ringing any more. Maybe if I'd stopped still for long enough I'd have noticed that it was still going, still warning people to get the hell out of the building!

'That weed's making you paranoid, sister.'

'Fuck you, Joe.'

'Any reason why someone would be following us, Joe?' I asked, slightly nervous of the answer.

'You kidding,' Mary said. 'Joe's got a thousand people would want to hunt him down and kill him.'

'Well. I left a trail of people I could have upset, Rip,' he said, a little too proudly. 'Preachers, storekeepers. The IRS. You shall know me by the trail of the dead butterflies, Rip! Slow down and we'll wave to him.'

Mary began to slow down and immediately the Plymouth came off at the next junction.

'See. He knows we know,' Mary said.

And that was that. I forgot about it. Until the next time.

'It's a Kodak moment!' Joe said as we entered the city limits of Rochester, a midsized city on Lake Ontario, and home to Kodak cameras. We stopped outside the George Eastman Theatre so I could take a picture of Joe and Mary on my little Olympus. Joe went off on one about the great entrepreneur and founder of the famous corporation: 'George Eastman was a travelling salesman before he got to this, Rip. Pounding the road. Pounding, pounding. You don't get to have a theatre named after you without a lot of pounding.'

I remember the name of the store where we sold next because it was the scene of my first sale. It was a florists called Rigby Bluff's. The woman behind the counter put me at ease straight away with a smile as warm as an armchair by the fire.

'Can I help you, sir?'

In Ithaca I had failed to deploy my main weapons – my voice, my charm – with any success. I had stuck rigidly to the sales script, and the more thwarted I felt the more by-rote I had sounded. I decided to go with Joe: be myself, let the product speak for itself, and make up whatever I felt like saying. Everyone knows that a pitch is a kind of lie; that what's really behind it is the cry of everyone's heart: love me, accept me, give me something to get me through the day!

'Good morning, madam. My name is Mr Jones. This is my partner, Mr Bosco. We specialize in making gift items for florists and if you have a few minutes I'd be delighted to show you what we have.'

'That's a lovely accent you have there. You must be from England.'

'Yes.' (Yes!)

'Well, we're always interested in new products for the store.'

'Well. Some products need to be explained but I think our products speak for themselves. When you see them I think you'll agree that they render words redundant.'

'Render words redundant. I like that. Marge? There's a gentlemen here who has something to show us.'

How lovely a product is when already lit by the eyes of approval. When I flipped open the case, the colours flew out and after that the tills were virtually opening by themselves.

'Oh, they're gorgeous.'

'This is just a selection,' I said, building the pyramid as Joe had taught me. 'We have twenty-six different species.'

Marge appeared brushing her hands on her apron. 'Oh, they are pretty.'

I reeled off the names, slowly. Joe added the Latin names for good measure and explained which faunistic region they came from.

'We see ourselves as trying to put a bit of poetry and beauty in people's lives. I think just looking at a butterfly can bring a little peace to a person's soul.'

'That is so true.'

I then used the one actual quote I knew that featured butter-flies.

' "We two will live and pray and sing, and tell old tales and laugh at gilded butterflies." '

'That is, well, that is beautiful, sir.'

'I can't claim the credit, I'm afraid. That was William Shake-speare.'

'Well, it makes the heart sing to hear it. Do go on. With the Shakespeare. Or anyone.'

That was the start of my fake quoting days.

'Well. I believe it was William Wordsworth who said . . . "There is in mankind a flickering gossamer soul searching for sunlight like a butterfly in June." '

'Well you paint a lovely picture, sir.'

'If only,' I said. 'It's all down to Mr Wordsworth, ma'am.'

Fake Wordsworth sealed the deal. It was a modest start – ten small and five mediums and a discount – but it was $195 in cash, and my virgin sale. The feeling it gave me was as uplifting as any pastoral scene or poem about a pastoral scene that I could recall. I gave Joe the green and black and white wad of rolled-up pres-idential promises and an unexpected elation came over me. I had persuaded someone to part with money in exchange for something I had that they didn't. The sweet maths of butterflies + poetry + charm + courage + bullshit = dollars. As we walked back to the car, Joe was beaming. 'What did I say? For every Ithaca there'll be a Rochester, Rip. That was beautiful. All that learning is paying off now.'

'I made it all up, Joe.'

'Who's going to know?'

'I wanted to be a poet; but maybe I am a salesman.'

'They are the same thing, Rip. They are the same thing!'

We arrived in Buffalo at Niagara Falls in the early evening, our day's work done. Mary was driving, Joe was sitting up front, I leant forward into the space between them, like a kid between parents, eager to see the coming natural wonder. We took the panoramic drive around the American side of the falls. A billboard advertised helicopter rides at $100 per person.

'Let's take a ride,' Joe said.

'No, Joe!'

'Come on! See the falls the way Jimmy Carter might see them.'

'We got $350. That would leave us with $50.'

Mary and I managed to overrule him on the grounds that we'd have no money for a motel. Instead, we opted for the boat ride and caught the last 'Maid of the Mist' of the day. Mary looked cute in her blue oilskins and sou'wester, the spume and foam of the Ontario flecking her face with droplets. Joe yelled like a lunatic, the spray on his face mingling with the tears that great natural beauty always induced in him. I confess that the natural wonder that was Niagara didn't make me cry. If you haven't seen it, don't let me put you off; but the feeling I got from looking at those roaring waters was as nothing to the feeling that selling two hundred dollars' worth of butterflies had given me just a few hours before.

Joe insisted on driving until we found a room for under twenty bucks. He was profligate to lunatic degree in the big things – cars, helicopter rides and giving alms – but thrifty as an ant in the small; gas, motels, clothes and food. There was always this wrestle between the poor kid who had grown up with very little and learned to make a dollar stretch, and the person who owned the world and everything in it.

We found a motel called The Western Promise. Rooms from $15. The Western Promise was a line of single-storey rooms with a reception one end, an angled slot for the car out front and a neon welcome sign. It could have been anywhere in America but it was my first motel and therefore special.

The room had two double queen-size beds. Joe took the floor. Mary took the bed near the bathroom. I took the one next to the window. While Mary went to the bathroom to shower, Joe took off his shoes, shed his clothes down to his underpants, lay on the bed with the remote control on his belly, and surfed the channels. He found a natural history programme about bears in Alaska.

'Denali National Park. That is a place, Rip. I sold some cases in Anchorage.'

His favourite programmes were nature documentaries and televangelists. The former he watched for the knowledge and the wonder; the latter for the sport and out of a sort of professional curiosity. He'd watch a documentary about Siberian tigers or a coral reef in wide-eyed urgency and shamelessly tear up at the images. But nothing got him stirred up as much as a televangelist asking for dollars. After watching the bears for a while he got bored and surfed until he found what he was looking for.

'Praise The Lord Ministries. These guys are total born-again crooks, Rip. Look and learn.'

On screen a preacher in a snappy suit was standing by a swimming pool in what looked like a theme park. 'We're having a great time in Florida,' he was saying. 'We want to thank all of you who have made that phone call to become a faith partner with PTL. I want you to praise God by praising him right now – in your home.'

Joe made no judgements about irreligious people behaving badly – which was just as well for me – but he hated immorality in the religious and he went out of his way to call it out.

The telephone number appeared across the screen and Joe picked up the room phone and dialled an outside line. He was through in seconds!

'Heritage USA? Hi. Yes, I'm fine. And God bless you too, Cheryl. Tell me, Cheryl. I'd like to pledge but I need to be sure you take my credit card. Great . . . One thing I need to know first. What percentage of the money I pledge will go to Pastor Joel and what percentage to the poor? Uh-huh. Oh. Really? Ninety per cent. OK . . . Let's do this. A million dollars. The number on the card. OK it's . . . fourbrif, thrcahhh, serooseeeee. You get that? OK. It's threeftsixteen brr. I'm sorry, I'm losing you . . . Cheryl? Pardon me, was that a yes to the million dollars? I can't hear . . . you're . . . fading.'

He put the receiver back. 'Seems they don't need it.'

'That's cruel, Joe.'

'Taking advantage of poor people who don't know better and spending that money on hair product and Mercedes is cruel.'

'I thought you believed in all that.'

'That's not the Gospel, Rip. Do you know what the great disaster of our age is? Apart from the gap between the rich and poor? It's that the most significant event in world history and the best news mankind ever received has been hijacked by wolves. It has become this twisted thing. Bad Theology is killing people, Rip. I have to do something about it. It's not religion that the world needs, Rip; it revelation. You gotta know the difference.' Joe was at his most righteously angry when it came to the religious people – 'The Hoop Jumpers' as he liked to call them – and especially the 'wolves who led them astray'. For him, these purveyors of an expensively coiffed and suited Gospel were the chief perpetrators of crime in the land, above drug dealers, duplicitous politicians or corporate thieves. These were the guys (it was nearly always men, he noted) who had the most to answer for given what they supposedly believed and knew. In his mind, they had taken something freely given, cheapened it, and then made people pay for it. I didn't believe in any Gospel, freely given or otherwise, but I believed Joe's indignation was authentic and righteous.

Mary emerged from the shower wearing knickers and a vest, her hair dyed blue.

'That ain't blue morpho blue,' Joe said. 'It's purple.'

'It's still wet.'

Joe went and did his ablutions. Whilst he flossed and dee-dee-deed Mary lay on the bed.

'How many cases you sell now?'

'We must have sold fifty.'

'How many did *you* sell?'

'Maybe fifteen.'

'It could take a few more days. Maybe weeks.'

'I can wait,' I lied.

Joe re-appeared.

'Well, Rip, that is one hell of a day. We should do the lakes. Head to Cleveland and then, when you really are blooded, we'll unleash you on Iowa' (he pronounced this Eye-Way). 'The very middle of Middle America. Your product makes it there, it makes it everywhere.' He took a pillow and laid it on the carpeted floor. He lay down and put his hands together in prayer, the way a child might. He said a prayer – the usual reverent and irreverent all at once – thanking God for the day, for sales, for stone-hearted liberals, evil televangelists, cheap motels, and me, and then closed his eyes and was snoring within a few minutes, breathing like factory bellows. It was a miracle he slept as well as he did. Like a man with no troubles and nothing on his conscience.

Mary and I lay there for a bit, listening to his breathing.

'Does he ever sleep on a bed?'

'I never seen it. He says most people in the world don't have beds so he won't.'

Mary was an arm's length away, lying there like a bay, a harbour, all calm and curled and inviting. Lights from the road make quadrilaterals in the room and a shadow on the roof filtered through the curtain and blind. It was full of the atmosphere I hoped to find. Charged. Seedy. Anonymous.

'You thinking about fucking me?'

'Shhh!'

'He can't hear. He slept through a tornado once.' She lay with her head resting on the palm over a hand angled across her ear. I looked at Joe lying on the floor and watched the rise and fall of his great torso, estimating how much time we'd have were we to try and do it.

'Shall we . . . check out the pool? Have a smoke?'

'Sure.'

So we went outside and sat on the plastic loungers by the pool; I rolled a joint and we listened to the sound of cars passing in the night – a sound full of sad desire and sex.

'We could do it here, no?'

'A deal's a deal.'

The dope turned out to be a helpful prophylactic, making me flaccid in body and intention. But where dope made me calm and glazed and contentedly mediocre, it made Mary paranoid. Her chief insecurity soon surfaced.

'You only want me for this,' she said, pushing her legs out to show the extent of her figure. 'Once you've had me you'll move on Isabelle, I know it.'

'I'm not interested in Isabelle.'

'You seemed interested, talking about books 'n' shit.'

'She's . . . not my type, Mary. I have no feelings for her. She's too serious. Too earnest and religious. I like a free spirit. You're a free spirit.'

'I'm smart, too. Just different. Isabelle uses her mind. I use this.'

'You are different. As different as the sun and moon. It's hard to believe you're sisters.'

'Maybe we ain't.'

'What do mean?'

She shrugged. 'You got to figure how I look like Pocahontas when Isabelle looks like Anne of Green Gables. Ma says my father was hardly around when I was born. How did Ma get pregnant with me when he was in a jungle in South America for nearly nine months? Do the math.' She stretched her mouth, as if trying wake herself, to sober up. She slapped her cheeks. I should have left it there, but curiosity justifies the picking of a thousand apples.

'What are you saying?'

'I'm not saying diddly. I'm just supposing. Don't you wonder if your parents were really your parents? I think that a lot.'

I hadn't ever thought it, much as I'd have liked a different father sometimes. Or my father to be different.

'Isabelle showed me a photo of him. In a book he wrote. He looks like a jerk. Hair and beard all wild like he doesn't care. Which he don't. Don't look like me.'

'Where is he now?'

'In hell, I hope.'

'Aren't you curious? To know what your father's like?'

'You can't call him my father. You gotta be around to be a father. He travelled all over the world chasing bugs then he disappeared. Look. He didn't give a shit 'bout us. He weren't even here for any of us being born.' This sounded like Edith talking to me. And suddenly that same power of paternal prohibition shut this line of questioning down. 'You should stop pushing in that direction. You might get bit.'

'I already got bit.'

Mary suddenly grabbed a towel, buried her head in it and screamed. When she lowered the towel her face was a patchwork quilt of fear and vulnerability – but also relief. Relief at having shared a heavy burden, perhaps? For surely that is what secrets are: little weights that grow heavier with the un-telling. That was my justification for pushing it. There is immense satisfaction in getting people to share their secrets with you. You feel you are being helpful, getting them to unburden themselves; you are flattered at their sharing a confidence; plus you get the prurient thrill of hearing the secret! I thought I was helping to bring things into the light. But really I was an idiot moth flitting too close to the flames.

'You better not say anything to Ma or anyone about that.'

'About which?'

'About me thinking I have a different father. You have to promise me.'

'Of course.' I said. And for the second time I made a vow to Mary I wouldn't keep.

'I feel awful tired. I'm turning in.'

I must have looked as disappointed as a dog for she repeated her terms. 'Two-fiddy cases and I'm yours.'

She did a dizzy pirouette by the pool and went inside.

By the time I returned to the room, Joe and Mary were asleep. I touched Mary's bare shoulder.

'You awake?'

She didn't answer me. Was she asleep? Or just pretending?

I lay on my bed, buzzing with a new speculation. Mary having a different father made sense; not just because of the physical differences; it also explained Edith's desire to control the story.

I thought I could hear a hushed roar of the falls beneath the sound of the air-conditioning and Joe's contented snore. I lay there watching the shape made by the lights of the passing cars and listening to the different noises they made as they passed. I dug out my notebook and tried to sublimate my still unsated lust into trying to write some lines about my first day on the Road and an Ode to Niagara, straining out a poorly disguised metaphor.

'Water falls near here
Splits a county in two
Makes one country
Out of me and you
Blood flows here
So let's me and you
Make one country
Out of two . . .'

After about ten minutes I put down the notebook. I watched Mary for a while. She turned, breathing in startled fits and jerks. She was lovelier in sleep, maybe because in sleep she had no suitors to try and impress. The air-conditioning had goosebumped her arms. She looked much younger. Isabelle was right. She was a little girl in a woman's body. But how I wanted the body. Just before I fell into a fitful sleep I said my prayers:

'Lord, let me sell those cases soon.'

CHAPTER TWELVE

In which I find my voice and Joe gets arrested.

For the next few weeks we enjoyed a rich seam of selling. I have proof because I made a note of every sale we made in my note-book, scribbling the amounts next to my poems. It became a kind of ledger of lust. We stopped at gift stores in Erie ($120 (just morphos)), Conneaut ('real pretty but no thanks'), a floral emporium in Cleveland ($350 and guaranteed re-order and a spectacular misquote of Winston Churchill). Joe sold in Toledo and Fort Wayne and I did $500 worth in Remington and Peoria, Indiana, after which Joe and I bought suits at J. C. Penney's and ties to match the colour of our favourite butterflies. Joe insisted that every leppar had to have a favourite, even if it changed. It was helpful, too, when it came to the collectors. A collector's favourite butterfly was usually the one they didn't have. I chose the emerald swallowtail and Joe picked out a spotted bow tie he said captured the markings and colours of his current favourite (he revised it monthly), the tailed jay.

I overcame my inhibitions about making things up, taking a leaf out of Joe's book (and everyone else's) and saying whatever I needed to win the sale. How lovely it was to leap into the lib-erating air of making things up and have my listeners hanging on and believing my every word; it was so much easier than follow-ing someone else's script, and a spiel lacking facts was harder to dispute. Statistics could always be made to sound true as long as they were delivered with confidence: 'Eighty-five per cent of our customers are likely to vote Republican'; 'Sixty-seven per cent of women tend to go for the double cases'; 'Indiana has the third highest amount of registered lepidopterists in the USA'. As a general rule, female staff seemed to prefer poetic, literary sounding quotes; male staff liked the reassuring, non-fictional truths of history or politics. My accent was a boon to both and in some stores I felt I could have said anything and I'd have sold something. And the further west we travelled – where my accent seemed more exotic – the more my powers of persuasion grew. On that trip we misquoted enough poets, politicians and prophets to rouse a quarrel of lawyers. Sometimes, Joe would be mid-pitch and then suddenly look at me and ask, 'What was it that Abe Lincoln said, Rip?' And I would say something like, ' "The flutter of a butterfly's wings stills the warring hearts of men." ' Or I would be halfway through my pitch and turn to Joe and ask, 'Joe, who was it who said "better the brilliant blue of a spotted emperor than all the emperor's clothes in China"? Was it Twain?' 'Nah. That was Confucius.' We took enjoyment in making ever more outrageous claims for our products, as well as for ourselves. And if one of us floundered the other stepped in.

By the time we crossed the state line into Iowa I had reached my secret sales target and Joe and I had grown into something of a double act, with Joe calling us the Flutter Brothers.

At the state line Joe announced our arrival with a little speech about 'the Hawkeye State' and how it was 'the very epitomacy' of Small Town America. It was the bellwether state, and not just for elections. When J. C. Penney wanted to know if a product would roll out in the rest of the country, they tested it in Iowa: 'You sell in Aiway, you sell in Americay.' Just before noon we entered a town called Centerville. It had a name that does not lie. It felt like the middle of something, geographically, culturally, politically. The extremes were left and right but this was the very middle of middle. To get to its centre you drove past a reassuring litany of fast-food outlets and tractor dealerships, past gardens with swing-seats and wind chimes and the outsized American flags on poles lest you forget which country you were in. And churches. Lots of churches. Centerville didn't look like a town where you'd expect to find trouble, unless you were the trouble.

'Look at this town, Rip. The people who live here have

achieved the very heaven of happiness as enshrined in our beloved constitution as being our fundamental right to pursue.'

Joe didn't really do sarcasm but this was sarcastic for him. The third element of the Declaration of Independence – mankind's inalienable right to pursue happiness – was another of his 'things', along with a US citizen's right to bear arms and the hijacking of the Gospel. He believed that the Declaration of Independence's claim that the creator had given mankind certain inalienable rights – life, liberty and the pursuit of happiness – was hogwash.

'Them first two sit well enough with the truth, Rip. But that third is without doubt a piece of Bad Theology on a level with a child being damned unless they are baptized, or saying the only people who get to heaven are the good folks who pitch up in a building for an hour every week, or that the only place you can locate the creator of the universe is in a piece of bread dispensed by a priest.'

For my part, the inalienable right to pursue happiness seemed like a good idea and I was happy for any government to protect my ability to pursue said happiness. But Joe really saw it as a kind of institutionalized evil. 'Is happiness what the creator made us for? Did the creator really make that a right? And how can a government protect such a right? That thinking has got a whole lot of people chasing happiness and complaining when someone – usually the government – doesn't give it to them. It's insane. And it gives birth to all kinds of evil children, like the American Dream, and self-help, and "if it feels good do it" philosophizing.'

I am lazy when it comes to assessing other people's politics. I see myself as being somewhere in the middle and that middle is intrinsically sane, good, liberal and has something to do with freedom (although when I think of freedom it's more the kind you associate with pleasure than ethics). Because I saw Joe as 'religious' (a term he despised) I assumed him to be a certain political hue and colour. When I first met him I'd have pinned him to my right. I'd have said red, Republican, rednecked; fiercely defensive of individual liberty, the right to say what he wanted and go where he pleased; a gun carrier and a Christian of the pointing kind. And yet. And yet he really didn't go along with that congregation. Not at all. He wasn't even in the building. He confounded my 'typing' from the very first day and continued to confound it. He, like me, cared little for politics; but unlike me it wasn't out of lazy indifference but from a deeper conviction about what or who was really running the world, let alone the country.

All was well when we parked up in the centre of Centerville in a vast square with blocks of stores either side.

We headed for a florist in the middle of the square. We'd hardly got across the threshold when the woman at the counter pointed straight past us to the door.

'Excuse me, sir. But you can see the sign.'

'No, ma'am. I did not. Which sign?'

' "No hawking." I don't know what wares you got in that box but you can't come in here with them. We are not that kind of town.'

'Well, I don't know about hawking, ma'am. But I'm a salesman. That's how I earn my living. Selling the trinkets of God's creation. It's how you earn your living, too, I suspect.'

'Salesmen are welcome. But not hawkers.'

'Ma'am, I'm not rightly sure there's a difference. I know that a hawker is someone who travels around selling goods, typically advertising them by shouting, but as you can see I am just talking calmly here.'

'Sir. You must leave.'

'Ma'am, it's a sorry day when a man can't show his wares to another and get a fair hearing. I mean we're all salespeople here. After all, you say to a customer: "Ma'am, could I interest you in these azaleas? Sir, there's some weed killer here that is just perfect for the roses." Is that so different to what is happening here? Let me just show you.'

Joe put the sample box on the counter and took out a couple of cases to make the pyramid.

The woman reached down and pressed something behind the counter. Agitated, Joe launched in.

'All of nature's trading, ma'am, so why can't we? Flowers and butterflies have a business relationship. Butterflies need the energy in the nectar that a flower produces to attract pollinators. When flowers trade with butterflies, they want a smart business partner. We are in the same business here: the business of taking nature and re-packaging it for people who crave a little beauty in their lives.'

'Have you quite finished, sir?'

'Oh no. I am only just getting started.'

'We make it very clear we don't sell to just anyone off the street.'

'But how else could I get in here other than off the street?'

'Sir, I don't like your tone. You are being aggressive with us. Unless you leave I will be forced to call the sheriff.'

'Ma'am, I am in no way being aggressive, here.'

In fairness Joe was not being aggressive but if you were this woman, without the benefit of knowing what Joe was like, without the benefit of having seen his gentler side, the hidden kindnesses and acts of spontaneous charity, you'd think him at best a fool and at worst a crazy dangerous fool. Joe was determined to put this woman straight even though it was clear she would not be bent from her position by him or anyone.

A man entered the store from the back. 'Is there a problem here, Betsy?'

'These gentlemen are hawkers, Mr Dean.'

Joe put his hands in the air, an unusual gesture of conciliation for him. 'We are just honest to goodness salesmen, sir. Doing what it is our right to do. Did not our own great president Lincoln say, "Deny a man the right to sell and you deny him the air to breathe"?' Joe looked at me for confirmation.

'I believe he did,' I said.

'I couldn't say whether Mr Lincoln said that or not, sir,' the man said. 'But you can't sell without making an appointment.'

'OK. Can I make an appointment?'

'Not like this, sir. I'd appreciate it if you and your friend left the store or I will have to call the sheriff.'

'Well, I don't think we can do that,' Joe said.

The man picked up the phone and started to dial. I thought I should rescue the situation. Or at least rescue Joe from himself and, by extension, myself.

'Joe? Sir. Ma'am. It's all right. My friend – my assistant is very passionate about our product and keen for you to see it but there's no need to call the police. Joe? Shall we leave? Respect their view? I am sure they have their rules for a reason. When in Rome?'

The man paused with his fingers over the black clickers of the telephone, willing to call it truce. But Joe didn't seem to hear me. Despite the futility of the cause, he continued with his soliloquy (for that is what it had become). 'People all over this country have been purchasing our butterfly cases, from Pough-keepsie to Buffalo. As I stand here now speaking J. C. Penney's are considering whether to invite us to pitch our product. But it seems I have driven into a part of America that is not America but a little country within it where freedom is unimportant. Where protection trumps liberty.'

'For the last time, I am asking you to leave, sir. I am calling the sheriff now.'

'I think you should know that you are making a judgement that condemns you in your own prejudicing.'

'Hello? Is that the sheriff's office?'

'I want to give you a chance to redeem yourself.'

'We have a disturbance.'

'Joe! Can we leave it?'

'No, Rip. This word hawker is made up by people who want to look down on the poor. Who think they are superior in some way. It's the poor who have to get out there and shout loud to be heard among all the powerful selling that is going on in this land.'

'Yes. Hello, this is Pat Dean from Floral Heaven. We are having some trouble.'

'Sir?' I stepped in front of Joe now. 'Please. We will leave. Joe?' I put the cases back in the case and snapped it shut. I cleared my throat, trying to make my intentions clear to Joe. But he was riled in a way I hadn't seen before. Was this about the definition of a word? Or was it – as Clay had hinted – he could not handle a man asserting authority?

'I understand that you work in a store in a town that thinks it's better than the rest of America. That probably looks down on the poor white people that live out there in the Appalachia where I myself come from. I understand that you may not have thought about what the rest of us might consider beautiful. But mark this. One day you will think of the day you turned down the possibility of selling a product that brings joy to many thousands of Americans, from gentlemen who will soon be running one of America's fastest growing . . .'

'Joe! Let's go!'

'I want to give you a chance. I will leave you this information leaflet. Should you repent and overnight wake up and say, what have I done? Call this number and order a few cases. Lucky for you I believe in a merciful God.'

I waited until we had got to the car before giving him a piece of my mind.

'Jesus. Joe, what was that about? They were hardly being rude. It was so . . . unnecessary.'

'They were denying me the right to make a living. That has to be challenged.'

'What you done now?' Mary asked.

'I was sticking to my guns.'

'They 'cuse you of hawking?'

'They don't know the definition,' Joe said.

'How did you know that, Mary?' I asked.

'He does this. I ain't helping you iotas, Joe. Not this time.'

'This time?' I asked.

We were not even at the end of Main Street when a patrol car with two policemen inside pulled up behind us, giving one 'wooo' of its siren. Joe slowed up at the city limit sign and annoyingly started dee dee dee-ing as though nothing serious was happening. The patrolman appeared at Joe's window and signalled for him to open it. The driver's side window of the Chuick was bust so Joe lowered the back window leaving me to speak on his behalf. 'Sorry, officer, the window's stuck. I keep meaning to get it fixed.'

The sheriff peered in and addressed Joe. 'Step from the car, sir.'

'A please would be nice, officer.'

There was a pause. I remember thinking what kind of policeman would he be? The trigger-happy type or the used-to-assholes type? I was so angry with Joe I remember thinking, 'Please, let it be the former!'

'I will ask you one more time. Step from the car, sir.'

'Just a please, officer. It's a simple courtesy is all.'

'Joe! What is your problem?'

The officer loosened his holster.

'Come on, Joe,' I said. 'It's not worth it. He's . . . Joe? Come on!'

'Sometimes freedom requires a sacrifice of protest, Rip.' Joe was seemingly intent on going from minor road traffic offence to electric chair in as short a time as possible. He sat there rigid, 'sticking to his guns'. The patrolman stepped away from the car and started talking on his walkie-talkie. I caught the word 'backup'.

'Joe. Can't you . . . just . . . '

'Don't waste your breath,' Mary said. She seemed so nonchalant about it, like she'd seen it all before. 'He is the stubbornest bastard on earth.'

'All I asked for was a "please" and he's loosened his holster.

He knows that I'll cooperate but out of his own law-bound pride, puffed up by the sense of power given to him by the gun and a badge, he refuses. I am a free-rider here.'

I opened the glove box to fetch my passport. My hands shaking. I noticed a gun – the gun Edith gave to Mary for the road. What seemed sexy now looked dangerous.

I got out of the car.

'Rip! What the heck?' Joe reached out to stop me.

The patrolman drew his gun. 'Raise your hands, sir.'

They were already up. 'Officer, I am so sorry about my friend. He's upset. He isn't thinking straight. I can vouch for his good character. This is not typical.'

The patrolman's walkie-talkie buzzed and he took it. 'Backup on Main Street. We have a Level 2. Sir, put your hands on the car.'

Level 2. What the heck was Level 2?

'Sir, place your hands against the roof of the car, facing the car.'

'Of course, officer.'

'You have your papers, sir?'

'They're in my bag, officer. My passport. In the front there.'

I'd seen these scenes a hundred times in movies and the person being pulled over always seemed so cool, so insouciant. But the idea of criminality is so much more appealing than the reality. As I placed my hands on the hot metal of Chuick's roof I felt a warm trickle of pee in my Fruit of the Looms.

'You too, ma'am.'

Mary got out, hands raised, and placed them obligingly on the car, standing next to me.

'He's doing a Texas.'

'What's a Texas?'

'He got accused of hawking and told the owner that when he was president he'd see to it her store was the first to be closed for violating his rights. They kept him in jail for a week. Ma had to drive down there and release him herself.'

'Why don't you say something?'

'Because he don't deserve it. He's too proud. I hope they kick the crap out of him and lock him up for good.'

Joe sat in the front implacable as a buffalo. I confess that, like Mary, I wanted them to beat the living shit out of him, put him in jail and leave him there to rot. For a few, red seconds I wanted them to kill him, I really did.

A second patrol car arrived – backup. The second patrolman was wearing shades despite the gloom. He asked the first officer to run the checks on the car. I wondered what trail of offence and felony might be revealed. I felt sick. What had I got myself into?

The second patrolman seemed more relaxed and put up a calming hand to the first patrolman, who couldn't have been much older than me. Lucky for Joe the second patrolman was immediately able to see that Joe was more of a dick than a danger.

'What have we got here?'

'The driver is refusing to cooperate, sir.'

The second patrolman went to the passenger door. Opened the door and leant in.

'We have a problem here, sir?'

'We have a problem, officer, but it has an easy and simple solution.'

'And what would that be?'

'A little more politeness from your colleague could have prevented this . . . escalation.'

'May I see your papers . . . please?'

'There you go! Of course, officer.' Joe pointed to the glove box. 'May I?'

'Go ahead.'

I had seen this scene too: a patrolman asks for papers as a prelude to the driver either taking off, pulling a gun on the policeman, striking the policeman, spinning the policeman a line.

Joe handed his papers to the second patrolman, who glanced at me and then at Joe's ID.

'If you'd step from the car, please.'

'Why yes, of course,' Joe said.

'We had a complaint you were hawking goods and that you then insulted the store owner, threatening her.'

'I merely asked the woman to explain the difference between a hawker and a salesman. Do you know the difference, officer?'

'Well, I believe a hawker tends not to have a licence to sell.'

'Well that is a good guess, officer, but it is not the case. There is no difference except that a hawker is, technically, someone who carries their wares with them. Soap. Life assurance. Bibles. Are you saying therefore that you'd arrest someone for selling Bibles?'

The second patrolman called back to the first who was on his walkie-talkie. 'You run the checks, Officer Flynn?'

It didn't look good: a complaint of a disturbance of the peace leading to a beat-up, dodgy looking car with unusual crew and cargo: a big clown, a little European guy, a girl not wearing shoes, a bald eagle in a box (a gun in the glove box), a hundred dead butterflies in the trunk.

'What is this car?'

'Well, sir, it's my own creation. A cross between a Chevrolet and Buick and I call it a Chuick.'

'Are those actual miles?'

'Closing in on a million, sir. And if I might add that in all those miles I have driven I have never encountered this kind of treatment for what is after all an everyday right of every American. The day it is an offence to sell your wares in this country is the day America dies, officer. A sore day. An apocalyptic day. What was it Nathaniel Hawthorne said, Rip? "If a man can't sell, he is lost"?'

I refused to corroborate.

'Is that beer?'

'That's mine, officer.'

He nodded. 'Should be in a brown bag.'

'Sorry, sir. I'm from Britain.'

The second patrolman then saw Jimmy Carter on the back seat.

'Is that a bird?'

'Yes, officer. The national emblem of this great nation. We're aiming to set him free in the Grand Tetons. I hate to think what he would make of this situation, officer. He's probably thinking, "Am I really the emblem of a nation that arrests people for trying to sell goods?" Maybe America needs another kind of symbol. I don't know what would be more appropriate. I guess it would have to be one that devoured its own kind maybe? Like . . . a spider.'

'Sir, would you open the trunk for me, please.'

The second patrolman seemed happy to play Joe's politeness game and Joe was cooperating. He popped the trunk. The second patrolman looked in. 'You have a licence to sell these?'

'Well sir, I don't need a licence. Except in some towns where they violate people's rights. Like Lubbock, Texas. Or Centerville, Iowa.'

The second patrolman examined a 6 by 4 containing a spectacular green-stained zebra wing. 'My old lady would like these.'

Incredibly, Joe began to sell it to him. 'Well, take one for her, officer. I'll offer it to you wholesale.'

'Where do you get the butterflies?'

'From official suppliers. This one comes from a farm in Costa Rica. And we have our own small butterfly house, too.'

The first patrolman, who had been back at his car, the black spiral flex of his radio pulled taut and as far as it would stretch, came back. 'Licensed to an Edith Bosco. PO box address in New York State.'

The patrolman handed Joe back his papers.

'Well. You are free to go. Just as long as you don't go selling in this county.'

Joe shook his head.

'I can't promise that, officer.'

The patrolman looked at Joe.

'Are you saying you will sell? Or that you intend to?'

'Well, sir, they are the same thing. I both will and intend to.'

'Then I guess you leave me no choice.'

'I just can't promise it, sir. We need monies for gas and food.'

'If you're telling me you're going to sell in Richmond County then I will have to arrest you now.'

'Very well.'

The second patrolman sighed.

'Then turn and put both hands on the roof of the car, please, sir.'

Joe did as he was asked, smilingly. 'Of course, officer.'

The patrolman did the Miranda and then frisked Joe. 'Feet apart.' He then had him turn, with a please and a thank you, and asked him to hold out his hands which he cuffed.

'I must say, officer, you have set a good example to your fellow officer there.'

I turned to Mary, pleading with her to intervene. She shook her head.

'I will have to ask you to accompany me to the station, Mr Bosco. I'm charging you for selling goods without a licence and disturbing the peace. You sure you want that?'

'I don't think there was real peace to disturb here, officer. It's just a peace maintained by control. And that is no peace at all.'

Joe had to duck down a long way to get in the back of the patrol car.

We followed them to the station, where we had to sit around for an hour waiting for Joe to be processed. He emerged, still smiling like this was all a wonderful experience. 'They're going to put me up for the night. It's going to cost five hundred bucks for the privilege.'

'Five hundred dollars!'

'Bail.'

We had $300.

'You take credit cards?' I asked the duty clerk.

'Cash only.'

'We'll need to sell some cases. How far to the next county?'

'It's about thirty miles to Bloomfield. But the stores will be closed by now.'

'What are we going to do, Joe?'

'You'll have to go sell first thing tomorrow. Just make sure it's in a town that respects the constitution of the United States.'

'OK.'

I looked at the deputy sheriff. 'Is there a reasonable budget motel around here?'

'There's a Ramada on Main. If you drive back east, there are some cheaper motels. You could drive on to Bloomfield from there tomorrow.'

'How long will you keep him?'

'Till someone pays.'

CHAPTER THIRTEEN

In which I discover that Mary isn't what I thought.

Black clouds lay ahead. We could see lightning in them but hear no thunder. Mary and I walked back to the car just as the rain started. Big, hot, generous American rain that started playing jazz on the roof. We sat listening to the tunes, our breath steaming up the window.

'Joe will get himself killed one day. It's a miracle he isn't dead already,' I said. 'What was that about? It was as though he wanted to get arrested.'

Mary shrugged. 'He don't like to be talked down to. That storekeeper must have looked at him superior. It's his hillbilly blood. Prolly.'

'But they didn't. Not really.'

'Look. My brother's crazy. You ain't worked that out yet?'

Joe was different. But he wasn't crazy. I could see a method in his madcapness: to me it was all a bit of an act, for effect; he knew full well what he was doing, I was sure of that.

I think we both realized at the same time that Joe's incarceration = imminent consummation.

'You must have done two-fiddy by now.'

We drove back out on the highway and pulled in to the first motel we could find. It was called Park Plaza Court. It had plastic Doric columns either side of the reception door – mock-heroic for my ersatz odyssey. Before I went to book a room Mary handed me a thick brass washer. 'Put it on your wedding finger. In case they make us take two rooms. Out here people still think you should be married if you take a double. I put it on when I travel with Joe. People don't always believe I'm his sister, on account of us looking different.' I let Mary put the ring on and went to sign in the newlyweds. I could barely write my name in the register with the anticipation. A month-long prick-tease was about to come to an end. I grabbed Joe's Big Deal Case with the freaks and fetched my passport again, seeing the Walther.

'You want the gun?'

'Nah.'

'You know how to use it?'

'I'm an American.'

The woman in reception had a gold plate name badge with black lettering that said Tammy McCarthy. Tammy asked me for my passport number and my mother's maiden name and made me sign the book. I wrote our names as Mr and Mrs R. Van Jones.

'Is that a Dutch name?'

'I'm from Britain,' I said, not wanting to go into how I had come by my new Dutch name. But just when I didn't want it to, my nationality became a matter of great fascination and an excuse for Ms McCarthy to list her ancestry back as far as her great-grandfather in 'Aberdeen, Scotland'. She drew her family tree for me on the motel stationery. I nodded as politely as I could and humoured her platitudes about England and the Queen and how my country would always be a special friend to America. Then she took an eternity to find a key that was attached to a key ring on a wooden block as big as a brick.

'That's just so's you don't go off with it. It used to cost me three hundred dollars a year in unreturned keys.'

I found Mary in the back seat giving Jimmy Carter a fresh litter of USA Todays. 'You get a room?'

I wiggled the key. 'Room 19. Another sign.'

'What do you mean?'

'Well. You're nineteen.'

'What's with you and signs? You're more superstitious than Clay. What we do about Jimmy Carter?'

'We can leave him,' I said. 'Check on him later, maybe.'

'He's been awful quiet.'

'He'll be fine.'

We left Jimmy Carter with some crackers and water and we went inside. The motel room was like any other but it was precisely that homogeneous functionality and anonymity that made it sexier than any Ritz or Grand. The ghosts of lust-filled nights were tangible in the brown counterpanes on the double double-beds and the flock wallpaper flecked with what looked like smeared moths. We weren't the first or even the hundredth couple stepping into that room intent on ecstasy but I'd wager few would have had the built-up desire we had. I pulled the door behind us and we kissed. She pushed me back against the door and tippy-toed, pushing herself against me before breaking off and going to test the springiness of the nearest bed. I joined her on the bed and we started to kiss again; but again she broke off and started to take in the decor of the room and in particular the painting that hung on the wall between the beds. It was of a wagon train passing along a red dust road through a canyon all bathed in an overly orange sunset. 'You think that's meant to be Arizona?' I looked at it, trying to see what she might be seeing, frustrated at the diversion. 'Maybe. It's just a fantasy of the West.' It was a terrible painting. 'I like it,' she said. The painting had no merit whatsoever and her liking for it should have been enough reason to stop right there, but lust trumps compatibility every time. I read her interest in the decor as just more teasing (oh my ability to read signs!). I started kissing her neck, deciding to take command, but when I tried to ease her onto the bed she stiffened her arms and held me back.

'What's wrong?'

'Nothing. Is the door locked?'

'Yes.'

'You sure?'

I went and tested it and put the chain on for good measure. I returned to the bed and resumed my love-making, which was – to be frank – not going well. When I tried to undress her, her hand slapped away my unbuttoning fingers. She looked afraid.

'What is it?'

'Nothing.' She shook her head then she said: 'I ain't done it before.'

'Oh.'

My reaction was one of genuine surprise and disappointment. It did not seem conceivable that she'd not done it before, the way she carried herself and talked, that knowing animal swagger. Then again, if I'd been thinking straight, thinking with my brain instead of my loins, I'd have seen it for the bravado that it was and the insecurity Isabelle had warned me about. That assurance, that innate physical ease I'd seen in the waterfall and witnessed in my room back at the house: it was all an act, an act that so many girls must feel obliged to perform for the benefit of horny boys like me.

'I didn't want to say when you asked me.'

'There's nothing to be embarrassed about. It's . . . fine.'

Virginity may be prized and revered in some cultures, but it's not what you want when you're expecting unadulterated physical gratification. With virginity comes responsibility and I was not feeling responsible. I wanted wild, dirty danger with someone wilder, dirtier and more dangerous than me. I didn't want to overthink or explain anything. I wanted mindless, thoughtless, irresponsible uncommitted sex.

'I been close to doing it. But he was a farm boy who just wanted to tell his friends he'd fucked a girl. Though they would have been impressed if he said he'd fucked a pig. We fooled around. I made him get off just short of Grand Central Station. I wasn't going all the way with him. He weren't the one.'

I pulled a strand of loose hair from her mouth tenderly. I drank in the implication that I might be the One. In truth, I didn't want to be the One. Not with Mary. But I was flattered she thought so. I said that it was important you went all the way to Grand Central Station for the first time with the right person. I reassured her that with me she was in good hands, and that I would never fuck a pig or any other kind of animal for that matter. I added – like a gentleman – that we didn't have to go all

179

the way to Grand Central Station. We could get off at Pough-keepsie or Yonkers or even Harlem if she didn't feel like riding the whole way. But she said she wanted to get to the main terminus and that I was the one to take her there.

Having anointed me as her deflowerer she leant towards me and pulled me to her with her hand at the back of my head. She kissed me, and it was a sumptuous fluid kiss. She then stood and took off her clothes until she was standing before me naked, as God made her, but not perhaps where God wanted her to be. I had already seen her naked – that first day back in the falls – but this was different. There was a voice telling me not to get on the train. But I ignored it. She seemed to interpret my awestruck reaction as hesitation because she asked me: 'You sure you want me?'

'Oh God, yes. I want you. Now. Tomorrow. Forever.' For five minutes of pleasure I would promise eternities!

'You have something?'

I didn't have anything. I hadn't thought any of this through. Thinking is antagonistic to hedonism.

'It's OK. Come like a Catholic.'

We made love with animal urgency. I was concerned that the long buildup would see me rush to a speedy, disappointing conclusion; but I think her virginity, the responsibility of taking it, the pressure to perform and set the bar high for her future lovers, as well as the terror of impregnating her, all focused the mind and took the edge off the pent-up lust, at least long enough to do myself justice and give her satisfaction. I came like a Catholic. Just.

Afterwards, I lay on my back and she lay on her side with an arm across my chest and her head over my heart; the bouquet of her body was powerful and complex and mildly repelling. With the lust fog clearing I became far more aware (immediately, I'd suggest) of all that I found unsuitable in her (but had ignored in the pursuit of this gratification), and I was filled with the utter certainty that I had made a mistake in having sex with her. Although I set no significance – legal or spiritual – on such things I felt I had bound myself to her in a primal way that could not be reversed and that would give her 'rights' over me and that she would exercise those 'rights' at some point, no doubt at a time when I least needed it. She lay there in my arms, more passive, more peaceful than she had ever been and more compliant than I felt comfortable with. I wanted the sassy, cool Mary back. But she was tender and, I'd say, sweetly vulnerable. I reached for the cigarettes and, in the time-honoured way, asked her if it had been good for her.

'It was . . . different.'

Different didn't sound good. 'Different good? Different bad?'

'Different. To how I imagined it.'

'How did you imagine it?' I offered her a cigarette but she declined. She was savouring a landmark moment in her life.

'It felt good but . . . it was like you weren't there. And I wasn't there.'

'Well, I can assure you I was right there.'

'No. I mean. You were . . . we were becoming one person.'

'Oh. OK.'

'You know that when a male butterfly fertilizes a female his sperm plugs her so she can't mate with anyone else?'

'Good job we're not butterflies.'

'You think you came inside me a little?'

'I hope . . . No. I got off at Yonkers or Harlem. Or wherever the last stop is.'

'But there's that little bit that comes out before you come. That can get you pregnant. That's what Ma told me. She said to make sure you get the guy to wear a condom.'

I didn't want to think about Edith, or Edith telling Mary this, or about my little spurts of pre-ejaculate getting Mary pregnant. Or her being plugged so no one else would use her. I wanted to go to sleep. I wanted to fall into a deep sleep from which I would wake and find myself somewhere else, having not made love to Mary or formed a bond with her in this way.

'Imagine if I was pregnant and you went back to England leaving a kid behind that you never knew you'd had. And then you met that kid, years later when he was maybe nineteen or twenty, visiting England.'

I imagined it and the thought shrivelled everything: my soul, my cock, my capacity to stay awake.

'What would you do?'

'If you got pregnant or if I met my child in twenty years' time?'

'If I got pregnant?'

'I . . . you won't.'

'But if I did. Just now. Would you want me to have the baby?'

Of course not. I was a selfish twenty-three-year-old who had had sex with someone who was physically ravishing but unsuited to my person in every way. These girly tests of loyalty were no fun. All I had wanted was to have consequence-free pleasure and go to sleep.

'I'd go along with whatever you wanted. It's your body.'

Mary batted back my sophistry. 'Except when *you* want it.'

Mary's head was still on my chest and her arm was now stuck to my skin.

'Am I sun or am I moon?'

'Huh?'

'You said I looked as different from Isabelle as the moon to the sun. Which am I?'

'The moon.'

'You sayin' Isabelle's hotter than me?'

'I'm saying you're more . . . mysterious.'

She sat up, and pulled the blanket around her, like a poncho.

'I weren't joking when I said we have a different father. I think I do.'

I started rolling a joint.

'You think, or you know.'

'I got a theory. Now I'm lying here with you and Ma's a thousand miles away I feel it even more.'

I was thinking, 'Don't tell me anything that binds me closer to you or makes me beholden to you in anyway'; but also thinking, 'Yes, tell me, because I need to know what's going on in this family, and it's wonderful to have secrets revealed.' Nosiness is a force as powerful as lust.

'Go on.'

'This one time, Ma got real drunk a few years back, at Thanksgiving. I was sixteen. She had been mad at me for getting caught smoking weed at high school. Even though she liked to smoke it herself with me sometimes. One night she starts telling me that when our father was away on expeditions she would get real lonely. She said she even went to a bar one night looking for company. I had the feeling she was trying to tell me something.'

'That she had other men?'

'Maybe. Or maybe that she went with a man who was maybe "my" father. She once described this guy she met. An Apache truck driver. Why would she do that?'

'Did you ask her? If maybe . . . you know?'

'She might kill me for asking such a thing. But I kept thinking it after she told me.'

'Maybe she needed to confess something.'

'It were more than that. I was sure.'

'You ever discussed it with Joe?'

'I told Joe what Ma had said. He said Ma was just drunk. It was the liquor talking. I asked him straight if he thought maybe I had a different father. He said you only had to look at us to see we were brother and sister. He thinks we have the same shape noses – which we do even though that nose is – was – like Ma's nose before the fire. He told me not to talk like that. So I forgot about it. But then you mentioned it and then it gets me thinking again. And the thought don't go away. It's become so's I gotta know for sure. Because I don't know who I am unless I know.'

I took her hand. 'It doesn't change who you are.'

She withdrew her hand. 'You think I'm crazy?'

I didn't. Her story and theory seemed plausible. I mean, you just had to look at her! But I was tired. I wanted to move on, to go to sleep. I took another deep toke. I wasn't thinking straight just when I needed to be.

'Maybe your mother had an affair, it doesn't mean you have a different father.'

'Maybe. Why do I get these feelings. Of being different? I know it when I'm behind the wheel. Maybe my father *was* a driver. I am a driver. Where does that come from? No one taught me that. Then maybe I think I just imagined it. Or I think maybe it don't matter. My father is either a lonely truck driver or a crazy entomologist who don't give a shit about no one. Sometimes I wonder what it must be like to have a child you never met. Maybe it don't matter. He don't care I exist. It means he can't reject me. It must be worse for Joe to know our father. To think that he's out there, living a life as though you don't exist. That must hurt. I think that's why Joe is the way he is. I think he is trying to prove something to someone who doesn't even care about him. But I don't know what I'd do if I was Joe and I met him. I'd probably kill him. Unless Ma killed him first. But I like that I don't even know he is my father. It means I'm free. Not like Joe. Or Isabelle. They think on him. In different ways. Isabelle through the collection. Joe trying to impress people. But I don't got to impress no one. He never knew me and I never knew him.'

She said all this with such touching ingenuousness.

'You listening to what I'm telling you?'

'I'm just thinking.' I should have let it lie but I have a meddling tendency. 'Why don't you find out for sure?'

'How can I know for sure?'

'Well, you could do one of those blood tests.' I don't know why I said this to Mary. It was more post-coital, drowsy stupidity than any desire to know the truth.

'How do they work?'

'I don't know exactly. They can test your paternity. If they took blood from your siblings and compared them.'

'I'd need Joe or Isabelle to give blood. They would never do that.'

'Isabelle?'

'You think she would?'

'I think she would,' I said. 'If she cares about the truth.'

'She wouldn't rock the boat.'

'What if I ask Joe.'

'Would you?'

'I'll ask him tomorrow.'

'Promise?'

'Yes. I promise.' I said this because it cost me nothing to say it and I wanted to go to sleep. But later, as I lay there with my eyes closed, I was wide awake. I was the very thing Isabelle suspected me of being: a hedonist, willing to take advantage of her immature sister for a fleeting pleasure and ignore the consequences; willing to egg on a childish fantasy, to make her feel wanted. If, at first, lust for Mary blinded me to the subtler attractions of Isabelle, it had also blinded me to the finer qualities of Mary, whom it suited me to see in a particular (diminished) way. She may have been self-regarding and a little too self-consciously brazen, but it was probably an act and, to be fair to her, an act I encouraged. A regret washed over me like a tiredness, a sadness I could not fully explain. I was sure that I had made a mistake, but then it's easy to be wise the far side of a fuck.

We woke at eleven, after checkout time. Ms McCarthy was standing where I'd left her, behind the reception desk. I handed her the ridiculous but effective keyring and apologized for being late. 'Don't you worry, Mr Van Jones. The sign says ten o'clock so we can get ahead. The cleaner comes at twelve, truth be told. And if newlyweds can't sleep in then who can?'

I paid the bill with my own cash, making a mental note to tell Joe that I couldn't keep bankrolling his alms-giving and bail monies. 'I hope you slept well, Mr Van Jones?'

185

It didn't seem appropriate to tell her that I had in fact had an uneasy night full of unsettling dreams that amalgamated three basic terrors: impregnating Mary, being caught by Edith, and then being tracked and hunted down by Mary's Apache father. 'Like a log,' I said, a phrase that made her smile and I had to repeat.

'And I hope your lovely bride slept – like a log, too?'

'We both slept like logs, Ms McCarthy. Like a whole timber yard.'

'Well. You've married a pruddy lady there, Mr Van Jones. Ya'll have a safe journey.'

I accepted the compliment on my new bride's behalf and thanked Ms McCarthy. Just before I reached the car I took the washer off my wedding finger and annulled our twelve-hour marriage.

My ex-wife was already waiting at the wheel, ready to sell a bail's worth of butterflies and set her brother free. We got the money in one stop. Mary did a $300 deal at the very first place we tried, a gift store in a strip mall some thirty miles out of Centerville. It was the only time I saw her sell and she did it with little fuss but no little charm. I could certainly see Edith in the way she sparkled and flirted in the initial exchange. As we walked back to the car with a roll of green she looked at me.

'We could still just leave the sonofabitch, you know.'

It was a nice idea: me and Mary setting out across America like a sexed-up Bonnie and Clyde, making love and sales wherever we pleased, living off butterflies for the rest of our days. The trouble is Mary wouldn't have been my first choice of companion and the feeling of regret had not lifted off me one bit. If anything, the change in her – a kind of accepting, sweet confidence, almost an assumption that we were together now – made it even clearer to me that we were not for bonding and that I had to work on some kind of withdrawal strategy before she made me put a real ring on it.

But I'd planted a seed (please God, not that kind of seed)

that had grown overnight into an idea. Her thoughts had started to travel a little too far along a particular road of thinking; in a direction encouraged by me.

'You're right, Rip. I should know who my father is. Or who my father ain't. I'm going to do one of those blood tests. I'll need to get Joe and Isabelle to do it. That'll be the hard part. Maybe you can help with that. The hardest part will be Ma. But maybe you can help me with that, too. She likes you. Will you help me?'

'Of course.'

'It's Joe that's the problem. You can't keep anything from Ma. Joe tells her everything. She's got him on a line.'

'Really? Joe?'

'He plays all footloose. But she's got him pinned. Why do you think he calls her every day?'

'Would it make you feel better to know? I mean. Which outcome would be best. That you have the same father or that you don't?'

'I won't know that till I get there. But I think you should say something.'

We got to the sheriff's office around noon. Mary waited with the car and I went in with the cash, filled out the paperwork and settled the bail. Joe was in his cell cheerfully evangelizing the duty guard in the habits of butterflies. He emerged, unrepentant, bragging that he had converted the sheriff to his way of seeing things about the meaning of hawking and the problem with guns and freedom being 'An American Paradoxical'. He gave the sheriff's department a blue morpho to remember him by; they gave us a police escort to the Appanoose County line where the sheriff gave us a blast of his siren and Joe waved to him, friendly as anything.

'Goddamn small-town freaks!' he yelled, smiling his smile.

CHAPTER FOURTEEN

*In which I challenge Joe about the past as we
head across the hard ocean.*

Having set Joe free we headed north through wooded valleys,
fields of corn and soybeans, hog sheds and cattle, and then west
across steadily flattening prairie. Joe made no apology for the
expensive and irritating hiatus his stubborn stance had caused.
Instead he riffed on how Iowa was America's most fertile state
and that the more fertile the soil the more backward the people,
although I think this was just sour grapes for his being arrested
by Iowans who seemed like fairly reasonable and friendly people
to me.

'America's a melting pie, Rip. You gotta swallow it all. Bald
Eagles. Indigenous genocide. Natural wonders. The 3/5ths
clause. The Road. Unlawful arrest.'

After Des Moines the landscape stayed the same all the way
to Nebraska where it would somehow find a way to become even
flatter and lonelier with horizons so distant you fancied you
could see the curve of the earth. Joe said that to see the curve
of the earth it had to be a flat nothing for 168 miles (a fact I still
haven't verified but believe to be true). At the state line we
would turn north passing through Sioux City and then continue
on up to Sioux Falls, South Dakota, which Joe claimed to be the
furthest point from the sea in the whole of the US. He called the
plain 'the hard ocean' and said that the further from the real
ocean we got the more you felt the sensation of being at sea.

It was in the middle of that sea – at the point where we were
furthest from stops, or any potential distractions or escapes –
that I decided to confront Joe with the question of Mary's
paternity. It was late afternoon, the hottest part of the day. Joe
was at the wheel, Mary was up front, I was in the back. The radio

was on but the noise from having the windows down drowned out the music. (Joe said it had to be 100 degrees before he'd put the air-conditioning on.) I had my elbow a little out and was holding my hand open, fingers splayed, catching the air until it felt like a ball in my palm, weighty and hard. I had been thinking about Mary being conceived in a truck-stop fuck. It rang true to me: the physical differences between her and Isabelle were undeniable, the personality traits too; Edith's husband's long absences, her drunken semi-confession years later; Joe choosing to believe his mother out of loyalty and a misplaced sense of needing to protect Mary. I worked myself up into a state of indignation. I felt anger at Edith for her management of the story and cross that Joe had maybe been the gatekeeper of her secret. I was not afraid of Joe; not once in my whole time with him did I fear for my physical well-being, even when things got fraught. He was a gentle soul, unsuited to violence, despite his great strength and erratic tendencies. He was always up for knockabout discussion and people speaking their minds, and well used to being challenged by his sisters, storekeepers, the law, indeed by all who crossed his path. But where I find it easy to challenge someone over an abstract philosophical, cultural or political matter, I'm a coward when it comes to the emotional and personal, even (perhaps more so) when I think I have right on my side. I had grown up tiptoeing around my father, of whom I had been afraid, and had adopted an anything-for-a-quiet-life approach to emotional disagreement, always taking the less bumpy way around an argument. But I now found myself in the role of knight errant, and I had sworn an oath to Mary to go into battle on her behalf. We were a thousand miles from Edith, in a flat plain of nothing, with a Joe contained. It had to be now.

As we passed a lonely church we saw a black clump of mourners gathered in a graveyard and I used this to segue into telling them about my father's funeral, how he wanted to be cremated rather than buried, and how I had been given the task of scattering his ashes because my mother had the shakes and was worried about the wind blowing his remains back over us. I told them how I had not been close to my father and how little sadness I had felt at his passing. From there I said that having a father around wasn't necessarily a benefit in life and that my life might have been easier (although technically not possible) without him. I asked Joe if he felt the same and he said he did and then I came out with it.

'Joe, can I ask you something?'

'Anything, Rip.'

'This sounds strange, but I look at Mary and I look at you and Isabelle, and I find it hard to believe you're related, one hundred per cent.'

The noise Joe made was the same noise he made when he had first told me about his father: a groaning hum, like a dying animal. It contained genuine sadness and weariness, I think, but when he spoke there was just the tiniest hint of anger this time, and anger – you must believe me – was a very rare emotion for Joe.

'Oh nooooowaah. Mary? You been blabbing on that old nonsense. Come on. Come on! Goddamn. You can't just say such things to people. That's not fair. It's not fair. It's settled.'

'Not for me.'

'You can't just say things like that.'

'You say all kinds of things, Joe. About your past. To get the sale.'

'That's different. That's business; that's causing no harm to nobody.'

I said, 'To be fair to Mary, Joe, it was me who raised the subject. I said I couldn't believe Mary and Iz were sisters on account of them being so sun and moon; I kept pushing it from there, until she told me what your mother said about having a fling.'

'Ma never said no such. Mary's been putting speculations in your ear, Rip. Pure speculations.'

'That's a damn lie and you know it, Joseph Bosco!' Mary

crossed her arms as if to stop herself lashing out at him. 'She said it and she meant it!'

'It's non-sense. Non. Sense. Shame on you, Mary. You can push that line all you like but it won't make it true. Shame on you.'

'Shame on you for being her flunkey.'

'I ain't no flunkey.'

'You been toeing the line all these years. Letting Ma have her way.'

'Come on, Rip. See what you done? You been stirring up a rebellion here.'

'Well, your mother can be a bit of a tyrant, Joe. I know she's worked hard; I know she is a woman scorned and wronged; I know she suffered – but maybe she's not completely straight about the past.'

'That's 'cos she is hiding something,' Mary said.

'Ma is not the enemy in this story. Let me make that clear. And that there is just a rumour. An ugly rumour.'

'A rumour Ma started herself! When she was drunk.'

'Aw . . . this is . . . I can't believe. That's . . . Well, I am shocked and surprised . . . disappointed, Rip. Really. That an educated, sensitive person like you would fall for that. It just ain't true. It just ain't. We shouldn't talk about this no more because it'll bring trouble. That's the end of it.'

'He's such a dick,' Mary said, turning to me and talking as though he wasn't there. 'He won't face up to it. He talks about good theology and bad theology. But it's bad theology not wanting to know the truth.'

'You don't know. You don't know, Mary.'

'You don't think it's possible, Joe? From what you've told me about your father being away and even your mother telling me how unhappy they were and . . .'

'Stop! Maybe this, maybe that. We ain't talking about that! I ain't talking about that . . . la la la . . . dee dee dee.'

Joe started to make his distracting dee-dee-dees and we

listened to his fake cheer, refusing to talk. He made a great pretence of it not being an issue, but I could see that he was ruffled. After a few miles more Joe asked me some total non sequitur of a question about Europe which I ignored. I had – for now – picked my side. I was with Mary on this one. It was the first time there was any real antagonism between me and Joe.

'Well, looky here,' Joe said.

'No, Joe!' Mary could see it.

'Why not?'

'Don't.'

'Let's do it!'

'No, Joe!' Mary put a hand out to the wheel. 'We ain't got the room, and we need to talk about this!'

'Yes we do got the room! You got the room back there, Rip?'

The subject of this dispute was sat on the roadside up ahead. I had no objection to picking up hitchers – it was part of the whatifness of the Road – but I couldn't help feeling this was more Cat-in-the-Hattery; that Joe was creating the next distraction in order to evade any further discussion about Edith. With a stranger in the car it would be difficult for us to probe private matters.

'Sure,' I said, annoyed at being thwarted once again. Joe wasn't waiting for anyone's opinion because he'd already slowed down and was preparing to pull over just ahead of the hitcher.

'He could be an asshole,' Mary said.

'He could be an angel though. "Don't forget to entertain strangers, for some people have entertained angels without knowing." Plus, he might give us gas money.'

'He looks like an asshole.'

The angel/asshole was sat on an upturned plastic red Coke case with his hitching-hand out and thumb barely to the vertical. He looked like he'd been trying for some time and lost hope of ever getting a ride. He was either very cool or he didn't realize we had pulled over for him because he stayed sat down smoking. When Joe tooted the horn the hitcher stood up and took a final drag of his cigarette before stubbing it out, then he hiked his bag over his shoulder and sauntered towards us. He wasn't going to rush for anyone.

'This guy could change our life. You just don't know. Think of the infinite perculations!'

I pulled Jimmy Carter into the middle of the back seat that was now free of the extra cases.

The hitcher held up his bag and pointed to the trunk.

Joe leant across Mary. 'Jump in, friend! We got a trunk full so you'll need to keep your sack on your knees.'

The hitcher jumped in and sunk into the seat across from me. He brought with him a whiff of perfume and tobacco.

'Thanks. Woah. Is that a bird?'

'This is Jimmy Carter,' I said. 'He's a bald eagle.'

'Is that legal?'

'Oh, he's a legal eagle,' Joe said. 'I'm Joe. This is my sister Mary.'

'Half-sister,' Mary said.

'And that's Rip. He's from Wales.'

'Mark.'

I shook the hitcher's hand, clammy from waiting in the heat of the day. Mark nodded at Mary, who refused to say hello to him. He was an asshole until proven otherwise. He didn't look like an asshole to me. He was a handsome man of around twenty-eight or twenty-nine, worldly and very cool, and I was immediately on my guard, sensing competition. I was no longer the most exotic one in the car.

'You been waiting long, Mark?'

'You were the sixty-fourth car.'

'Well, there are no accidents in the universe. Rip here's the superstitious one. He'll find some significance in that number sixty-four. Where you headed, Mark?'

'Rapid City. Then on to LA – eventually.'

'Where you travelling from?'

'New York.'

'No way! We're from New York too. State, that is. Up in the Catskills.'

'Hippies and hillbillies, right?'

'Right. But which category you putting us in?' Joe asked with his least intelligent sounding hillbilly inflection, doing his 'dumb and proud' act. I think he was still angry at me and Mary and trying to get back at us in some way. The hitcher looked at Joe and then at me and then his gaze rested on Mary – way too long for my liking. He was trying to fit us to some stereotyped line-up in his mind. 'The car says hillbilly. But no hillbilly travels this far from home. I'm leaning toward hippy.' In truth he must have been in a state of confusion about who he'd got into the car with.

'How about you guys? Where you headed?' he asked, not sounding like he cared much. He had that air some people have – an air that says 'my life is way more interesting than yours and I am quite content with it and unthreatened by anything you might be doing or have done but will ask anyway'.

'Wyoming.'

'Business or pleasure?'

'I don't compartmentilate those things, Mark.' (Although Joe genuinely muddled words I think he sometimes did it deliberately to get people to underestimate him.) 'Our business is always a pleasure for as long as it allows us to roam free. I mean, it's only work if you wanna be doing something else.'

Mark deigned a little smile. 'That's the truth. And what's your business?'

None of your business, is what I wanted to say. How possessive of my experience I had become. I didn't want someone from the outside world to come in and break the spell.

'Rip'll show ya.'

Reluctantly, I lifted the sample case and opened it on my lap. For some reason – maybe it was the whiff of sophistication I was getting from Mark – I felt embarrassed about showing him the butterflies because, when I stopped to think about it, it was odd to be selling bugs for a living and I could tell that whatever Mark did it would be a cooler way of getting by. I handed him a case with a malachite.

'Wow,' Mark said, although it was more of a 'I thought it would be something cooler' wow than a really impressed 'wow' wow.

'Is this what you do for real?'

'For real,' Joe said, hearing no criticism or superiority in the question. 'It's like a currency. We sell butterflies and we keep moving. Experiencing the joys and wonders of this life.'

'Interesting equation. I got a real thirst on out there. I could get behind a beer.'

I had not had a beer, or any alcohol, since meeting Joe. I'd been happy without it but now, all of a sudden, I wanted one as though it was a thing I'd craved all along. There was a gun in the glove box but no beer.

'This is a dry vehicle, Mark, but there's a warm Coke there.'

'What kind of country prohibits beer in a vehicle but not a gun?' I asked, trying to be clever and impress our passenger.

'One that wants to shoot straight?' Mark said, quick on the draw.

Joe laughed, a little too enthusiastically for my liking. Rubbing it in, he said, 'Now that's a sharpness we could use, Rip.'

I handed the two-litre bottle to Mark who guzzled down a quarter of it, without shame. I noticed him eyeing Mary as he glugged. He looked at her in an obviously lustful way and I felt outraged at how little he did to disguise it. One's own hypocrisy is hardest to see – Jesus and Joe were right about that – but I was jealous, not for Mary's sake but for my own. Mark was cool in a way I coveted. He had an economy of movement and words; it was as though he'd studied Westerns or something, learned all his manners from movies. He didn't instigate much talk but it wasn't from shyness; I think it was calculated to make us do the running. Annoyingly, Joe made it easier for him by being his infuriatingly un-judgemental self. In fact, he was being way too nice to a guy who to my mind had an arrogant superiority and an entitlement to this ride that he certainly hadn't earned yet, considering he had just met us and was beholden to us for said ride.

'Mind if I smoke?'

'Go right ahead.'

Since we'd left the Catskills I'd tried not to smoke that much around Joe. It's not that he would have told me not to, but more that his natural vitality took away the inclination. When I was alone with Mary the desire returned and when Mark started lighting up and smoking a spliff out the window I was drawn into that world again. I don't mean the world of smoking, I just mean everything that goes with it: some degree of intelligent subversion, a cultural edginess, anti-establishment feeling that equates to the illusion of freedom.

'So what's in Rapid City for you, Mark?'

'My friend's got a small part in a movie. They're shooting it around there.'

'No way!'

That had us all sitting up. Even Mary adjusted her slump. In the pecking order of seductive things – unaccountable freedom, sexual gratification, drugs, money and panoramic landscapes – involvement, any kind of involvement, in a movie ranked highly; to even be able to say to someone, 'I know someone in the movie business,' bestowed superpowers beyond what wealth and education could buy. There I was thinking my life was the most interesting life currently being lived in America and then he gets in our car. Damn him! But it was about to get worse.

'So what's the movie?'

'It's a Western. It's about this cavalry officer who goes native.'

'Oh my God! That's awesome!' Joe went on, mindlessly. He was doing it deliberately, I was sure, but he was at his worst – his most try-hard and embarrassing – when around cool, sophisticated people. I wanted to disown him completely.

'So what line of work are you in, Mark?'

'I'm a writer.'

It was like a punch to the solar plexus. Of all the people we could have picked up in that flat nothingness we had to pick up a writer.

Joe was giggling like a kid. Oh, he was tickled pink at this. 'This is great! Only in America. So now we got two writers in this car! Think it's big enough for the both of ya? Rip here wants to be a writer.'

'I'm a dabbler,' I said, before Joe announced me as Nobel Prize-winner or something.

Mark didn't blink. He didn't even look at me. My self-deprecation was at least meant to lure him into asking me what kind of writing I dabbled in. But no, that was beneath him. The arrogant fuck. The way he said 'I'm a writer' in such a non-chalant and matter-of-fact way; I wanted to kill him.

'Say, what kind of car is this?'

'It's a Chuick, sired out of a Chevrolet and a Buick.'

'It's neat.'

Well great, no one was asking for your opinion, I thought. I had transferred my anger at Joe to this guy. But God how I wanted to know what kind of writer he was and I had to swallow a lump of pride fit to choke a horse to ask him.

'What kind of writer are you?'

'Right now, a broke one.'

Oh God, a self-deprecating writer.

'I'm a script writer. Mainly. And I got a novel going.'

Right. Neither have I.

'Like movies?' Joe jumped in.

'Like movies.'

'That's awesome. I got so many ideas for movies. Like you wouldn't believe. So many stories. So many. Rip here's going to write a book about me and our travels. Maybe you should write the movie.'

'Why not?'

'So how comes you're hitching? A big Hollywood hotshot

like you? You should be flying to LA. Or behind the wheel of a Corvette.'

'I like to see the land I'm travelling through. You get a feel for something better. Plus, you meet people and people are stories. I get most of my ideas from just hanging with people. Listening. Hitching is great for that. Every ride's a story.'

'Well, you picked the right car for that,' Joe said. 'I got stories you would not believe.'

Don't do it, Joe. Those stories are yours – and mine. Don't give him your pearls. Don't just piss away the magic on this stranger. We barely know the guy. He says he's a writer but you don't know that. And writers are thieves. He might steal your story, claim it as his own, use your life – and mine – and ruin us. It's my story!

Too late. Joe gave himself to this stranger, body and soul, lubricating everything with his overstatements and fancy flights of fantasy. He started with the full-fat version of the family history, throwing in some other details I had never heard before; he told him about his father's collection of aberrations, and the five-winged blue morphos, and how we were heading to Wyoming with 'a million-dollar butterfly' to meet a man called the Wizard. I have to commend Joe for the energy and the drama he put into the telling. He was virtually projecting the pictures on the road ahead. It was as if we were driving into this movie he was describing. The scriptwriter listened intently, occasionally smiling, sometimes interjecting to clarify a point. But mainly he just listened. He wasn't physically writing anything down but you just knew he was scribbling away furiously in his mind, the way true writers probably did, and that he was already formulating the plot for a movie that he would pitch in LA that I would one day, in the not too distant future, see a poster for in the foyer of a cinema back home: *The Million-Dollar Butterfly*.

Joe ended his story – a story in which I featured merely as the English Assistant – with the bold claim that if he sold the collection to the Wizard he would make the movie himself and pay Mark to write the script. It was hard not to conclude that Joe, as punishment for my betrayal in questioning his own story earlier, was getting me back with this reckless, giddy giving away of his life story. I had been usurped as his chief chronicler!

'What do you think, Mark? Think it'll make a movie?'

Mark stayed silent for a while. I could tell he was captivated by Joe's energy and crazy dazzle – as I had been – and that he, like me, wanted some part of it. But he was acting like the prospector for gold who pretends he hasn't seen the nugget in the river bed.

'It's got something.'

'Really?'

'Really.'

'The story has to have a happy ending, Mark. Life's a comedy. Even though it threatens all the time to be a tragedy, it winds up a comedy. That's the gospel truth. The trouble is, people stop at the tragic part. It's almost easier to take. People say happy endings are for fools and crazies. Well I'm with the fools and the crazies – and the kids. I have more where that came from. That's just a brief outline there.'

Mark wanted to know more, particularly about the rare butterflies, and the collector we were going to meet. He also wanted to know about Joe's father. If he was still alive. Joe furnished his new best friend and chronicler with all kind of details (details I had been trying to extract myself). My usurpation was completed with Joe's inviting the scriptwriter to join us in our onward journey to meet the Wizard – and even to come stay in the Catskills when he was done, meet the family, interview his Ma, meet Isabelle. Everything I thought was mine was being offered to this total stranger who then rubbed salt (he must have known) into my wound by asking if I had some quarters so he could make some calls to reschedule things and travel on with us. After that Mark was practically casting the movie of Joe's life, the movie Mark was going to write.

When we stopped for gas I announced our need for help

with it but the hitcher, no doubt drawing on the unspoken right of the writer to pay for nothing, kept his money in his jeans. He said he was waiting on the green light for them to start shooting his script, any minute now. Joe, who was well used to spending the collateral of nothing, was more than sympathetic to this and told him not to worry. He could pay him back when they made the movie! Mark went to break my five dollars into quarters, Joe starting waxing mystical on our good fortune in meeting Mark.

'You see, Rip. There is a law in the universe that says you keep your eyes open and you will meet who you should meet.'

'He's an asshole,' Mary repeated. 'And I'm going to tell him some truths.'

'Mary, with respect. You and the truth are not great buddies.'

'I don't like him,' I said. 'I don't trust him. He says he's a writer but what's he written? And why did you tell him all that stuff – about your father? And the five-winged blue morphos. A complete stranger? You gave him your pearls, Joe.'

'Aw, Rip. Come on! There's enough to go around. You were a stranger not so long ago.'

As Joe talked to the attendant I went to buy some cigarettes, in a petulant funk. Mark was having a cigarette out the back, looking out across a grassy, flat nothing. I went and asked him for a cigarette and we stood side by side, writer and manqué writer.

'He's not for real, right?' he asked. 'The million-dollar butterflies? It's hot air, yes?'

'Oh. It's all bullshit with Joe.'

'It's unique bullshit though. And the butterflies are poetic. But the million-dollar butterfly. I could use that.'

'Use?

'It's a great title. I just need a pitch to go with it. Is he being serious about that part? He really has a bug that valuable?'

'Joe makes a lot of claims he can't substantiate.'

'That's clear. But I'd like to bottle some of that wild energy. And the girl should do a screen test.'

'Screen test?'

'Screen test. That bone structure. The colouring. The whole . . . aura she gives off. She really his sister?'

'So he says.'

'Crazy scene. Selling bugs for a living. Makes for a good story though.'

I watched him saunter off. I was envious, of course. But my aggravation was also born of a possessiveness, an appropriate jealousy for Joe and his story. I had come to feel that these people, and my adventures – going to see a man called the Wizard, 'million-dollar butterflies', rags to riches, crazy beautiful sisters, terrifying mother, genius crazy father, maybe another father – were all mine. So you can see how I might feel bad about someone coming and 'taking' them, saying 'I can use' them. Unlike Joe, who was profligate and generous with himself and his life, I didn't want to share the story with others and it wasn't until he started telling this guy these things that I realized just how much I felt that sense of ownership, that they were my stories to write about, not someone else's. I didn't want someone coming along and taking them, telling them and selling them; I wanted to be the teller and I would do – if not quite anything – quite a bit to keep it that way.

While Mark was making his call I walked back to the car, striding purposefully. Mary was at the wheel and Joe was in the back. He'd fetched his attaché case from the trunk in order to show Mark the freaks. I got in the car, calm and said, 'Drive!'

Mary looked at me quizzically.

'I'll explain. Trust me on this. Drive!'

She fired up Chuick.

'What are you doing?' Joe asked, looking to see where Mark was.

'Trust me, Joe. You don't want that guy in the car. I'll explain. Let's go!'

Mary floored it. Chuick screeching off the forecourt and onto the road. I didn't even look back.

'What's going on, Rip?'

When we were about a mile from the gas station, I told them. I told them that whilst having a cigarette with Mark, I noticed that he had a small tattoo on the inside of his arm, a serial number. And when I asked him what it was he said he'd done time, and when I asked him what for, he'd said armed robbery, and that when I asked him if he really was a scriptwriter, he'd said he wasn't but he felt he had to earn his keep, to sing for his supper as it were, so he invented a different person for each ride, to fit with what might best impress the drivers, that when we picked him up he'd decided to be a Hollywood scriptwriter, and when I gave him the money for the phone calls he said it wasn't to LA or anyone in Hollywood, but to his parole officer in Detroit. The guy just got out of prison for armed robbery.

I stopped then, for fear of overreaching myself (if you're going to lie, lie hard but not too long).

'Goddamn.' Joe was properly flummoxed.

'That's why he was interested in the five-winged blue morpho, Joe!'

'Goddamn!'

'He probably intended to call his partner or someone, and steal it. After you'd blabbed about it.'

'I read him wrong, Rip. I totally read him wrong.'

As Joe pictured the implications of my outrageous fib, he shook his head, still properly mystified, but relieved.

'Wow, Rip. You did good.'

'Sometimes it pays to be a bit cynicalistic about people, Joe.'

And then, over the noise of the wind, Mary yelled back at her brother.

'I told you he was an asshole!'

I think we were all equally irritated with one another after that. Joe at me for siding with Mary. Mary at Joe for disbelieving her in front of me. Me with Joe for flirting with the writer and me with myself for doing such a shitty thing to someone who, if I had met under any other circumstance, I would have liked, made friends and gone on to make movies with, maybe even a movie called *The Million-Dollar Butterfly*.

Silence reigned for about a hundred miles. Even Jimmy Carter was quiet. Too quiet, it turned out.

'Jimmy ain't moving,' Mary said. 'We should never had brought him.'

Jimmy Carter died, somewhere on 10.

Joe looked at the limp bird and lifted him from the box. 'Poor Jimmy. He's deader than a pound of roadside stew.'

We buried Jimmy Carter on the side of the road where Joe said a few words.

'We commend Jimmy Carter to you, Lord. Forgive us for not being more careful. I'm sorry we didn't get to set him flyin' free in the Tetons. Rest in peace, little bird.'

If you wanted an ill omen, there it was. Hindsight is useless (I know this now!) and hindsight about a piece of foresight is particularly worthless. But I had a piece of foresight during the ceremony, a vision that I was heading towards trouble; a formless trouble on that bright, lying horizon.

CHAPTER FIFTEEN

In which we meet the Wizard and everything changes.

We had been driving for hours through the summer-yellowed grass of Wyoming, towards the Grand Tetons where Joe had hoped to set Jimmy Carter free. Poetic descriptions of scenery won't change the facts of what was to come and have little bearing on the essential events of my story, so I'll not go on about those mountains too much. I wouldn't want to put you off seeing them. There's nothing more irritating than someone describing something wonderful they have seen that you haven't and then insisting you see it because 'you haven't lived until you do'. It's hard not to hear the implicit brag in that urging: my life has been more interesting than yours. Panoramas may stop hearts of men but they rarely change them. That said, if you haven't seen the Grand Tetons, try. They are something to behold. The best mountains are always the ones that start from a low base, like a flat plain, and these seemed to do just that, rising seven thousand feet straight from the plateau. There are higher mountains in this world but not many as sudden as those great, jagged teeth that appear as the first serious obstacle on your journey westward across the American flats. Poor Jimmy Carter would have loved whirling and careening in the air here. In the excitement of Jimmy's death, ditching the hitcher, Mary's theories about her paternity, and my annoyance towards Joe for refusing to discuss the subject, I had almost forgotten that, for Joe, the real purposes of this trip was to go see a man called the Wizard about selling the collection. It all seemed so far-fetched. Even for Joe. But then he suddenly stopped to make a call. 'They told me to call once we got to Wyoming.' He was given instructions as to how to find the house by Roth's private secretary. She told Joe the Wizard's real name: Truman Roth III, and said Truman was looking forward to meeting us and seeing the five-winged morphos. She told us that the entrance to the property was halfway between Dubois and the Continental Divide, just off Highway 26. We were to look for a small Exxon gas station and count five miles west from there until we saw a gate and a cattle grid and a sign saying 'Hexapoda'. When we found the gas station, Joe started to sing like a crazy man.

'Who wants to meet a trillionaire? I do!

Who wants to sell bugs everywhere? I do!'

My hair was almost solid from the dust that had filled the car on account of having the windows down, Joe's shirt had a cruciform sweat stain on the back, and I could smell Mary's spice in the mix; add to that the lingering smells of Jimmy Carter and we were a reeking bunch.

'You think we should smarten up a bit, Joe? They may not let us in, dressed like tramps.'

'Truman Roth III ain't going to be interested in our apparel, Rip! He probably sees the best dressed, the best educated, and smartest people day in day out; I doubt he gives a flying fish about any of that. We should be ourselves. Authenticulacy is what counts. And it's not what we're wearing. It's what we're carrying. We could be arriving in a twenty-car presidential cavalcade of shiny black limousines, dressed in cashmere suits and silk pants, speaking Latin and still not be allowed in to see him. There is only one thing that gets us through the gates of this particular heaven, and it's four inches tall and six inches wide, a heavenly blue with something not even the Angel Gabriel has. That's what allows us to enter the throne room of this trillionaire and speak as equals. That's the thing that makes us righteous in his eyes, Rip!'

Initial security at the gates of this particular heaven wasn't as stringent as you'd expect. It consisted of the cattle grid, a single-bar gate and a sentry box with a bored Hispanic guard, shelling peanuts, sitting in the shade of the little shelter. A three-foot-high cow fence ran off in either direction – Canada one end,

Mexico the other. The name of the house was crudely painted on a piece of junkyard wood with an arrow pointing onwards: 'Hexapoda'.

This had Joe chuckling.

As we pulled up to the grid Mary said what I was thinking:

'Don't look like the gates of no trillionaire to me.'

'You think he wants everyone to know where he lives by building some fancy gates and a wall?'

Joe had to open the door to speak to the guard, once more cursing the broken window and promising to get it fixed.

'We have an appointment to see Mr Roth. My name is Joseph Bosco. These are Mary Bosco and Rip Van Jones.'

Saint Peter didn't look like he was expecting us. Our names weren't on any list.

'Wait here, señor.' The guard stepped away and started to speak into his walkie-talkie. We could hear the squawk of the receiver but not what he said. He spoke fast and in Spanish.

'If this guy's so wealthy how comes he lives like a cowboy?'

'I don't know, Mary. Maybe he likes horses. You think he has one home? He's got homes all over.'

The guard kept giving us sideways glances. His conversation was going on a little too long for my liking and Mary's patience.

'He's got no idea who we are, Joe. This is bullshit. We drove all this way for diddly squat.'

The doubtful guard was gesticulating at Chuick, no doubt thrown at having to admit such a shit heap.

'He's real pissed.'

Joe started humming 'who wants to be a trillionaire' again. It was hard not to agree with Mary, that this was as far as Joe's bullshit was going to get us; that we'd reached the end of the blagger's road. Then, just like that, there was a transformation in the guard. He stopped talking mid-sentence with his mouth open and his eyes widening and he started to nod his head slowly and look back over at us. *Oh, OK.* He came back a new man, all smiles.

'Go right ahead, Mr Bosco. Go straight up the track. After fifteen miles you'll come to a second set of gates. You'll have to clear security there. They'll take you to the complex. Buenos dias.'

'Muchas gracias!'

Joe saluted the guard and we juddered over the cattle grid and into the Wizard's land. We were not in Kansas and the road wasn't brick, but the bleached stubble and sandy dust bisecting grassland, with cattle one side and horses the other, was almost yellow. The road ran in a straight line toward the mountains. Behind us, Chuick left a delta of dust that consumed our past.

'O ye of little faith!' Joe said.

'Yeah, we'll see,' Mary said.

'You know that they say if your drive is a mile long you're a millionaire,' Joe said.

'They?'

'People. The people who say things. It's true. And if your drive is ten miles long you're a billionaire.'

'Or a cowboy.'

'So if it's nearly twenty miles long you gotta believe he could be doing pretty good for himself. A double billionaire. Which gotta be a trillionaire.'

'He probably ain't even a millionaire.'

'Mary, your cynicalistic ways continue to blind you to the potential joys and wonders of this world.'

Even accounting for the 'math of Joe', Roth would at least have to be a millionaire. The fact the guard called Roth's house 'a complex' was promising, as was the twenty-mile drive to get there; but I still didn't believe we were going to meet a man described by Joe as one of the world's richest men, the owner of the single largest private collection of butterflies on earth.

'Look!'

Joe was pointing ahead, to the mountain where, halfway up, we could see the straight, hard lines of a building growing out of the rock. It created the strange effect of looking as though the mountain had been landscaped to fit the property rather than the other way round. The house – we were about to learn – had been built into a rocky outcrop of the Tetons in homage to the ancestral pueblos of the Navajo at Canyon de Chelly in Arizona. From below it did not look that big but that was because it was nearly all facade. Its most visible feature was the huge jutting balcony. The real house must have been within the mountain.

'It takes some dough to put a house there.'

The road started to camber down into a gully which formed a natural funnel to the next entrance. Here we were left in no doubt that we were on the property of a very wealthy person indeed. The gates were wrought iron and the fencing high and electric. There were two security guards with weapons hanging at their hips, standing either side of the gates, which opened automatically as we approached. We passed through the gates and a third guard directed us to a parking bay. Chuick must have been the most beat-up car ever to make it this far up this drive, but if the guard was bothered he wasn't showing it. He asked us all – 'Señora y señores' – to 'exit the vehicle' and said that a transport would take us to the house. Joe joked that he didn't have time to valet Chuick and the man said he'd have it cleaned and offered to jiffy lube it. We were searched and asked to step through a metal-detecting arch. Joe's attaché case was opened and a device like a Geiger counter run over it and then over us. We were then sprayed with a liquid before being led toward a shuttle bus. On the bus Joe pronounced loudly on the perils of wealth.

'Be glad you ain't so rich you have to search your guests, Rip. With great wealth comes great fear. Security guards. Electric fences. Insurance policies. Cameras and walls. The very thing you thought you were getting from money – freedom – gets lost. And then there's the separation. The distance between you and your neighbour increases. You end up with no friends. No community. And then you have all that guilt about the people you squished to get what you got. Because there's no success without squishing someone. No palace put up without a pauper put down.'

'I agree, Joe. Just don't say any of that to Mr Roth. Not if you want to sell him the collection for a decent amount.'

'I ain't being no sickiphant, Rip. I intend to be fully myself here.'

Joe continued to share his views on economic relations between employer and employee and the travails of great riches. Joe asked the driver a few questions – how long you worked here, have you met Mr Roth? Does he pay you a fair wage? – but he answered with an 'I'm just doing my job' shrug. Unlike Joe, he lived in a world where the keeping of livelihoods trumped the speaking of the mind.

It was a short ride to the 'front door', technically a lift taking us up to the house. As we ascended Joe allowed himself a little told-you-so smugness. The actual was beginning to outdo the imagined. Only an hour ago, at the first gate with the Mexican guard, I had braced myself for the underwhelming moment when this all turned out to be one of Joe's flying fat pigs. But even Mary was impressed as we rose up through the mountain.

'The guy's got to be doing OK for himself.'

When we stepped from the lift we found ourselves inside a very clean, very minimal entrance hall where a man in tie and tails stood waiting for us. He made a little bow and introduced himself as Foster. 'Welcome to Hexapoda. Mr Bosco. Ms Bosco. Mr Jones.' He knew our names and whose name went with whom and gave a little bow to each of us. 'If you want to freshen up after your journey I can show you to some guest restrooms. Then, when you are ready, Mr Roth will take lunch with you on the terrace.' Foster – who had a faint Scottish accent – had that egalitarian acceptance that the best staff have to have, that ability to treat any guest – however uncouth or dishevelled – like royalty.

The restrooms had views across the spine of the Tetons towards Jackson Lake, a view framed by a wall of glass. The drop from the window was around five hundred feet to the rocks and river below. I felt too filthy to touch anything so I washed my face and wet my hair and then combed it with the tortoiseshell comb supplied. There was a knock at my door and it was Mary, washed and hair up but defiantly still wearing her vest and cut-offs, and proudly announcing that she weren't dressing up for no man. She went to the window and looked out over the landscape. 'I ain't met a butterfly collector who ain't a nut job.'

'Credit to Joe though,' I said. 'For once, he wasn't exaggerating.'

'There'll be a catch. There's always a catch with Joe.'

I joined her at the window and kissed her on the neck. But she was too on edge to reciprocate. Since that night in the motel she'd been distant.

'You still mad at him?'

'The sonofabitch knows the truth. When you asked him, you could tell.'

Joe was calling our names and we joined him in the corridor. He'd gelled his hair and looked fresh. 'Let's keep it real and do this deal.'

Truman Roth was waiting for us at the top of the staircase on the upper level of the house. He was a spry man, probably in his seventies. He was wearing a navy sailor's peak cap, French blue blazer, slacks, espadrilles and darkened but not fully dark glasses. He looked like a character from a Jules Verne adventure, ready to set sail in some crazy transport that he had docked at the side of his mountain.

'Welcome to Hexapoda. How was your journey?'

'Swell, Mr Roth. We took in some sights. The greatness of this nation truly lies in its natural wonders.'

'I envy you that. To feel the country through the wheel. I must do that again. Note to self.'

'You should, Mr Roth. You should. No point in having all these riches and not being able to enjoy your life.'

Roth paused and looked almost pained. I thought Joe had

blown it already. But then Roth smiled. 'That is so true, Mr Bosco,' as though Joe had pronounced a wisdom he'd never heard before. 'And please, call me Truman.'

'Well OK, Truman. And feel free to call me Joe. This is my sister Mary-Anne. And this is my best friend and business partner Llew Jones although we call him Rip on account of all the sleeping he does. Rip is from the United Kingdom.'

'My apologies if the security was a little zealous.'

'No problem. You got a heap of things to protect, I'm sure.'

'It's not thieves I fear, Joe. No. It's carpet beetles, which, as I am sure you know, are the plague of the collector. They find a way. You know there's a plague of carpet beetles at the Natural History Museum in London right now? Which is why I house my collection underground, using the natural temperature, the lack of light, and the dryness. That said, it's a mystery how these got in. We think the French ambassador's wife had some in her luggage. It's all futile really. The insects will do for us in the end, Joe, I'm sure you know.'

'*Anrivenum sarnicus!*' Joe said. 'My sister Isabelle has nightmares about those critters. She's the one who looks after the collection.'

Roth's face came alive at the mention of the collection. 'Which I am very much looking forward to discussing with you. You have the aberrations?'

'The freaks are in the house, Truman!' Joe held up his attaché case. The sight of it seemed to throw Roth.

'Good. Good. Yes. Well. I can't wait. But lunch first. I am very fond of your country, Rip. Some of the finest lepidopterists come from Britain. Which part of the kingdom are you from?'

'Wales.'

'Ah. Now that is fascinating. You know the American painted lady?'

'No, I don't.'

'Ah. There's a great tale to tell. Pound for pound – or ounce for ounce I should say – the most epic traveller on earth. I'll show you later. But we must eat. You must be hungry.'

'We could all eat horses, Truman,' Joe said.

'Horse is available if you desire it.' We laughed. Roth smiled. But of course horse would have been available if we had desired it. 'We prefer to ride horses around here. Do you ride, Mary-Anne?'

'Never tried, Mr Roth.'

'Please, call me Truman.'

'I don't feel I know you well enough yet, sir.'

'Mary's got her own criteria, Truman.'

'Call me whatever's comfortable. You are here as my guests first, business second.'

'We're all God's children, Truman. I mean look at us. Nothing to separate us. 'Cept maybe a few billion dollars. Plus, you got better nails than us.'

Roth looked at his hands and smiled. I had noticed Roth's nails when I shook his hand, which was smooth and cool as cream; they were immaculate with perfect half-moons. As we followed him through to the balcony Mr Roth explained that the house had been built to be as one with the mountain.

'It was modelled after the temple of Queen Hatshepsut at Deir el-Bahari in Egypt. You enjoy art, Joe?'

'Truth be told, Truman, when I look at art I realize that it won't make a difference to my life no matter how long I stare at it. I still never seen a painting that could match nature, or colour that could compete with the radiance of a malachite. I like the way nature does it better.'

'Well, that is hard to refute. As I am allowed one true obsession, I have limited my art collecting to one work per century.'

Roth had something crucial from every era and culture, displayed in chronological order, and to walk from entrance to balcony was to pass through four millennia of artistic expression, at roughly a stride a century. A beaker from Susa. A ceremonial mask from the Belgian Congo. A bark drawing of Mimi spirits from Australia. Roth's favourite piece was a little pencil drawing by Rembrandt; a self-portrait of the artist as an old man.

'He looks lost, Truman,' Joe said, gurning at the old chap. 'Kind of like he's saying, "How did I end up here, in the glass cabinet of this trillionaire, in a country that was not even a glint in the founding fathers' eyes when I was alive?"'

Roth seemed to be coping well with Joe's singularity so far. He laughed quite heartily at this and my nerves that Joe was going to blow this deal by offending our host and buyer began to settle.

On one of the pedestals I saw a Greek plate carrying a depiction I recognized.

'Dionysus?'

'Yes!' Roth was delighted, as was Joe, who beamed at me, taking vicarious pride in having employed such a well-educated fellow. 'There are two opinions about what is happening in this scene. *Dionysus Sailing on the Sea.* Some think that Dionysus has just been captured by pirates and that he's turned them into dolphins. Others say the god of wine is on his way to his own festival. I prefer the former story myself. I like to think the better story is usually the true story. You like wine, Rip?'

I had almost forgotten what wine tasted like. 'Yes. Very much.'

'Well, I collect wine too but I don't count it as collecting. Come. Let's go up to the balcony, have a drink, take in the view. And talk about the most beautiful creatures on earth. I want to hear how you came to be the possessors of such treasures.'

We walked from the gallery out onto the platform – the feature we'd seen from the car – and took in the view. We could see the road we'd taken all the way back to the first gate, fifteen miles away, where it joined the highway which ran like silver lining to the horizon. Our destination was, literally, the end of the road. There were no houses or people visible, just land, stretching to a horizon which Joe joked Roth probably owned too.

Foster brought us cocktails. As far as I knew, Joe didn't drink. I don't know if it was nerves or a need to appease his host, but he took a Manhattan, slugged it back like a glass of milk, licked his lips and took a second from the tray, with Foster still standing there. 'That was delicious,' he said.

Roth seemed amused. I think he was prepared to forgive this hick anything as long as he got what he wanted.

Lunch I remember for many things: the view, which was vertiginous and not conducive to digestion; the fact that all of Roth's food came pureed ('A stomach condition. I cannot break food down'); Joe getting a little drunk which – despite having twice the surface area of a normal-sized man – happened quickly and had an endearing effect on his personality. His face became more plastic and rubbery. He and Roth certainly struck up a fine rapport that augured well for the sale but I did wonder if this drink was a tactic to soften us up so I took the cocktail slow.

Joe was, commendably, his 'authenticulate' self throughout the encounter. I always envied this ability to see everyone as flesh-and-blood beings of equal worth. And Joe proved during that lunch that his equalizing eye was not a pose. Not even a man with the means to change his life affected his flight pattern.

'Do you like being rich, Truman? 'Cos I been telling myself all these years that it ain't all it's cracked up to be. That money don't make you happy. You know, just in case I get none. I can see it had its up sides. But when our Lord said it's harder for a rich man to enter the kingdom he must have meant something by it. Is it the getting and the having the riches that keeps you out of the kingdom – all the squishing of the poor you have to do to get it – or is it the fact that you don't get into the kingdom 'cos you got all you think you need? It's not the riches that keeps the rich man out. It's the not wanting for anything else.'

For every person Joe offended upon first encounter (I'd put the proportion at around seven out of ten) there would be the one who understood him immediately, the person who was able to work out that there was more to him than the considerable amount that met the eye, and that his angle on life could prise open new realities. My hope was that Roth would be one of these.

'You think all this collecting stuff is filling a void, Truman?'

There was a bit of a pause. Roth looked quite serious and troubled again.

'Well, Joe! You have asked the very question that keeps me awake at night! When I was a child I used to collect anything. Stamps. Cheese labels. Mersenne primes, swizzle sticks. I keep the stubs of cheques and I have the entire set of 1986 Philadelphia Phillies player trading cards. Yes. I think it gives me a sense of control. There's a great thrill in having the ability to withdraw one member of a set and behold it singly. I'll collect anything although with the butterflies it is different. I have fallen out of love with stamps, cars, even art. But not butterflies.' Roth paused, as if aware he was making a confession. 'And of all the collectors, butterfly collectors are the worst kind; the most obsessive. There are people who will go out into the field and collect sought-after specimens and rub their wings to make them uncollectible for other collectors. It's a lethal affliction. There's always something you don't have. And I can't abide the thought that someone – even you, Joe – has something I don't. And then, when you get the thing you wanted, the joy of possession is soon lost to the sorrow of not having what you know still to be out there. There is always something I do not have. And it is the something I do not have – flying free in the world, or pinned in some dedicated collector's collection – that eats away. It is not the carpet beetles that keep me awake at night, Joe. It's the butterflies I don't possess!'

When he had finished his teeth were gritted and I sensed the initial warmth and tolerance had lifted off him for a moment.

'Which is, of course, why you are here.'

'Well, I confess that it's sweet knowing that I got something that a man of your taste and wealth don't, Truman.'

Roth was probably surrounded by people who dared never

make a joke, or challenge him on anything. And, like an emperor bored of obsequiousness, desperate for someone to answer back or disagree with him, he seemed to tolerate Joe's undisguised critical remarks. I think Joe could have told Roth that he was the ugliest, dullest little man he had ever met and Roth would still have put up with him. By the end of lunch Joe was giving Roth financial advice and offering him a way through the needle.

'I don't mind rich people, Truman. But I do not like it when they forget about the poor. I hope you give some of this wealth away.'

'Well, Joe. I do. But, let's be honest, my giving is all about tax efficiency. All done by my accountants.'

'Well, that's not a heart decision, is it?'

'No. But you are right. I have always consoled myself with the thought that my businesses employ thousands, which feeds tens of thousands; but perhaps that is not enough?'

'I'd say it ain't.'

'So what do you suggest, Joseph?'

'I work on a simple Jacob principle – of a tenth before taxes. That's just the bottom line.'

'And if I purchase your collection you will follow this law to the letter?'

'To the last Zee!'

After lunch Roth took us to see his collection, which was housed in the bowels of the mountain. At the entrance to the display galleries there was a sculpture of a caterpillar the size of a beer barrel and made from a single piece of amethyst. Roth paused for us to admire it.

'It's right we honour the caterpillar. The butterfly gets all the publicity but the caterpillar does all the work.'

'So true, Truman. I always say the caterpillar has to munch a lot of leaves to become the thing it dreams to be.'

The collection was set in a darkened gallery, like a bowling alley, with cases in simple glass desks, lit from within. Instead of sitting in hidden drawers, as they did back at the house or in a museum, everything was visible. It was divided according to the five faunistic regions, had all the major species and most of the minor. The room was one hundred metres long and had the luminous, subterranean brilliance of an aquarium.

'Most collections, by necessity, must be hidden out of sight. As a consequence, the butterflies people see in museums are not the interesting ones. They see the most colourful ones perhaps but they generally see the second-rate bugs and the crown jewels are kept locked away. I want to be able to see everything.'

Joe went from case to case, piecing the logic of the layout together, calling out the names of the wonders. His knowledge always surprised me and I think it impressed Roth.

'Lobster moth! Look at this, Rip. It mimics the bird dung and then mimics the larva and the ant that eats that! Not only does it mimic a leaf, but look, it mimics the grub-holes so as to put other insects off! We got three of these, Truman.' (Later Joe would tell me: 'Rip, he had everything you'd expect; but I weren't looking for what was there; I was looking for what weren't.')

'I can see you only got a pair of Queen A's here, Truman. Fine examples though, for sure. I'm looking for the zebra wings . . . no.'

I'm not sure if Joe was being ingenuous, doing this deliberately, or if he was just a little drunk, but it started to piss Roth off. By the time we'd reached the end his face was saturnine.

'Truman, this is wonderful. Truly wonderful. This is how butterflies should be displayed.'

'I think it's time you showed me what *you* have, Joe.'

Joe had brought the catalogue of the collection and he handed it to Roth. He explained how Isabelle had taught herself the art of mounting butterflies years back, and that to date they had cased up over two thousand specimens. Roth sat at the lightbox, admiring Isabelle's meticulous work and marvelling at the range, depth and rarity of the Bosco Collection. It could have been the florescence but Roth looked to be turning greener as he sat there.

'Four *hesperons*?'

'We got all the Big Four. Five times over.'

'*Vanessa virginiensis*. Large copper. Palos Verdes blue?'

'Yes, sir.'

'*Homerus*.'

'Six.'

'How have you preserved your collection?'

'Good old-fashioned mahogany drawers and moth balls.'

'The climate in the Catskills must be a disaster for that kind of preservation.'

'My sister's scruplous, sir.'

'Mmm.'

Roth's continued ability to see and accept Joe as an equal was being tested to the seams and they were beginning to tear. I could see his sense of entitlement and superiority returning, firstly around the mouth, where the humble smile had turned to a superior sneer, and then in the way he now addressed Joe. He could no longer disguise his suspicion toward the upstart country boy and the thinly veiled prejudice he had just beneath that. I could read his mind and it was saying: 'Where did this damn hick get these treasures?'

'Astonishing. There's no doubting the brilliance of the collection. I think it's time you explained how you came by it, Mr Bosco.'

Maybe using Joe's surname was a genuine mistake, but there was a big shift in the way Roth carried himself now and I'm not sure Joe noticed it. The way he said 'it's time you explained'! As though Joe had done something wrong by owning it; and the way it was 'Mr Bosco' now that we were drawing near to the business end of our visit. I began to feel a defensiveness for Joe rising up, as well as alarm that he might suddenly take exception to being talked down to like this.

'How did someone like you . . . come by such a thing? No offence.'

'None taken, Truman.'

In this version Joe had his father disappear in a gulch in Colombia. He described him as having a beard and long hair. Always wearing shorts and able to speak five languages. Joe cleverly made the five-winged morphos the central characters of his tale, knowing full well that it was these mythical critters that held the key to the deal. As Joe told Roth about his father, Roth started to hunch his back with the tension, his face grimacing. When Joe was done he could wait no longer.

'Let me see them.'

Joe lifted his 'big deal case' onto the light box. And Joe – again, I am not sure it was a ploy – was teasing things out. As he fiddled with the combination locks of his attaché case he seemed to forget the number.

'Now let's see . . . . Did I change it?'

He chuntered on whilst turning the dials through various combinations.

'Truman. You will not be disappointed. When you see them. They seem at first glance no different to their twenty-dollar cousins. And then you see it. The magical fifth wing.'

Roth's expression as Joe fiddled with the locks! You'd think that case contained life's elixir. His eyes grew, as if trying to X-ray through the fake lizard skin to the treasures within.

'I'm sure it was 3344 . . . Mary, did you change . . . ?'

And then the right lock clicked open. And then the left.

When Joe opened the case he (miraculously) had the sense to remain silent and let his precious butterflies speak. Roth looked in and stared for a minute before saying anything. His face was a mix of venal craving and innocent wonder; for a few seconds his privilege, his sense of entitlement, the jaded boredom of the impossible-to-impress super-rich evaporated. His reaction was not much more sophisticated than a child wanting the thing they didn't have in the shop window. Until that moment, Roth had everything he wanted in the world; he had it all ordered and categorized, had all his Ming ducks in a row. Here was something we had that he didn't and wanted. How quickly he reverted to being the man whose ancestors had 'squished' people to get what they wanted. The slow erosion of manners and kindness in Roth was fascinating to watch.

'How much for these and the entire collection?'

It was absurd – but perhaps a good thing! – that we had not discussed money in any serious way, other than a notional 'we'll get hundreds of thousands if we find the right collector'; and the precedent of having got $50,000 for a set of Big Four. Joe took in a large gulp of air and let it out through his nostrils. He stroked his chin, doing a terrible impersonation of a hard-nosed businessman. At first I thought, don't do this, Joe. Not with Roth. Don't haggle. He'd never had a more willing or wealthier purchaser. He wants the collection. He has the money. Just name your price. But Joe continued to stroke his beardless chin and then, worryingly, scratch the scars on his hands. Finally, he looked to me. As if to say, 'What do you think, Rip?'

'Well, I don't know, Truman,' he said. 'I had a number in my mind.'

'Name the number.'

'I can't. I can't remember what it was.'

'A bit like the combination locks,' Roth said. 'Give me a ballpark?'

Either this was a brilliant tactic or Edith was right: Joe was a terrible negotiator.

Roth was thinking that Joe had no idea and I was sure he thought he could take advantage of this God-loving country boy who'd be happy with anything more than a few thousand.

'I'll pay you $150,000 for the morphos and the collection, subject to verification.'

Joe was nodding. I could see he was on the verge of accepting this (in my view, derisory) offer.

'Well. That's an interesting number, Truman.'

'But not the number we discussed, Joe,' I said. And then I turned to Roth and decided to take over. 'I think it has to be a million dollars, Mr Roth,' I said. 'As we discussed, Joe. Yes? Back at the house. With Isabelle and your mother. One million dollars for the entire collection. The swallowtails alone are worth a hundred and fifty thousand.'

I stayed quiet then, not from cunning but from pure amazement that I'd said it. There are larger sums of money in this world, like two million dollars, but they don't have the same ring as a million dollars, and when it comes to deals it's the ring of it that matters. 'I made a million dollars today.' To be able to say that! Well, who gets to say that?

Roth said nothing. Although he was well past the point of being ruffled by the sound that a million dollars makes, he still had the bully genes of his ancestors coursing in his blood.

Joe was chewing his lip. Oh God. He seemed to be in a trance. I couldn't look at Mary but I could feel her interjection coming. Joe cleared his throat and I thought he was going to offer Roth a lower price!

'Your offer is very gen . . .'

'A million dollars for the entire collection,' I repeated. 'A collection that includes a butterfly that no one in the world has, Mr Roth.'

'For that I'd want all twenty-four five-wings.'

The lust of the incomplete allows for no mercy.

'All twenty-four? Joe? Do you think Isabelle would be happy to let all twenty-four go?'

Joe was speechless, which was helpful.

'Damn straight,' Mary said.

'We are on a promise not to sell all the five-wings.'

'Isabelle don't have the final say so on this,' Mary said.

'Who has the final say so?' Roth asked.

'We all do,' I said. 'It needs to be unanimous. And I say a million for everything.'

'Well?' Roth asked. 'Would a million dollars do it, Joe?'

A million dollars would do it. A million dollars should do it. A million dollars usually did do it, for most people in most situations: the ransom on the kidnapped daughter; the hitman for the assassination of a despot; the prize winner of the lottery. Yes, everyone has their price and a million dollars usually does it. And yet here was Joe – the same Joe who had been scrambling for years to make a hundred bucks here, seventy-seven there – on the cusp of making more money that he'd dreamed of (maybe the exact amount he'd dreamed of) and standing there like a giant mummy.

Roth turned to Foster who hovered so stealthily you didn't know he was there until Roth asked him to do something. 'Foster, would you go to my safe and bring one million dollars in cash?'

Foster left the room and reappeared five minutes later with the money on a silver platter. It was vulgar but sublimely effective. I had not seen a million dollars. It looked exactly the right size to me. Roth took a wad from a block of one hundred hundred-dollar bills.

'Smell it. Something my grandfather taught me: the best way to tell money is real.'

We each took turns in smelling the wad. One thick band of a hundred hundred-dollar bills. The money had a bummy smell, like varnished cheese. Roth handed the ten thousand to Joe.

'This is yours. A non-refundable deposit of ten thousand dollars. The rest you will get when my people verify the collection. We can tie up the deal in New York next month, on a date that is convenient. And I'll throw in a case of wine for you, Mr Jones.' His mouth was dry; you could hear it. Was he going to offer more? Probably not. He could see that it wasn't about the money. He'd guessed the million to be the summit no trailer trash could turn down no matter how talented and charismatic they were.

'I think that is a very good offer, Mr Roth,' I said.

'Damn straight,' Mary said.

And then Joe put his hand out. Steady and strong. And Roth put his mitt into Joe's and they shook on it.

'A million dollars for the entire collection,' Roth said.

'A million dollars for the entire collection.'

'Subject to verification.'

'Subject to verification.'

'Deal.'

'Deal.'

'Excellent.'

'Amen.'

— *Rip? Rip. Wake up!*

— *Joe?*

— *Wake up, Rip!*

— *Joe?*

— *Yes!*

— *You're alive?*

— *Of course I'm alive.*

— *What are you doing here?*

— *I've come to set you free. You ain't guilty, Rip. Your sins have been washed clean away.*

— *You really are alive, Joe?*

— *Sure. Feel.*

— *And . . . we're free?*

— *They couldn't pin any of it on you in the end.*

— *Where's Larson?*

— *He sent me in here. To bring you the good news. He thought I should be the one to tell you. You don't believe it?*

— *I don't know. I'm so tired.*

— *You need a little respair, Rip.*

— *Respair?*

— *Sure. That feeling of new hope you get after despair. You need fresh air, Rip. The Good Theology of cold water and sunshine. That'll wake you up. And then we start over.*

— *With what? We lost everything. You lost everything. In the fire.*

— *That's super-negative talking there. You never lose everything. If life shows you anything it's that it comes again. You ready? You got your things?*

— *I don't have much.*
— *Where we're going you don't need anything . . .*

❁

— *Mr Jones?*
— *Larson?*
— *It's me. Sorry to wake you.*
— *What time is it?*
— *It's ten. I brought you coffee. And the cinnamon buns you like. Plus I got the pens you asked for.*
— *Thanks.*
— *You OK? You were having a dream there.*
— *I . . . was. About my friend. Again.*
— *Butterfly Joe?*
— *Yeah. He told me he was alive. And that I was going to be set free.*
— *Let's hope that's one of those prophetic dreams. I sent the postcards to your mother. 'The green, green grass of Wyoming.' You seen more of this country than me. You OK? You been sleeping a lot.*
— *I didn't sleep well when I was a child. I'm making up for it. Plus this writing is tiring.*
— *How's it coming?*
— *Slowly. There's a lot to remember. Everything hinges on my ability to remember things correctly. Then I wonder if I am remembering a particular thing as it was or because I want to remember it that way. Then I'm afraid I'm muddling my memories and dreams. The dreams I'm having in this place – so vivid. Then I have this other thought that I'm not really awake. I mean, when Rip Van Winkle woke up after twenty years he must have had doubts that he was really awake. That it was just another dream. During the twenty years he was asleep he must have had dreams within the dream, including dreams where he thought he*

was waking up from a dream but was still in the dream. You think I'm going crazy, Larson?

— Maybe you should stay away from dreams, son.

— The sheriff said to write down everything that is relevant to the case. 'Down to the smallest detail.' The lawyer said to 'remember without prejudice'. Who can do that? Remembering and recalling things without prejudice is an impossibility. This idea that I can stand outside of myself and see me as someone else, without the knowledge of what was to come, is a fiction. A total fiction.

— Woah. Take a deep breath. You're overthinking this. From what I read, I'd say you are remembering plenty.

— It's enough detail?

— It's plenty. It's plenty.

— What then? You're looking at me.

— A couple of things are puzzling me. Guy like you, reading all these books, and spends a whole lotta time dipping inside people's heads figuring out what you're thinking and what they're thinking. How did you not see what was coming?

— It was hard to. If you were there, in the moment.

— But there was signs all around. You said it yourself.

— I only understood them when it was too late.

— Wise after the event.

— Not wise enough. Hindsight won't get me out of here, Larson.

— Well keep going. You may not have cases to sell but you still got a case to make.

— I like that.

— I'll give it to ya for free. You're writing a book there. I see you got chapters and everything.

— It helps me make sense of it. Order it. It's not quite the book I had in mind.

— What did you have in mind?

— It doesn't matter now.

— Try me.

— I had this notion I'd write an account of my travels in America, in verse, like The Odyssey.

— Can't say I know it.

— It's a tale of an epic journey made by a Greek hero. The hero is trying to get home and what should have taken a week takes ten years. Things happen.

— So, this hero. Does he make it?

— Yes.

— Well, I hope you make it home, son. And let's hope it don't take as long as the Greek.

— I could lose the best years of my life, Larson.

— Hey. Tears won't help. You got to hold your nerve. You got to hold your nerve and then you will remember things better. There's a lot riding on you doing that. You are your own witness. Right now you are the only witness. It's your story, and no one else can tell it. Remember that.

IV.

And so we made a killing
On the Road out West
Took dough from the Wizard
For a dead man's chest,
'Cept the man weren't dead
In the strictest sense
And the million ain't raised
Till the collector collects.

CHAPTER SIXTEEN

In which we head home feeling like millionaires.

Oh the whooping as we exited the Wizard's property in the valeted Chuick, now two shades of blue lighter and smelling of lemons. We'd tried to remain cool when Roth agreed to pay a million dollars for the entire collection, lest our celebrating show us to be happy hicks scraping by rather than experienced business people for whom million-dollar deals were two-a-penny, dime-a-dozen. Joe's parting line even made it sound as though Roth had got a bargain:

'Truman, you sure know how to do a deal. I guess that's why you're the trillionaire and I'm the hick.'

'I don't know what you are, Joe Bosco. But you are no hick. Of that I am certain. And your friend has a ruthless streak – watch him.'

Walking to the car we clenched our hands and held our arms straight down to keep our fists from pumping; the held-in hysteria forced little squealing noises from us like air trapped in a pipe. We just about managed to keep it together until we were through the main gates where we let rip with a pure hollering that was like the ecstatic praise of revivalists.

'Waaaah! Rip! When you asked him for a million I thought: "Oh my Lord, what are you doin'? He will surely throw us out the door." But he didn't blink. Not once.'

'But the way you hesitated, Joe. I thought you were doing that to make it look like it wasn't enough. As though you wanted more!'

'It weren't a strategy, Rip. I think I was drunk. Really couldn't think. And then I just couldn't believe what you said. A million!'

'He was patronizing you, Joe. He was waiting to see if you had the hick mentality. He thought he'd buy the collection for peanuts. These rich are tightwads. It's how they get to where they got. And I knew how much the collection was worth. Even Isabelle would have wanted more than $150,000. And he wanted them. He really, really wanted them.'

'Oh God he did. He wanted those little five-winged freaks more than any person wanted anything. Did you see his face?'

'Of course! I knew he would pay whatever we asked. And I thought, the more we ask for the more seriously he'll take us. It had to be a proper amount. A million is peanuts for a man like Roth.'

'It's horse feed!'

'It's chicken feed!'

'It's fish food!'

'It's small change.'

'It's diddly squat.'

'It's crumbs from the table.'

'It's nothin'!'

'It's dick!'

'It's a game-changer, Rip. It's a game-changer.'

'We made a killing, Joe.'

'We killed it, Rip!'

'A million dollars, Joe. A fucking million!'

The deal had exceeded my expectations – by about a million dollars. That is to say, I – like everyone else in Joe's family – hadn't taken the possibility of him selling the collection seriously. I don't think Joe himself really did, and nor did he know how much he wanted for it. In the heart of his own exaggerating heart I think he'd have taken Roth's opening offer.

While Joe and I were singing each other's praises, the voice of reason sounded from the back of the car.

'We ain't got the dough yet.'

'Come on, Mary!'

'You didn't sign diddly, Joe. He could change his mind.'

'A man like Roth don't change his mind.'

'Feels too easy,' she said. 'Maybe it's like a test. Maybe God's testing you. Showing you the riches. Then taking them away. That's what he usually does.'

Mary had a negative streak that wasn't a pose; it was a learned and inherited pessimism that pushed back her hopes whenever they started to rise.

'I don't know how much the Devil's paying you to be his advocate, sister. But God don't tempt you with riches and then snatch them away. That's the Devil's method.'

'I'm just trying to keep a lid on things, Joe. We had disappointments before.'

'Look, the worst that happens is we still have the rarest butterflies on earth,' Joe said. 'Plus, we had an adventure and got paid ten thousand dollars for it.'

'Right. You better give that to me, too. Before you throw it to a bum.'

It was just as well the Wizard didn't give Joe a larger deposit because he would have found a way to spend it before we made it back to the Catskills. Mary (our designated purser) took a thousand dollars from the stack and handed it to Joe saying, 'There's your God Money.' The first one hundred went to the Mexican guard on the outer gate. The guard's face – a mix of baffled gratitude and alarm – was a picture. He touched his chest in thanks, made a little sign of the cross, and thanked 'Jesuchristu'.

'Don't thank Jesus, señor,' Mary said. 'It ain't Jesus that gave you that money.'

'We're his hands and feet, Mary,' Joe corrected her. 'We're his body. And that's his money.'

'He ain't having my body and he ain't having my money.'

Joe's giving – as random and chaotic as everything else he did – could have been more effective but at least it was consistent: ten per cent before taxes.

'Are you hoping to get to heaven with all this giving, Joe?'

'Rip! No. Are you not learning here? You can't pay to get into

233

heaven. You can't raise your deeds to the level of infinity! That is dangerous thinking. Only the Lord can pay that currency.'

'OK, but how do you decide who to give the money to?'

'I don't overthink it, Rip. You overthink it, the money stays in the wallet. You gotta look out for the last, the least, the lost and the left over. Sometimes it ain't that the person is economically poor. Like that guard there. He's probably doing OK. But you see his reaction when we gave it to him? I'd pay a hundred dollars to see that reaction.'

'So the hundred thousand? Who will that go to?'

'I promised that to the orphanage in Albany. The one where we found Celeste.'

'You told them already – before the monies was confirmed?'

'I told them that if I ever pull off a big deal, they get the tithe.'

Joe gripped the wheel and sighed. He had tears in his eye and those tears started rolling down his cheeks. These weren't the drummed-up tears of a forced sentiment, or a swell of gratitude for the wonders of nature surrounding us in that God-thanking Wyoming landscape. They were the sweet tears of relief and disbelief. My guess is Joe was getting a glimpse of what that million might mean for him: an end to the hand-to-mouth, day-to-day existence, the contingencies of the road, and the burden of being the bread-and-butterfly winner – a burden he never complained of and carried with great humour and cheer, but that must have weighed him down. He let the tears roll and the snot drip and he hung his jaw in gormless disbelief, shaking his head and muttering 'provision, provision, provision' over and over.

'This deal is going to change things, Joe. Right?'

'Right.'

'What do you think it'll mean?'

He shook his head. 'A ton of stuff, Rip. A ton of stuff.'

Then a Tourette's of unedited possibility poured out of him, in no particular order, but all expressed with the equal enthusi-

234

asm and conviction that it would come to be. 'We buy and fix the house, we extend the butterfly farm, we open Butterfly World; we have a cafe where people can drink coffee and butterflies fly all around them; Isabelle goes to college; Mary gets a shot at NASCAR; we diversify into other areas, like making jellies from the indigenous fruits of Jamaica where they have fruits called custard apples, starfruit, tamarind and ortaniques – that's a cross between an orange and a tangerine; and when it's all up and running and taking care of itself you and me will travel the world! Think of the wonders that are out there as yet un-glimpsed upon by us.'

I don't think Joe really knew what the money would go to, despite this list. But the prospect of that million revealed his heart's desire: he didn't want to sell on the road anymore, he didn't even want to sell butterflies, or even be rich; he just wanted to be free. I thought of Edith, her face lit up with the surprise of this deal happening and me being its author! I thought, too, of Isabelle and what such a windfall would mean for her. College. And then Mary, quiet and thoughtful in the back seat. The deal would set them all free from and for different things. And I was their chief liberator.

'We should call Edith, Joe.'

'We should do that. Maybe you can tell her yourself.'

'No. It's your moment.'

Joe called his mother from somewhere in the middle of America in the middle of the night. I was surprised he'd waited so long, but maybe he wanted to enjoy his dreaming for as long as he could before hitting the hard wall of Edith's doubt. It was touching that he called her as much as he did. Edith still exercised considerable centrifugal force over him. As well as a natural resistance to the emptying nest, she must have also had a fear that Joe might, like his father, disappear altogether one day.

He made the call from a booth at the gas station. When he came back he looked disappointed.

'You tell her?'

'I told her.'

'She pleased?'

'She weren't.'

'Don't tell me: she'll believe it when she sees it?'

'You got it.'

'*She* should have more faith. Well, I am looking forward to seeing her face when Roth hands her that cash.'

'Take a picture of that, Rip. Ma being impressed by something I done. Now that'll be a sight as rare as a Palos Verdes blue.'

Joe chuckled but I could see that this time he was – despite being used to years of scant praise from her – disheartened, perhaps even a little angry at his mother's reaction.

'She should show you a little more appreciation, Joe. I mean I get the need to be realistic and that there have been disappointments in the past; I get all that, but she is a little harsh on you.'

Joe didn't reply, but nor did he disagree with me.

'I mean, did she ever pull off a million-dollar deal?'

'She nearly did once. With A and P. But she took exception to the guy staring at her face.'

'Well, I'm proud of you, Joe. Even if she isn't.'

We drove from Wyoming to the Catskills, a distance of two thousand miles, in not much more than thirty-six hours, stopping just four times for ablutions, gas, to swap drivers and to help some road workers. Joe gave the last of the God Money to an old woman at a gas station in Pennsylvania. His one other gratuitous act of kindness was stopping to help some navvies dig a ditch, after which he handed them all business cards and told them that 'a super huge' business opportunity awaited them working for 'America's most exciting theme park'. He drove most of the way and he would have driven all the way had Mary not made him let her take the wheel. When they swapped Joe took to the back, lay down and fell asleep in seconds. I waited for his snoring and then started to rub Mary's neck.

'You've been quiet. Ever since we did it. You've hardly said a word to me.'

'I got things on my mind.'

I told her that I couldn't wait to do it again and that when we got back we were going to flout house rules and do it whenever and wherever we could get away with it: in the closed garret of the house, in the library, in the back of Chuick, behind a tree in the lake for the benefit of the cranes and in the butterfly nursery, among hatching nets, with the kisses of blue morphos tickling our butts. Maybe even in Isabelle's bed in front of all those Russian novelists.

'If you want me you gotta back me up against Ma. 'Cos I'm gonna make her tell me the truth.'

The deal made me over-confident, cocky really. It gave me the idea I could achieve anything. And it was in the fertile soil of that cockiness that this idea of myself as the great liberator of this family – Joe from the demands of the road, Isabelle from the demands of her mother, Mary from the uncertainty of her paternity – all of them from the tyranny of Edith – began to grow.

'I'll back you, Mary.'

'Promise.'

'Promise.'

And there I was again: making promises about the future to get what I wanted in the present.

Somewhere between Des Moines and Joliet, I reached over and brought Mary to a climax whilst she gripped the wheel and her brother slept like a man who'd made a million.

❖   ❖   ❖

We arrived at the house around eight in the evening, Joe at the wheel, Mary flat out in the back, me drifting in and out of sleep, keeping a half-eyed vigil in case Joe made some unplanned detour. The house was silhouetted against a moonlit sky and with its crenellations, spikes and gables it was at its most castle-like. Sleepily I fancied us as heroes returning from a quest almost accomplished: the fleece found, the grail grasped.

Chuick's headlights picked out the four red slits of the dogs' eyes as we came up the drive. But apart from Nancy and Ronnie, no one else came to greet us. Not even Ceelee. I know the money wasn't in the bank but some sort of fanfare would have been nice. Tickertape's been thrown for less. At the end of a two-thousand-mile drive and a million-dollar deal we deserved a little more gratitude. Clay appeared, coming up the side track from his house. He chained the dogs and walked toward us, bending down to inspect the front of Chuick.

'Look at the bugs in this grille. How was the trip?'

Joe got out and gripped Clay by the shoulders.

'We are millionaires!'

'Huh?'

'Ma not say?'

'Miss Edith been busy.'

'We ain't sold them yet,' Mary said, mussing up her hair.

'We got complications, Joseph.'

'Complications or trouble?'

'I'd say complications leading to trouble. Them bailiffs came back. They demanded the rent. Six thousand bucks.'

'We got six thousand bucks, Clay. Pretty soon we'll have six hundred thousand bucks!'

'Well, Miss Edith will be relieved to hear it. We all been busy trying to get orders done. We got a huge order in from Cleveland. Five hunnerd cases.'

'Hey, Rip! That was the gift emporium you charmed. You see. A natural born salesman! Where is everyone?'

'Everyone's in the factory, working hard to get it done.'

I followed Joe up to the factory and watched him – a big shot entering a saloon.

'Stop your grinnin' and drop your linen!'

Ceelee ran from the table to Joe, leaping into his arms. Elijah was using the silicon gun. Isabelle was setting a butterfly on a twig. Only Edith didn't look up. She stayed sat on her throne, fixing stickers. I hoped, for Joe's sake, she might at least say, 'Well done,' but instead we got: 'No one's counting chickens here.'

Looking back with distance and hindsight and all those other wise-after-the-event luxuries that are unavailable at the time, Edith was right: we should not have counted any chickens until the chicken was standing right in front of us, wearing a suit and writing out a cheque for a million dollars. Of course, her unwillingness to acknowledge the deal was sensible, it was protection against disappointment; it showed a healthy scepticism towards a lifetime of Joe's over-claiming. When you've been around a loudmouth with a congenital hyperbolic condition for so long it must be hard to take when they deliver on what they've promised. But still her 'welcome' could have been a little more encouraging. And despite being used to his mother's stone-cold scepticism about pretty much everything he said, Joe looked a little woebegone; I got a glimpse of what Joe the boy looked like. His need for approval was as deep as mine, he just disguised it better.

'You should be excited, Edith,' I said. 'This man is the real deal.'

'I'll decide when I'm excited and no one ever "shoulds" me – ever. The deal means dick till the money's in the bank. Right now we got to find six thousand dollars for the rent or we are out of a home.'

'Ma, the deal's a forgotten conclusion,' Joe said. 'And we got the monies for the bailiffs.'

Joe produced the deposit and threw the dollars on the factory table, counting out the first few before tossing it all in front of her.

Edith looked at the new money, picked a single note and sniffed it.

'What do we know about this man?'

Isabelle had kept her head down when we'd entered, taking

a lot of time to fix a glass-wing to a twig; but whilst her fingers fiddled, her ears were burning. The sale of the collection was going to be hardest for her.

'How did he make his millions?'

'The usual way, Iz,' Joe said. 'Squishing the poor. But he had a teachable heart. Wouldn't you say, Rip?'

'Yes. Joe gave him plenty of guidance there.'

'You shouldn't go around saying it like you got it, is all,' Edith said. I don't want another Yo-Yo.'

Joe had failed to tell me about Yo-Yo. Yo-Yo, Isabelle later told me, was supposedly a collector from Japan who was interested in buying the entire collection. Joe had met him at the Annual Bug Fair in LA and after showing Yo-Yo the catalogue he'd offered a hundred thousand for it. He invited Joe to his house in Kyoto and bought him a plane ticket. But then cancelled without explanation.

'This isn't a Yo-Yo. This guy has real bona fides.'

Isabelle left the room; she'd heard enough.

'You think he has that kind of money?' Edith went on.

'Ma. He showed it to us. On a plate. It was unbelievable.'

'Right. It is unbelievable.'

'Roth's got the money,' I said. 'You should have seen his place, Edith.'

It was hard to describe Roth's place without sounding like an insane fantasist, but I gave it a go.

As I was describing it, Mary entered the room. She gave Ceelee a hug and then mumbled something about 'turning in early'.

'You ain't even got a hello for the mother that bore and raised you?'

The self-pity-in that question wasn't going to win Mary back. Not this new, emboldened iteration of Mary.

'We got a hundred cases to make by morning here.'

Mary muttered something that sounded like 'I ain't doing this no more' and made for the door.

Edith hollered. 'Hey! Get back here. You ain't doin' what no more?'

Mary paused, thought about ignoring her mother, then turned and half faced her. 'I ain't got time for this no more.'

'Time? Time for what?'

'For your . . . tyrannical bullshit.'

Of all the words Mary could have used she has to use my word! Edith was on it like a one-eyed hawk.

'Well, that's a fancy word for a girl who claims she don't read.' Edith looked at me rather than Mary when she said this. 'There's only one person in this house uses a word like that and maybe two who know what it means. And you ain't one of them.'

As it was, Edith was just like a tyrant in that moment, a tyrant whose subjects had returned from lands that enjoyed greater liberty than their own and who needed to re-establish the hierarchy.

As Mary walked off, Joe stepped in.

'Ma. Mary's fatigued. We just drove two thousand miles in two days to get here and we did the deal of our lives and you're hollering about nothing.'

'Nothing? I had two men threatening to take everything I own today. I ain't livin' off your maybes no more.'

Joe picked up some of the tossed dollars.

'This ain't a maybe, Ma.'

❖   ❖   ❖

For a few weeks, we lived in the tension between the possibility of a life-changing windfall and a 'nothing's changed yet' industriousness. For Edith, it was business as usual and the usual business was getting out that order of five hundred cases and a hundred-case order of yellow swallowtails (to match the colour of the bridesmaids' dresses) for a wedding in White Plains. Despite the million-dollar promise, she would not countenance talk of it. Joe, however, acted as though it were a done deal, and I was inclined to agree with him. I had been inside the Wizard's house and glimpsed his vault. I had seen the look in the collector's eye when Joe had shown him the sample case. And something of Joe's hope was starting to rub off on me. I had become less 'cynicalistic', more credulous, more expectant of good things. I had begun to think like an American and it was more fun than being my old, sceptical, no-can-do European self.

Joe decided to throw a 'Thanksgiving dinner' in lieu of 'the great harvest we were about to reap'. Like any rational person I was superstitious about celebrating something before it had transpired but Joe, of course, dismissed this as more Bad Theology on the grounds that God was outside time. When Edith pointed out that actual Thanksgiving was still two months away Joe said that those Pilgrim Fathers had got the calendar all wrong and that actual Thanksgiving was just another bogus concoction of man's making. He wanted to serve up 'a surf and turf cornucopia of American produce', including New York strip steaks and Maine lobster. He was going to get the ingredients from Poughkeepsie, where he knew someone at the Culinary Institute of America who could source 'the best produce in all the land'. The idea of this meal was not completely spontaneous because Joe had kept back some monies for it – three hundred dollars. He called it the Feast of the Assuming because he was assuming we'd have plenty to thank God for.

When we set off to buy the produce I realized that it was the first time I had been alone with Joe in a while. He seemed calmer (if Joe could ever be calm). I think the promise of Roth's million had lifted a great pressure from him and exposed the butterfly business to be expedient rather than essential to his being. The imminence of that financial windfall had reset his ambitions, and allowed him, perhaps for the first time, to think of the things he really wanted to do with his life.

As we followed the flow of the lordly Hudson on Route 9, passing former presidents' homes and billionaires' follies, I reminded Joe of the prophetic wish he'd made as we'd gazed from the lookout point over the Hudson River, on the day he'd re-named me.

'Someday, the Hudson. You think that day's coming? A house on the Hudson?'

He nodded absently, his mind elsewhere.

'Is that really your dream, Joe? To be rich. Live in a big house. Hobnob with society.'

'I do live in a big house. Hobnob? What's that?'

'Mix it with high society.'

'Society is who you meet, Rip. And it's high enough for me.'

'But what *is* your dream, Joe?'

Joe twitched and made a squirming sound. 'Aw. I don't go for all that dream talk. I got plenty to do when I'm awake.'

'Come on.'

'So many things.'

'Name one.'

'I can't! So many.'

'You're afraid to name it in case you don't get it. That's it, isn't it?'

'Don't be ridiculing me! Look. A deer!'

I looked and there were deer, in the grounds of one of the great houses he no longer aspired to live in.

'OK. What do you hope for? Really? If this comes off what will you do?'

'I got a heap of things planned.'

'You still want to be the Henry Ford of lepidoptera? Take butterflies to the masses?'

'Sure.'

It didn't sound like he did.

'Isabelle suggested that you're only doing the butterfly stuff to impress a father you never knew or had. That you'd rather be doing something else.'

'Are you shrinking me, Rip? I don't need no shrink here.'

It is a measure of Joe's brilliant evasions (and my solipsism) that it had taken me until now to make a connection between his

243

restlessness and his fatherlessness. Isabelle's comment seemed so obvious at the time that I had dismissed it. But there it was. Clear as.

'Personal is good, Joe. Is it true? About your father?'

Joe made a nervous giggle. 'Are we done here? This has gotten way too personal.'

'We both have father issues, no?'

'I don't got a father so how can I have father issues? Anyways, I really don't need a father. I got a heavenly one. If I wanted to find my earthly one, I would.'

'So why don't you?'

Joe started to dee-dee-dee.

'Joe! Come on. Why don't you?'

'Because.'

'Because your mother tells you not to!'

'Because he ain't going to satisfy, Rip. He ain't what I'm chasing.'

'Then what are you chasing?'

Joe dee-dee-deed again. 'Dee- d- d- dee, dee, d dee- dee . . .' to the tune of 'Dixie'.

'I think you don't know what you want.'

'I know. I just ain't coming out with it.'

'To find an entomological wife?'

'Ha!'

'Is that it?'

'For real.'

'But you have never mentioned having a girlfriend, Joe.'

'It just ain't happened. You know this stretch of road is where the first automobile was driven?'

'No. Is that a fact?'

'That is a fact. Think what those early century folk would make of Chuick, Rip.'

'They'd think the world hadn't progressed much.'

'Chuick is a wonder of modern science and homemade

ingeniousness. And one thing I would like to do when we get the money is to get this car gilded up in gold.'

As we came into Poughkeepsie the car suddenly drifted into the next lane and I had to pull the wheel back to the sound of an angry honking.

'Woah, Joe! Where were you going there?'

Joe had been looking in his wing mirror too much and lost track of the road.

'We're being followed, Rip. There's a Plymouth sitting on our tail. He's been following us since we joined the highway.'

I watched the Plymouth in the vanity mirror.

'Didn't Mary say we were being followed by a green Plymouth?'

'She did. Although there's more than one green Plymouth in this country.'

Joe slowed to a dangerously low speed, to see if the tailing car did the same. It overtook us, as any normal car would, and drove on ahead.

'Could it be the bailiffs? The IRS?'

'Probably nothing.'

After we had picked up the lobsters and steaks from the culinary college, Joe suggested we go see Washington Irving's house in Tarrytown. He said I needed to see the house where the author wrote the story that had brought us together.

'We have the time?'

'One thing I have observed is successful people always have time and are never on time, Rip. Rockefeller was famous for his tarditude.'

'You're making that up. The fact as well as that word, which I like by the way.'

'It's true! I read it in *Time Magazine*. Ha!'

'He could afford to be late, Joe. He was a multimillionaire.'

'So can we.'

'Not yet. If we get this deal.'

'When, Rip. Not if. When.'

Irving's stone mansion was as made up of gables and as full of angles and corners as an old cocked hat. The actual house was closed but we got out and looked around the outside. As we stood there, Joe put an arm around my shoulder.

'Just think. If Irving had never written the story of Rip Van Winkle, you might never have met me. You might have been reading something else that didn't have that same effect on you. You might not have tarried by the Falls that day. I might have missed you by a chapter or a paragraph. And Mary might not have liked the look of the book, never taken it, and I'd never have come back to give it to you. Or offered you a job selling butterflies. That's a butterfly effect right there, Rip! You know that Butterfly Effects was going to be our company name but Isabelle said it was cheesy and Ma said we'd probably get sued. So we called it Butterfly World. When are you going to write this book, Rip?'

The question jolted me back to my former self; the self who wanted to make a statement on the page. I liked it when Joe talked about me being a writer, even though I knew there was a credibility gap between my ambition and the actualizing of it. In the weeks on the road I had secretly continued with my 'Americodyssey', scribbling lines in motel rooms or in the back seat of Chuick, but experience had superseded the writing, and my desire had been sublimated into other things. I had a notion – romantic I see now – that at some point I would stop and take stock and put pen to paper or fingers to the Remington and that all my adventuring would pour out onto the blank page. But I'd hardly thought about writing during that time. I hadn't had time! My ambitions had been focused on more immediate pleasures and achievable goals: see America (check), screw Mary (check), sell butterflies (check with an A+) and challenge Edith (pending).

'Someday someone will be driving by the house you wrote your book in, Rip.'

'That's a fine thought, Joe.'

'Will you use your real name or write under a pseudopen?'

'I don't know.'

'Well. Rip Van Jones is a good name for a writer. I been thinking about titles for this book you're going to write. I was thinking "The Adventures of Joe Bosco".'

'Oh. So it's all about you?'

'Well, mainly, sure. But you can call it "The Adventures of Joe Bosco and Rip Van Jones" if you can fit it on the cover. It'll be about our adventuring, about America, and butterflies and the search for True Freedom. It'll be a book that will get people inspired about the beauty of America. And leps, too.'

'I don't see when I'm going to get the time to write this book. I'm having too much fun.'

'We get this deal done, I'll set you up in a cabin in the mountains.'

'Would you even read the book, Joe?'

'I wouldn't need to. I'd be livin' it.'

'You should read more. You're a smart guy. There are worlds in books. You can't just read *Butterfly Monthly* and the Bible.'

'I read other things! I'm always learnin'.'

It was true. Joe was a scattergun autodidact, making up for the years he'd been selling on the road instead of studying by being fascinated – infatuated – with life.

'But I have a difficulty with words.'

'You?'

Joe nodded as if giving himself permission to admit something to me. 'When I see words on a page they come at me in a strange order. I have to really concentrate. To see them in the order they were intended. Sometimes I read something and I put them in a different order and I get a sense, a different story to the one other people see.'

'You're dyslexic.'

'That's what they told me. But it's not quite that. It's hard to explain but it swells my head when I read. I get this bubble feeling. Sometimes, when I speak, I can't think of the right word so I say a word – any word – and I know it's not the right word, but I say it anyhow and then, to cover up for that word, I say another word, and to cover up for that word that I know is not quite right, I say another, building words on words in a kind of panic, and even though I know that each word I add ain't right I say it anyway; and rather than stop, I have to add a word and then another. Until I have this tower of words. Like Babel. That's why I need you by my side selling and that's why I need you to write my story, Rip. Keep it from toppling over.'

'Have you ever thought about checking on the meaning of a word before you use it, Joe?'

'If it sounds right, Rip, that's all that matters. Like lyrics in a song. No one cares about the words really. The melody is what matters. As long as the words fit in with the melody.'

Joe may have been dyslexic but he didn't have difficulty with words. The numbers of words, that is. He had lots of words in him, and when they came out they usually found a curious eloquence. It hadn't occurred to me (how much hadn't!) that he might be talking fast in order to stay one word, one step, ahead of the impediment. Even speaking was an act of plate-spinning for him.

'So are the most successful people dyslexic as well as late?'

'Everyone knows that. It's self-evidenturing.'

As we walked back to Chuick, we both saw the green Plymouth across the street.

'Our friend's back.'

I could see a man in the driver's seat with a telephoto lens. It was trained on the house, and us. As soon as he saw us looking at him, he stopped, started the car and pulled away with a guilty squeal of rubber.

'Such a purdy colour,' Joe said.

On the way back I decided to clarify something that had been bugging me.

'Can I clear up one thing, Joe?'

'Go ahead.'

'Mary said you took that book. At the Falls that day we met.'

Joe looked at me, checking to see if I might be joking.

'And you believed that? Man, Rip. You're right to give her the benefit but you gotta handle what Mary tells you with nuclear gloves.'

'Why?'

'Because Mary tells lies all the time. Come on.'

'Like the one about your mother having her by another man?'

'Yes and I ain't going there. You got something going with her? I seen the way you look at her. Rubbing her neck in the car.'

'It's just . . . flirting really. It's nothing serious.'

'Now you are blushing like *Euthalia aeropa*. I thought you'd be more Isabelle's type. But either way, I'd be happy to have you as my actual brother. Then we really can be a family business. Keep up the tradition of the special relationship between our countries. You'd be a big improvement on Mary's boyfriend.'

'She had a boyfriend?'

'Ricky Fountain. He was in the Marine Corps. He went overseas some place. El Salvador. He was a total crazy. He asked her to marry him and everything.'

'And she accepted?'

'Yeh. But then he disappeared.'

'Jesus.'

'There you go again, Rip. Praising.'

'She never mentioned him.'

'Like I said. He dumped her in a bad way.'

'She told me she'd . . . never had a serious relationship.'

'Maybe that's because she likes you. She's trying to impress you. She lies to make herself seem more interesting. Or make things happen. It's like a disease with her.'

I felt nauseous. The revelation threw me into a sulky silence all the way back to the house.

CHAPTER SEVENTEEN

In which a thanksgiving feast becomes a last supper.

The table was laid with assorted cutlery and crockery and American produce. It made for a still-life that a deranged Dutch master might have dreamed up: lobsters piled high in a steaming pink-red tower, steaks like plates, tomato ketchup, butternut squash, hammers (to smash the lobsters), Mickey Mouse mugs and a set of fine crystal goblets – one of the few relics left by the previous occupants. The uneven heights of the chairs made it look like a council of giants and pygmies. Celeste a foot higher than Isabelle, Edith's head at Elijah's shoulder. No two people were at the same level, the lesser were greater than the taller. The only person not present was Mary.

Joe's grace had the tone of a departure and was – I know now – charged with the prophetic.

'Friends, pilgrims, sisters, brothers, mother. I'm calling this the Feast of the Assuming because I am assuming that pretty soon our lives will change. That we are about to receive a blessing which I would like to thank the Lord for now. We have food from the oceans of Maine and the fields of Kansas, as well as vegetables from our own allotment. It's a spread of goodness.'

Mary entered the room. I had my eyes half closed for Joe's still unfinished grace, and I pretended that I hadn't seen her.

'I ain't done yet. Ceelee? Hands off. I want to thank Rip here for his contribution on the road. He proved a fine salesman. And when it came to the big deal, he delivered big. So here's to Rip.'

'Rip.'

Joe raised his Mickey Mouse mug.

'Roth said this case of wine is from France. It was made in 1964. Same year as me. It's called La Tour. Which I'm pretty sure means "damn fine" in French. I know those Pilgrim Fathers would have frowned on it but those zealous nuts should have read their Bible better 'cos even pagans know the Lord's first miracle was turning water into wine. So let's raise it and praise it!'

Apart from Mary, we all raised our assorted receptacles. 'Raise it and praise it!'

'And . . .'

'Come on, Joe,' Edith said. 'We're all starving here.'

'Just one more thing. Ma says never count your chickens. We got two chickens on the table. They are definitely hatched so it's safe to count them. And whatever happens with this deal, it don't change the good things about us. We stay humble and kind. Amens?'

'Amens already!'

I was sat between Celeste, who towered over me on a bar stool, and Mary, who slumped back in an armchair with her plate on her lap, withdrawn. Up until that day I had ignored her immature posturing, fibs and attention-seeking in the pursuit of pleasure, choosing to see it as sexy rebellion. With the veil lifted, her smouldering glower – so sexy before – looked petulant and self-indulgent now.

Clay poured the Chateau La Tour into whatever receptacles he could find.

'Join us, Clay,' Joe said.

'I'm all fine, Joe. The spirit is enough for me.'

How I disliked his pious phraseology. When Joe flung God into things it was somehow more natural. With Clay it was hard not to hear some kind of judgement. I misread a lot of people and was wrong about a lot of things during my butterflying days, but about Clay I was right.

Joe, as he had done at Roth's, knocked back the wine like it was milk. Isabelle took small, appreciative sips. The only person – other than me – who looked like they understood what they were drinking was Edith. I noticed her savouring it, swirling it expertly in the glass, a gesture I'd never have associated with her. As she looked into the dark liquid she decanted a memory:

'I can tell this is nice.' She held out her glass and I charged it for her. 'Your father liked wine,' she said, addressing no one in particular. 'He always used to do this. And it drove me insane. Pretentious fucker.'

'What's a pretentious?' Celeste asked.

'Someone who tries to be someone they're not,' Isabelle said.

'That could be pretty much anyone here,' Mary said, a little scattergun. She finished her toothpaste beaker of wine and poured herself some more.

I was being a bit slow. My mind was on other things: the wine, the food, the excitement of the deal – Mary's secrets and lies. But I began to see what was about to happen: Mary was steeling herself for an assault on Edith. That glower – usually directed at 'everything and everyone' (the world, me, men, her brother) – was for her mother.

I tinkled my glass with a fork, cleared my throat and tried to head her off at the pass.

'I know you think it bad luck to count chickens, Edith, but let's just imagine. Let's assume our chickens hatch. The deal comes to pass. Let's go around the table and each of us say one thing they'd like to buy with the money. If you could have one thing. Edith, you go first. What would it be? Don't be superstitious now. It's not bad luck to speculate.'

'It ain't that it's bad luck. It's that I just don't have a mind for it.'

'OK. But let's just imagine. You can have one thing. Starting to my right. Ceelee. What would you like?'

'Frillies.'

'Frillies? Is that a butterfly?'

'Frillies are dresses,' Isabelle translated for me. 'Where from, Ceelee. Bloomingdale's?

'Yeah. Yellow.'

'OK. A yellow dress for Celeste from Bloomingdale's. Edith?'

'Between the IRS and Joe's goddamned phone bills I can't say there'll be a whole lot left to spend on frillies.'

'How about a nice dress, Ma?'

'A dress won't hide what is so obviously so,' she said. She paused, uncomfortable with this speculative sport. She was so used to a making-ends-meet, backs-to-the-wall defensive approach to life, she never allowed herself thoughts of frillies. Edith's indulgences were emotional not material: her dramatic reaction to things, her exuberance with an expletive, her controlling of the family story. But I pressed her, and the others, getting brave with the wine, did the same. 'Come on, Ma! Treat yourself.'

'Well, OK. A vacation would be nice. I ain't had a vacation since a long time. Not since before Joe was born.'

'You can't be serious. Not even a few days?'

Edith thought about it. 'Well, I have had some weekends. When we lived in Michigan we'd drive to Superior. My sister had a cabin there.'

'But weekends are weekends,' I said. 'I mean holidays.'

'Nope. Before the kids. Mexico. Canada. But that don't count.'

'OK. So where would you go? One place,' I persisted.

'The Taj Mahal. I'd like to see that.'

This wasn't randomly plucked just to fob me off; she'd thought about it, you could see in her expression and hear it in her voice.

'OK. Good choice. Edith gets to go to see the Taj Mahal. What about you, Iz?'

Isabelle had said nothing to me about the deal since we'd returned. Other than asking who Roth was and whether he'd made his money in an ethical way. And then walking out when Joe and I had tried to describe the encounter with Roth.

'Maybe Yale is possible now?' I said.

'Maybe. I don't know,' she said. 'It'll be good to have a little more financial stability.'

That was the straight truth, but she wasn't playing my game.

'OK. Stability for Isabelle.'

'Clay?'

'Oh no, not me.'

'You got to play, Clay. Everyone must.'

'I want for nothing, Mr Rip. I got everything I need. The Lord's given me . . .'

'Play the game, Clay!'

'Well. I love my Ford but if I could get me one of those Japanese pick-ups. An Isuzu. If that's too much then a season ticket for the Jets.'

'OK. The Isuzu pickup for Clay. And a season ticket for the Jets.'

Eli was next. Despite my half a dozen 'English' lessons, his monosyllabia had not improved in my time at the house, nor had his capacity for abstract thinking.

'Nothing.'

'But if you could have one thing, Eli.'

He shook his head.

'Imagine it, Eli,' Isabelle coaxed.

'Eli's like me,' Edith said. 'No mind for speculating.'

'OK. We'll come back to you.'

I was next in the sequence. I asked for a year to write my book. And a room with a view to write it in. By the time I came to Mary she was on her third glass of wine.

'Mary?'

She swirled the goblet, mimicking her mother's twirling.

'I think I'd like to buy me a blood test.'

Elijah laughed for some reason. It sounded funny. Unless you were me. Or Edith.

'One of them blood tests for telling if I got the same father as you all.'

Someone snapped a lobster claw. We all braced ourselves for the storm. I couldn't look at Edith. I couldn't have her thinking

I was at the root of this. But my casually tossed seeds of subversion were about to erupt like field mustard.

'Why would you want that, Mary-Anne Bosco?' Edith asked in a soft, controlled voice, saying Mary's full name to remind her who she was, and then turning to me and saying, 'Mary-Anne gets these crazy notions in her head.'

'A crazy notion *you* put in my head!' Mary came back.

Edith smiled. It was a cold, lizard smile; rather than look at Mary throughout this she kept her eye on me.

'I don't think Rip wants to hear about your wild fantasies.'

Mary turned to me. I was holding the pink gristle of the lobster, using the shell as a shield.

'What do you think, Rip?'

'Stop now, Mary-Anne, come on,' Joe said.

'Let her talk,' Edith said.

'Rip? You said yourself Iz and me are sun and moon. Chalk and cheese.'

I looked at Isabelle – sun and cheese in this dichotomy – and she was watching me too, almost as if this outburst were my fault.

'You look the same and different. Like any sisters.'

'That's because we are different. 'Cos my Ma fucked another man. When she was lonely. When Joe and Isabelle's father was away all the time. That's why!'

'Mary. Don't do this.' Isabelle widened her eyes at her sister, in a plea to be reasonable.

'Yes, honey,' Edith said, her voice getting quieter. 'You are different. But everyone here is different.'

Rather than fight fire with fire, Edith was more like a sandbank or a moat, absorbing the heat, drawing it.

'You treat me different 'cos I am different. Even if you hadn't told me. I would still think it. I always been thinking it.'

Mary looked at me for backup but my coward heart – and the new information about her relationship – kept me mute. She had entered this brave new world of 'stand up to your mother' a little too prematurely for my liking. From a thousand miles away the idea of taking on Edith seemed a lot easier.

'That's the prollem with this. What I want can't be paid for, not even with a million dollars. A little truth is all I want.'

'Honey. You know you have a problem telling truth and lies apart.'

Edith continued in this faux-sweet way and her words, so clearly not matching her thoughts, sounded like those terms of endearment maintained between a couple even when they wanted to kill each other. She was either unfazed because she had nothing on her conscience or because she was, like her youngest daughter, one of the finest actresses this side of the Rockies. Trying to discern the fakers from the real in this family had become a subtler challenge than I'd first thought.

'I think that's enough now, honey. We all got a little excited. Maybe it's time you stopped with the weed. Don't mix well with the liquor neither.'

Mary looked at me. Tearful now. Eyes bugged and watered. 'You think I'm telling the truth. Or her?'

I don't know what would have hurt Mary more: her family closing ranks or my last-minute treachery.

'Ain't got an opinion now you got what you wanted?'

I feel wretched recalling this scene because, if I am being honest (and I am trying to be honest), I believed that Mary was telling the truth about this particular thing. Edith's manner alone told me there was something in her younger daughter's claim. But I had to make a difficult decision and make it quick: back Mary, face expulsion from the house and the end of my adventuring just when I had achieved something significant and was about to make some real money; or back Edith, face the wrath of Mary and keep this adventure on the road. I was not prepared to give the latter up even though, in my heart of hearts – that bit inside us that doesn't need to reason with itself but *knows* – I believed she was telling the truth.

'I think you've had a little too much wine,' I said.

There wasn't much time between the word 'wine' leaving my mouth and the actual wine hitting my face. And although it was an unpleasant shock her action was helpful to my cause: it got me off the hook and won me sympathy. If she'd kept her calm, she might have exposed me for the cad I was; but her violence towards me had everyone on my side.

'Goddamn crazy woman!' Joe said.

'It's OK. I'm fine,' I said, sounding sensible and magnanimous.

'Cowards. You are all cowards! I'm not putting up with this chicken-shit family anymore. I'm done with youz!'

Mary slammed her plate on the table with a crash. She stood up, wiping her lobster juice and butter on her arm. (She looked great again, damn it!) She was angry with Edith of course, but her last words were for me.

'You can fuck *her* now.'

We all sat there for a few seconds. No one said anything. I took in air and breathed it out slow. I pulled my T-shirt away from my skin. The silence was broken by the scrape of Isabelle's chair as she got up and went after Mary; not for the first time trying to rescue her sister (it was already half-sister in my thinking) from self-destructing.

'Leave her be,' Edith said. 'She'll drive to Cassie Rose. She can cool off there.'

'Cassie Rose?'

'My sister.'

A minute later we all heard the muscle growl of the super-charged Camaro roaring up the drive.

A minute after that Isabelle re-entered, upset at having failed to stop Mary and, I am sure, blaming me for what had happened. She was tight and started to clear the plates away with a clattering anger.

'She was quite drunk, Ma. We shouldn't have let her go.'

'She drives better drunk than most people sober.'

I started to help Isabelle clear the plates, wanting to put my

257

case forward. But Edith signalled me to join her and as I went to sit with her Isabelle left the room.

I sat on the stool and Edith topped up my glass.

'How's that shirt?'

'It's nothing.'

'You better soak that.'

The wine spatter on my T-shirt made me look like I'd been attacked with a dagger.

'My younger daughter is a liar, Rip. She's full of falsehoods.'

'I'm beginning to see that.'

'They all have dealt with not having a father in different ways. Joe keeps talking, Isabelle keeps reading. But Mary ain't landed with who she is. She has one crazy notion about being a NASCAR driver one week, or an actress, then a dancer the next, but she don't know what she wants. So she's invented this idea she has a different father. What did she tell you? She tell you I got drunk once and had an affair?'

'Something like that, yes.'

'Uh-uh? Who was it? She say I went with an Apache truck driver?'

I nodded.

'Well, I knew an Apache driver. But he ain't her father. The lyin' gives her another life, see. The trouble with you, Rip, and I been noticing it, is you get taken in too easy. If you believe everything people in this family tell you you'll get in a creek.'

Edith continued watching me with her one eye. It narrowed as she smiled.

'You plant that seed in her?'

This question gave me fibrillations. I pictured my seed shooting over her daughter's nut-brown belly.

'The one about me being a tyrant? That weren't a word she'd use. I knew you been talking.'

I tried to look innocent.

'Well. I might have watered it, but I didn't plant it.'

'Anyway. Enough of that. Tell me about this deal. Is it true

258

that it was you that asked for a million? With Joe all tongue-tied?'

'Roth offered a hundred and fifty thousand but, from what little I knew, it didn't seem nearly enough. I knew he'd pay. So I plucked the number that sounded right.'

'Is this guy as wealthy as Joe's mouth makes him?'

'To be fair to Joe, he undersold it.'

'That ain't possible.'

'I think Roth will be good on his word.'

'A man's word means nothing until it's something.'

'Maybe put the champagne on ice then.'

'I ain't drunk champagne since my wedding day. And that's something I don't like to be reminded of. Anyway, you've come good, you little punk. I didn't think you would but it seems you've come good. Here's to you.'

We chinked glasses and drank them dry.

Later, after throwing my claret-stained T-shirt in the sink to soak overnight, I went and lay in bed and contemplated the day's events. I could still feel the glow of Edith's endorsement (I'd suckled that tit of praise like a famished piglet); but Mary's duplicity ate away. I don't know what was worse: the fact she'd lied to me or that I hadn't noticed it. She'd made such a convincing virgin, responding exactly as I'd expect someone having sex for the first time to respond. But the thought of her having had another lover left me feeling more foolish than hurt. And it made me feel less bad about stabbing her in the back. I managed to convince myself that my 'betrayal' in not supporting her at dinner was of a lesser order than her betrayal of me.

A purposeful knock at the door jolted me from my justifying. I thought it might be Mary come to get revenge.

I opened the door to find Isabelle standing there wearing a look that suggested I was in trouble.

'I need to talk to you? May I?' She pointed to the alcove,

where she stood, hugging her arms, more from modesty than from the evening chill. I left the door ajar, not wanting her to think I had anything to hide or any intentions towards her, but she went and closed it, signalling the reprimand to come. I lit a cigarette in cocky provocation, and then I lay on the bed in idle pose, smoking my cigarette in the manner of a man who gave not ten thousand shits.

'When I told you that Mary is more vulnerable than she lets on, I thought you understood that – that it was obvious. She got let down badly by someone. You showed her approval. Even if it was for shallow reasons.'

'What are you saying?'

'I'm saying that you took advantage of that vulnerability.'

I laughed, a little haughtily. 'She didn't seem so vulnerable this evening.'

'You shouldn't have encouraged her.'

'To throw wine at me?'

'To think such things. She was clearly expecting you to say something. Why did you encourage her?'

'Because I believed her?'

'Because you want her.'

I laughed but this stung.

'Well?' Isabelle asked.

'Well what?' I was not going to make this part easy for her.

'It sounds like you got what you wanted. That you "had your way with her" – isn't that how you would phrase it?'

Impressively, Isabelle didn't blush. Her skin kept its true hue. Instead it was I who blushed and, damn it, I didn't want to lose to her in a game of embarrassment tennis.

'I didn't have *my* way with her! We had our way, with each other. Jesus, Isabelle. What are you? The sex police?'

'I don't care about the sex. I care about my sister.'

'Your half-sister.'

'Don't start that.'

'Well, it's possible, isn't it? You never wonder if your Ma

might not be telling you everything? I mean, given the history, the way Mary looks, the way you look. Do the math!'

'Mary is my sister.'

'You're prepared to live with the lie? I thought you believed in truth.'

'We all live with lies – our own and other people's – every day. Sometimes you have to believe the best of people.'

'Except for me, it seems.'

Isabelle turned back to the window. She didn't deny it. She then sat in the armchair and leant forward with her hands together, a gesture that seemed almost conciliatory.

'You haven't even mentioned this deal. Or said thank you for it. The fact that we've sold the collection for an amount of money that will make a big difference to all of you. I know this guy isn't squeaky clean but who is? From day one you've been untrusting towards me, Isabelle. Prickly. Suspicious of my intentions. Superior.'

'I appreciate what you've done. And yes, I'd rather the collection went to someone more reputable. Or a public museum. But I understand we have to sell it. It'll make a difference to things – especially Joe.'

'And you. You won't have to play Mummy all the time.'

'Is that what you think I do?'

'Well, yes. You've said yourself you delayed university because you needed to help your mother. This deal will enable you to go and study. Follow your dreams.'

She winced. 'You really think life is about following dreams? What if the dream is a ridiculous dream, or dangerous one? Or a selfish one?'

'Oh. What is life about then – do tell.' My sarcasm was slightly forced but I sensed that a little fight was needed here, to open her up.

'You come here and make these pronouncements and judgements about us.'

'Maybe it's easier for an outsider to see things clearly.'

'And you think you see things clearly?' Sarcasm from Isabelle – good!

'I see a family trapped, trying to get by by doing one thing and struggling. I see a family with the means of making money in another – legitimate – way. And that this could free them from that trap. It'll free Joe from pounding the road. It'll free you from having to keep house so you can study. It'll maybe help Mary get out and pursue dance or acting – or whatever it is.'

Isabelle pulled at her earlobe.

'That's a fine speech but I don't believe it. I don't believe you. I think you are here for what you can get. I don't think you care about us. You will say what it takes to get what you want. Even now you're doing it. Because you want the deal!'

'You're not so pure though are you?'

'OK. No. But now you're going to tell me something I don't know about myself?'

'I mean you've lied.'

She waited for me to reveal the lie.

'About your father. Writing to him. Incognito.'

'What I did . . . what I did then . . . is not your business. And what Mary thinks I did and tells you is not to be trusted – as you know.'

'You really are impossible to please, Isabelle.'

Isabelle stood up from the chair, waving away my cigarette smoke.

'Why should pleasing me – or anyone – be your main goal in life?'

CHAPTER EIGHTEEN

In which Joe is arrested – again – and I decide to quit.

The morning of doing the deal – or 'Do-da-deal day' as Joe called it – I awoke with two varieties of butterflies hatching in my gut: Butterflies of Excitement and Butterflies of Anxiety. Excitement that I was about to close a deal that I had set up and that would justify my position in this family; anxiety that some natural disaster or intervention of history would snatch it away. I kept these thoughts in the gloomy recesses where they belonged and instead focused on the likelier outcome that today would be a million-dollar day.

When I pulled back the curtains and looked out across the grounds of the house I saw a silver canopy of spider webs spreading from the drive to the edge of the lawn, across the croquet-smooth grass that Joe had manically cut the night before with a hand-pushed mower in an effort to do as Edith had instructed and remove the 'whiff of hick' from the premises in case Roth's representative needed to come and see the collection. The jalopies (minus Mary's Camaro) were parked the other side of the outhouses and the dogs were in their kennels. The hazy sunrise gave the dilapidation of the grounds a golden grandeur; and if you squinted you could believe it was a house in its heyday, a place where great things were going to be accomplished.

I donned the suit Joe had bought for me at J. C. Penney's and the tie that was flecked with the green of my favourite butterfly and went downstairs. I wasn't the first one up. Or even the second. Edith was sat at the kitchen table drinking coffee and Elijah was playing with the free toy from the cereal packet.

'You're up early, Edith. Excited?

'It's just another day, Rip.'

'Really?'

'So far.'

She was wearing crimson lipstick, and a light dusting of foundation.

'You've dressed up. I thought you never dressed up for any man.'

'I'll put lipstick on for one about to pay me a million dollars.'

There was something touching about this prettification. It was easy to forget that she wanted and needed this deal as much as anyone. Maybe more. She couldn't keep up the 'it'll never happen' act for ever.

'Maybe you should come with us to New York, Edith. You should be there, really, not me.'

'Believe me, I want to be there. But a company needs a face and it can't be this one. When I pitched Atlantic and Pacific the man looked at my scars all the way through. He didn't barely look at the product. He kept asking me if I wanted anything. In the end I got so mad I said, "Yes, I want you to stop looking at me, you dickwad." It kinda killed the deal. Just see that Joe gets there and signs the papers and don't talk too much. The boy has a disease of words. He gets excited and, well, you know. It's time for you to justify your existence, Rip. Bring home the bacon.'

Joe entered singing, 'It's Deal Day. It's Deal Day. It's Do-da do-da-deal Day!' He looked at his mother, then sniffed ostentatiously. 'Ma's got all coochie for the Wizard's man.' Even in the cheap suit he looked a million dollars.

'How do I look, Ma?' He twizzled his clip-on bow tie.

'Same as always.'

'Rip?'

'Entomological and entrepreneurial,' I said, telling him what he wanted to hear. 'Like an educated, mad-scientist-explorer-poet.'

'What's with the dicky bow?' Edith asked.

'Gives me a gravitational pull, Ma.'

Another phrase that Joe mutated into something even better than the original. He clasped me around the shoulders.

'Our lives are about to change, Rip, I can feel it!'

The dogs heard them first, their crazed barking telling us someone was coming:

'Car! Car! Car!'

We were all drawn to the window. Two cars were coming up the drive at funeral-cortege speed, cautious, anticipating resistance. A patrol car escorting a green Plymouth, the same make, model and colour of car that we'd dismissed as a manifestation of Mary's dope-fuelled paranoia and that had spooked me and Joe in Tarrytown.

'What's this?' I asked.

'It's the catch,' Edith said. 'There's always a catch.'

I could feel a swell of panic that I was about to discover something else I could and should know about. The feeling in my stomach was more a rising than a sinking feeling.

'Who is it?'

'It's the FWA,' Joe said.

'Who?'

'They're like the FBI for critters.'

As the convoy swung around the island of the circular drive the insignia on the doors declared: US Fish and Wildlife Agency. A man wearing shades, a white short-sleeve shirt, grey flannels and brown shoes stepped from the Plymouth and walked towards the house. He had a real sheriff's saunter on him and he sauntered as far as the bottom step, placing one shiny toecap on it.

'What do they want?'

Joe wasn't explaining. He'd left the room.

'We'd better go find out,' Edith said. 'Give me your arm, Rip.'

As I escorted Edith downstairs, rather ominously she said, 'Look like they mean business this time.'

'This time?'

'They stopped me once for selling butterflies they thought were on their goddamn special list. Maybe Joe's been selling something he shouldna.'

The driver of the Plymouth had been joined by two officers who shadowed him from a distance. They must have wondered if they'd stepped back in time. The whole family – less Joe – was now gathered on the veranda. With Edith, the grand matriarch, at the centre of the group and Celeste in her petticoats we looked as if we were about to pose for a box camera.

'Can I help you, officer?' Edith asked.

'We're looking for a Joseph Bosco.'

'Is he in some kind of trouble?'

'Is he here, ma'am?'

'I believe he is. Elijah, will you go see where Joe's got to?'

Elijah went back inside.

There was a box of small- and medium-sized cases on the step, ready to be Fedexed to that wedding in New Jersey. The agent looked at the box.

'Go ahead, take a look. You like yellow swallowtails? I can sell you a case. Ten dollars for the small.'

Edith had charm, a deep well of it when she bothered to lower the bucket, but the agent wasn't tempted. I noticed he couldn't look directly at her. I'd got so used to her deformity, I had to remind myself what it was like seeing her for the first time. This guy would have failed 'The Test' for sure.

'Is he in trouble, officer?'

'He is, ma'am. A heap.'

'What's he done?'

'Well, I got a sheet of paper here listing it but he needs to hear it first.'

'Hullo!'

Joe suddenly appeared, brushing some dust from the lapels

266

of his suit. He walked right up to the agent and shook his hand as though he was a long-lost friend. Joe did it all so fast the agent didn't have time not to shake his hand back.

'How can I help you, officer?'

'Are you Joseph Bosco?'

'That is me. Six foot five and two hundred and ten pounds in my Fruit of the Looms.'

'I have a warrant for your arrest.'

'For real?'

'For real.'

'Could you . . . could you arrest me tomorrow, officer? You see we got real important business in the city today?'

And then, with the entire family watching, the agent announced that he was arresting Joe for selling Appendix I butterflies in contravention of the Lacey Act (which said same officer would later explain to me with great solemnity). That on three different occasions in the last eighteen months Joe had sold protected species to undercover agents disguised as collectors. He told Joe that he would be taken to the Federal court in Hudson and charged with the illegal import and selling of contraband. He said that the FWA would be returning on the morrow with a warrant to search these premises for further contraband. Joe, doubtless familiar with the wording, added a harmonizing hum to the Miranda. Had he ever exercised his right to remain silent?

Edith stepped towards the agent and he actually took a step back and reached for his holster.

'I think all this is unnecessary, officer.'

'Agent.'

'I think it's uncalled for. These butterflies all belong to us.'

'I am taking your son to the court in Hudson where he will be charged. You will have to make your case at the hearing.'

'How long will this take, officer?' Joe asked. 'You see, I have to be in New York. At 3pm today.'

'I can't say with certainty, sir, how long it will take. It depends on the magistrate judge. And on what other cases are in court. I'd suggest you won't be going anywhere today.'

'Do I get a phone call?'

'Yes. You do.'

Joe was either putting on a wonderful act of nonchalance for the benefit of his watching family and me, or he really wasn't concerned.

'Well, officer, agent, this is most inconveniencing. Can I speak to my friend?'

'You may, but keep it brief, sir.'

'You have to go to the meet on your own, Rip. You have to buy some time.'

Buying Joe time. Who had enough resources to do that?

'What do I say?'

'Do your thing, Rip. You'll think of something.'

'Mr Bosco.'

The agent came forward with a pair of cuffs. Joe offered his wrists, very compliant and still annoyingly nonchalant. 'Is that your Plymouth, sir?'

'It is.'

'I love the Grand Fury. I seen you tailing me that time near Rochester. And just a few days back – in Tarrytown. It's hard to forget a car like that. It's a great colour. It's the same colour as the *Argema mimosae* moth from Senegal, which is a moth to match any butterfly. Do I get to ride in it?'

'You'll be in the patrol car.'

'Aww.'

'Is Joe in trouble?' Ceelee asked as they led Joe away.

Isabelle tried to reassure her: 'They're just asking him some questions, Ceelee.'

'But the man put the chains on him.'

'That's just what they do when they want to question someone. Joe will be fine. He'll be back soon.'

Just before he got into the car Joe turned to me. 'I'll try to call, Rip. If you don't hear before midday then you better go to New York without me.'

And then, for the second time since I'd known him, I watched as he tried to duck his massive frame into the back of a law-enforcement vehicle.

'Damn fool,' Edith said.

Celeste was as upset as I was, albeit for a different reason. 'Will Joe go to jail, Ma?'

'Let's hope so,' Edith muttered. 'It might put an end to all this bullshit. Like I said. A deal is never a deal until it's done. It's just words. I'm getting on with what's real.'

Edith stood and put out an arm for someone to take. Clay obliged her. 'You better take the phone call. I don't want to speak to that ape, unless he's calling from hell itself.'

Edith went in with Clay, Celeste and Elijah leaving just Isabelle and me standing there. We both watched the convoy until it had disappeared around the bend, carrying my friend away and with it – I was sure now – the prospect of the million-dollar deal. My million-dollar deal!

'Was he serious?' I asked. 'About confiscating the collection?'

'I guess. But I don't think they can take it away from us,' Isabelle said.

'But they can stop us from selling it?'

'Maybe,' Isabelle shrugged.

'Well at least you'll be pleased about that,' I said sarcastically, sure she was taking secret pleasure in this turn of events.

She looked surprised by my sharpness. 'Am I not allowed to be?'

'You can be what you want, Isabelle,' I said, sulkily. 'You just carry on being yourself.'

She looked at me as though I was a hopeless case and went inside.

I felt sick. Actual sick rose up, an acid reflux making me swallow and grimace. There was one cloud in that damn sky and the sun managed to find it. The loss of light and warmth was as sudden as a switch, bringing with it a chill of reality and a frame of mind I thought I'd banished. I was so cross and disappointed that I decided to go for a walk, get my head round this turn of events, see if I could get some guidance from nature. I reached the end of the drive and looked out over the Catskills. It was hard to believe that just over those mountains there was a metropolis busting with millions. And somewhere in the heart of that metropolis Roth's representatives were waiting for Joe and me to sign off on a deal that was no longer possible.

I continued to stare at the vista. Even though I knew that nature did not give a damn about how things appeared to us, I looked for a sign and the fates offered me a chevron of geese flying in the direction of New York City, full of purpose and instinctive direction; I envied those geese: without the benefit of a classical education they knew exactly where they were going. How I wished I was one of them at that moment.

'I don't believe this.'

I said this out loud but I should have believed it. When you make your bed with the unpredictable, you ought to be ready to lie down with it at any point. I had wanted to believe I had been working for someone different; a great exception, a beautiful aberration, a holy fool, iconoclastic adventurer, idiot savant; when really he was no more than a huckster, duping people with his fool/clown act, with me the latest to be duped: you shall know him by the trail of the suckers. Everything that the agent had said about Joe – selling legal butterflies to the masses, and illegal butterflies to the chosen few – sounded plausible. All too plausible. Joe had been 'up to something' and this was the something he was up to. For the first time in all my time with Joe I contemplated quitting, leaving this place. I was done with this Joseph and his technicolour dreamcoating.

I must have walked for a couple of hours for when I returned I could hear someone calling my name.

'Rip! Rip!'

It was Celeste and she was standing on the veranda holding out the walking phone.

'It's Joe. He says this is his one call.'

'Thanks, Ceelee.'

I took the phone and my ear was filled with the breathy high-pitched sound of Joe yelling a garbled message that wouldn't quite get to the point.

'Rip! Can you hear me? This is my one call so you need to listen! Can you believe it? That hairy guy who arrested me? He's called Agent Moroni!'

'So?'

'He's named after a bogus angel! The goddamned same name as a bogus angel from the Book of Mormon!'

I don't know which part Joe was asking me to believe or not. The arrest. The name.

Tell him you quit!

'I can't believe this. I can't believe it!'

I can believe it. Everyone else in the world who has ever met Joe can believe it! Now quit!

'He wants to lock me up for twenty years!'

Sounds like a wise man to me.

'They have arrested me for selling my own bugs. It ain't illegal to sell your own bugs. But this bogus angel is like a maniac. And now I got into an escalating situation here, Rip. I upset the magistrate judge and they're gonna slap me in jail for contemptuanity.'

I sighed.

'I told him he weren't the judge that mattered to me. He gave me thirty days and when I said to him thirty weren't so bad when you figure our Lord spent forty in the wilderness he slapped ten days more! Rip – are you there? Don't bail on me. I'm at FWA in Hudson. I can't call you after this. It's plain fool-ishness. This guy don't know his own rules. Says now he's caught me he's not gonna let me go! That's how he's talking. He calls me "Butterfly Joe"! Which I kinda like but he says it like I'm Al

Capone or something. He's like a guy who thinks he's found cocaine when it's just baking powder. Anyway. You gotta go to the meeting, Rip. You got time.'

'I don't know, Joe.'

'You don't know what?'

'I don't know if I can go on with this.'

There was at least enough of a pause to show Joe was listening.

'What are you saying?'

'I'm saying that maybe I should quit.'

Silence again. And then a giggle!

'You can't quit, Rip. I'm counting on you. We're all counting on you. You gotta go meet Roth's man. You just gotta meet them and buy me time. Rip? You hearing me? This deal's still on. This story's not done.'

Quit now, Llewellyn!

'You gotta buy us time here. Say whatever it takes. Tell them I died if you have to.'

'Joe?'

But the phone went dead.

❋   ❋   ❋

My father had a motto: anything for a quiet life. To me this was the epitome of smug incuriousness and the opposite of how I wanted my life to be. But as I stood there, holding the phone, listening to Joe's bluster, I had an image of my father saying this to me and it came with such unexpected force that I wondered if my conscience was trying to steer me along a safer road. My conscience – essentially on holiday for a few months – was suddenly back with a tan and a new-found clarity and, like an admonishing parent, insisting on calling me by the name I'd been born with:

Time to take a safer road, Llewellyn. Ramifications are stacking up, consequences waving at you from the horizon, portents yoo-hoo-ing at every corner. They're all telling you the same thing: you're working for a huckster who you should never have agreed to follow in the first place. He promises you this and he promises you that but he never delivers, this Cat In The Hat. I know you have not exactly won glory through any great deeds and your homecoming would be tinged with the what-might-have-beens, but you really should quit while you still have a head!

I walked towards Chuick just as Isabelle appeared at the entrance.

'What news of Joe?'

'Who knows. He hardly made any sense.'

'Are you going to New York?'

I took off my suit jacket and threw it on the back seat. 'Maybe,' I said. 'I really don't know.'

And with that I got in the car and drove off, enjoying the fact that it was my turn to be irritated and taking a cruel satisfaction in leaving Isabelle just standing there, none the wiser. I'd even suggest that she looked concerned about me.

It was good to be alone in Chuick. Sometimes inanimate objects are all we can trust. Dear Chuick, I will write an epic ode to you when I have the time. You are faithful as a hound. As reliable as gravity. You were transport, sanctuary, and at times my home. And I thank you! I didn't completely know what my intentions were for the first few miles. I think I wanted to know what quitting would feel like. And perhaps I needed to glimpse the Quiet Life. I was, in effect, taking two roads at the same time: one to New York; one back to my aunt's. It was convenient that they happened to be the same road.

The sight of the house and the barn of ten thousand books was like a battering ram crashing through the fourth wall of my adventuring. Perhaps it was time to go back to reading of the escapades of imagined heroes and heroines instead of having the hubris to think I was one of them. Of course, as is always the way with these things, the place was at its most appealing. The trees were in their full fall glory, all burning reds and glowing golds. There was a sleek Buick Riviera in the drive. There were lights on inside the house and, intriguingly, in the barn (a light that would have been my light had I stayed). I parked across the road, switched off the engine and sat there taking stock. The idea of quitting and resuming my old walks and habits, returning to the life I had been leading before I met the man known to the Federal authorities as 'Butterfly Joe', was compelling. I just had to walk up to the house, ring the bell.

I turned the radio off, closed my eyes and projected what might happen from here, were I to step from the car and knock on the door. Images of a Quiet Life flashed before me: my aunt embracing me with open arms and full bosom; me calling the Boscos to tell them I was quitting; a proven-right Edith saying 'I told you so'; a relieved Isabelle. A Mary cursing my name; and a still-incarcerated Joe despairing that I had back-slidden into being boring. From there my quiet life reduced to a quick succession of scenes: my mother saying, 'It's lovely to have you back, Llewellyn.' My friends pleased to see me but their interest leavened by healthy indifference and having their own lives. My brother sarcastically asking how the great Welsh-American novel was coming on. The safe course of this life led to a sensible job that didn't require me to misquote poets and presidents, or use the exaggerated tragedy of someone's past to get people to buy things from me. A girl who listened with interest to my half-tales of selling butterflies in glass cases in America and thought me imaginative for having even done such a thing. The images accelerated through the stages of life: a wedding, children, setback and disappointment. I grew fatter and lost my hair but at least I grew old knowing the difference between delusions and dreams. The Quiet Life. It didn't seem so bad.

The side door of the house opened and someone – a tall man – walked across the lawn towards the barn. He was carrying something under his arm: a file, papers, a manuscript! It was Garton Lake, the novelist who used my aunt's barn whenever he needed to 'get away and do some hard yards on a book'. He'd said this to me when I met him at my aunt's apartment in New York. I was fresh off the plane and my aunt had thrown a dinner in my honour and invited Lake to encourage me in my own writing endeavour – and to make an impression. At some point in the evening I had the temerity to ask what his book was about and he'd turned to me and said that his first rule of writing was 'never to discuss the work whilst it was still nascent'. This seemed deeply impressive to me at the time. But as I sat there thinking about it now it just sounded pretentious. I watched him cross to the barn and he seemed lost in whatever world it was he was creating. Was that the book? I wondered. Had he nearly finished it? It looked substantial. Would it be good enough to be one of the books in the Barn of Ten Thousand Books, as I'd hoped my own might be – one day. I felt an envy and frustration rising up again. Damn him, for writing that book. Just as Lake reached the top step of the barn he seemed to notice Chuick for the first time. I sank down in my seat, like an undercover agent. He stood there for a while, watching, and then, seeming uncon-cerned, he entered the barn, closing the door behind him. I could have gone up to the barn, said hello, asked him what the book was about now that he'd finished it. But I didn't care what his book was about (a book I decided I despised without even having read a single word). I needed to know what was going to happen to Joe. To Isabelle. To Mary. To Edith. To the butterflies. To me! I couldn't quit because, despite Joe's latest misdemean-our, the sensible advice of my father's ghost and my own conscience, this story wasn't over.

I drove to New York, playing the radio loud so as not to hear myself think. When I crossed into Manhattan over the Alexander Hamilton Bridge the sight of the mighty monoliths of Midtown lifted my spirits. This was a city that forced you to look up and think soaring thoughts. And whilst my thoughts weren't lofty they were at least focused on what I had to do. And what I had to do was save this deal.

Around 45th I started looking for a parking space but drove block after block without any joy. It was two thirty-five and I must have been ten minutes' walk from the Roth Building. What would Joe do? I thought, knowing full well that he'd ask God to provide a parking space, as he had done in Cleveland, an event that triggered an argument between him and Mary with me taking Mary's side. Mary: 'Why would he bother to help us find a parking space with a whole universe of serious things to be dealing with?' Joe: 'He's either involved in our little bitty lives or he ain't. You think he's drawing the line at parking?'

Without the Creator's help I found a car park that held no more than a dozen cars and resembled a basketball court. The sign said FULL but I could see two free spaces. I drove up to a wooden signal box where a man sat playing with a roll of tickets.

'Sign says full.'

'You have two spaces there, I can see. There.'

'For emergencies.'

'This is an emergency.'

The man looked at me. 'Oh yeah?'

'My friend . . . is dying.'

'Yeah, right.' Then looked at Chuick. 'The hell is this anyway?'

'It's a Chuick,' I said. And I launched into a hagiography of my most trusted transport, using every scrap of poetry Joe had uttered in its defence. 'Made before Motown made them to break down.' 'Two tons of Pittsburgh steel.' 'Someone hits this car they're as dead as snot.'

The Ode seemed to tilt things. He nodded and gave me a ticket from his roll.

'Take the one on the left. Hope your friend gets better!'

'Thanks. So do I,' I said as I ran off toward the Avenue of the Americas.

The Roth Building was over five hundred feet tall but I'd never have noticed it had I not been attending a meeting there. It was anonymous among the lovelier skyscrapers of Midtown. I ran into the entrance and took a lift to the reception on the twentieth floor where I stepped towards the reception desk and announced my name and the time of my appointment. It was a relief and a thrill to see my name already written down, next to Joe's, in the 3pm slot in the appointment book. I explained that my companion was unable to attend the meeting due to being 'indisposed'. I chose this word as it seemed to cover most even-tualities, including the possibility that the receptionist wouldn't ask for fear that she didn't know what it meant or that the answer might be too distressing. She offered me a seat in the reception area. I couldn't sit so I stood for a while and watched the traffic and people passing up and down the avenue below. So many people with lives I knew nothing about and who in turn knew nothing about mine.

'You can go on up now, sir. Take the elevator to the fortieth floor.'

As the elevator rose slowly through the floors, the buttons lighting up the numbers, all the little lights started coming on in me. For weeks Joe and I had confabulated shamelessly to make the sale – killing off his mother in the fire in one store, his sisters asphyxiated in another; his father falling into a gulch in the jungle one day, killed by a jaguar the next. I was going to have to confabulate. The ding of the bell indicating that the lift had reached its destination only confirmed my thought.

It was time to justify my existence by ending Joe's.

'Mr Rip Van Jones. Butterfly World,' I said to the second receptionist.

She led me to a room, knocked on the door, and leant in.

'A Mr Van Jones is here to see you, Mr Eliot?'

I prepared my face for the faces that would be staring back across the table at me by looking in the glass door beside me.

Appropriately enough my suit and black sample briefcase gave me the air of a mourner. I looked as sombre and sober as hell.

There were three people in a room which had leather-padded walls (to soundproof the screams of those who were being fleeced by Roth's lawyers, perhaps). Roth's lawyer (Mr Eliot), Roth's head of acquisitions (Mr Matthews) and the curator of Roth's museum (Ms Daniels). This was the three-headed Cerberus that stood between me and the death of the deal.

'We were expecting two of you, Mr Van Jones?'

Mr Eliot, the lawyer (the middle head), wore heavily horn-rimmed glasses and resembled a hornet. He was, I detected, the power in the room and I decided to meet his insect gaze with a piercing look of my own. I took my time. I was weighing up the depth of the dive I was about to make, just as I had done that first day I'd met Joe. (In a way, lies are like dives: the greater the height the more impressive they look; once your feet have left the solid rock of fact and propelled you up and out into the air there is no stopping it; you are committed.)

'I . . . I'm afraid . . . my colleague Joe Bosco cannot be with us.'

Mr Eliot detected the heavy burden in my expression and tone. 'Oh?'

I took a final look over the ledge (making sure I had all six eyes on me) and then I dove.

'I debated long and hard this morning as to whether I should cancel this meeting in the light of recent events. But, after much discussion with Mr Bosco's family, and in light of Joseph's own wishes, it was agreed that I should come here today. But it is with a heavy heart that I have to tell you that my colleague, my friend, Joe Bosco, is dead.'

'Oh,' Mr Eliot said. 'That is . . . most unfortunate.'

'What does this mean?' Mr Matthews asked. Roth's man seemed quite put out. To be fair to him, he'd just flown in from London, where he'd purchased a set of sooty moths from Bonham's. He couldn't quite disguise his terror at the thought the collection he'd been sent to secure for his boss might have gone the same way as its owner.

I'd only just decided to kill Joe – in the moment. And whilst less is more should have been my guiding principle, I felt I owed them some kind of explanation. For a few minutes I experienced what it must be like to be Joe – to be the Cat In The Hat – starting something and having to keep going lest everything collapse for the stopping.

'He went lepping up near the Kaaterskill Falls, three days ago. He was looking for late season butterflies. When he didn't return that evening we went looking for him the next day. And found him at the bottom of a creek. He'd fallen some sixty feet, off the edge of a hidden bluff. He died from the fall.'

As I was killing him off I kept thinking how much Joe would have enjoyed my delivery. Of course, had he been there, I would not have been able to kill him quite so cleanly, or execute my speech without that wretched self-consciousness which is the crusher of all true poetic expression. But I gave him an end that was more poetic an end than he was likely to meet. Joe's death was easily my most convincing sell. A competitive need to prove yourself, a reckless abandon, desperation and disregard for the outcome make for a potent mix. In business there's probably no better way to pitch. Joe had taught me well. The Cat In The Hat had begat another cat.

Mr Eliot put his fingers together in a pyramid, respectful enough. 'I'm sorry.'

Mr Matthews offered commiserations, too.

Seeing that I had their sympathy I moved on to the real reason we were there.

'I realize, Mr Matthews, that you have come a long way. The family obviously want to honour the deal to sell the collection. But they will need a period to mourn Joe.'

'Of course, Mr Jones.'

'How long do you think the family will need?' Mr Matthews asked. 'Just so that I can inform Mr Roth.'

'Well, grief is no respecter of rules. I know this myself from the recent death of my father. But if you can give us a few weeks. Maybe forty days or so? Perhaps I can contact you when the family are ready. Would that be acceptable to you, and to Mr Roth?'

'Of course. Please offer our commiserations to the Bosco family.'

I should have left it there, but I was enjoying myself too much. 'It's no compensation for a life, of course,' I said. 'But perhaps in some small way the sale of this collection will be a fitting memorial to my friend.'

CHAPTER NINETEEN

In which I meet the man who caught 'Butterfly Joe'.

After killing Joe, I went to see him in jail. I was on a high from the thrill of the kill and I felt no shame for what I'd done. If anything I felt justified: the deal was alive. Joe's death was a blessing; and it wasn't even one in disguise. That meeting gave me renewed enthusiasm for butterflying and a confidence in my ability to save impossible situations. It is true that I had sacrificed Joe in the process, but I was sure that was a detail he could live with. All I had to do now was let everyone know that Joe was dead. Anyone can walk into the underworld, that door's always open; it's just that they're expected to stay there.

The FWA facility was in a brick office in a nondescript strip of buildings that if you had to describe you'd say looked like an underfunded school. The name 'Fish and Wildlife Agency' carried more farce than threat. I thought Joe's situation would be resolved quickly; it was just another fix Joe would talk his way out of and walk away from. All I had to do was turn up, pay a fine, set him free and drive back to the Catskills. At the desk I presumptuously announced that I was here to pick up a Joseph Bosco. The duty officer asked me to take one of the three plastic chairs in the waiting area. She didn't act as though she was expecting me or as though she knew who Joe was. I sat there for half an hour – time enough to think that perhaps I wasn't going to be leaving with Joe. Eventually, a man wearing shades, a six o'clock shadow, a white short-sleeve shirt, grey flannels, brown shoes and a job-done smirk entered the reception area. He looked more like a *caporegime* protecting a crime racket than a man protecting rare species. It was the man who had arrested Joe. He of the bogus angel surname. I tried not to think of him in those terms but when the good seed's been thrown the idea keeps growing. Right from the start I imagined him with wings tucked away beneath his shirt.

'Mr Jones?'

I stood. 'Hello, yes.'

'Or is it Mr Van Jones?'

'It's both. The latter is my working name.'

'My working name is Agent Devon Moroni. I need you to come to my office. I have some questions to ask.'

'How long will that take?'

'Am I keeping you from something?'

'I was told to come and pick Joe up.'

'Mr Bosco won't be going anywhere today. Or tomorrow. And – hopefully for many days after that.'

The sign on his office door said 'Agent Devon Moroni' in white lettering printed against the black strip. A photo of a butterfly was stuck crudely beneath his name, a handwritten, taped strip of card said 'Bug Patrol'. Moroni's office was stuffy ('airconditioning is killing the planet'). There was an office chair behind the desk, the kind of IBM electric typewriter that I coveted, and 'an interrogation chair' opposite the desk. On the wall was a single shelf with reference books on butterflies, as well as other insects. There was a framed giant horn rim beetle on the shelf next to what looked like small elephant tusks.

'Walrus ivory,' he said, seeing me wondering. 'Twelve years.'

'Twelve years?'

'That's what they got for smuggling them. Two schmucks – same age as you and your friend.'

I didn't like what Moroni was implying.

'Such a waste. Imagine. You're twenty-three, twenty-four years old and to go to jail for twenty years, you come out my age, fat, bald, your balls hanging down, your best days behind you, and all for what?'

I saw a pack of cigarettes on his desk but I resisted the temptation to ask for one, associating such an action with a signal to confess. When he offered me gum I felt sure he was going to try and get something out of me, get me to tell him things about Joe, betray Joe. That was what his manner was telling me.

'I have a few questions for you, Mr Jones.'

'Do I have to answer them?'

'No . . . but it might help your friend.'

There was a cork 'suspect' board with photographs of people and lines of string joining up the suspects to a map of the world. There was a photo of Joe, wearing his suit and bow tie. A line connected his image to a spot in the Catskill Mountains.

'So how long have you been working for "Butterfly Joe"?'

'"Butterfly Joe"?'

He reached up to the filing cabinet and pulled out a blue dossier which he set with a thud on his desk.

'But-ter-fly Joe,' he said savouring the name as if Joe were a notorious outlaw. 'The FWA have been trailing your friend for some time.'

A survival instinct made me decide to play the idiot. 'FWA? What is that?'

'Fish and Wildlife Agency. We're the FBI of the animal kingdom. Except the FBI has ten thousand agents and we got a hundred and twenty. Crazy really when trafficking in wildlife ranks just behind drugs and humans in terms of profit. We are the thin green line between the protected species and extinction. Your friend is a one-man environmental wrecking ball. There are nineteen protected species. He claims to have all of them. He even admitted it! I didn't even have to drag it out of him. He tried to sell some Palos Verdes blues last year. And that's like selling a dodo.'

Moroni finally took off his sunglasses, revealing mussel-shell rings around his eyes, quite lovely violet eyes with great long lashes. He looked tired from keeping all the species from extinction. I could see great dedication in the exhaustion. But someone was going to pay for that.

'We could have arrested him twelve months ago for selling Palos Verdes blues to an undercover agent posing as a Japanese buyer. But it's like poker with these guys. You gotta know when to play your hand. When he sold a set of Big Four at the LA Bug Convention he was bragging he had more where they came from! Said he had five birdwings. The Smithsonian only has two. But like all these guys he couldn't stop bragging. Said he had all nineteen species on the endangered list. Claimed he has a set of five-winged blue morphos. A butterfly that don't even exist.'

I began to think about the Miranda and my own right to silence. I was being very slow to see that I was intimately involved in this.

Moroni opened the file and pulled out some papers and photographs. He tossed a photo at me.

It was Joe wearing his bow tie and carrying his attaché case. The grainy quality and the bow tie and glasses made Joe look like a clown up to no good.

'This is your friend just last month. Selling to one of our undercover agents, pretending to be a buyer for a collector.'

I shrugged. 'Is that bad?'

Moroni spread photographs of rare species of butterfly on the desk. He picked out the most spectacular. I knew what it was. It was an Alexandra birdwing. Mounted and framed by Isabelle's fair hand. The Latin inscription in her spidery cursive.

'You know what this is?'

'No.'

'You are a butterfly salesman and you don't know what this is? That would be like being a car salesman and not knowing what a Cadillac is. Except this is rarer than a Cadillac and more valuable. It's more of a . . . Bugatti. It's an *Ornithoptera alexandrae*. That's an Alexandra's birdwing. One of the rarest butterflies in the world. There are more white sperm whales roaming the oceans than there are birdwings in Papua New Guinea.'

'Blimey.' I continued to play the role of entomological ignoramus.

He laid three more photographs of butterflies on the desk.

'So if the Alexandra's is the Holy Grail for collectors, then this is your Golden Fleece: Homerus. Named after some Roman poet.' (Moroni knew his bugs if not his Roman poets. I decided not to correct him. Not with what was at stake.) 'Then this one with the pretty flare is a chika. And this, from Corsica, is a *hospiton* which don't look much but believe me when a *hospiton* has baby *hospiton*s it's laying gold.' He set the four photos side by side now. 'Together you are looking at the Big Four. You know what some people would pay for that set?'

I shrugged. 'A lot?'

'Ten years, my friend. Or a $250,000 fine. And that's just these. There are nineteen Appendix I butterflies listed under the Lacey Act. Your friend has, in the last eighteen months, offered to supply people with all nineteen at various points. We got it on tape. I can't even say what that equates to in jail time, Mr Jones. We woulda got your friend in the end. These guys can't stop bragging about what they got. And your friend certainly had something to brag about. I mean Palos Verdes blues? Do you know how rare they are? I mean we're talking Tasmanian tiger rare, Barbary lion rare, great auk rare! Namely we're talking extinct rare!'

'That's certainly rare.'

'Why are you laughing? You don't think I'm being serious?'

'I'm not laughing.'

'You're smiling.'

'I'm just trying to . . .'

'Two hundred years ago there were whales in the oceans and buffalo on the plains. Then they brought in the Endangered Species Act. You ever heard of that?'

'No.'

'No. That's the thing. It has no power. You laughing again?'

'It's nerves. I'm sorry.'

'Well, let me educate you. A little history lesson. They brought in the Lacey Act. In 1900. They had to do something to prevent, and I quote, "the extinction of all God's creatures". It prohibits trade in wildlife, fish and plants that have been illegally taken, possessed, transported or sold. There are serious civil penalties for anyone who violates these rules and your friend is a violator, make no mistake. And now I got him I ain't letting him go in a hurry.'

'I didn't know about any of this, Mr Moroni.'

'Agent.'

'Agent. Sorry.'

'How can you not know? You're his partner in crime.'

'Not at all.'

'The other Flutter Brother, right?'

'What?'

'That's what he called you. The Flutter Brothers. Tells me you sold butterflies all over America.'

'So he did talk.'

'He didn't talk any sense. He just talks in fairy tales. About the Wizard. The Lord. And the Flutter Brothers.'

'I've only known Mr Bosco a few months.'

'Right. He said you're practically family. You're going to marry one of his sisters.'

'Joe exaggerates sometimes.'

'Not about his bugs. It's quite some operation he has going. Selling legit bugs to stores and running this on the side. Pretty smart cover. Are you the cover?'

'Joe is no criminal.'

'You know, in my experience, the best conmen don't know they're conmen. Like your friend. He just doesn't realize it. He's a bit crazy, too. Is he all there?'

'All where?'

'In the head. You know. Sane. You know he got forty days for contempt for saying the judge weren't the judge that really counted. He's quite the biscuit. Right now, he's in that cell, acting like this is a joke, singing songs like it's a holiday.'

'Joe isn't a crook. Or crazy. He's a lot of things. But not a crook or crazy.'

Moroni laughed. 'Tell me what you know. And I'll cut you

a deal. Plea bargain. You seem like a sane young man. And I imagine your six-month visa is up for renewal soon. You wouldn't want links to a felony to force you to leave this country prematurely. Why don't you tell me where he got these bugs?'

'They came from the family collection.'

'Right, and I'm Elvis.'

'His father was – is – a respected entomologist. The butterflies were caught by him.'

I gave Moroni a full-fat version (the one in which the father was alive – the truer version). 'He must have told you this?'

'Sure. He told me that story. And the magistrate judge gave him forty days to prove it.'

'What do you mean?'

'If his father can prove the butterflies Mr Bosco sold were his then he goes free.'

'And if not?'

'Twenty years.'

I had no reason to disbelieve Agent Moroni. But Joe must have wound him up something rotten for the agent had a seething suppressed rage, a mad revenger's glint. I'll admit I felt a powerful urge to put distance between me and Joe, to disabuse Moroni of the nature of our relationship. Tell him how Joe was elusive at best, untrustworthy at worst. That he made promises he couldn't deliver. That I was never sure of what the truth was when I was around him. All the bad bits. But the more he talked the more I believed Joe was right about Moroni: 'he'd bitten the wrong end of the carrot.'

'You know why I joined the service, Mr Jones? To catch people like your friend. People who plunder the treasures of the planet and then profit from them. Now your friend says you knew nothing about what he was doing. That you just work for his legit butterfly business. But I think he's set you up. Played you for a fool. Used you – and your English thing. It gave him a look and sound of being legit. That big redneck was never going to get into some of the places without your help. I think he

287

invented this story about inheriting them just to get around the law. But unless he produces his father he's going down.'

'Can I see him?'

Moroni led me back down the corridor to a room that had a glass pane dividing it in two. The room through the glass had a cushioned low armchair, a bed and a basin. Joe was lying on the floor (I assume in solidarity with the world's poorest majority), his hands behind his head. It wasn't the body language of the guilty man or someone looking at twenty years in jail. At least here Joe couldn't do any more deals, set more plates spinning. Here he was unable to menace the world with his Joe-ness. He was singing one of his 'made-up' songs, loud and annoying.

'Way out West where the weather is fine
I met a sweet girl and I made her mine
We lived in a hut . . . by the oceans sweet
And wrote fine poems and ate sweet meats!'

'For someone in the kind of trouble he's in he's acting pretty breezy. He's been doing that ever since he got here. He can't see or hear us.'

It seemed unfair being able to watch someone and talk about them without them knowing you were watching them. But I found it oddly reassuring that Joe was still Joe whether he was being watched or not. Still annoying. Still singing his songs. Still eschewing the bed. Joe being watched acted no differently to Joe alone.

'You got twenty minutes.'

Joe leapt up and embraced me. He was so big and strong that he held me slightly away from himself, afraid he might crush me. The height difference meant he planted his feet two feet away from me and leant over to stoop down. It was awkward but endearing and the first time he'd really hugged me like that. He always found new ways to win me over, and it was usually when I was at my wits' end with him.

'Rip! Thank the Lord. I am so bored. Here, take a seat on this lovely federal state chair.'

'Moroni says I have twenty minutes. And you're getting twenty years.'

'Bogus angel.'

'He seems pretty sure you're going down, Joe.'

'Moroni Macaroni Baloney. That was him in Rochester. And Tarrytown. They set me up, Rip. Those ads in the bug magazines. "Rare butterflies wanted". Enough of him. You see Roth's guys OK?'

'Uh huh.'

'You did?'

'Yep. I bought us time.'

'That's great! The deal's still alive then!'

(I made a face to show Moroni was the other side of the glass and could hear.)

'Oh, don't worry about him. Come on, Rip. Tell me what you told Roth's people. How did you do it?'

'I told them that you died.'

'Ha! No. Seriously?'

'No. Seriously. I told them you died.'

Joe looked at me and seeing I meant it his face opened up into that great shit-eating grin. Then he belly-laughed for about ten seconds. 'Oh boy. I taught you well! Was it a beautiful death?'

'It was a death you didn't deserve, Joe. Heroic.'

'Why, Rip. That is wonderful! How did I die? You need to describe it to me!'

'Really?'

'For real.'

'I had you chasing a swallowtail – no a yellowtip – in the Kaaterskill Falls.'

'That would be unusual at this time of year, but not impossible. Go on!'

'And you were so preoccupied with the chasing that you missed the drop. I got quite into it. Almost cried myself at the end. I thought you'd be the first to agree that sacrificing you was a price worth paying to keep this deal alive.'

'Absolutely solid, Rip. Good Theology, too. Substitutional atonement. Makes the world go round! Didn't I tell you I'd achieve more dead than alive!'

'My thoughts exactly.'

'Death opens doors to hearts, you know. *The Death of Joe Bosco*. I like it. Was it as good as *Saving Ma From The Fire* or *When My Father Never Came Back from the Jungles of Yucatán*?'

'It had to be. Roth's people weren't florists.'

'Think, Rip, if you can manipulate the hardnosed business heads of America what more can you achieve?'

'Look Joe, I have twenty . . . fifteen minutes. This guy Moroni is saying you have been selling illegal specimens. This is all well and good. But what now?'

'I ain't no illegal dealer. Those were my butterflies to sell. It ain't ever been a crime to sell the family silver.'

'Joe! Can we be serious for a bit? You know what they're asking? You have to prove your father caught those butterflies!'

'Rip, you are handsome when you get angry! A lover!'

'I can't help you unless you start being honest with me. No more twists. No more "I gotta meet a man about this", or "I gotta go see so and so about that". Deals on the side. No one tells me the truth in your family – except Isabelle.'

I waited to see if he'd pick up on this but he was too tied up in his own yarn.

'On the way here I nearly quit, Joe. I thought seriously about going back to being Llewellyn Jones. I went by my aunt's. That close!' I held up my thumb and index with a gossamer-thin wing gap between them.

He looked stung for a fraction but he didn't believe me.

'I shown you wonders and I'll show you more if you stick around. You want to go back to being a guy drifting along and tripping over because he can't look where he's going 'cos his nose is in a book? Getting high and depressed and telling people he's going to be a writer when he's got nothing to write about! I'm giving you stories here, Rip. Like bread to a duck.'

'It would be good to have a . . . normal story. One where you didn't go to prison.'

'Well . . . that is . . . that is the most depressing news I heard all day.'

'No, Joe. The most depressing news is that you got arrested and face twenty years in prison.'

Joe scratched his hair as though he had nits.

'Why didn't you tell me you were selling on the side?'

'I wanted to tell you. But I had to work out what I can tell you. Because you'd choke on it if I did. I gotta feed it to you in pieces you can swallow. And like I said I wanted this deal to be the real deal. I'm protecting other people.'

'From what?'

'From . . . disappointment.'

'Truth! You are always telling me the truth will set you free.'

'It does, but it can also be like a sword, cutting people in two. I ain't lied to you. I just couldn't reveal all the information. I sold a few bugs. We needed the money. For college. And other things. For the house. How do you think we pay for it all? Ma thinks the business is enough but it ain't. We can't get loans. We got no credit anywhere. I had to sell some bugs, Rip. But it weren't illegal. You think I'm as foolish as I look? I got my reasons.'

'So why be secretive?'

'Because . . . I can't prove they were caught all those years ago. And if I got caught there's always this danger that they would ask me to prove it. And that would mean having to go get . . . my father.'

'Moroni said you didn't ask for a lawyer.'

'I screwed up with the judge. But maybe it buys us some time.'

Joe stopped there and looked to the glass, suddenly caring about being heard. 'Look. I'll get out of here. Those butterflies were caught long before Fish and Wildlife was even an idea. They were mine to sell. I'm exempt from that law because of the previously existing law when those bugs were caught. It's called a grandfather clause. I already knew this because Ma once sold some aberrations years ago.'

'Joe, they're saying unless your father confirms that they're his you go to jail.'

'There's other ways to prove it.'

'Such as?'

'It's a storm at a tea party. It'll blow over.'

'How?'

There was no other way to prove it. I knew it and I knew he knew it; but the alternative was too much for him to admit. Joe didn't have a plate for this part. He'd run out of plates.

'OK. What if I go and get him?'

'Get who?'

'The Unmentionable One.'

Joe emitted that strange low groan he'd let out that first time I had asked about his father, the day he drove me to the house.

Moroni's voice came through the speaker. 'Five minutes, people.'

Joe took off his glasses and cleaned them, even though they did not need cleaning. He made little contortions with his nose, rubbed his mother-saving, plate-spinning, thorax-pinching hands. Events were catching up with him.

'That can't happen.'

'But why?'

Joe shook his head.

'Joe! Think about it. He can prove they're his bugs. Then Moroni and all his other bogus angels will fly away and bug someone else. And you go free and we can do the deal.'

'I made a promise to Ma.'

'Break it!'

'That's the devil's advice.'

'No. The devil's advice is to have nothing to do with your father because your mother tells you to! I'll go and get him. You don't have a choice, Joe.'

'I don't know where he is.'

'Isabelle does.'

He flinched, and stretched out his neck. 'What?'

'She wrote to him once.'

'No, no, no.'

'Yes, yes, yes. She wrote to him at Princeton.'

'No. No. No.'

'Yes. I think she knows. I know she knows.'

'Dee-dee-dee. La da di,' Joe covered his ears.

'He could be a day's drive. Less.' I waited until he'd un-cupped his ears. 'Joe, listen to me. I'll go get your father. Ask him to help. I'll take Isabelle with me. And who knows, you may like him. You may even get to know him.'

Joe started to pace the room, covering it in three strides there, three strides back.

'She can't know. Ma can't know.'

'I'll tell Edith . . . something.'

'Oh Gee. Isabelle won't go with you. Under false pretences.'

'I'll talk her round, Joe.'

'This is . . . this is . . . gonna be trouble, Rip.'

'Joe. You're going to jail if we don't find him and if we don't get you out of here this deal is dead.'

– Lew?

– Julia?

– Oh my.

– That bad?

– Well. You look like you could use some sunshine. Are they treating you OK?

– It's not as bad as you'd think.

– You sure?

– I went to boarding school. The food's nicer here and there's no Latin. I'm fine.

– You're being stoical.

– I am and it's not easy for a hedonist to be a stoic. Although the hedonists were more pragmatic than people think.

– I talked to Robert Peabody, my attorney. He's looking at some kind of extradition. It's all so . . . unjust. But we'll get you out of here, Lew.

– No hurry. There are little pleasures to be found. I've had time to think. And sleep. The guard, Larson, has been a good friend to me. And I'm getting the book done, you'll be pleased to know. Prison's good for writing.

– Do I get to read it?

– Maybe.

– Garton is fascinated by your situation. Thinks there's the basis of a book in it.

– I hope not.

– I didn't mean for him. For you.

– Well. I don't know. The ending's not clear.

– It'll come. I still feel . . . this is my fault somehow, Lew.

When you told me you had got this job I thought it sounded great. I should have . . .

– What?

– I don't know. Asked more questions. Something.

– You weren't to know. Things took a turn.

– But these people, Lew. How . . . I mean. They sound . . . crazy. Real freaks.

– Ha!

– Is that funny?

– More than you know. But they weren't all crazy. I'd say eccentric. It's hard to explain. Without meeting them.

– Not sure I want to!

– Well. I'm sad you won't get to. Especially Joe.

– He sounds like he was the craziest of them all.

– Well, maybe.

– You got mixed up in something.

– I'm not innocent, Julia. I did my bit. I'm a people-pleaser. It's my hamartia.

– Your what?

– My tragic flaw.

– That's not true, Lew. You're charming. That's not a flaw.

– It is. I want to have my cake and eat it.

– You're a young man. It's what young men do.

– That sounds like something my mum would say.

– She called again.

– You didn't tell her, did you?

– I did as you asked. I said you were travelling all over. She said she got a post card from Niagara, and then Mount Rushmore. Just last week.

– I bought them on the road. I've been sending one every two weeks: Larson posts them for me. I don't want her to worry about me, Julia. She's had enough to deal with. What with Dad.

– I don't know how long I can keep lying to her, Lew. She wants to come over.

– What did you say?

– I said maybe the summer. She'd get suspicious if I said no. She really has no idea about you, Rip. She didn't know about you selling butterflies, or these butterfly people. Didn't you even say?

– I told her I had a job selling hand-made products. It sounded too weird saying butterflies. I tried to write and tell her about it – several times – but I couldn't find the words.

– That doesn't sound like you.

– I almost didn't want to tell her – or anyone – about it in case they didn't believe me, or laughed at me or dismissed it. I wanted to preserve it, in my head, to keep it from flying away. Anyway. She'll have something to read soon enough. You all will.

V.

Oh, My!
America:
What have you done?
You raised my hopes
And from the heights you had them flung.
You're a stage for a hero that never comes
I bought a ticket for the show
That always runs:
The synthetic myth
Of the one who saves the day.
Now I'm through with your fake transcendencies
The full-fat promises, the endless what-if-you-sees.
Get me back to cups of tea
And nothing to achieve
A hero-free town of mediocrity
And Ordinary Joes.
Spare me the thrills of your wide extremes
And keep your dreams
Where they belong:
In dreams.

CHAPTER TWENTY

*In which I persuade Isabelle that there's a time
for lying and a time for truthing.*

I was brought up to believe – and do believe! – that you deceive
only yourself with the deceiving, that a lie will find you out. I am
as aware as the next person of the consequences. Of how lies
give birth to other lies which elope with each other and have
baby lies that you don't even know you've spawned until they
turn up on your doorstep, asking for a grandfather's help! But
there is a time for lying and there is a time for truthing. The
truth may set you free, but it was going to take a few more lies
to get Joe out of jail.

It was dusk by the time I reached the winding road to the
house. The mauve sky was clear, the mountains cleanly outlined,
and the hemlock trees muttering to themselves, making judgements about me: 'There's the guy who'll say what it takes to
get what he wants.' Well, it's all right for trees. How wonderful
it must be to live without choices, without conscience. To be
natural all the time. Oh to be a tree for a day!

When I entered the house I affected the pose of someone
who had had a tough day at the office, my suit jacket slung over
my shoulder, my electric-green tie loose at the neck. Everyone
was in the factory, even Isabelle. Since Joe's arrest it had been a
case of all hands on deck to put together the five-hundred-case
order for the Cleveland Gift Emporium. Joe's day-old promise
that no one would have to make a case again when the deal was
done seemed like ancient history already. Ceelee saw me first
and she ran to embrace me and pepper me with questions.

'Is Joe in jail, Rip?'

'Well, yes, just for a few days, Ceelee.'

'Will he have those chains on his hands?'

'They took them off, Ceelee.'

'Does he get Hungry Jack in jail?'

'I'm sure he does. He's fine, Ceelee. He says hi. And that he'll be home soon.'

Edith brushed her hands and the production line came to a halt.

'Give us the news,' Edith said. 'And leave out the sugar.'

I started with truths: Joe had been given thirty – then forty – days for contempt and was to be moved to a correctional facility in Hudson.

'Someday the Hudson!' Edith said.

I told them that if charged for selling Appendix I butterflies he could go to jail and the FWA impose a very hefty fine but that Joe was confident he could prove the butterflies were his to sell.

I told them a lie about the truth that Joe had to prove provenance by saying that the FWA wanted to interview Isabelle in her capacity as curator of the collection, and that I needed to take her in for questioning as soon as possible.

Isabelle looked startled but I reassured her that this was standard procedure. I tried to make a face at her, hinting that there was more I couldn't say here.

I then countered with the good news – still true at this point – that the deal was still alive.

'How's that?'

'I managed to buy time from Roth's people. They were very understanding. I told them Joe . . . well, I told them that he . . . was indisposed.'

'Indisposed? Talk American, Rip.'

'I told them he had died.'

Isabelle shook her head and then left the room whilst I was talking (not for the first time). I was a constant disappointment to her. At least in this I was consistent.

'You did that?' Edith asked.

'I had to give them a damn good reason for Joe not being there. One that would stop them asking too many questions. And with the hearing being scheduled for his release in forty days, it needed to be a proper excuse.'

Edith started to laugh, mercifully unruffled. 'You been taking too many leaves from that boy's book. But you killed him before I did, you little fucker!'

'He obviously needs to stay dead – so to speak – until we complete the deal. So if Roth's people call about the collection we all need to have our story straight. Joe died whilst lepping in the mountains. He fell into the ravine near the falls. When it's safe, we'll resurrect him.'

'You bad, Mr Rip!' Elijah said, getting loquacious.

For now I'd won favour. In just twenty-four hours I had morphed from being someone ready to quit this whole circus to someone who thought they could save the day! There is nothing quite like feeling you have the capacity to rescue people from themselves. No wonder Saviours look so smug. This self-belief hadn't come from nowhere. I think I'd found my voice in that leather-padded office in Manhattan, Killing Joe so convincingly – and all with words!

Having delivered the good and bad news, I went to look for Isabelle. I found her checking the inventory of the collection in the library. The task gave her an excuse not to look up when I entered, but she was expecting me. Her first lines sounded rehearsed.

'Is there nothing you won't say to get what you want? To say something like that, to manipulate someone with that kind of lie. It's not OK.'

'It's no different to what I've been doing on the road, selling cases with lies and exaggerations and stories.'

'You can't see the difference?'

I shrugged. Given Isabelle's position on lying, it was going to take all my powers of persuasion to get her to accept the necessity of the next lie I needed to tell. I closed the library door behind me and continued just one up from a whisper.

'Look, Isabelle, I'm sorry I killed Joe but I had to.'

'This is all a joke for you, isn't it?'

'No. Well. I can see the funny side, and I'm not going to apologize for that. Look, it just came to me in the moment and I went with it. But it's the least of our problems. There's a more serious issue.'

Isabelle stopped leafing through the index. She'd been making a pretence of checking off the inventory, but it was all displacement activity, to stop her facing me, and whatever it was I was going to tell her next.

'I lied just now to your mother – about Joe being released.'

'I could tell.'

'You could?'

'When you're not telling the truth, you do this thing with your mouth.'

'I do?'

'Yes. You make this little twist. And pout a bit. I noticed it when you argued with me all those weeks ago.'

'And to think I actually believed what I was saying then.'

Be completely straight, Rip. Go on! See if you can manage that.

I continued, trying not to think about the shape of my mouth. 'The guy who arrested him – Moroni – thinks Joe could get twenty years. And they can impose a fine that would bankrupt you.'

'But . . . the butterflies were his to sell.'

'As usual, Joe thinks this is just "another storm at a tea party". That it will blow over and we'll carry on; but this guy has been following him for nearly two years, he's built a case, photographs – even a tape of Joe boasting about the bugs he has. He says Joe will go to jail. He's sure of it. Unless he can prove these butterflies were caught twenty years ago. The magistrate judge says Joe has to prove provenance.'

Isabelle closed her eyes; she'd worked it out.

'There's only one person who can prove the specimens were caught before the law. We have to get your father to come to the hearing.'

The F-word caused Isabelle's eyes to flicker, as if she were trying to blink him away. She put her head in her hands and rubbed her temples.

'No.'

'Yes.'

'We can't do that.'

'I don't see that we have a choice.'

Isabelle stood up and started to pace the aisle of the mahogany canyon. I started my pitch.

'You said you knew where he lived. And you told me he logged every bug he ever caught. I told Joe I'd go and find him, with your help. Even Joe accepted that it's what we have to do – as long as Edith doesn't find out.'

'You had no right to do that! To tell him that.'

'I had no choice! I had to. I'm sorry. Joe thinks this will magically disappear, but it won't. I don't want Joe to go to jail.'

'You just want to save this deal!'

Isabelle shouted this at me and I put a shushing finger to my lips.

'Yes. I do want to save the deal, because the deal is a good thing.'

'For you!'

'And for you!'

Isabelle started to walk up and down again, her face displaying proper anguish. 'This is all wrong.' I felt for her. She was a prisoner of her own conscience, incarcerated by loyalties and vows, blood ties and moral imperatives. And now she was caught between loyalty to her mother, needing to help her brother, and being open to the possibility of meeting her father.

'Look. When you wrote to him all those years ago, you were

doing something completely natural. You wanted to know what he was like!'

'That was not for you to share.'

'I will go and find him myself if necessary. But it might help if you come with me.'

'No! No, I will not!'

'Isabelle, keep it down. The walls have ears.'

'I don't care. I can't do this.'

'Why? Because of this stupid rule your mother made? I understand your loyalty to her. But this is an emergency.'

'It's not just about loyalty to her.'

This was going to require a different tack.

'Isabelle. You are an adult. Free to make your own choices. How bad can he be? Really? Are you going to live a life without ever meeting him? Only ever knowing him through your mother's one-eyed description? Or his books? When you showed me the collection that first time it was obvious that you have a desire to know the man behind it. You're suppressing your natural curiosity and that's not good. What if he's not got in touch out of respect for your mother's wishes? That inscription you showed me. "For the ones that got away." What if that is you? The point is you don't even know that. Even if your mother is right about him maybe he's changed? People change. Curiosity alone should get the better of loyalty here. I'm not even his child and I want to meet him!'

She took a deep intake of breath and then exhaled in broken stutters.

'I know my mother might be exaggerating, of course I do. And yes, I am curious and I think about it. A lot. But . . . this is not the way I'd want to meet him for the first time in twenty years.'

'Then let me meet him.'

'No!'

'Why? Why won't you come with me? Are you afraid of being

disappointed? Or rejected? Afraid he'll be this Big Bad Wolf your mother makes him out to be?'

Isabelle finally looked at me and there was a vulnerability in her I'd not really seen before.

'I'm not afraid of him being a terrible person. I'm afraid of him *not* being a terrible person. I'm afraid that he *won't* be a monster. I'm afraid I *will* like him. That he will be brilliant and handsome and charming and that I will want to get to know him and that he will want to get to know me and that my mother will be proved a liar and hate me for knowing the truth and that I will not be able to see her again.'

I hadn't thought of that. I'd been too caught up in my own scheming to think about such a thing, reading Isabelle's resistance wrongly. In that flash of temper I saw her in a different light. Her aversion to subversion, her incapacity for mendacity – traits so irritating to me when I first met her – now made her more attractive.

'OK. But. You have to break free. At some point. Look, Isabelle. I know you think me a chancer. What was it? "Willing to say whatever it takes to get what you want". Maybe that's half true. Maybe one hundred per cent true. But I need you to help me. I don't want Joe to go to jail and, yes, I want this deal to happen.'

'I'm not good at lying. Ma will see through me.'

'Let me do the lying. I've got good at it these last few months.'

'It still makes me a liar.'

'It's just a white lie.'

'Lies are lies. There are no grades or shades.'

'It won't even be much of a lie. A lie of omission. I'll say the FWA want to interview you. Which – they probably will want to do. We can kill all our ducks in a row.'

She at least smiled at the Joe-ism. 'Maybe we just tell her the truth.'

'If we tell her the truth she will not allow it. And Joe will go to jail.'

'I don't want to believe that.'

'Don't be a Cordelia about this, Isabelle. Sometimes one little tweeny weeny lie – "Dad, I think you're great, whatever the other two say" – can save a lot of trouble.'

I was wearing her down with my wiliness. Absently, she started restacking the index books and opened the one at the top of the pile.

'I kind of knew this would happen.'

'What?'

'That the butterflies would lead us back to him. When I first took an interest in the collection Ma told me not to get too attached to it as it might make me want to meet him. She always said this thing: don't think these beautiful bugs tell you what he's like.'

'Well, there you are then. You can find out if that's true.'

'If we do this I will have to tell her. At some point.'

'All right. But you can't tell her yet. Not until Joe is free. Isabelle? Yes? Agreed?'

Isabelle shook her head *no*. And then nodded her head *yes*.

❖ ❖ ❖

Three days later, we set off to find her father.

To minimize the possibility of Isabelle giving the game away before we left, I told her to avoid being in a room with her mother and to leave the white lying to me. Edith was so distracted by having to get the huge Cleveland order ready that she didn't even bat her single eyelid at me when I told her I needed to drive Isabelle to the headquarters of the FWA. One morning I took Chuick to get some groceries and made a call to Princeton University. I pretended to be a journalist interested in interviewing the great American lepidopterist Professor Shelby Wolff, and established that the professor was in town. The secretary at the department of entomology informed me that as well as giving his usual weekly lectures he would be delivering the Annual von

Humboldt Lecture at the Princeton Chapel that Friday ('tickets available at the door'). I thought this would be a fitting way to see him, before meeting him.

By the time we set off, Isabelle was sick with the subterfuge. She had dark rings under her eyes from lack of sleep and looked paler than usual. She sat stiffly in the passenger seat and had the look of someone wanting to get it all over with as soon as possible. Even without the secrecy it would have been a momentous day for her, so I let her be until we'd left the controlling force-field of her mother (a range that extended to the very edge of the Appalachia).

'Are you all right?'

'I get car sick.'

'I'll try keep it smooth. You want the window open?'

'OK.'

'Thank you for doing this. I know it's a big thing.'

'I'm not doing it for you.'

'No.'

Isabelle looked straight ahead, to keep from being sick. I thought I'd ask her what I was actually thinking.

'Why don't you like me?'

'I don't know.'

I laughed. Her candour was somehow appealing now.

'So you *really* don't like me.'

'What do you want me so say?'

'I don't know. That I'm not as bad as I think you think I am?'

'I don't think you are bad.'

'That's not what you said the other night. What was it? That there was nothing I wouldn't say to get what I wanted? That's pretty bad.'

'I was upset. I shouldn't have said that.'

'It was true. I seek approval from others by saying what I think will make them like me. Or make them happy. Usually both. I'm shallow that way. And if I can't win someone's approval I decide that I don't like them. As a sort of protection. It's what

I told myself when I met you. But, the truth is, I do like you.' And as I said it I felt it, a welling up.

Isabelle didn't show any outward sign that this news made any difference to her. She stared resolutely ahead, still trying not to throw up.

'I don't know what to make of you, Rip.'

I nodded, encouraging her to try.

'When Joe "found" you he came back all excited, saying he'd met someone interesting who wanted to work for us. Said you were a bit lost, a bit depressed. But clever and charming. When you first turned up I thought that you were, although I wasn't sure why you would work for a family like us. But charm and cleverness impress Joe – they even impress Ma – but they don't really work on me. I don't say that as a brag. They just don't. They slide off me.'

'I thought you disliked me. You seemed pissed off with me.'

'I saw you looking at Mary, the way so many guys do, and I thought, OK, that's what he wants.'

'I was . . . I am . . . a sucker for the obvious. Although Mary fooled me. What will you do? If you find out that Mary was right? About your father not being her father.'

'Whatever happens, she's still my sister.'

I warmed to Isabelle, with every passing mile. On that journey, I began to see that it wasn't a generalized need for approval I wanted from her, but a specific one. I wanted to please her because I liked her and, if I was being honest with myself (always the hardest person to be honest with), I hadn't allowed myself to show it yet, not just because of her more distracting sister, but for fear of her rebuff. I had the notion that Isabelle had some salvific quality. That if I was honest enough about my sins she would accept me and maybe even save me.

'Joe was right. I was depressed. And a bit lost, when he found me.'

Picking up on this candour, Isabelle looked across at me and nodded for me to continue. It really was as though this was the only language she was prepared to speak.

'Why was that, do you think?'

'My father had died only a few weeks before. I'm in a foreign country. I was alone. I had got a little introspective.'

'Were you close? To him?'

'Close enough to feel sad, not close enough to know exactly why or for it to hurt.'

'You were grieving perhaps.'

'If I grieved anything it was the lack of a relationship.'

'What was your father like?'

I didn't answer her for a while. Partly because it was so uncomfortable thinking about someone whose image gave me a sinking feeling. Yes, sinking is exactly what I felt I was doing when my father came to my mind. I was also quiet because he belonged to a different world. I mean the world I'd come from which seemed unreal to me now, and to which I wasn't sure I wanted to return.

'It's OK if you don't want to talk about it.'

But I wanted to talk about it and not for any gain.

'He died two weeks before I was due to fly here. When my mother rang to tell me she said I shouldn't change my plans. "Your father would have wanted you to go." Out of kindness to her and respect for the dead I didn't correct her revisionism. Months before, when I actually told my father about this trip, his enthusiasm wasn't that apparent. We were having what turned out to be our last supper together. When I mentioned my trip he asked me why I'd give up my job (he thought I was working for a publishing house). I told him it was a stop-gap and he said, "Between swanning around and fannying about?" That was how he saw me. A bit of a waster. It was true: I had no vocational certainty (his phrase). Unlike my brother Michael, who is already a doctor, or my sister Fran, who is not only a solicitor but married, I had little to show for my expensive education and I still had no clear sense of where to head, just a vague feeling that the universe would point me in the right direction. For my father tertiary education was meant to be a stepping-stone to respectable employment. He was conservative, a lawyer. He valued vigour, intelligence and plans and people who had all three. I was not so much the black sheep of the family, more its snail. We are a competitive family and I think value was measured in Darwinian terms, and success reduced to a rarefied checklist of A grades, university, a career in either law, banking or medicine and a mortgage before you were twenty-five. Put me in an average family and I'd have been considered a moderate success; but among the Joneses I was a runt. I didn't have enough high grades and I had a low-grade drug problem. It's partly why I was keen to get away. I had a vague idea that some sort of reinvention would be possible in America.'

I felt myself getting hot with the telling. I put the air-conditioning on.

'You mind?'

'You were saying. You were looking for reinvention. A reason to come here.'

'When I told my father about the trip he quoted Shakespeare at me. "*I'll not lend thee a penny.*" When I said, "I'm not asking for money," he said, "I'm just quoting: it's what Falstaff says to Pistol. 'I'll not lend thee a penny.' Then Pistol replies: 'The world's mine oyster which I with sword shall open.' "' Quoting lines was a family sport and my father was its champion. It irritated me when he did it. I felt he was using other people to say what he wouldn't say himself. He could slap me down with Shakespeare, vanquish me with Virgil, dismiss me with Donne but really he was letting other people's truths do the dirty work for him. You can't really have the last word with other people's words. He said something like, "One day, you're going to have to choose a proper profession, Llew. When I was your age I was engaged to your mother. I had responsibilities. You'll be thirty before you know it. You have to be ready to do things you don't enjoy if you want to get on in life. The point of that quote, the bit that people miss, is that the world is not just *your* oyster. It's everyone's. And they are all fighting to get to the pearl. You have to decide, what are you going to do that makes you stand out, Llew?" That was when, foolishly, I shared my pearl with him. I told him that I had an idea for a book. A travel memoir in epic verse. He laughed. It was the laugh of a man who has read the classic canon and thinks that unless you're capable of adding to it, forget it. For him literature was something that had arrived fully formed, having been created by great people who were all dead. "Dream on," he said. Those were my father's last words to me.

'Dream on!'

I had to blink out the tears to stop the road multiplying. For months I'd kept these thoughts, these feelings, at bay and lost myself in the immediacy of my adventuring. But they were not that far beneath the surface. It all came out without forethought or guile, in a clear flow, without caveats or second-guessings, or consideration for which bits were true.

'So you see, having a father around isn't necessarily better for your health and happiness. I have even thought I needed him to die to amount to something. You know, where I had failed him in life I would show him in death. A dead parent can be a potent source of motivation. Is that an awful thing to say?'

'It sounds like a true thing to say.'

'My mouth did that thing?'

Isabelle laughed. 'I didn't notice it . . . Well,' she went on, 'perhaps you should convert his "I told you so" into an "I'll show you so".'

'How?'

'By writing that book.'

'Maybe.'

'Are you serious about wanting to be a writer?'

I shrugged. 'I was when I arrived in America. I'm not sure now.' This sounded weak – if there's anything that should never rest, it's ambition – but at least it was honest. 'I have been so immersed in events I haven't had the chance. I've managed a few verses. The other night I actually wrote a stanza. About my father. I thought it might make for a beginning.'

'Do you have it with you?'

I nodded, coming over all shy. 'It's in my notebook, in my bag. There.'

'Can I look?'

'Sure.'

Isabelle reached into my bag for the black notebook.

'It's the last entry.'

She found the last page and read it out.

' "So I scattered his ashes
  On a butterfly breeze
  Then flew away
  Across seven seas . . ." '

'It's not much. But it's a start.'

'There's more.'

'I'd rather you didn't.'

Isabelle respectfully closed the book and put it back in my bag.

'Thanks for letting me see it.'

'I think . . . I'm afraid of failing.'

'Isn't that the risk anyone takes, when trying to say something true?'

I nodded. Honest confession is like a song, one verse opens up and flows into another.

'But more than that even, I think I am most afraid of all this ending.'

'This?'

'This . . . time. This adventure. With Joe. With you. I don't want it to end. My constant thought these last few months is "How can I keep this going?" Keep this story on the road. How can I be this person – Rip Van Jones – who is having this extraordinary time? I fear going back to my old life. My old self.'

'Your old self?'

'My slightly cynical, lost, depressed self? I think it's why I was so drawn to Joe. It takes real confidence – belief – to be that un-cynical. I used to wear my cynicism as a badge of honour but I secretly loathed it, knowing it was really a cloak to cover my essential uncertainty about myself. I envy his hope, his faith. And yours. I'd like some of it myself. What is it? It's a mystery to me.'

Isabelle was fully engaged now.

'Well, it's not magic; but it's hard to explain it. It's a bit like a butterfly. It's beautiful and true but elusive – and fragile.'

'And the moment you catch it you kill it!'

'Yes,' she smiled at this. I was rather pleased with the meta-phor, not least because it combined her two great loves.

'Then maybe that's the answer. Not to catch it. Or try and explain it. But let it fly.'

How good it was to be able to just talk without an agenda. And to have – after Joe, and Mary – a listener. That drive was, I see it clearly now, the point when I forged a new appreciation for Isabelle. And she, in turn, for me.

'I think I've judged you harshly,' she said. 'I'm sorry.'

'Don't be. I misread you, too. Deliberately.'

'You did?'

'Yes. Your lack of need for admiration frustrated me; it deprived me the use of a core skill: saying what I thought people wanted to hear. Instead of what I want to say.'

'It must be a tyranny. Trying to be all things to all people.'

'Yes.'

'You end up lying to someone. Which will make it hard to write something true.'

She hadn't misread me at all.

'You're a rare one, Iz. An American girl who isn't susceptible to flattery. Who doesn't drive, knows the ontological argument – and its limitations – and who – as far as I can tell – isn't inter-ested in boys.'

'You're embarrassing me now.'

'I like it when you change colour. It's like the opposite of camouflage.'

Isabelle looked better now. She had got a little of her colour back and I felt as though I'd recovered a little bit of my soul.

New and historic bits of America were passing by but if there were landmarks and fine sights, I missed them. I don't know how long we talked this way, but we failed to notice the fact we were in a new state or that it was already late, too late to get to Princeton for the night. Somewhere in New Jersey, Isabelle fell asleep and I felt my eyes getting heavy with the strain of looking into and away from the on-coming lights of trucks and cars. I eventually pulled over at a truck stop to catch forty winks. I covered Isabelle with my jacket and watched her sleeping for a few minutes. Not long after that I fell asleep lying across the back seat, one of the sweetest sleeps I have ever had.

CHAPTER TWENTY-ONE

In which we encounter The Big Bad Wolff.

The university threw me back to a time I'd tried to forget and gladly left behind – the cloistered world of academia that I had failed in and that had failed me. The fact that it was all modelled on, and similar to, my own university only unsettled me further. The fourteenth-century-style architecture of the Princeton Chapel compounded this sense of transportation to a time and place with which I had unhappy associations. We pulled up in the square and I could see already one or two people forming a queue for the lecture that Isabelle's father was going to be giving in about an hour's time. I insisted we have something to eat, so we found a coffee shop and took a table near the front window from which we could see the street. We ordered coffee and apple pie and cream. Isabelle – brave and resolute until now – started to lose her nerve. That vibration in her voice re-surfaced. She coughed and tried to clear her throat which was all clogged up with phlegmy emotion and fear's constriction.

'I feel sick.'

'I'm sure it's nerves, Iz. I mean, I'm nervous.'

But, of course, my nerves had a different root. For me, this trip was about saving the deal, freeing Joe and sating a curiosity; for Isabelle it was potentially life-changing. I tried to encourage her by making light of it.

'The first lecture you attend at university will be given by your father. Not many people can say that.'

'I don't think I can do this, Rip.'

'We'll sit at the back. He won't know we're here.'

'I feel faint,' she said.

'Whatever happens, and whatever he is like, he is still your

315

father and you have a right to hear him. More than anyone else in this place. Come on, eat your apple pie.'

The sad reality of twenty years without a father seemed to be summed up in the moment of having to purchase tickets for Isabelle to hear her own father speak, and the fact that these people, these strangers, probably knew him as well as if not better than she did. Her father had certainly drawn a crowd. It was hard to identify a single type from the queue of people now filing inside. It seemed to be a mixture of students, teachers, academics. Entomologists, lepidopterists, amateur and professional. A poster on a billboard outside the chapel carried his picture beneath the headline: 'The Annual von Humboldt Lecture'. And the title of his talk: 'Signs At The End Of The Age'.

Again, I tried to joke. 'It's not the end of the world.'

But Isabelle wasn't hearing me now.

Inside, the front pews were already taken but Isabelle was happy to be near the back and out of sight. She had an understandable but irrational fear that her father might spot her in the crowd and single her out. We took our pews and waited. I watched the stage eagerly, Isabelle played with her nails unable to look. I put my hand to her back and continued to tell her that all would be well.

At exactly midday, two men entered from the side. One of them was wearing a ceremonial academic gown, the other dressed as though clothes were an inconvenient afterthought. The man in the gown approached the lectern.

'Welcome everyone to the twenty-fourth Annual Alexander von Humboldt Lecture. It's with great personal pleasure that I introduce today's speaker. I have known Shelby for nearly twenty years. I could say intimately as we once shared a tent in Colombia for three months. He is widely regarded at one of the finest entomologists this country has produced. He's known by many of you for his book *American Lepidopterist*. But it's upon his mammoth and still unfinished work that his reputation in science has been built. He knows more about life on earth than almost anyone I know. He also has a thing about time and people using it up. So without wasting another second, I will hand him over. Ladies and gentlemen, the American lepidopterist, Professor Shelby Wolff.'

My picture of the father was a distorted, identikit image, like the face on a Wanted Dead or Alive poster made up of blockish segments. Joe's crazy energy and hope. Isabelle's cerebral seriousness and calm. Mary's fire. My idea of him had largely been informed by Edith's one-eyed rants and Joe's fantastic pitches. Of course, all were exaggerations; the versions they needed to live with, and I expected the reality to be somewhere between Joe's fantasy and Edith's bitter prism. But neither quite worked for the man who stepped up to the lectern. I knew it was Joe's father before he'd said a word. He had Joe's scale. He was tanned in a deep way, in a 'been in the sun for long periods' way. He had long silver-streaked yellow hair. And for a man who spent his days closely examining the cinnabar-spotted jackets, emerald dew-dropped socks and lily-white striped coats of nature's best-dressed creatures, the professor had little regard for his own apparel. It looked as though he'd been to a thrift store in the 1970s and bought his entire outfit so as not to have to think about it ever again. No doubt his disregard for human interaction was down to his busy and beautiful inner life. His physical presence was given added intrigue by his limply hanging left arm (the result he'd later explain of rheumatism from sleeping rough in the field too long). He was clearly not only admired, but loved; the applause was not far off rapturous.

All this induced a nervous foot-tapping in Isabelle. I looked at her looking at her father and thought I could read several diametrically opposed feelings in her expression: pride, regret, possessiveness and loss. Anger, too.

Like his daughter, the father didn't seem to need or want approval. He made the clapping stop with three little karate chops and started his talk. He spoke with an unfailing fluidity; no fat on any of it. Unlike his son. There was nothing homey, or

317

hick about him. You immediately got that he was a man of precision. And pedantry. Every word uttered was being weighed, sifted for irregularities. Where Joe was a great big bulldozer of words, churning up the earth of anything that might be used for vocabulary, his father used words like precious drops. He was as precise and cold as a snow crystal. He was serious about what he had to say and there was not sufficient time, you sensed, for him to say what he needed to say. He spoke without notes or stopping for breath for an hour. I was attracted to him from off the bat.

'I was fifty-eight last month. For over half of my fifty-eight years I have been overseas, looking for butterflies. For ten of those fifty-eight years I have been in my study, studying. Or writing. Writing books is a far harder job than crashing through jungle in the foothills of the Andes looking for butterflies. And much less enjoyable. I like to travel and spend as little time in this country as I can. Our culture is hazardous to concentration. We have more entertainers, drug companies, food manufacturers, cars, brands of dogfood than we need. Too many businessmen. Too many preachers. Not enough scientists. However, science is reliant on capitalism's crumbs. Without its patronage, I'd be unable to do my work and institutions like this would not exist. Perhaps, one day, wealth and learning will not be co-dependent, but until that day we must be grateful. You may think the title of my talk a bit of hyperbole. It's true that I usually get to write papers with titles like "Milkweed butterflies and their reproduction". But the title comes from a conviction that these days we are living in what could well be our last – this generation's last. And sometimes you need to get people's attention. I wasn't looking for signs when I became an entomologist. I wanted to find, to collate, to compare. Not predict the future. I am not a star-gazer or sign-reader in any superstitious sense. I was not looking for signs indicating the end of any age. But, as is often the case, it's when we're not looking for something that we make a discovery. People looking for signs usually find them. And it's never just one. And it was while I was busy going about my usual business of studying butterflies that I noticed things. People, that is *Homo sapiens*, have always looked at butterflies and seen them as signs. A lonely butterfly on the slopes of Mount Fuji is a geisha. Two butterflies signify marital happiness in Java. In Costa Rica, four butterflies are bad luck. In Eastern Congo, butterflies are witches. To the Ancient Greek, a butterfly is psyche – or a spirit. In Madagascar, the butterfly is the creator who flies over the world searching for a place people could live. Butterflies bring dreams in Corsica. In Umbria they come from the tears of the Virgin Mary. Migrating sulphurs are pilgrims on their way to Mecca. In England butterflies steal butter. In Sudan the dye of a butterfly wings make your pubic hair grow strong. A black butterfly signifies death. Hordes of butterflies signify famine in India. White butterflies foretell rainy summers in Maine. Someone in love has butterflies in their belly.'

I could feel the bench shaking. Isabelle could not sit still, her tension tapped itself out through her foot which I had to stop with my own. *All right?* I asked with my eyes. But she didn't reply.

'Now, I confess I once looked down upon such things, with an anthropological smugness, as mere wives' tales. Indeed, it was because the creature I study lends itself to poetry, to fancy, to metaphor – that I was cautious. But I have in time learned not to dismiss the poetry. Not all folklore is garbage. Indeed, I have found so-called local superstitions to contain highly accurate prediction. When there is a red sky in the morning there is an eighty-seven per cent chance that it will be a wet and stormy day. When hordes of butterflies flock to the Ganges plain it's because there is a lack of water further south, which suggests precipitation is down. Poetry is after all a deeper seeing. And whilst I am no poet, and I would gladly rid the planet of superstition, I confess that I have come to recognize the deeper seeing in some of these observations. Butterflies, as any leppar will tell you, have always given us clues as to the state of the environment, and if you were to denote a weather report based on current data you'd have to conclude that the world is in a critical condition. Perhaps terminal. In my lifetime I have discovered a hundred and seventy-four new species of butterfly. And moth. Let's not forget them. But I have witnessed the extinction of two hundred and thirty-five – as of last month. This year the Palos Verdes blue was declared extinct. And although creatures come and go, always have, the extinction rate is increasing. And it's clear that *Homo sapiens* are responsible. Butterflies in the Neotropical zones are moving northwards in great numbers, seemingly seeking cooler temperatures. Butterflies are emerging in spring earlier than usual. In the Sierra Nevada in California butterflies are fleeing to a higher elevation to escape warmer temperatures. Those already on the mountain tops had nowhere to go but heaven. So, whilst you might feel that the title of this lecture is a trifle over-dramatic, I'd suggest to you that it's an understatement. If the butterflies are telling us anything, it is that "we are not long for this world".'

I was mesmerized. And not just because I was looking at Joe's more intellectual precursor. His father held your attention in almost the opposite way Joe held your attention. He spoke with an authoritative gloom underpinned by a vast, glacial knowledge of which you felt sure you were merely seeing the tip. Edith – to be fair – had said he was brilliant; she had grudgingly described him as having a brain too big for his head; but she'd said nothing of him being engaging, charming, witty, humane even. And still less of him being – in a grizzly unkempt way – quite beautiful. Was ever a monster so attractive in both physique and intelligence?

The audience listened with rapt attentiveness. Joe would have appreciated the delivery of this preacher, if not the theology. I read Isabelle's fidgeting as stimulation and agitation – and probably antagonism. This was a vision in which man was not the centre of the world, or even its keeper. That the very notion of being the planet's husband, or having dominion, was a distortion that had led man to think he could do what he wanted with it. The world didn't need us, he said. It was an icy, clear and brilliantly convincing pitch. When he was done he simply said, 'Questions?'

Whilst he fielded these with verve and wit, I thought about Joe. What would he have made of it? What question would Joe have asked? Of course, I had many. Not many of them entomological in the strictest sense. I was desperate to ask him: why did you leave your wife and children? What really happened twenty years ago?

Isabelle held the pew in front of her as though about to faint. She had the same nervous tic as her brother, folding one hand into a fist and scratching the back of it with her other hand. What must she be thinking? Was she thinking what I was thinking: look at the man, listen to the man, behold the man? He's brilliant and he's your father!

After the fifth or sixth question, she got up and walked out.

I found her sitting in Chuick. Her tears could have been for any number of reasons, of course: the shock of seeing her father, the shock of him being magnificent, the shock of the what-might-have-been encounter and having to recalibrate so much of what she had known. To have discovered her father to be so interesting, so beguiling, and leading an interesting and fulfilled life – without her. To realize that her mother had proved to be a false witness.

'I see where you get your good looks and your intelligence,' I said, unable to find the right thing to say.

'I can't do this.'

'No?'

'No.'

'But . . . You should be glad, Iz: your dad is a brilliant man who is great at what he does.'

'Don't call him that.'

'I don't understand.'

'I can't meet him like this.' Isabelle looked panicked.

'But. I need you to come, Iz. He can't turn you away if you're there.'

Isabelle reached into her bag and produced one of the Freaks. She'd removed it from the main display case and laid it in a glassine envelope along with the original card upon which her father had scrawled the date, name and place some twenty years ago. *03. 11. 67. Morpho wolffii. Los Perdos. Col.*

'Do I tell him you're with me?'

'I'm not ready to meet him.'

'What if he wants to meet you?'

'He won't.'

'How could he not?'

'I just know, he won't.'

'OK. I'll go.'

❄   ❄   ❄

In the visualization of my heroic mission to lure Shelby Wolff from his lair, I pictured a long drive into the Far North, followed by a canoe ride, a treacherous hike through bear-infested forest to a lonesome lodge where I would find the reclusive, genius scientist, hirsute with hermitry, cantankerous from contactless-ness, his life wrecked by an obsession and unfulfilled ambition, raining abuse at me and chasing me off his land. But the Big Bad Wolff lived a twenty-minute drive from Princeton, in an easily accessed suburban house set back from a manicured lawn, hedged in by rhododendron bushes. The house resembled a house Celeste might have drawn: three windows up, two windows either side of the front door. His car was the car of someone who didn't care about cars, an oxidized red Datsun Cherry. To get to this monster's gates, this hero had to cross the road. With its speed bumps and pedestrian crossings, the odds of an unexpected death had been narrowed. There was no impenetrable swamp to cross, and no disorientating mist descended. The greatest danger this hero faced was getting sprayed by a sprinkler on a lawn that someone

– perhaps he – had mown. He had a mail box with 'Wolff. S.' written in black square lettering on the side. The tidiness of everything was suggestive of someone who lived alone. A lone but contented Wolff.

I rang the doorbell and set my gaze up, anticipating height. The Freak heavy in my pocket, my calling card if all else failed. Maybe I'd save time and just show it to him straight away – like a police badge. The door opened and a short, dark, oriental face looked up at me. The woman was wearing a black pinafore like a maid in a large, smart hotel.

'Can I help?'

'May I speak with Professor Wolff?'

'Professor warking.'

'Walking?'

'Warking. Always warking afternoon.'

'Will you tell him it's urgent. Please.'

'Not disturb.'

I pulled the Freak from my pocket and held it out to her.

'Please show him this. He will understand. Very important.'

She looked at the butterfly and shrugged. What was so special about this butterfly, she was thinking.

'You wait.'

She went inside, closing the door on me, and I stood there thinking that I should have not handed such a precious thing to a total stranger. The minute I waited felt like ten.

Then Joe's father appeared. I was temporarily struck dumb. Close up, he was the same scale as his son. Same height, same wingspan. I could see his weathered lines, and the grey peppery flecks in his beard. His reading glasses were pushed up against his hair like an Alice band. He held the freak out in the palm of his hand.

'Where did you get this?'

'Isabelle, your daughter.'

'Who are you?'

'My name is Rip Van Jones. I apologize for turning up

unsolicited but I need to speak to you as a matter of great urgency. It concerns your son, Joe. And the butterflies you caught twenty years ago.'

'Is he dead?'

I almost laughed. 'No. No he's very much alive. But . . . he's in trouble.'

'And why should that be a concern of mine?'

I did laugh this time. 'Well. He's . . . your son. Although . . . I understand the history. No. He's been arrested for selling some butterflies that you caught – before it was illegal to catch them.'

The professor had a brain that seemed to be able to think about a number of things at the same time. He looked at the morpho. He looked at his watch. He seemed to be waiting for the second hand to get to the twelve.

'Very well.'

Inside the house was the distilled essence of neatness and order. Every single object in the room, from the paper knife to the books on the shelves, was in its right place. Even the curtains hung in their predestined folds. If this was an indication of the man's character, it was superficially easy to see how incompatible he and Edith were. The place would have been an open goal for Joe. Given the choice between Joe's chaos and his father's order I know what I'd have taken. The ultra-perfection made me want to flip everything over. I followed him through to a study which had a different kind of order to it, an order perhaps only the professor understood. There were reference books opened and marked – with postcards. Curiously, I couldn't see a single butterfly anywhere.

'Take a seat unless you prefer to stand.'

'Thanks.'

The professor set the Freak on the desk, moving it an inch to the side. Then back to the spot he'd first set it. He then flipped the hour glass.

'It's a thirty-minute timer, if you're wondering. I am currently a hundred and forty-six writing hours in deficit, thanks to speaking engagements, lectures and a three-month trip to Papua New Guinea. Add to that social intercourse and unexpected interruptions, and it all adds up, eating into my precious time, like worms.'

'Or carpet beetles. *Arrivenum sarnicus*?'

The professor seemed impressed. 'Precisely.'

'I'll not waste another second of it, Professor.'

'It's Mr. I was stripped of my tenure. But it's too embarrassing to explain it every time I speak. The world of entomology has more Torquemadas in it than the Catholic Church. And I am a heretic, Mr Jones. A burnable heretic.'

'You have . . . controversial views?'

'I have discovered and described many new species in my life – including this fellow.' He poked the morpho. 'Paradoxically, I have discovered many more being destroyed because of the ruthless destruction of the ecosystem. Contemporary man is too besotted with economic trivia to comprehend the consequences of his avarice. In short, we are destroying the planet.'

'Why would you lose your professorship for suggesting that?'

'I boycotted the institution that paid my salary. But let's stick to the point.'

The timer and the fact that I was looking at a man whose visage contained the imprints of at least two people I knew and who had a lot more than twenty minutes of questions to answer for made it hard for me to get to the point. I had already used up half a teaspoon of sand before I got there.

'I am a friend of your son, Joseph Bosco, and your daughter Isabelle. I have been working for the family business for a few months.'

'What is the business?'

'Um, well, they sell, we sell, common butterflies in glass cases, to gift shops and florists.'

He widened his eyes.

I then found myself pitching Joe to his father: 'Joe's dream is to make this country into a nation of butterfly lovers. He's evangelical about it, turning the most indifferent hearts – mine included – into enthusiastic believers. His ambition is to get a butterfly in every home in America. To popularize an interest that has become . . . well, academic. He wants be a kind of Henry Ford of entomology.'

Shelby Wolff wasn't buying it.

'I realize that me coming to you may seem inappropriate after all that has gone before.'

'Why?'

'Well. The separation. You know, the . . . upset.'

'What does it have to do with anything?'

'Right. Well. Joe tried to sell some specimens to a collector. They were butterflies that you caught. Rare – Appendix I butterflies. The FWA arrested him. And he has to prove their provenance or go to prison. I understand – from your book – that you keep a written record of every butterfly you've ever caught. And I am hoping – for Joe's sake – that you might have the records of the butterflies in question.'

He said nothing. He said nothing for maybe twenty seconds. A second for every year he'd been gone. He squinted, looking at the Freak on the table. He looked as though he was working through something, like a chess player only going back over old manoeuvres made rather than ones he was about to make.

'So they're pimping butterflies.'

'No. Not at all.'

'The mother was always trying to persuade me to sell them.'

'You mean Edith?'

'Yes. How is she? The mother.'

'She's well.'

'As vivid as a malachite. As volatile as a sprite. The Appalachian Cleopatra. She came from a family that would shoot you rather than argue with you. But she had that Southerner's tolerance of the aberrant – which I am. Still a fanatic? She was always trying to convert me.'

'No.'

'Should never have yoked myself to that woman, to any woman. It was a mistake marrying her. Having children also.'

I glanced at the sand timer. There were things I had to know and he seemed to be opening the gate a little.

'Why was it a mistake?'

He picked up the Freak and turned it in his hand. 'Twenty years ago, whilst looking for these, I had what some might call a revelation. I realized that if I was to achieve my ambition I could not serve both family and work. I had to put these creatures above everything else. Wife. Children. Wealth and Health. Edith was not the wrong person. Marriage was just the wrong idea. Those children were the spawn of a bad idea. Quite literally ill-conceived.'

I couldn't tell quite if this was a confession of remorse. He delivered it all so deadpan. He didn't sound like a man who had been rolling the rock of regret up the mountain for the last twenty years. But I was warming to him.

'Why couldn't you . . . do both?'

'Entomologists are like mountaineers. They're not doing it for the view. It's all or nothing. I wasn't a hobbyist. So I chose all. And, since then, I have been able to pursue my work – without interruption or a false sense of duty. The man who creates or discovers something does not do it by chance. I did not catch this butterfly by chance, Mr Jones.'

'I understand,' I said.

I was brought up to revere intelligence above all else. ('Are they intelligent?' I hear my own father asking when I asked if I could bring a friend home. My father's idea of heaven was a library packed with people who could complete *The Times'* crossword in one sitting.) So I was happy to indulge his deficiencies. We can forgive a thousand flaws in a person if they produce something great. We overlook their obsessions, infidelities, narcissisms, social ineptitudes if they rise above the rest of us in achieving something no one else can. And Shelby Wolff had done that. I was sitting with 'America's greatest living leppar'.

327

The more we talked the more the conviction grew that Edith had misrepresented and maligned her ex-husband and deprived her children of a connection they might have enjoyed.

He stood up quite suddenly and walked across the room and started looking at the book shelves for something. He pulled a book out and then another, and then reached an arm into the gap and produced a bottle of whisky. He found a glass and poured a triple. He fetched a second glass and poured me a single. He screwed the cap back on and sat down again.

'Despite what people tell you, blends are more interesting than single malts.'

I raised my glass but he held his, just staring at it. He used up another precious minute of my thirty with another cogitating silence. I suppose he had a lot of catching up to do. He then stood up again and fetched a set of black accounting books. He sifted through them and pulled one out. He opened it and flicked through it to the page he was looking for and then showed it to me.

'There. Bottom of the page. That's the butterfly you brought today.'

And there it was: '*Blue morpho. (Abb) March, 11. 1967.*'

'So what butterflies was he arrested for selling?'

'Joe? Well, the Big Four. And a set of Palos Verdes blues. Which you mentioned in your talk today. I was there. With your daughter Isabelle.'

I waited to see if he'd bite on that.

'I don't even have to look up the Palos Verdes blues,' he said. 'I caught them in the summer of 1966 near Long Beach. The Big Four I'd have to check, as I caught a number of them several times over and all in different countries of course.'

'So you *can* prove the butterflies Joe sold were caught by you?'

'Of course. Where are these butterflies now?'

'At the house. In the Catskills. I brought a catalogue of the collection. Put together by your elder daughter, Isabelle. She has for the last few years worked on setting and mounting them into a collection.'

Again he didn't take the daughter bait. But he flicked through the catalogue, using a magnifying glass. He took off his glasses and cleaned them absently, squinting, widening his eyes into a stretch big enough to take it in.

'These have been mounted in the old way.'

'Isabelle mounted the entire collection that way, Mr Wolff.'

'They have been well maintained,' he said. 'I see she's used the old British method.'

'Yes. Do you have a favourite lep?' I asked, wincing at how crass this question must have sounded to him, but wanting some morsel to take back to Isabelle.

'The angled castor. *Ariadne ariadne*. An ugly and unassuming creature.'

'Well, "Beauty is in the eye of the beholder", as Shakespeare said.'

'I believe it was Margaret Wolfe Hungerford.'

'Right. Yes, of course.'

'She's done a fine job.'

I thought of Isabelle a few minutes away. I wished she had been there to receive this accolade.

'She's here, Mr Wolff. If you want to meet her?'

'Who?'

'Your elder daughter, Isabelle.'

'I only have one daughter. To my knowledge.'

I could feel the breath of Mary's 'told you so' at my prickling neck and then a wave of sadness for her. But I decided not to enter that dispute at this delicate moment.

'Yes. I meant Isabelle. Would you like to meet her?

'Perhaps when the provenance of the butterflies has been established.'

'Of course. So you will help?'

'We don't want these butterflies falling into the wrong hands.'

I handed him Moroni's card. And Joe's case number. 'This is

the agent at the FWA who is responsible for arresting Joe. The hearing is on November 5th. You will be called as a witness, for Joe. If you can match your records to the butterflies they have in their possession then Joe will go free.'

He looked at the card.

'This is . . . wonderful, Mr Wolff. Really. Isabelle and Joe . . . they'll be very grateful. Thank you.'

Finally, his eyes welled with tears. What were those eyes filling with? Regret? Anger? Sadness? It didn't matter. It was enough they were filling with something! He had a heart after all.

He then handed me back the Freak. 'I thought I'd never see them again,' he said.

CHAPTER TWENTY-TWO

In which we return home and the good news turns bad.

'He's going to help, Iz!'

My excitement echoed in the nave of the cavernous chapel where I found Isabelle sitting in an attitude that could have been despair or prayer. She snapped from whatever conversation she'd been having with her maker and looked at me. She was, in that moment, like a little girl, expectant of good things and wanting the promise of happy endings. I realized that, at this point in time, I had exchanged more words with her father than she had. I actually knew more about him than she did. 'He still has the notebooks recording every butterfly he's ever caught. He even showed me the entry for this little Freak! And he was hugely impressed at what you'd done with the collection. Knew exactly what method you'd used and everything. And then, right at the end, he said that he'd be happy to meet you after the hearing. I mean, he was eccentric in that brilliant sort of way, and there's no doubting where his priorities lay – the work comes first for sure. He had me on a timer, for God's sake!'

'You liked him?'

'Well, he was not the man I expected. Or the man your mother described. He was obsessive but admitted that he had put the work before everything. Said he was unsuited to being a husband or a father. He hinted at regret – for not having seen you grow up. Just at the end. After I'd asked him if he'd meet you. He said, "I thought I'd never see them again."'

'He said that?'

'He did.'

If I had any doubts about the accuracy of what I was saying, the look on Isabelle's face was enough to reassure me I'd done the right thing in saying this.

'He's not the monster, Iz.'

She looked as if she was going to cry but she held the tears in. I put out my hand, placing it over hers. And she let it rest there. That small surface area of hand was the whole world for a few moments; I took her hand then dared a squeeze and to my delight she returned it with her own pressure. It was a touch lovelier – more meaningful – than the full union of flesh I'd experienced with Mary. Mary would have set fire to us both if she'd seen it, but I no longer cared about that prohibition. I lifted Isabelle's hand to my mouth and kissed it, old school.

'All will be well, Iz.'

I won't lie, the sense of being the hero in my own adventure was at its peak on that drive back to the Catskills. I had killed nearly all my ducks in a row: I had succeeded in getting Joe's father to attend the hearing; I was going to help bring about Joe's liberation, not just from jail but from years of pounding the road potentially by saving the million-dollar deal that the zealous Moroni had threatened to wreck; I was going to free Isabelle from her mother's grip and facilitate a potential reunion for Joe and Isabelle with the father that had been denied them by twisted maternal prohibitions. My hunch – that Edith had held history captive and denied her children access to and a possible relationship with the man (whose only offence was a dedication to his work) out of bitterness – had been proven right. As I drove, I talked excitedly of what this might all mean, how good it would be, for everyone. I painted a picture of a great reconciliation, where all misunderstandings were understood, all wrongs turned right, and where everyone had been set free from the prison of the past. Yes, a part of me did wonder if perhaps I had exaggerated the depths of Isabelle's father's regret in an effort to say what I thought she wanted to hear, and in order to bring about what I wanted to happen; but I believed I had done the right thing and that things would turn out for the best. For all my cynical pretentions, I had a simple faith in – and an expectation of – a happy ending.

While I described this new world, Isabelle sat in silence, pale again and sad with a melancholy recognition that things had changed.

'Thank you,' she said.

'For what?'

'For helping Joe. For asking for my father's help. For going without me. I think it was always going to need someone from "outside" to help us break free.'

'You think you'll meet him?'

'I don't know.'

'I think he'd have been happy to meet you. Both of you.'

'Both?'

'You and Joe.'

'He didn't mention Mary?'

I'd almost forgotten this detail. 'When I described you as his elder daughter, he said he only had one.'

'He didn't know?'

'He spoke of Edith's "understandable anger" at his long absences. He seemed to be implying that he didn't blame her for not wanting to have anything to do with him. Maybe he knows but wasn't saying. But Mary was right.'

'Poor Mary.' Isabelle seemed to accept this as confirmation.

'You suspected it?'

'I thought it possible. But chose to believe Ma. It's one of the main reasons I didn't want to meet him. I didn't want to find out.'

'Will you tell Mary?'

'It's not for me to tell her.'

'How are we going to play things? When we get back?'

'Ma will need to know where we have been sooner or later. And if my father comes to the hearing and she finds out, which she will, then it's best to confront her now.'

'She doesn't have to know about you coming with me. We

can say I acted independently. After all, you didn't actually meet him.'

'It can't be put back now.'

I thought about persuading Isabelle to keep her convictions in her britches until the hearing but she was resolved. Her tolerance and her loyalty could not hold off the truth of these things any longer.

'My days of grace for Ma are over.'

I reached across and took her hand and she let me hold it while I drove one-handed. She looked ahead and in profile I could see her lovely neck, all pale against her black hair, and the little freckles around her nose. All the marking you see and care about when you get closer to someone.

'You're a rare specimen, Iz. I'm just sorry I've been so slow to see it.'

'There are more dazzling specimens around.'

'I'm no longer dazzled by her now.'

'I wasn't thinking of Mary.'

'Oh?'

'I was thinking of Joe. I think it's Joe you really love.'

I laughed. I couldn't deny it.

Those hours on the road home with Isabelle, before the unravelling that followed, were among the sweetest of my butter-flying days. We had made an unexpected, if delicate connection – our individual needs and wants finding common ground and roots; I know that it was partly the subliminal themes of lost fathers that joined us, but it was more than this; I was finally able to appreciate her for who she was rather than who I was trying to make her be; after the manipulations and stimulations of Mary, the honesty and the calm were liberating, and it was this freedom that conceived a desire. Not the quick-shallow satisfaction of a lust, but a more profound feeling of gladness that I was with her and a hope that I'd still be with her in the days to come.

*

The day had an hour of light left in it when we reached the Cat-skills. The landscape was on fire, the mountains aflame with all those lovely shades of orange, red and purple and the thousand tones between that have those names writers pretend they use every day but have to look up when they are called upon to describe the spectral phenomena that is the American fall: ochre, magenta, persimmon (you know the ones). The 'leaf peepers' were out in force, pulled over at the roadside vantage points to take photographs of the splendour. Of course, it would be remiss of me not to point out that the dead leaves, given new life by the wind, resembled butterflies swarming. Good luck? Trouble ahead? The end of the world? I'll leave it to the rune readers to interpret what they signified; we drove on, into the heart of the leafy furnace.

When we arrived at the gates a figure was coming up the main drive. It was Clay. He put up a hand to stop us and came to the passenger-side door to speak to Isabelle. When she low-ered the window, I could smell the blood of a double-crosser blowing in.

'Miss Isabelle.'

'Clay.'

'It's prolly best he stay out of the house. Until things cool down.'

'What is it?'

Clay glanced towards the house by way of explaining. 'Miss Edith's threatening violence.'

'Nothing new there,' I said.

'She seems stirred up by something *he* done and has been cursing his name to high heaven and low hell these last few hours. I'm sure he got an explanation for it but I don't rightly know as she's not in the listening mood.'

Clay wouldn't look me or address me directly throughout this impartation. 'I'm here, Clay. You can talk to me, you know.'

He made a rueful, conspiratorial smile that suggested we were in this together.

'The Lord knows she don't make any sense in this mood, with no Joe here to calm her down. And she's oiled up on that wine. I ain't the judging kind, I ain't even had anything against you and I think you mean well, but I'm just here to warn you.'

'Why's she mad at me?'

He wouldn't answer at first.

'Clay?' Isabelle said. 'What's going on?'

'Miss Edith says you been stirring trouble. Puttin' thoughts that don't belong. Miss Edith thinks you plotting. And she knows where you done been.'

'And how does she know that?' I asked, convinced he knew and had told her.

He stiffened at my aggression. His nastiness lay millimetres beneath the nice.

'Miss Mary told her.'

My ripples were finally coming back as waves.

'How did she know?' Isabelle asked.

'Maybe you told her, Clay. I've seen you listening at doors.'

Clay couldn't disguise his reaction quick enough to my eyes. Whatever his words were saying.

'I think you'd best not go to the house. I see that look in her before. It ain't pretty.'

'I'll take my chances.'

'She got Besse wid her.'

'Besse?'

'Her shotgun.'

'I don't have time for her threats now,' I said.

'Let me talk to her first,' Isabelle said.

Edith certainly knew how to create a little drama. She was sitting on the veranda in the rocking chair, a goblet of wine in her hand, the shotgun across her knees. And there was Mary, sat on the ledge behind her mother, legs dangling, smoking a spliff, smiling at me without mirth or affection, with that far-away, indifferent smirk of the stoned. It was all familiar and faintly comic on the surface but no joke underneath. I wondered if Edith had consciously choreographed the scene.

'Hey Edith, hey Mary,' I said. I was going to keep this civil and beat them with my civility (as well as the rightness of my cause).

'That's as far as you go, boy,' she said as I stepped onto the first step.

Edith hadn't called me 'boy' before. Lamo, Limey, Punk, Motherfucker, Shithead. But these were all names I had learned to absorb with good humour and little offence.

'Ma, Rip is not to blame for this.' Isabelle was brave with righteousness, too.

'I'll deal with you later. For now, I'm gonna speak to the meddler.'

'No, Ma. This isn't his fight. This is about us.'

'How could you, Isabelle Bosco?' Edith made a grimace and spat.

'I've been telling you she ain't the saint you think, Ma,' Mary said. 'She prolly ain't a virgin no more neither now. Not if she been on the road with Rip. He likes to get a girl when she's on the road.'

A gun-toting, drunk Edith with a stoned but spurned Mary for cheerleader. This was looking bad for me. I couldn't quite see Edith's face as it was half in the shadow, but I felt sure she was smiling. Isabelle stood in the light thrown by the porchlight, one arm crossing and holding the other arm which was straight. She was not made for confrontation any more than I was, but she was sure of what she was doing.

'We had no choice, Ma. Joe has to prove that the butterflies were caught by . . . my father.'

'Don't call him that.'

'It's what he is.'

Edith charged her glass with more claret.

'Rip went and asked him if he would testify at the hearing. Prove the butterflies Joe sold were his. And he's agreed.'

'Did he now?'

'He did.'

'And ya'll best friends now.'

'Ma. I didn't meet him.'

'You sent the meddler.'

'What would you have us do, Ma? Let Joe go to jail?'

'Might be no bad thing. Might be better for all of us.'

'You're drunk.'

'What's got into you, girl? Right now you never looked more like him.'

'They prolly got married or something.' Mary sucked in and blew the smoke in big dragony clouds.

Celeste appeared and went and hugged Isabelle but as she came towards me Edith clapped her hands in warning. 'Stay away from him, Ceelee.' Celeste stopped mid-step. 'He's got a disease you don't want to catch.'

'It's OK, Ceelee,' I said. 'I'm OK but do as Ma Edith says.'

'Is it true you went to see the bad man, with Izzy?'

'You get to bed now, Ceelee,' Isabelle said.

Edith didn't seem to care whether a child witnessed this or not. 'She should stay, maybe. Needs to see who you really are.'

'Ceelee?' Isabelle pointed to the door and Celeste obeyed and went inside.

Edith sucked her teeth and took a sip of the claret.

'Ain't you going to join us, meddler? Or you going to stay lurking in the shadows there where you belong?'

The situation was so combustible I decided I should do whatever it took to keep it from catching fire. I went and sat on the armchair. Mary shifted her position and raised one leg revealing her knickers. I felt sadness for her. For what she didn't yet know. Poor Mary. Her blood was more at fault than she was.

Isabelle went and sat on the balcony step, half in half out of the house.

'What about you, miss? Are you too holy to drink with us?' Edith asked her.

'I don't feel like drinking.'

Edith poured me a claret and handed it to me. There were bits of cork floating in the glass and I had to pick them out by dabbing my finger at them. She then raised the glass.

'Blood of Christ.'

I raised it. Isabelle continued staring out across the lawn wanting none of this bad communion.

'The priest said I couldn't take communion no more. On account of being divorced. Anyway, Meddler. How was he?'

'How was who?' I wanted her to say his name!

'Don't make me shoot you already.'

The metal muzzle of the shotgun was lit up by the moon. I felt confident that she would not use it on me but a gun is a gun, a woman scorned is a woman scorned, and a drunk woman scorned with a gun is to be handled very carefully.

'Oh. You mean Shelby?'

Edith actually shivered to the sounding of his name. 'You know, sarcasm right now ain't going to charm me, Meddler.'

'He agreed to come to the hearing.'

'What did you say to him, Meddler? I know you are a slippery-tongued snake, but he ain't coming for the love of his children.'

'Well, maybe not but he said he would like to meet them.'

'Bull crap.'

'It's what he said. He said he never thought he'd see them again. That sounds like regret.'

'Like I say: you gotta have a heart to have regret.'

'Well, I'm just reporting what he said. He would like to meet his children.'

It didn't feel fair or right that I should be the one to break the news to Mary about her paternity, but I wanted to give Edith the chance. Edith looked at Mary. It was very quick but it was unmistakable. But she said nothing. I was close enough to see her eye now and it was trained on me; I was in its cross hairs.

'Ever since you came here I had this feeling that you were

up to no good and that you would bring no good. Seems you been stirring things up.'

'Pointing things out.'

'Pointing things out. That's thoughtful.' Edith scrutinized me from the recess.

'Mary been telling me about what you did on the road. Taking advantage of her. I could shoot you for that. Assaulting my daughter. You are quite the piece of work.'

I let her describe the piece of work I was (and some of it was true).

'You pitch up all charming. Playing like you don't know much of what is going on. And then get to make people like you. Then you start to stirring. Stirring where you should never think to stir. Planting little malignancies. Calling me names. Tyrant. Ain't that what he said, Mary?'

'That's it exactly, Ma. That was even the very word. And other words.'

'Times is a tyrant is what the people need. I don't mind the description. But I do object to the describing. I object to you going behind my back. Stirring, meddling, planting.'

'Ma. Please. Stop this.' Isabelle put out her hands in a gesture of supplication which Edith ignored.

'You like him, Meddler? "The Professor".'

'He was polite enough.'

'I knew that aberration better than anyone. Better than he knew himself. I can see he charmed you.'

'I don't know if he charmed me, Edith. But I know he's coming to the hearing.'

Edith tried to top up her glass but the bottle was empty and that was the last of Roth's vintage. 'This is one thing you did good, Meddler. This wine. I'll remember you for this.'

'When we do the deal I'm sure you'll be able to afford some more.'

Edith laughed. Shelby's description of her as an outlaw seemed spot on in this moment.

'The deal is off. I'm cutting you loose.'

Edith pulled back the hammer on the shotgun. Funny how such a precise and delicate action is prelude to great mayhem.

'Ma!' Isabelle stepped between us.

'Lookedy!' Mary laughed. 'She'll lay down her life for you, Rip! True lurve.'

Mary walked to her mother's side, lest we be in any doubt about whose side she was on.

I should have been afraid, the way I had been when guns were involved in Iowa, but I felt madly emboldened. The adrenalin acting liked a hundred shots of coffee on my system. Maybe being a finger-pull from death tipped me into it.

'That's enough, Edith. Enough of your control. Your self-pity. Your domination. Enough of your manipulations and accusations. And your bullying. Your boring anger and your bitterness. The way you constantly run Joe down, the way you patronize Mary and take advantage of Isabelle. You *are* a tyrant. A petty one. You are a burning martyr. A foul-mouthed martyr who got burnt! And who wants the whole world to know it. That whole world being those you can control.'

I had the sensation of floating outside myself as I said this; of watching the scene, and wondering why I was being quite so bold when cowardice would have been the better part of valour. I don't know what possessed me. In my family, disagreement was suppressed and then dressed up in non-saying, with the most patient and unemotional person (usually my father) winning the argument. Threats were never physical, always psychological. With Edith you were of course dealing with emotional threat that carried with it this physicality, this animal ferocity. Plus she had a gun. But on I went, happy to dig Rip's grave. 'It isn't just Joe who had the monopoly on exaggeration around here. This one-eyed story you tell of being married to a selfish man and raising the children on your own, this story is all very well, but there's another side to it. And you didn't share that. But you know what, Edith? The real issue is that he isn't the monster here. You are.'

There was a pause, and it was like that pause you get between a child falling over and hurting themselves and the actual cry of pain that follows, where the longer the pause the greater the injury. A few seconds passed and then gunshot sounded. I looked at my chest to see if Edith had put her bullet where her mouth was. But the absence of blood, the flakes of wood and the smoking gun barrel pointing up at the ceiling told me that I had survived. And then the second noise. I don't even like recalling it. A purring growl that turned into words screamed through a whisper. 'Get. Out. Of. My. House. Or I *will* kill you.'

I didn't even bother fetching my things, such as they were. I walked back to Chuick with Edith firing a volley of invective at my back. It wasn't until I reached the car that I realized that Isabelle had followed me. 'Rip?' I turned, wondering if she might want to come with me. 'Where will you go?'

'I don't know. Maybe I can stay at my aunt's. I have Chuick. What about you? Come with me?'

Isabelle looked back toward her mother and half-sister. She was tempted. I am sure of that.

'I have to be here.'

'I understand.'

Isabelle then took my hand in her two.

'Thank you.' She then kissed me, on the cheek, still holding my hand in hers and squeezing it with a passionate gratitude and a tension that contained a promise that this was not the end.

I pulled away in Chuick at breakneck speed. As I descended the winding road through the forest, the headlights caught the reflection of a thousand eyes watching from the understorey. I fancied that landscape – loyal to its indigenous inhabitants –

and was ready to spring to Edith's defence. I was so pumped with the adrenalin of the face-off and this feral threat that I continued to drive as though being pursued by a thousand hell hounds until I had left those mountains. I drove as far as the gas would take me, eventually stopping at a small motel on the Hudson. At the time, I felt quite proud of myself. I had stood up to the tyrant and I had done it in front of the people I hoped to liberate, including the one I was keenest to impress. But while being banished with a death-threat singeing my neck hairs made for a thrilling send-off, I had no inclination to go back and test the sincerity of the threat. I realize now that Edith was showing great restraint in not shooting me that night. If I put myself in her calipers, knowing then what she knew that I didn't, I think I'd have pulled the trigger.

CHAPTER TWENTY-THREE

In which Joe meets his father at the trial.

Is it possible to be homesick for a person? Because that is how it felt in the days before the hearing. Indeed, I thought about Joe more than Isabelle, or Mary. More than anyone. I missed him with such a deep longing that it made me realize Isabelle had been right: it was Joe I was in love with. The thought of him being in jail for forty days worried me, not because he couldn't handle himself, or even because of his preternatural ability to wind people up and get into fights; but because incarceration for Joe was about as bad a punishment as you could devise for him. Twenty-four hours would have been hard; but to be unable to ramble unaccountable for forty days and nights, and not be allowed to stretch those great wings.

When I arrived at the courthouse, Joe was standing in the car park with his guard. He was wearing the bow tie and suit he'd been arrested in and his face made an effort to light up at seeing me.

'Hey, Rip.'

'Hey, Joe. You look good.' This wasn't true. He actually looked diminished and seemed enervated.

'I was thinking that when he sees this suit he'll think I turned out OK. That I'm an intelligent, stylish man who can afford a decent suit.'

I wasn't sure if Joe meant his father or the magistrate judge but I didn't have the heart to check. He then became distracted by something on the ground and squatted down on his haunches, to examine whatever it was. 'Look at this, Rip. This is wonderful.'

There, next to Joe's shiny black Oxfords, were two monarch butterflies feasting on a dog-turd.

'These critters must have missed the migration. Got blown east on their way to Mexico.'

We stared at those two lost, shit-eating butterflies.

'How would you interpret this sign, Rip?' he asked, teasing me.

As signs go it wasn't exactly a shooting star. 'I'd say that it's a sign we should go to Mexico after we've done with this shit?'

'I'd like that, Rip,' Joe said. 'I'd like that very much.'

When he stood up I saw that, despite the familiar garb, he really did look different. He had lost weight and the volume of everything had been turned down a few notches. There were crinkles of anxiety on his brow. He looked a bit grey around the gills and he had a fat lip. It was clear, close up, that forty days and nights in jail had taken its toll.

'How was it, Joe? Being locked up?'

'It were super-interesting, Rip. An insight into the condition of man and the state of this nation.'

'How did you kill time?'

'I did some cogitationals. And I got my fellow incarcerees into bugs big time.'

'You get that lip while you were in there?'

'Aww. This is nothing.'

'Theological argument?'

'A man wanted to rape me, Rip. That was one cheek I weren't turning.'

'You fought back?'

'I hit him once. I ain't never hit a person before that.'

'I imagine that once was enough.'

'It's true, he didn't get up for a few hours. But I got some regard after that. I turned him round. I made a lep lover outta him. Then I converted the guard, too. He gave me some materials. Let me have a metal box with a glass lid. Some cotton so I could make some sleeving. I gave my fellow prisoners some lectures. Showed them how to raise their own butterflies. And they were hungry as caterpillars for knowledge. I told them to think of prison as a kind of chrysalis stage before they flew free. They were lovin' on it.'

'So. You ready for Joe Bosco v. The United States of America?'

'I'm ready, Rip.'

'It doesn't sound like a fair contest to me. It'll be over in seconds.'

'I know,' he said. But he didn't sound like he believed it.

'How do you feel about meeting your father?'

'Huh?'

'Your father. You ready to meet him?'

'I appreciate him turning up. To exonerify me.'

'You nervous?'

He tweaked his bow tie. 'Are you kidding? I don't do nerves, Rip.'

Just then Moroni pulled up in his Plymouth and parked next to Chuick. He greeted us both, 'Mr Jones. Mr Bosco.' His eyes were hidden behind shades but they were smiling, I was sure of it. He seemed disconcertingly at ease to me; no longer a man hell bent on capturing, killing, stuffing, mounting and hanging Joe on the wall of his office. More like a man confident of an outcome going his way. We watched him saunter into the courthouse.

'Looks like he got promoted,' I said.

'Bogus angel.'

Joe Bosco v. The United States of America deserved a better arena than that grotty magistrate's courtroom in Hudson. The room was just clearing from the previous hearings and two court guards were escorting a felon in cuffs from the room, the felon muttering, 'Ain't no justice in this county.'

We found a room with a few dozen plastic stackable chairs, strip lighting that flickered and buzzed. A guard wearing a food-stained shirt, overweight even by American standards, was all that stood between enraged felons and a judge's judgements. A magistrate judge who looked to have other – more important – things on his mind, like the itch at the end of his nose, was already sat at his desk going through the paperwork. Joe and I took our chairs on the left. The prosecuting lawyer was already sat on the groom side. Moroni wasn't in the room, nor was Joe's father.

'Seems that tarditude runs in the family,' I said to Joe, who was dee-dee-deeing, making an unconvincing show of ease.

The hearing was set for 11 a.m. and the magistrate judge started it bang on time.

'OK. Let's start. We're calling now Mr Joseph . . . Bosci? Bosco. I'm sorry. Please come forward. OK. Mr Bosco, good morning, sir. You have been charged with selling Appendix I butterflies in contravention of the Lacey Act. I understand you are representing yourself?'

'It's the only way to be sure, Your Magisty.'

' "Sir" is fine, Mr Bosco. And I must warn you against a repeat of your previous contempt at the arraignment.'

'I apologize, sir. I believe I learned my lesson. And although I still say that the land of the free is being strangled by legalism and religious bigots I'd like to let that be water passing under a bridge of no returning.'

'Very well. And you are calling your own witness today.'

'Yes, sir. I want to thank you for giving me the opportunity to set the records straight here and prove my innocence in this business of selling protected species and I am sure that when my witness arrives and takes the stand he can exonerify me and put this case down like a litter of kittens.'

Judge Breece looked at his notepad, squinting at it and frowning. It was the gesture of a man who hadn't given it more than a few seconds' preparation and had a lot of cases to get through that day.

'Is this witness here?'

'Not yet, sir.'

'I understand your witness will be able to prove that the butterflies you have been selling were grandfathered.'

'Oh yes, sir. The witness is one of the leading entomologists in the world, respected in all continents for his erudiculation, caught those butterflies twenty years ago and can prove it.'

'Well, I look forward to seeing this evidence. I understand this is your father?'

'Uh-huh.'

'Did you confirm a time with him?'

'Oh no, sir. I ain't talked to him in twenty years. Not since he left for Colombia to look for the butterflies in question. Although I can recall the last conversation I had with him in full, sir. He was just about to catch a plane from LA. Dressed in his shorts. Always wore shorts. He had his lepping gear with him. And he leans down. And he says, "Joseph. I am going to bring you something no man has ever seen." And I ask him what. And he says it was a butterfly with five wings. And then he tells me. "Keep them safe." This was before the fire. And most of my father's butterflies being destroyed. Apart from the most valuable ones which we kept in a trunk. That was the trunk I pulled from the fire, sir.' Joe held up his wrists to show the judge the scars. 'That was 1967, sir. Twenty years ago. Or one whole Van Winkle, as my friend Rip here would say.'

'Right. And it is these butterflies that you have been selling recently that you claim to be grandfathered. The ones caught back then. Before the Endangered Species Act made them illegal.'

'Correct, sir. A set of the Big Four. A case of Palos Verdes blue.'

'And your father can prove that these were his?'

'He kept records of everything, sir. He's an Einstein of entomological accounting.'

'Well. Is there any word on where he might be?'

The prosecuting lawyer raised his hand.

'Yes, Mr Kelly?'

'Sir, Mr Wolff is with agents from the FWA. Going through the notebooks. Trying to match his records with the contraband inventory. Agent Moroni has asked for another fifteen minutes.'

'Well, we can wait till 11.15, Mr Kelly. Mr Bosco, do you have anything else to add before that?'

'I can share some insights on the penal system, sir. That may be of interest to you and might even make your job a little easier.'

Breece smiled, gamely. 'I'm all ears, Mr Bosco.'

'Well. I should say that the forty days and nights I have endured in the state prison were no great deprivation and that unlike the Lord I got fed and watered and not a single devil offered me the earth. But, it seems to me you got too many 'tel-ligent and useful folks locked up doing nothing much for having done nothing much. For exampling, I shared a cell with a man who made a bomb out of beer just to see if he could. Now that man might better be used to work for the government or the military than "sitting in Sing Sing doing nothing", which is a song I wrote while I was in there. It works to the tune of "Singing In The Rain", if you'd like me to sing it for you.'

'Please, continue with your penal analyses, Mr Bosco.'

'Sure. Let's just say that I have learned even in this short incarcerating what it is to be a free man and to appreciate that. It were a levelling experience, sir. A reminder that we are all broken vessels. I should say that the Lord's presence was thick behind those bars, sir. I'd say I encountered him more clearly there than in any congregation I worshipped at. It was illuminating.'

It was a relief to hear the Joe I knew and loved, full of his usual epizeuxes, exaggerations and escalations – and the inter-breeding and mish-mashing of words that weren't meant to mate with each other; making pronouncements on the law and state of the nation and what the Holy Spirit was up to. It was a pity Joe's father was not there to hear it.

At 11.15, with Joe in full flow, the door opened and Joe's

father entered, followed by Agent Moroni still looking far too pleased with himself for my liking. Joe's father sat without a glance at his son – or me. He stared resolutely ahead at the judge. His expression betrayed no emotion or even any sense that his son, unsighted for twenty years, was sat a few feet away from him. He had the same look he'd given me when I had turned up asking if I could talk to him: a look of impatience at the valuable time being eaten up and the inconvenience of it all.

The entrance of his father muted Joe.

Agent Moroni whispered something to the prosecuting lawyer, who smirked.

The judge was waiting expectantly for Joe to say something.

'Please continue, Mr Bosco. Perhaps you might introduce your witness for us.'

But Joe was stymied. When he started speaking, it was in a mumble that only I could hear. His countenance melted, his facial muscles slackened like someone having a stroke. His arm – in a subconscious mimic of his father's – also fell slack at his side. The zing that made him zing was gone. It was as if those twenty years of non-fathering hit him like a train.

'Mr Bosco? Are you with us?'

'Sir.'

'Now that your witness is here, perhaps you would like to introduce him?'

Come on, Joe, I thought. Don't stop being Joe now! Show your father what an extraordinary individual, what a singular creature, you are. Show him what he's been missing! I had the awful thought that Joe's Joe-ness was just compensation for a cavernous emotional emptiness he could no longer fill, a persona to compensate for his fatherless life, an ordinary rather than extraordinary Joe. He looked over at his father and his expression was pathetic. His little smile and the raised hand a touching attempt at familiarity. The fact that signal went unrequited, that not a blink came back from the father, made it all the more painful to watch. If time slowed for me in that moment, for Joe it reversed as he travelled back through all his instars to that five-year-old boy seeing his father off on that expedition.

'I kept them safe, Pa.'

'Speak up, Mr Bosco?'

Joe continued channelling his five-year-old self, but muttering the words so quietly only I could hear him. 'I kept them safe, Pa. I did as you asked. I kept them safe. You said they were the most precious things. That's why I didn't get Ma out totally. I did a little bit. But I remembered what you said. I dragged the trunk out of the fire. Ma started it but it were an accident. Ma said we should keep them after that. She said they belonged to us. They were our inheritance. I had to sell them. We had no choice. They helped us some. But I never sold the five-wings. Never. Until recently.'

'Mr Bosco? You're mumbling. What are you saying there?'

Joe unclipped his bow tie and loosed his top button. He took off his jacket, revealing sweat patches at his armpits and a column on his back. He was burning up. Having such a vivid flashback to the conflagration that I think he believed he was on fire. He flapped his arms, cooling himself. I wanted to put him out. Grab an extinguisher and spray him with it.

Breece's patience with Joe's idiosyncrasies (impressive till now) finally ran out, which was a small mercy for I didn't know where Joe was going and neither did he.

'It would help your cause and this case if you could introduce the witness. If you intend to prove your innocence, Mr Bosco.'

Then more words tumbled out of him, again too fast and quiet to hear. Edith was right, Joe had a disease of words, a connection Tourette's not unlike the clang association you can experience on good weed; but where I could usually hear the poetry and the humour in the muddle, this was the sound of someone breaking down. He became tangled and mangled in words and memories, and enmeshed it trying to communicate something to his father who, to compound the awfulness, was utterly unmoved and indifferent to his son's crashing. Joe was falling. I could hear the shouts of 'Tim-ber!' I wanted to catch him. But it was too late. I stood up but the prosecuting lawyer had already raised a hand.

'If I may, sir?'

'Go ahead, Mr Kelly.'

I sat down and bid Joe sit. He sat and wiped the sweat from his forehead. When I put a hand on his back to steady him it was like touching a man who had malarial sweats.

'Mr Wolff has shown the proof of provenance to Agent Moroni and the office of the FWA. And we are satisfied that the contraband was grandfathered and that therefore Mr Bosco was acting within the law when he sold them.'

I clenched my fist in a silent tribute. 'You hear that, Joe?'

Joe didn't seem to hear it.

'However, Mr Wolff has asked if he might say a few words. Mr Wolff?'

Shelby Wolff stood and came to the front. Joe quickly glanced at his father and then looked down again. His father still wouldn't look at Joe; but I looked at him, just as I had looked at him that day in the Princeton chapel.

'I confirm that the butterflies Mr Bosco has been arrested for selling are specimens that I caught on separate expeditions over twenty years ago. In 1964, 1965 and 1967. I have already shown my records to Agent Moroni of the FWA and they are satisfied that my records match the butterflies in question. I want to thank the FWA for their important work in stopping the illegal trade of endangered species. They play an important role in the fight against the wanton destruction of the planet by unscrupulous characters intent on making a buck here and a buck there or, in this case, a great deal of money. I understand that Mr Bosco intended to sell the collection to a Mr Truman Roth, a man whose family made their fortune destroying the planet he allegedly now seeks to save. For the record, I must have it noted that the butterflies that Mr Bosco intended to sell to Mr Roth are not – nor ever have been – his to sell. They were not left as an inheritance. The only reason these butterflies remained in possession of Mrs Bosco is that at the time of our separation she had lied, telling me they had been destroyed in the fire that Mr Bosco seems to have suggested in his rambling account that she started. A fire in which I believed I'd lost around five thousand papered specimens, including a set of twenty-four five-winged blue morphos, which constituted a major scientific discovery at the time.'

'I thought I'd never see them again!'

'This collection includes twenty-three new species as well as all nineteen of the rarest butterflies on Earth. They were caught with the financial assistance and commission of the Smithsonian Museum and that is where they rightly belong. Indeed, these butterflies do not belong to Mr Bosco. Nor do they belong to me. They belong to the nation. And it is my express wish that the collection goes to the rightful owners. I realize that this dispute of ownership reaches beyond the remit of this hearing, sir, but I have been advised that it is in the gift of the FWA to decide to whom the confiscated butterflies will be returned. And Agent Moroni has assured me that the entire collection will be returned to its intended owner with immediate effect.'

Joe started to rock back and forth in his seat. I thought he was either going to explode or take flight.

Oh Joe. What have I done?

'Thank you, Mr Wolff. Well this all seems quite straightforward. The charge is dismissed and Mr Bosco will be allowed to leave this court a free man. The FWA will release the contraband to the original owner for collection at a time convenient to both parties. Mr Wolff, do you have anything else to say?'

'No, sir.'

'Mr Bosco?'

Poor Joe. He'd spent all his words. Sometimes, when you get bad news you can't compute the information. It just sits there, obliterating thought. That's how I think Joe was in that moment. He sat there dumb. His old self nowhere to be seen. His father was, as Edith had described, a man chillingly free of sentiment, compassion, remorse and all the characteristics of a sensitive heart that affect the likes of you and me. I felt the rejection of his son as a rejection of myself and everyone else. I had never really believed Edith when she said she would shoot her former husband if she saw him again, but by the time Shelby Wolff was done, I would have shot him myself had I had a gun.

I left the crumpled chrysalis of my friend in his chair and I ran after his father, catching up to him in the corridor. 'Mr Woolf!' I sounded hysterical to myself. No wonder Moroni stepped between us.

'You didn't even acknowledge him! Your own son.'

'I think we're done here, Mr Jones,' Moroni said. He seemed unable to stop himself smirking.

'Fuck off,' I said, feeling suddenly very British.

'Careful, Mr Jones.'

'It's all right, Agent Moroni. Let him speak.' Joe's father looked at me. If I could have taken up twenty years of his time I would have!

'How could you do that? After all that you said when we met. And all that I told you. And then you just ignored him. Your son!'

'Mr Bosco has his freedom back. Isn't that what you came to see me for?'

'Joe! His name is Joe!'

'I don't understand your anger, Mr Jones.'

'You said that once you had attended the hearing you would meet with your son and your daughter.'

'I said I would think about it. And I have thought about it. And I have concluded that it would be a bad idea. I would only be doing it out of false sentiment and misplaced guilt. And these are never good reasons for doing anything, Mr Jones.'

'You really are a monomaniac.'

'It's the monomaniacs who get things done.'

A butterfly may flutter its wings in one place and cause a hurricane in another, but my flapping was having no effect on this man. I'd have got more remorse from a rock.

'Your . . . your son is in that room. And you don't even want to talk to him?'

'I don't.'

I stared at Joe's father, flabbergasted. This man who'd spent his lifetime looking for and studying the beautiful aberrations in this world had missed the most beautiful of all.

'You shake your head, Mr Jones. But is that so difficult for you to understand? I came to retrieve what I thought I'd lost and would never see again.'

CHAPTER TWENTY-FOUR

In which I return to the house for the last time.

I realize I've been infected with Joe's disease of amplification, but I have never been as angry as I was in the moment his father walked off having got what he wanted, leaving his son slumped in a chair, disinherited and abandoned for a second time. The wise tell us not to act out of anger but their proverbs and aphorisms, bons-mots and smart-arseries are of no use in the moment of true anger. Of course, my anger wasn't all righteous. I'll admit it was as much for my loss as for Joe's. I was angry at myself too, for this situation was of my making. Out of a vain need to please, a naive belief that I could get Joe out of jail and a prideful desire to prove I could keep the deal alive, I had manufactured a disaster. Without my meddling the events that unfolded might have remained folded, the crap brushed under the carpet, the sleeping dogs snoozing, the cyclops in its cave etc. I had, again, been one step behind what was going on, and, again, I had misread someone's intentions. My sanctimonious conscience was very clear about all this, telling me (in a loud voice) to make amends and (in a quieter voice that I chose not to hear) to do so within the bounds of the law.

When I walked back to the courtroom I was practically in tears. The guard thumbed me towards the entrance. 'I took your friend outside. He don't seem in his right mind.'

I found Joe sitting on a bench overlooking the car park. He was bent forward, elbows on knees, fingers picking nails. He was looking down at his feet. Had Joe ever looked down? He was always so busy looking up. It didn't look right.

'Joe? I'm sorry. I really am. I don't know what to say.'

Joe didn't respond at all. I don't even know if he could hear me.

I led him to the car and helped him into the passenger seat, the way one might help an elderly person or a badly wounded war veteran. As we set off for the Catskills I launched into a rant about his father; how he had totally blanked Joe, how he had failed to meet his promise to me.

Joe was still mute. Not even a dee, dee, dee. A downcast, silent Joe was a disconcerting thing: a creature not being itself, like a great white that ignores the skinny legs of the swimmer or a tiger scared of the antelope. I was still half hoping that at any moment a great smile would burst forth from him, and he'd say, 'Just kidding!' It took me several miles to get over myself and see that it was Joe who needed consoling and that my grievances were secondary. I tried to be cheerleader to his cheerless heart, to wake him from his catatonia. I lobbed ropes of hope into the pit he'd fallen into, trusting that he might grab one and pull himself back up. I talked about the utter injustice of what had happened. That he had been robbed of his inheritance – by his own father! How he had been the real father in the family, the bread and butterfly winner. I listed all that was singular about him and said how proud I was of him and as I said these things I believed everything to be true. But still he remained silent, staring off into himself. In desperation, I sang his theme song:

'Will you buy my butterflies,
From all around the world?
I brought them here for you to see
How much d'ya think they're worth?'

Nothing. I found a radio station playing country music and I sang along in my worst Americanian, but still he remained out of radio contact. I had wanted Joe to get real, but not too real. Not this real. Where have you gone, Butterfly Joe? Please come back. I need you.

'Joe? Say something.'

Still no words. He was a stunned bug. A butterfly trapped in a killing jar and I was unable to set him free. Perhaps he didn't want to be freed. Perhaps he needed to be defeated, to get to the end of himself. Perhaps he was tired of being the Cat; tired of being all that. It was easy to forget what a massive energy it must have required just being Butterfly Joe.

I decided to let him be for a while. He would bounce back; he always bounced back from setback and disappointment. When I first met him, I thought he was afflicted by a surfeit of unreasonable hope; something I saw as an American condition. But he carried this unreasonable hope with him wherever he went even when others doubted him. He remained the super-optimistic poor kid who says, 'With all this horse shit around there must be a pony somewhere.'

I hummed a tune of my own making for a few miles more. When he spoke he sounded different.

'He didn't say anything about my suit.'

I wanted to laugh, but Joe delivered this with the gravity of a deep revelation.

'I thought he might . . . at least notice it. Anyway, it doesn't matter,' he said. 'They weren't worth it. The butterflies weren't worth it. After all that.'

'What do mean?'

'I should have left the trunk in the fire. And I should have got Ma out, instead of going back for the bugs.'

'You can't blame yourself, Joe. You were five!'

'I could have saved her from getting hurt. And I shoulda.'

'You were trying to do the right thing. Your father gave you an instruction.'

'Turned out that the person giving it ain't worth listening to.'

Joe sounded different because there was no artifice. He wasn't trying to sell me anything. His voice was an octave lower. The tone gentle, accepting, almost resigned. It was as if the encounter with his father had forced him to set down his plates, drop the act.

'Maybe he was getting back at Ma.'

'For what?'

Joe started to free other memories that must have lain there somewhere, unable to get out until now.

'For Ma going with another man. When he was away. I don't blame her for it. She met him in a bar. A driver. Not Ma's type, not at all. I didn't like him, although he was nice to me. But she didn't want to be with him. She was just lonely, I guess. The night he called to say he was leaving she tried to destroy my father's study. I don't think she meant to start that fire but she meant to hurt him for leaving. Ma lied about the butterflies. She told him they were destroyed in the fire and maybe that weren't OK.'

'He didn't deserve them back. Your mother wasn't exaggerating. He's a monster. I should have trusted her. I fell for his act. I took him at his word,' I said. 'I'm such an idiot.'

'You did right to take him at his word, Rip. You have to take people at their word or you get caught up in a cynicalistic spiral.'

'But you saved them. That makes them yours. No?'

Joe shook his head. 'Maybe it's time to let them go.'

Something important was happening to him but I was still so caught up in the needs of my own saga and forging the outcome I wanted for it, that I didn't quite give the moment its due.

'You don't mean that,' I said. 'About the butterflies?'

'I do mean it.'

'You are just going to let the collection go back to him?'

'I wanna be free of them. They've been a kind of curse.'

I shook my head. 'But . . . That wouldn't be fair, Joe. That isn't justice.'

'Men's laws don't always deliver justice, Rip. They'll be going to the Smithsonian. Maybe that's where they should have been all along.'

'So what are we going to do?'

'Nothing.'

'Nothing? We just turn up and tell your mother that the butterflies are going back to your father and forget all about it? She won't let them go without a fight.'

359

'She don't got no choice.'

'Come on, Joe. That's not the Joe I know talking.'

Joe shook his head. 'I got a glimpse of something that I don't ever want to see again, back there, Rip. I felt fire then ice. And then a numb nothing. I felt what it was to not exist. To never be again! And for there never to have been anything other than what "we make of it" and our perceiving of things. A place where there was no higher truth to trust and where Death and the Devil win. But it's OK. Sometimes you have to see the other side of a thing to know what matters.'

Joe's personality was powerful enough to bend all things to his will and for the good – which he believed coincided most of the time. But now he seemed done with trying to make things fit his preferred narrative; to bend things to a comic shape. Perhaps it was no bad thing for Joe to think – for a few moments maybe – that the universe was an indifferent Godless space and that the essential comedy of life was an illusion that would forever be shattered by random rocks being hurled by a careless cosmos. Because that is, indeed, what it might be. But I needed his hope. And I needed *him* to believe all that stuff even if I didn't believe it myself.

'We can't let him win, Joe.'

'I'm done with the bugs.'

I was blind to what was really going on with Joe. I was still charging on towards the flames like that idiot moth, but he wanted to hold back; he was unwilling to fight something he couldn't beat and continue chasing something he couldn't catch. In the last hours of our adventuring, Joe Bosco was seeing things way more clearly than me.

It was only when we reached the main gates that I remembered that Edith had forbidden me from ever passing through them again.

'Your mother said she'd kill me if she saw me again, Joe.'

'You seen too many movies, Rip. It's all smoke with her. Ma wouldn't hurt a fly.'

That might have been true, but we hadn't factored in that Edith would be ahead of us. Twenty years ahead of us.

'Red sky at night,' I said.

A sunset-orange glow lit the tops of the trees, making a hearth in the middle of the purples, blacks and maroons of the sky either side. But these signs in the sky – of which I thought I was a fluent interpreter – were misleading. I was again failing to see the forest of reality for the trees of symbols and images.

'That's no sunset,' Joe said. 'The sun's behind us.'

He was right; I could see the sun, dipping down behind the Catskills.

'Probably Clay's bonfire,' he said. Then Joe suddenly sat forward.

'What is it?'

'Look!'

He was pointing ahead, along the line of the car's bonnet. A blue morpho had landed dead centre on the bonnet at the top of the radiator. It sat there wings out, the shimmering grille insignia of a new automobile. A miracle for this time of year and this climate! The lone morpho took off and flew up into the cold air, where we saw the brilliant flashing wings of another blue morpho, and then another, and another. They flew in confused lines, searching for sunlight. A mini-swarm of butterflies released from their tropical glasshouse into the hard bite of this temperate Appalachian night.

'What are the chances!' I said.

Joe saw what it really meant. 'Someone's left the butterfly farm door open. Pull over. I'll go see to it. You go on.'

'But I can't, Joe. Not without you.'

'Don't be scared. I'll see you at the mansion.'

Joe set off towards the morpho farm, his long, loping gait eating up the ground, carrying his great frame twice the distance of the average mortal. As he walked he put out his arms and started to corral the butterflies back towards the nurseries, herding them to safety. Then he was gone. I watched the spot where he'd disappeared for a few moments and then drove on.

'Come on, Chu,' I said, geeing myself up.

I'd barely travelled fifty yards when I saw two figures running down the drive towards me. It was Isabelle with Celeste. Isabelle was holding Celeste's hand and Celeste was holding her doll by the hair; like two displaced people fleeing a raging conflict. I got out to greet them and Celeste embraced me. She was sobbing. 'Mama Edith gone crazy.'

Isabelle, out of breath, her eyes red from tears – and maybe smoke – spoke in a croaking, cracking voice.

'She's burning them. I couldn't stop her. Where is Joe?'

'He's . . . Wait. She's burning the collection?'

Isabelle nodded and caught her breath, choking back the emotion. I could smell the residue of burnt butterflies on her skin. The sensible thing to have done in this situation – the thing that Llew Jones would have done – would have been to have let Isabelle and Celeste jump in the car and driven away, leaving Edith and the others to their fate. But sensible had not been my friend or confidant for a while now and I still thought I could win.

'I have to stop her,' I said.

'It's too late. Don't go there, Rip, please.'

'She can't destroy them!'

'Rip! You can't stop her.'

'Get Joe, I'll go on.'

The thought of those dollars fluttering into flames was painful. Every second's delay meant another rarity up in smoke. I was still so sure of myself, of my ability to fix things, I drove on.

As I reached the house I could see the source of the fake sunset: Clay's bonfire, burning high and harder than ever. It looked as though he was burning more than leaves for I could make out a chair in the orange flame. Clay's flat-bed Ford was parked up by the outhouses, a tarp tied over a highly stacked container, the weight of the chattels tilting the vehicle and giving it an Okie look. The library window was open and a cloud of smoke was spiralling out and up into the purple sky. A lick of flame reflected from inside onto the open window. There was a sound of smashing glass. This was a slash-and-burn operation, or a scorched-earth policy. Leave your lands but burn everything of value before the enemy gets here.

I took a deep breath. Mary's Walther was still in the glovebox. I had never used a gun but how hard could it be? It was cool and solid and a satisfying weight in the hand. I worked out where the safety catch was. I cocked the hammer. I opened the chamber. (Although I am not sure that these are even the right terms for what I was doing.) I gripped the gun and stepped from the car. There was no sign of the dogs. I ran into the house and up the staircase towards the sound of shouting and breaking glass and the smell of burning, holding a gun I had no intention of using, busting moves I had learned from a hundred cop movies and Westerns, all crouch and poised anticipation. I reached the top where I met Clay coming down the landing with two empty canisters of gasoline. When he saw me he stopped, calmly set down the canisters, then held up a hand like a traffic cop blocking my path.

'You ain't welcome here.'

'Don't do this, Clay.'

'You better turn round and leave,' he said. 'Or I will gut you like a trout.'

Clay had always shown deference towards me, but now all pretence at being the meek and humble servant was dropped. He even dispensed with my name and the interesting thing is that, shorn of the nauseating religious prefixes, he sounded better. I actually preferred the real nasty Clay to the fake nice Clay.

There was another crashing from inside the library.

'Why are you doing this?' I cleared my throat to try and hide the fear in my voice.

'She ain't letting them go back to him.'

'She'll go to jail for it. We might all go to jail.'

'You ain't stepping across this line.'

Clay was twice my age but he was in shape, scrawny and streetwise. In a hand-to-hand fight he'd overpower me easily. But – and this is the lovely thing – I had something that made me far more powerful than him: a gun! Yes. Joe was right: guns give superpowers to idiots and wimps. And I was at least one of those things. I pointed the gun in the direction of Clay's head. I'd like to say I said something cool. Something like, 'Step aside, motherfucker!' But I was too nervous to construct a decent put down so I simply said, 'Outside!' Clay took me seriously enough; he raised his hands and moved over. I'm glad he did – for my sake as much as his – because the thrill of saying even that one word whilst holding the gun gave me such a powerful sense of righteousness that the slightest hint of resistance might have made me do it. And that would have got me into more trouble than the actual trouble I was about to get myself into.

'Miss Edith was right aboutchoo. You is a malignancy. The Lord will have vengeance.'

'I'm counting on Him having a better sense of justice than you. Now get out of the house. Or I will shoot you. And if you set the dogs loose I will shoot them. Which would be a pleasure.'

I liked the sound of my gun-toting self. Guns definitely give one a temporary sense of self-worth. I felt this forcefield around me, projecting power and assertiveness. It was a shame I only had an audience of one. I waited until Clay had descended the stairs, left the building and closed the door behind him.

I still don't completely know why I entered that library or felt so strongly (enough to risk my life) about saving those butterflies. Perhaps I had the walk-through-fire-fearlessness of the already condemned. It did have something to do with saving the collection for the collection's sake: the thought of its incineration and people never seeing them and all Isabelle's hard work coming to naught. I think I also wanted to save Edith, too. From her raging self, as well as the law. And of course, I still had the wild hope of saving the deal. But the thing I really wanted to save was myself. My reputation. I somehow conflated the saving of the butterflies with the saving of my name in those final, fiery moments.

What a scene: Elijah, at the top of a step ladder, pulling the upper drawers from the cabinet and dropping them to the floor, with a crash; un-cased butterflies lying all over the floor, some easy-over some sunny side up; Edith standing at an oil drum, that Clay must have dragged into the room from the back yard, picking up the freed specimens and dropping them into the barrel like stray leaves into the bonfire, their colours offering one more flash of delight before disappearing into the pyre. The smell of it all was quite particular – a tangy smell like cinched pinewood – and the heat was astonishing. Edith, her hair tied in a gingham scarf, was wearing gardening gloves and a vest that revealed bare shoulders and skin that was scarred from the fire she'd started twenty years before. She'd never looked more Appalachian. Standing on one crutch and with her eye patch she was a crazed pyromaniac pirate, taking demented pleasure in tossing the specimens into the flames, sometimes pausing to pull off the wings, and speak some last rite. The noises of cracking glass underfoot and the crackling of a thousand flaming thoraxes in the furnace added sounds and furies to match the madness of the moment.

'Edith!'

She was so utterly absorbed in her ritual that she failed to notice me standing at the door until I shouted her name for the third time. When she finally did look at me she seemed unconcerned.

'Meddler. Is that you?'

She dropped a pink and black butterfly into the flames.

'You look a little shocked, Meddler. A little disappointed. Like you didn't get what you hoped for; like you didn't know what you were dealing with there.'

'Edith. Please. Why are you doing this?'

'I should have let these fuckers burn twenty years ago.'

'Don't do this, Edith. You'll go to prison. This is wilful destruction. It's not worth it. He's not worth it! You were right about him, Edith. Shelby doesn't care about people. Except himself. But that's not you. You do care, I know you do.'

'Listen to you. All enlightened now. It's not just about that son-of-a-bitch. It's about these cursed butterflies.'

Of course, this wasn't just about Edith denying Shelby his bugs. She may have been making a bonfire of his vanities, but she was also constructing a pyre for her unhappiness, getting rid of the thing that was the source and supply of her trouble and pain. By destroying the butterflies she was breaking the curse and getting free of the past.

'I want to thank you for one thing, Meddler.'

I waited for the unexpected compliment.

'I want to thank you for starting this fire.'

'I'm not responsible for this,' I said, feebly.

'Oh, I'm pinning this one on you, Meddler. You definitely started it. I got witnesses.'

I could see Elijah looking down at me. He looked scared and conflicted about what to do next. 'Elijah! Please. Stop.'

He looked at me and he looked at Edith and then at the gun that I was waving. He seemed scared and that made me even more afraid. Some people can handle a gun as though it were as everyday as a toothbrush. But I wasn't one of those people and my arm trembled and my hand shook with the holding of that pistol as I pointed it at my former host, the mother of my good and dear friend, Joseph Bosco, a woman whom, despite all that I knew about her and what she was doing, I quite admired, and even had some sympathy for. She knew I wouldn't use the gun; and even if she thought I would, I don't think she cared. She'd crossed the line of caring. So much so that my instruction to her to stop what she was doing was ignored completely and my repeating of the instruction only made her laugh. It was too late anyway. All the drawers were emptied. All the cases smashed. And a thousand specimens were already in the pyre. The heat and the increasing airlessness was making it hard to think. I never took the measure of Edith's unforgiveness, her sense of rage. But I knew then nothing was going to allay it. Not the restoration of her ruined face. Or even the winding back of time. I think the rage had become a part of who she was. It was her identity. And she wanted to burn that, too.

I couldn't shoot her. The only thing I could do that didn't involve killing her was to kick that damn furnace over so that she had no way of burning what was left of the collection. This sounds like a logical sequence of thinking now, but in the moment it wasn't like that. I pictured myself kicking it over and then – in the same thought-second – I *was* kicking it over. I ran towards it and kicked it from the side so that it wouldn't topple on her. As a result it fell towards the alcove and the contents – wood, singed butterflies, paper – spilt out onto the carpet and towards the great silk drapes. I had no time to stop the fire igniting them because Edith was now lunging at me with the broken shard of a smashed case. I backed away making an effort to look like someone who would actually fire the gun that I was still, lamely, pointing at her with the safety catch on.

'I will do it,' I said.

'You don't have the balls.'

It is true what they say, that when someone faces a life-threatening situation time seems to slow down and almost stop. It might have been the intense heat and the imminence of total disaster, but I had something like terminal lucidity, that ultra-clarity that sick people are said to experience in the hours before their death. Despite my perilous position (or perhaps because of it) I had the sure sense that I was here – in this place, at this time – for a reason, that all this mess would be made right, that violence and destruction would be transformed into something good, that there would be an exchange of beauty for ashes. And then, almost exactly as I had this revelation, I saw colours and stars fizzing against a black velvet backdrop.

— *Rip?*

— *Llew.*

— *?*

— *I've gone back to being Llew. I'm going to ask the prison chaplain to un-baptize me.*

— *OK. Llew.*

— *I know. It doesn't sound right to me either. But I thought that I might experience a change of fortunes if I reverted to my old name. Reclaim my old, dull self. Rip was trouble. Thought he could save everyone. Thought his actions had no serious consequences.*

— *I think Rip tried to do some good, no?*

— *Not really. He meddled and got burned. Your mother was right about that. Anyway. It's nice to see you, Iz.*

— *Sorry it's been so long, since my last visit. It's been difficult. What with Ceelee. But I found a school for her and my cousin's putting us up for as long as it takes. At least until I go to college.*

— *You got a place?*

— *Yale.*

— *Iz. That's wonderful. Scholarship and everything?*

— *Yes.*

— *Well, that is . . . brilliant.*

— *Thank you. You are partly responsible.*

— *How?*

— *You challenged me. When you said I should quit mothering everyone. You see. Rip wasn't all bad. And Ceelee liked him.*

— *How is the little sprite?*

— *She's been drawing a lot since we left the house. Mainly fires and butterflies. She's done you a picture.*

— I see she's put me behind bars.

— She's given you a pen though.

— Is that to pick the lock?

— Maybe it's prophetic.

— I have to write my way out of this confinement? Like one of your Russians.

— You look a bit Russian. With that red hair and that wispy moustache.

— Tolstoy or Dostoevsky?

— More like Gogol.

— Handsome dude?

— Clever. Charming.

— Those things don't cut it with you though.

—

— You were always out of my league, Iz. As was Mary for that matter. I didn't deserve either of you. And I treated you both with . . . I was careless.

— I'm sorry.

— Don't be. If there's one thing prison does it strips away the ego. Shows you what you are. I've had time to discover some things about myself – and grow a beard.

— What have you discovered?

— That I can't grow a beard.

— It actually suits you.

— Well. The other great thing about prison, other than growing a beard and reflecting on the murky colour of my soul, is the time I've had to read. I've read your Big Russians. 'Man is a creature who can get accustomed to anything!'

— Dostoevsky.

— Yes. And it's true. I've adapted. I've become like one of those peppered moths you showed me. Blending in with the grime.

— Is that your confession there, on the table?

— Yes.

— You've written a lot. It looks almost Russian!

— Joe was right. There's a time for reading stories and a time for making stories; but there also a time for writing them.

— Have you finished it?

— Almost. Why?

— I have some news. Can I sit?

— Sorry. My manners have deteriorated in this place. Here.

— Mary turned up – at my cousin's.

— Oh.

— She wants to give a statement. Saying that you were not responsible for the fire.

— Really?

— Really.

— That's more forgiveness than I deserve.

— That's the point. Of forgiveness.

— What changed her mind?

— We got that blood test. The one you suggested.

— And?

— We have different fathers. Not that that really matters. What matters is that she knows the truth. We know the truth. But it loosened her loyalty to Ma's version of events.

— She's willing to back my version?

— She wants to say the butterflies were destroyed in the fire and that it was an accident. She wants you to do the same. If we say that it was an accident then my father won't sue us. And no one will be convicted.

— He really is a piece of work. You've seen him?

— No.

— You've forgiven him? After what he did?

— I don't have a choice. You know what I believe.

— Well. That's impressive. I couldn't believe in a God that forgave someone like that.

— What kind of God would you like to believe in?

— I don't know. One that dispenses fire. Gets even. Or evens things out.

— *Now you sound like one of those preachers Joe's always baiting.*

— *Joe.*

— *You miss him.*

— *I miss him. In a way I haven't missed anyone. He's been haunting my dreams. Almost every night. Barging in uninvited. As if to say, 'Hey, this dream is boring. I'll make it more interesting.'*

— *I miss him, too.*

— *I miss his hope. He was completely unable to resist hope. Except perhaps that one time – after the trial. It's all my fault, Iz. None of this would have happened without me . . . trying to fix it, at the end.*

— *You can't blame yourself for what happened.*

— *I can. I created a disaster. I messed it up for all of you.*

— *You helped set us free.*

— *Except for Joe. I might have actually killed him.*

— *You didn't kill him.*

— *I got myself into a situation from which I needed rescuing. And he rescued me.*

— *Yes.*

— *But you don't think he's alive, do you?*

— *I don't know.*

— *They didn't find a body.*

— *No.*

— *And it's just like Joe to disappear.*

— *I suppose.*

— *And someone saved me.*

— *It's true.*

— *That's my hope. He's alive. I'm going to keep believing it until they find a body. Yes?*

— *Yes.*

— *Yes.*

— *You really loved him, didn't you?*

— *Love. Present tense. There's no past tense with love.*

— *Yes. Love.*

VI.

There's a raging fire
At the heart of this house
Its flames lick the ones
We love the most
And burn the hearts
Of those who've lost
And turns their treasure
From gold to dust.
It's one part fiend
And one part mother
Two half-sisters
To one half-brother
It roars, scolds
Singes and shouts
It sears our dreams
Will not be doused!
Into that fire
I saw him go
To save my butt
If not my soul;
To grab something
Worth more than gold
And leave this
Story to be told.

EPILOGUE

A year had passed since I first encountered Joe Bosco and his half-sister, Mary-Anne, at the Kaaterskill Falls; and six months since I woke up to find myself in the New York State's Hudson Correctional Facility. The blow to the back of my head (delivered by Mary with the butt of Besse the shotgun) made a hiatus of time, turning seconds to years and making the years seem like seconds; for several days afterwards, I remained in a confusion of understanding about what had happened, as though shrouded in one of those witchy Catskill mists. My mind was filled with beguiling visions of those final, fiery seconds at the mansion. One moment I was facing a shard-brandishing Edith, the next I was lying in the drive, on my side, the house on fire and giving off such heat I could smell the singe of burning hairs on my arms. I saw a man – or the silhouette of a man – enter the house; I tried to tell him what was so obviously so – that the house was on fire and he would quite likely die if he went in – but the words remained choked in my throat. When I came to, in the medical wing of the Hudson Correctional Facility, they told me that I cried out Joe's name several times and insisted that the medics stop my friend from entering the burning house. A doctor told me – and I wanted to believe – that this vision was likely the result of the blow to my head and I had probably not seen anyone enter the burning mansion. After being treated for concussion and shock, I was told that I was being held under suspicion of arson and wanton destruction of government property. The FWA and Shelby Wolff accused me of destroying the collection, an accusation given credibility by the fact that I was the only person found at the scene and had been heard telling Shelby Wolff at Joe's hearing that if I had anything to do with it, 'he would never see those bugs again!' In jail, the days passed slowly and the weeks went quickly until, in the sixth month of my incarceration, Clay was spotted by the tenacious Agent Moroni in a trailer park in Tucson, where Edith and he had started a new business selling dried flowers. After cross-examination, Clay suggested that the fire was most likely an accident. A claim backed up when Elijah overcame his monosyllabia and testified, saying he thought the fire had been caused by the collecting materials igniting. Edith refused to say anything about my innocence or guilt. But all charges that had been pinned on my sore head were eventually dropped when Mary (against all expectation, and everything I deserved) testified that the fire had already started by the time I arrived at the house and I was released almost exactly a year to the day of my arrival in America.

Whilst in jail I had often dreamt of freedom, and was often deceived by dreams! When actual liberation came it did not seem real. I had been reprieved but I felt no gladness. I experienced no renewed hope after the despair, or 'respair' (the word Joe had used when visiting me in my dream). In prison I had at least found a new sense of purpose – of meaning – in the writing of my confession; and I had the time to reflect on these events and what they said about the condition of my soul. And, although he was not with me in person, I had kept Joe alive in my imagination and through the words of my statement. Indeed, Joe had been so present to me in my daily reconstruction of events that once I had finished, I immediately felt his absence like a death; I was bereft and alone, and almost tempted to invent and write down new adventures simply to be with him again. In prison I believed Joe would appear at any moment to liberate me once more from the chains of my existential frustration if not prison itself. I refused to countenance the prospect that my friend was, as the authorities declared, missing presumed dead, and even in the first moments of my release I was expectant. Stepping through the gates of the jail I hoped to find him sitting in Chuick, gunning the engine and announcing our next adventure. But it was not to be.

Some believe we are permitted – if we are lucky – one great adventure in life. As I took a bus back to my aunt's house in the Catskills I felt the heaviness of knowing that I had already had mine and that the person who had given it to me was not around to thank or remember it with. My aunt was sweetly welcoming. Her scatty kindness helped me make light of the time that had passed in jail and the happenings that had happened. She did her best to make me feel as though I'd hardly been away and that six months in a state prison was good experience and grist for the writing mill.

'What a thing you have been through, Llew. I hope it hasn't put you off America.'

'I love this country. I'm a born-again American. We have unfinished business, America and me.'

'You know you can stay here. Visit with me. Write more books.'

'I don't know. About the books part.'

'But you finished the book you were writing, yes?'

'Nearly.'

'Maybe I could pass it on to someone. I know people – in the literary world.'

'That's kind, Julia. I'm not sure it'll be their cup of tea. I don't even know if it counts as a "book".'

'Well. I'd like to read it.'

A copy of my confession – kindly typed up by the stenographer at the Hudson Correctional Facility – sat on the desk in the Barn of Ten Thousand Books, next to the Remington upon which I had started my Americodyssey. I had not read it since my release and had put off the moment out of a fear that I might hate the sound of the vainglorious young man who had caused trouble for this family and had the hubris to think he could save them. When I placed a hand on the manuscript, I was surprised that all those words had come out of me. Imprisonment had at least given me the one thing even billionaires can't buy enough of: time. Time to reflect, to get memories back, to get my story straight. Although having tried, I don't know if it is possible to write a straight story, be honest with what are essentially slippery happenings and elusive truths. I'd probably be accused of being another of those unreliable narrators (as if there were really any reliable narrators out there!). I do know now that in the writing I silenced the voices – mainly my father's – that had held me back. I performed an exorcism of that particular ghost; I was writing my way out of a hole of grief and depression as well as a set of expectations (many of them imagined) that had shackled me. I know too that it was an act of preservation. It pained me that the wonder and magic of this time and the singular brilliance of Joe might remain unknown to the world. In writing my statement I was trying to preserve something of his sayings, his doings, as well as those of his extraordinary household. Trying too, to recall the glory of this country. America, I am not done with you yet. Your wildness, your weirdness, your wonder. Joe always said that the land of the free and the home of the brave was not an actual place but a state of mind and I will continue to search for that state. As for 'True Freedom', well, all I know is that it took being incarcerated without to free things within. We were all incarcerated in our own prisons when we first met and it took a strongman to bend the bars back far enough for us to escape. I know too, above all this, that this confession is an act of self-preservation; a way of leaving a mark. Yes, that vanity goes deep! Some nights in the cell I felt like one of the ancients drawing on the walls of a cave, recalling their dreams and trying to capture them so their descendants might know their story in the centuries ahead. I remembered the day I finished it. Larson brought me my coffee and bun, whistled at the word mountain, then told me I looked different and, whilst I make no claim for transformation, I felt different. A burden had lifted off me and I felt as light and bright as a swallowtail, happy to go wherever the wind blew me. As I looked at the manuscript in my aunt's barn, I realized that I didn't care what people thought, whether they liked it, believed it, or admired it. It was – as Larson had said to me – a story only I could tell.

In my last days in America I finished writing my story and then tried to escape to other stories, taking books with me on walks in the mountains during the day. But Joe's ghost was too easy to find in that terrain, and every time I opened a book I could hear him telling me to put it down and get out there and start living the next chapter of my life.

One morning just a few days before I began my journey home, I received a letter postmarked in Jamaica, addressed Mexico, and dated about a fortnight before. The letter was written in an angular, childish script, with the capitals printed decisively and the t-bars strong and high and visionary. (That, or it was the handwriting of someone who was nuts.) The words were Americanly optimistic: generous, big-hearted and full of preacherly cadence and the kind of statements that excite fallacious hope. The spelling was creative as were some of the words. But I didn't need a graphologist to tell me who had written this letter, what its author was like; or an entomologist to tell me the name of the five-winged, large blue butterfly that was in a glassine envelope taped inside the letter.

Mexico, someplace

Rip!

 Glory be. I am not dead. You will be chokin' on your marmalade to hear it, I know you will. I can see that cynicalistic smile I could never get you to lose. And hear your voice – boy how I miss it! Hear it sayin', 'Where the heck is Joe Bosco now?' I imagine you'd think this is a situation that will 'render words redundant!' I sent this letter to your aunt's place figuring that it would get to you somehow. Well for reasons that don't need explanating I can't give an exact address. The one I wrote is probably old by now. Just know that it's somewhere in the

379

Neotropical region. And that it has the second largest butterfly in the world for its national emblem.

I am sorry for your incarcerating. And for all the trouble I left you with. I did not expect them to blame everything on you. But I guess families will always circle the wagons. And Clay is as loyal as a dog. When Iz found me at the nurseries and told me that you'd gone on to try and stop Ma I didn't believe it; especially after what I told you about those bugs not being worth it. (Not all of them anyways.) That was a crazy notion. What were you thinking? You were lucky Ma told me you were there. I don't think she would have left you there to burn – so don't feel too rejected. I hope you can forgive her. You gotta forgive if you want to keep flying!

Turns out you weren't the only thing that needed saving from that fire. I moved the freaks the day Moroni arrested me and I put them somewhere no one would look. Iz and me always joked that in the event of a fire one of us would grab the freaks. I have all twenty-four of the critters. Less the one I sent you. I trust the little freak arrived safely in this letter and that you have him somewhere no one can see him. Keep him safe, Rip. Do what you want with it. Maybe give it to your own Natural History Museum in London. Or sell it. Or keep it as a momento memorial – to me!

One thing you should know is that I think I might have found a wife. As I am writing this, Amelia is sitting next to me. She is not only skilful and pretty but entomologically minded, Rip. Her favourite lep is the same as mine (currently the chocolate albatross). You think maybe the Lord put me through all that just to help me find a wife? Didn't I say she gotta be 5 feet 8 at least, maybe a hundred thirty pounds; she gotta have no intention of settling down, and have Good Theology. She blushed when I told her what I was writing just now which I will take as a yes. I been teaching her about the five faunistic regions. The life stages and the classifications.

Don't feel disappointed I didn't get to make a reunion with my father. Some things can't happen this side of heaven. Of course I always wondered what he might be like and I knew Ma was putting a bad spin on it. But I also knew she weren't lying. She was protecting us. I don't say what Ma did is right – back then or now – but I understand it. In her clogs, I think I might have done the same. You were hoping he'd have changed from what he had been and I have commendation for you thinking that way – that is uncynicalistic for a European like you, to believe a person can change. Don't give up on that notion. Although remember that when St Francis converted the wolf the wolf was still a wolf. My father was still the same Wolff!

There is a funny side to all this. In truth I split my melon thinking on it. Not out of being cruel, but on account of you getting more than you paid for! But I am trusting that you will be true to that promise that you would write the story of our adventuring and I know that it will be better for having met me. I almost cry with laughing when I think of you having never met me and writing the kind of book you said you were thinking of writing. A book full of things that will impress folk who don't never get out into sunlight and mountains. Make sure this book contains all the things I said. America and lepping and the search for True Freedom, which I think you got some qualifications for now. Write it in full-fat Panavision!

This isn't the end of the story, Rip. You and I both know that. I don't feel our butterflying days are over. That's a little flame you should keep burning. Don't let the winds of trouble blow it out, Rip! There! Is that one of your epic similarities? I know you like a metaphor like some people like junk food. So here's another one for you. Remember that life is an apple and you have to bite it to the core, not peel it and cut it up into slices!

I had a dream the other night and you know I don't go in for dreams. I had this visitation. I am not joking about this. Fear not! This visitation involved no particular message and there's nothing to add to what the Lord's already said on almost everything that needs to be said. But he came to me as a blue morpho. He told me that my task in life was to help the last, the

*lost, the least and the looked over, and get people to see the joy
and the wonder of living. I said count me in. And then he was
gone. It was so real, Rip. Realer than life itself. When I woke up
I thought, am I going crazy? Is this another bogus angel founding a religion? You gotta test the spirits, see. You gotta discern.
I'm going to have to weigh it up, but I'm leaning t'ward it being
the Almighty.*

*Things work out, Rip. Life is too full up of joys and wonders
to give up on it. One thing you can count on: the seasons will
change, eggs will hatch, small caterpillars will grow into big ones
and pupate and then the butterfly will emerge and dry its wings
and then, pretty soon, it will make its first flight. People say
happy endings are for the fools and the crazies. Then I'm with
the fools and the crazies. This story ain't done yet and no matter
what happens in between, it will end well.*

Joe

I was so stunned it took me a while to get to the end of this letter.
Joe on the page was no substitute for Joe in the room – damn
him, he was right about that! – but his words were all I had. I
read the letter several times, a bit like a lover trying to capture
the essence of the sender; I read the lines and the lines between
and the words and the gaps between the words, trying to conjure
Joe's presence. When finally I stopped reading it I felt an aching
for its author's company.

Three days later, I took my swimmers and my *Classic American
Stories* with me up to the Kaaterskill Falls for one last dip in the
still icy waters and to finish the story of Rip Van Winkle. Thanks
to Mary's bibliokleptomania, I'd never managed to finish it and
the completist in me needed to put a full stop to my American
adventuring. The day was overcast but warm enough for a Brit
to think about a swim. Perhaps I would un-baptize myself in the
waters while I was there, shed that skin and officially return to

being Llewellyn Jones, leave Rip's grave clothes floating at the foot of the falls. I arrived at the waterfall as the sun broke through the cloud cover. The waters were full – fuller than the year before – from the heavy snows that, thanks to my incarceration, I had missed completely. Everything was as I remember it. Less the naiad in the water; less the colossus on the rock. I saw the empty ledge where I had been lying that day Joe had first appeared and I went and sat there with my book. The sun was almost at the point in its orbit where Joe had blocked it out. I started to read the story of Rip Van Winkle again, from the point where Rip wakes up, but I couldn't focus on the words. After several times of trying I gave up. I realized that I didn't want to finish Rip's story because I didn't want to finish *my* story, so I set the book down and left my namesake lying asleep near the cold waters beside the Kaaterskill Falls. And a profound sleepiness then came upon me and I laid my head on the rock, eyes nearly closed but with lashes touching to allow a little vision, letting the sun warm my face to the point of burning. I lay there indulging a nostalgia. I won't lie, I was hoping for a sign, willing a butterfly to flutter by, as one had done that day I first met Joe; but no butterfly came and the lack of a sign brought on that sad-sweet melancholy for what was not and what was, and as I gave in to this feeling the tears began to flow like the winter melt waters of the Catskill River. It was good to let go and I lay there blinking, creating multiple suns in the refractions of my tears, listening to the hissing rush of the fat falls, imaging Joe turning up with that marvellous expression that contained wonder, gratitude and the promise of new adventures. And then, just as I pictured him, I detected a vibration in the understorey and thought I could hear, rising above the abundant music of water, the sound of a man singing to himself and laughing at the world.

Acknowledgements

I wrote this novel all by myself; but I couldn't have done it without the inspiration, encouragement and agency of some special people:

Joseph Simcox, who once offered me a job selling butterflies and promised me I'd see America.

Adam Leyland, who agreed to ride shotgun and let me drive even though I had no licence.

Harry Armfield, who encouraged me to write this book and helped plot its route as we walked around Richmond Park.

The two Steves – 'Silent' Steve Matthews and Steve Robinson – for letting me run bad ideas by them at inconvenient moments.

My agent – Caroline Wood – for backing my decision to write a book that was a little bit different to my last.

My editor Kris Doyle and publisher Paul Baggaley for taking the book on when still in chrysalis stage and having faith it might hatch and take flight.

David Kosse for being involved in and connected to this story from egg through to imago. And maybe to another 'stage'.

My son Gabriel and daughter Agnes for putting up with me staring into space during dinner and offering elegant solutions to conundrums.

My wife, Nicola. Words don't cut it really.

The Author Of All Things.